15 JUL 2019

THE
SPIDER

Dublin City Libraries
Withdrawn From Stock

By Leo Carew and available from Wildfire

Under the Northern Sky
The Wolf
The Spider

THE
SPIDER

LEO CAREW

WILDFIRE

Copyright © 2019 Leo Carew

The right of Leo Carew be identified as the Author of
the Work has been asserted by him in accordance with the
Copyright, Designs and Patents Act 1988.

First published in 2019 by
WILDFIRE
an imprint of HEADLINE PUBLISHING GROUP

1

Apart from any use permitted under UK copyright law,
this publication may only be reproduced, stored, or transmitted, in any form,
or by any means, with prior permission in writing of the publishers or,
in the case of reprographic production, in accordance with the terms
of licences issued by the Copyright Licensing Agency.

All characters in this publication are fictitious and any resemblance
to real persons, living or dead, is purely coincidental.

Cataloguing in Publication Data is available from the British Library

Hardback ISBN 978 1 4722 4703 2
Trade paperback ISBN 978 1 4722 4706 3

Typeset in 10.5/13 pt Zapf Elliptical 711 BT by Jouve (UK), Milton Keynes

Printed and bound in Great Britain by Clays Ltd, Elcograf S.p.A.

MIX
Paper from
responsible sources
FSC® C104740

Headline's policy is to use papers that are natural, renewable and recyclable
products and made from wood grown in well-managed forests and other
controlled sources. The logging and manufacturing processes are expected to
conform to the environmental regulations of the country of origin.

HEADLINE PUBLISHING GROUP
An Hachette UK Company
Carmelite House
50 Victoria Embankment
London EC4Y 0DZ

www.headline.co.uk
www.hachette.co.uk

For Dad, with love

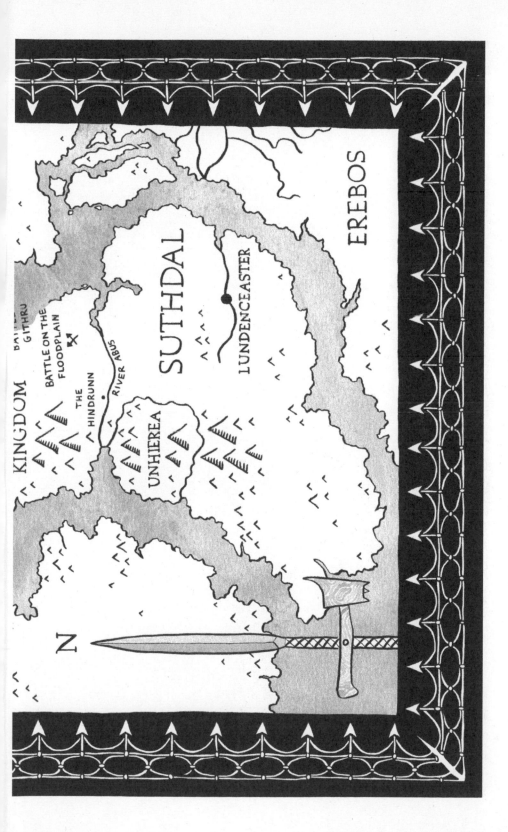

Contents

Map of Albion   vi
Prologue   1

Part I — The North

1 The Drop of the Body   9
2 The Blaze   18
3 When the Dead Rise   25
4 The Accomplice   38
5 The Stones   49
6 Unhierea   63
7 The Man in the Mountains   77
8 The Trials of King Gogmagoc   91
9 A Flush of Red   111
10 The Trial   125
11 The Hand   132
12 The Great Canal   137
13 Into Suthdal   145

Part II — The South

14 The Spymaster   149
15 The Empty Lands   163
16 Lincylene   175
17 A Broken Crow   184
18 The Passes Are Shut   188
19 Thingalith   197

20 Under Siege   201
21 The Quiet War   214
22 The Rock   224
23 Silence   236
24 The Weapon   247
25 Brimstream   255
26 Like Locusts   269
27 Sickness   282
28 Hunger   299
29 The Earl and the Giant   318
30 The Spymaster Unleashed   328
31 Reciprocity   338
32 Help Me   352
33 The Incantation   364

Part III — Lundenceaster

34 The Smell of Blood   371
35 The Tunnel   378
36 Ellengaest   393
37 The Walls of Lundenceaster   407
38 The Breach   422
39 The Suthern King   450
40 The Witan   463
41 The Fire   479

    Epilogue   485
    Roll of Black Legions   489
    Houses and Major Characters of the
      Black Kingdom   491
    Acknowledgements   495
    About the Author   497

Prologue

Through the rain that fell soft as down, two figures sat in a little boat, on a sea like tar. Moon and stars were hidden, the only sounds the splash of the oars and the waves lapping at the hull. The dark mass at the oars heaved and grunted, puffing a fine spray of water from his lips. His passenger was a black silhouette crouched at the back of the boat, so huge that his weight lifted the prow from the water.

'I still don't know the plan,' said the oarsman.

The darkness clotted at the stern made no reply. It just hoisted a hood against the rain, and stared out over the pitch sea.

'You could take an oar,' said the oarsman, whose name was Unndor. 'We'd be faster.'

The shadow flicked a hand towards his own enveloped arm, held in close and vulnerable at his chest. 'We would not.'

The boat was drawing towards a bright pinprick, far across the water. The waves knocked on the hull, rocking the pair as the distant light slowly resolved into a ship, twinkling silently as dark figures crossed the deck. It grew huge: a rolling, sweating, round-bellied hog of a ship without porthole

Leabharlanna Poiblí Chathair Baile Átha Cliath
Dublin City Public Libraries

or mast, fastened to the sea floor by two hemp ropes running beneath the waves. The top was awash with yellow lamplight, obscured as the little boat passed into the shadow of the hull. They had been spotted, and a silhouetted head protruded over the side. 'Ellengaest, is that you?'

'It's me,' replied the shadow from the stern.

The head retreated at once. 'They were expecting you?' asked Unndor.

'I am their only visitor who arrives at night.'

A rope was tossed over the side, a pair of hands appearing above to lash one end onto the rail. Unndor took the rope and knotted it onto an iron ring at the bow, and then a rope ladder tumbled down the hull, its end coming to rest just above the boat's knocking gunwale. The passenger, the Ellengaest, did not move, and after a moment, Unndor took the ladder and began to climb. When several hands had reached from the ship to help him over the rail above, Ellengaest followed.

He was pulled aboard a solid acre of planking, bordered by a low rail, and gently curved like a fragment of an enormous barrel. The deck bristled with posts, each bearing a pair of blackened storm lamps, and the whole vessel gleamed with tar and rain. The men on the deck wore beaten expressions and heavy black cloaks, each emitting the smoky reek of tar, rain beading on the stifling garments and drifting through the lamplight. The captain, Galti, was small and hunched, and stood a half-pace further back from the towering form of Ellengaest than might have been normal. 'What can I do for you, sir? Leave us,' he added to the deckhands.

Ellengaest watched them go. 'This place is hell,' he said.

Galti did not disagree, staring up at his visitor, the rain running down his face.

'We have come to see one of your prisoners, Captain,' said Ellengaest. 'Urthr Uvorenson.'

Galti's foot twisted beneath him. 'What do you want with him, sir? I ask as he is quite a high-profile prisoner.'

'Not your concern, Captain. Lead on.'

Galti hesitated, gritting his teeth, and then turned away, leading them to a hatch at the heart of the deck. He pulled it open to unleash an abominable stench: damp, excrement, rot and urine in one potent gust. Unndor staggered back, but Galti swung himself down onto the rungs of a hidden ladder and disappeared into the cavity. The two new arrivals paused by the entrance.

'Ellengaest?' asked Unndor. 'Why Ellengaest? Sounds like a Suthern word.'

'You next,' said Ellengaest, without looking at Unndor.

'My brother has been living down there for three months?'

'Go and ask him yourself.'

Unndor screwed up his face and plunged in, having to twist slightly to accommodate his shoulders. Ellengaest delayed long enough only to take a fortifying breath before he followed inside.

Beneath the deck, the air was a poisonous fume. Ellengaest advanced, guided by half a dozen flickering candles lining the corridor, ignoring the gleaming eyes that followed his progress from behind iron bars. The passage rocked and swayed, and there was a soft clink from either side as the prisoners stirred.

By the time he reached Galti and Unndor, the cell before them stood open. He stepped inside, taking a candle from Galti, which illuminated two wooden bunks. The top one was empty. The bottom supported a shackled prisoner, who sat up stiffly to face the newcomers, squinting in the candlelight.

'Leave us,' said Ellengaest. Galti retreated, his footsteps fading down the passage, and Ellengaest, Unndor and the prisoner were left observing one another.

Urthr Uvorenson had been put in this fetid belly by Ellengaest himself, though he probably did not know that. He had served three months of his sixty-year sentence and already looked a broken man. He was thin, his hair matted, his face watchful. Open sores covered his hands, and his nails were tattered from the endless work of grinding flour, unpicking tarred ropes and shattering metal ore. 'Brother,' he said, eyeing Unndor. He turned his attention to the other visitor. 'And I know you. You are Vigtyr the Quick—'

'Ellengaest,' he overrode. 'My name is Ellengaest.'

Urthr stared at him, then he shrugged. 'Why are you here?'

The visitor – the Ellengaest, Vigtyr the Quick – smiled at Urthr. 'I've come to see if you would like to walk free.'

Urthr gave a brief, flat laugh. He looked bitterly at his brother, sitting in the other corner, in rebuke at this cruelty.

'I do not make idle offers,' said Vigtyr.

Urthr shrugged. 'And how could you arrange that?'

'I could take you with me tonight,' said Vigtyr. 'Your brother and I arrived by boat, tethered outside. It is as simple as you agreeing to help me, and then the three of us will take that boat back to shore.'

Urthr examined him. 'They would stop us.'

'The captain,' said Vigtyr, leaning forward to watch Urthr's reaction, 'is quite considerably in my debt. We have a good arrangement. I maintain silence about what I have done for him, and in return I have access to the prisoners I need.'

There was a look of incredulity on Urthr's face. 'What have you done for him?'

'If I told you, it would erase the debt.'

Urthr held up his hands, showing his manacles. 'I am tempted by any agreement that gets me out of these. So what do you want from me?'

'It is not what I want from you. It is what I want *for* you. For both of you,' he added, indicating Unndor. 'Revenge. On the man who killed your father and put you in here to rot for crimes you did not commit. We are going to tear down the Black Lord.'

There was a slight movement as Urthr examined his brother's face, then turned back to Vigtyr. 'And why do you want this?' he breathed.

'Your freedom is in your hands,' said Vigtyr, 'but you may startle it away if you're too rough.'

Unndor spoke then, leaning forward from his corner. 'But you cannot simply expect us to trust you. There are rumours about you. How can you bring down Roper? How could you do it, when our father could not?'

'There is a man below the Abus,' replied Vigtyr. 'A Sutherner of unusual cunning, who has let it be known that he needs spies.'

'Bellamus,' said Urthr, unimpressed. 'Perhaps the Black Kingdom's greatest enemy. You want to use him?'

'I will use him. And I will use the Kryptea. And you will help me, or you'll rot here. Those are your choices.'

The darkness thumped as someone walked the deck overhead, and the three could almost sense the straining ears tracking their every word. 'I know you,' said Urthr at last. 'I know your reputation. You come here offering a great deal, but there is no payment I can imagine that would satisfy you. What would it cost me to be in your debt?'

Vigtyr shrugged. 'Nothing you treasure. Nothing you haven't already lost. I need messengers. I can't regularly head south of the Abus to contact the spymaster, it would be obvious, and I'd be missed. That is where you two come in. No one will miss you. You will have your freedom, and you will have revenge on the man who killed your father. Will you take it?'

There came a pause. Then Urthr began to laugh. It was a noise so uncontrolled that even Vigtyr leaned back a little, eyeing the prisoner. The laugh rattled beneath the deck like a die in a wooden cup. Urthr fell silent, his wrists tugging at the shackles that linked them. 'Yes,' he said. 'Get me off this hulk and I'll do anything you want, but especially kill Roper Kynortasson.'

'And you?' said Vigtyr, looking at Unndor.

'Of course,' he said. 'Of course. Though I doubt you will find the madmen of the Kryptea easily controlled.'

'The Kryptea are the smallest part of this,' said Vigtyr dismissively. 'In the war that is coming, every soul will be involved. Suthdal is weak. We will need to uncover every enemy that Roper has and rally them against him. And not only him. Those close to him will die too.'

Urthr was smiling still. 'Who?'

'His brothers are first,' said Vigtyr. 'If they are not dead already, they will be within days. The man I have set on them does not fail.'

The pair eyed Vigtyr for a time, the only sound the creak of the boat's timbers. 'When do we begin?'

Vigtyr smiled. 'We have begun already.'

Part I
THE NORTH

1

The Drop of the Body

The Black Lord was a tall man, though not as tall as often supposed. He held his back very straight; his hair was dark, his face robust and stern at rest. But that was an illusion, and his attention, if you gained it, was consistent, personable and intelligent. He was a man of sharp edges, concealed by a practised and deprecating manner. It was only the very few close to him who saw the ticking heart like a clockwork spring that drove him on, on, on. And at this moment, his face had assumed the distant mask he often wore in times of turmoil.

Because his brother was dead.

He stood, wrapped in a dark cloak, on a white sand beach at the head of a long lake. The only person within ten feet was a tall woman with black hair and poisonous green eyes, she too enfolded in a dark cloak. Her name was Keturah, and the pair of them stood slightly apart from a score of mourners, buffeted by the wind rushing the length of the water.

Along the lake's edge, some fifty yards away, a procession was approaching. A dozen boys, no older than twelve, walking together in two parallel lines.

They were carrying a child's body.

A grey, limp presence held awkwardly between the lines.

The mouth was a dark ellipse. The arms, like slim boards of willow, bounced with each step. The flesh was naked but for a layer of charcoal, and a chain of raptor feathers clutched at its neck, and behind the procession a vast stretch of a drum thumped with each step they took.

Dow. Dow. Dow.

Roper did not notice the drum. He did not see the mountains enclosing them on three sides in a sheer verdant wall, or the grey waves swept up by the wind. He was lost in the memories that swarmed this place.

He remembered a still day on this very beach, when he and the dead boy had been engulfed in a cloud of midges. He remembered how they had run up and down the beach to try and lose them, but wherever they went, still more waited for them. How they had plunged into the waters of the lake to wait for the return of the wind, and found it too cold. They had finally taken refuge in the smoke of their fire, which though he had to breathe hot fumes, Roper found preferable to the swarm beyond. He had said he was going to make a dash for their cloaks, and his brother had declared that the midges would have reduced him to a skeleton by the time Roper returned. They had joked that together, they would spend the rest of their days attempting to find the Queen Midge, should such a tyrant exist, and destroy her as a favour to all humanity. Surely they could do no greater good.

He remembered the moon-blasted night they had fished together on a promontory at the far end. How he had been surly because his brother had caught two fine trout, and he had managed nothing. He remembered the last time he had seen Numa, standing on this beach with the iron clouds stretching behind him. Roper had turned in his saddle as he rode south with two unfamiliar Pendeen legionaries. He remembered how Numa and his twin had looked back at him and had not waved: merely shared one last look before Roper turned away. He remembered the steady metallic hiss of the rain stinging the flat lake. He remembered the cold of

it running down his cheeks and over his lips. He remembered it all, but could feel no grief. All he had was the restless
ticking in his chest, seeking revenge.

The procession was drawing near the grave at Roper's side,
its earthen walls impressed with interlinking handprints,
like a canopy of leaves. As it came close, the mourners began
to sing: a gentle lament that quivered and shook, swelling
with the body's approach, and presently becoming a funereal
howl that almost drowned the reverberations of the drum.
One of the singers standing by the grave was the double of
the corpse, his face a tear-stained mirror to the scene before
him. Gray was next to him, singing with the others, and
placed a hand on the boy's heaving shoulder, eyes not leaving the swaying body.

It was manoeuvred into place above the grave, head facing
east, and close enough that Roper could see the lacerations
in the skin, cut to ribbons to hasten the moment his brother's
bones rotted into the earth. The dark limbs were folded to
the body's side. For an instant it floated above the grave.

The reverberations of the drum faded and the singing fell
away. Even the wind fell still.

Then the body dropped.

It plunged into the earth, a filthy embrace whooshing up in
reaction. There was a distant thump as the corpse hit its resting place. Then Numa's peers and his stricken twin began
pressing the piled earth forward with their bare hands, filling
in the grave. Roper turned away then, receiving a momentary
assessment from the green eyes at his side.

'Now we find out who killed him.'

'Master.' Roper caught the eye of a stooped, ancient man
robed in black, and hailed him, remembering too late to lift
the thunderous frown from his brow. The Master of the haskoli
and Roper met amid the embracing mourners and shook
hands. The Master's was a swollen talon, cold and lumpen,
and the face above it so lined it resembled a piece of

parchment stored at the bottom of a travel-sack. Keturah and another woman in dark robes joined the pair of them, and the Master offered Roper a gentle smile.

'A sad day, lord.'

'Yes, a sad day,' Roper agreed. 'But my priority here is discovering why this day has come at all.'

The Master's smile did not relent. This was the man who had overseen Roper's own time in the haskoli, whom Roper had feared and admired without limit as a student. The Master had been a Sacred Guardsman once, but injury had forced him into the mountains. He still possessed an unmistakable aura though: that of a man who has had the threshold at which he becomes agitated breached and reset so many times that it was now near unreachable. 'I'm so sorry, my lord. Events such as this are not unheard of.'

Roper narrowed his eyes. 'I'm not sure I understand.'

The Master interlinked his fingers over his chest. 'These boys are pushed very hard, my lord, as you will remember from your own time here. We initiate them into the sacred art of war. They learn not to back down under any circumstances, and there is a fierce rivalry between their groups. Sometimes, that gets out of hand. I have seen it several times now. It is usually a fight that has gone too far. No malice, nothing out of the ordinary – just an accident, from boys who are testing their limits.'

'You think one of Numa's peers did this?'

The Master nodded. 'That is the most likely explanation, lord.'

Keturah, who had been listening closely, made a brief impatient noise. 'Hm, do you really think so?' she said, tucking her hair behind one ear. 'Perhaps that would be true if this were a normal student, but Numa is the brother of a Black Lord who has just defeated a very powerful enemy. This is surely the remnants of Uvoren's power-block at work. I'm sure the Inquisitor will support me,' she added, gesturing to the woman by her side, who gave an approving smile. Her name was Inger and she was a little over a hundred years, with greying hair and a round, pale face. She wore black robes with a dog-headed angel inscribed on her chest in silver thread, and white eagle feathers rippling through her hair. Inger usually seasoned these marks of office with a vague smile, giving the impression that she was unaware of even her immediate environment. She had spent most of the journey here making their party laugh with awkward and singular observations, but Roper knew that she could not possibly be as hazy as she appeared. It took a mind of unusual insight and dedication to reach the rank of Maven Inquisitor.

'Not impossible,' the Master replied to Keturah. 'I can only tell you what seems most likely to me, as someone who has overseen this school for two dozen years. If this had been Uvoren's men, they would surely have wanted to make it clear this was not a random act and chosen a more overtly violent method. Unfortunately, Numa seems to have been killed by hand.'

'The timing is more significant than the means,' opined Keturah.

'I agree,' said the Inquisitor, distractedly.

'We will discover the truth, one way or another,' said Roper abruptly. Not for one moment did he believe this had been an accident. 'I am leaving two guardsmen here: Leon and Salbjorn, to aid the Inquisitor.' Roper indicated two armoured men who stood nearby, observing the conversation silently. Leon was massive and dark, with a crudely carved rock of a face. Salbjorn, standing next to him, was his protégé: small, wiry and blond, with a pointed chin and angular cheekbones. 'Salbjorn will help with the investigation. Leon will protect Ormur.' Roper named Numa's surviving twin.

The Master inclined his head. 'As you wish, lord. They can have quarters up at the school.'

'I thank you for your help, Master,' said Roper. 'Time is against me. I will speak with my brother, then I must go.'

The Master bowed and Roper tried to slip into the crowd

of chattering mourners. But they shied away from him, every
one of them aware of his person and backing away swiftly.
Roper ignored this, casting around for his younger brother.
He saw him almost at once: a solitary figure standing at
the water's edge, the lake lapping at his bare feet. Roper
went to join him, the two of them staring out over the water
together.

Ormur was small for his age, as Roper had once been. His
features were still expressive and endearing, yet to develop
into the strong mask of a mature Anakim, and reminiscent to
Roper now of the Sutherners. He tried to think what to say to
the boy, who did not seem to have noticed Roper's approach.
'Are you all right?'

'Yes, lord,' said the boy.

'What happened?' asked Roper, unable to think of anything more helpful to say, so succumbing to the question he
most wanted to ask. 'I heard you found his body.'

'I found him, lord.'

'Don't call me *lord*, Ormur.'

'I found him. We were fishing off Cut Edge,' said the boy,
giving a listless wave up the lake to a steep drop, overhung
with branches and beneath which the trout liked to linger
for the insects that fell into the water. It had been a favourite
fishing spot in Roper's own time here. 'We'd had no luck, and
he wanted to go and set some baited lines by the shore. I kept
fishing.' Ormur's face began to warp and Roper placed a hand
on the boy's arm, turning him away from the water.

'Look at me, brother.' He stared into Ormur's grey eyes.
This was not the roguish, impish character that he remembered. 'Take a deep breath.'

Ormur seemed steadied by Roper's touch. He closed his
eyes for a long moment, drawing in the mountain air.

'Are you ready?'

Ormur nodded. 'He didn't come back. I stayed fishing until
late. We had a moon, I was waiting for him. It was dark before
I packed up and went to find him.'

Ormur's grief began to resurface, and Roper intervened quickly. 'Did you get any fish?'

'I got a char,' said the boy. 'Not a big one.'

'I miss char,' said Roper, watching his brother carefully. 'That is the smell everyone says they associate with the haskoli, when they have moved on. Char, roasting over the fire.' The break in the conversation had given Ormur a little time to gather his energy, and Roper waited now for him to go on.

'I found him down on the shore of the lake,' said Ormur, his voice grotesquely suppressed. 'He was so pale, under the moon. One of his arms was underneath him, and one of them trailing in the waters of the lake. I didn't realise he was dead. I thought maybe he'd slipped and hurt himself. And then I turned him over—' Ormur coughed, his eyes dropped, his chin followed, his chest heaved, hiccoughed, and then he broke over Roper. His head leaned into Roper's chest and he sobbed wretchedly, a keening so animal that Roper could feel it plucking at his flesh. He raised his hands to the boy's shoulders and held him there, leaning his head into his brother. Ormur was trying to go on, and Roper shushed him, but the boy would not be stopped. Between each heaving breath, each gasping sob, he forced the words free. 'He . . . was . . . strangled!' He hauled in three rapid breaths. 'His *eyes*!'

'Stop,' said Roper, firmly.

They waited there, the two of them. 'I'm sorry, brother,' he murmured into Ormur's head. 'I'm so sorry. We will find them, you know. Whoever killed Numa. We will find them and make them pay.'

Ormur's shoulders were no longer heaving, his sobs replaced by deep, slow breaths.

'I am leaving an Inquisitor here with two guardsmen. The Inquisitor and Salbjorn will find Numa's killer. Leon will protect you.' The boy made no reply. Roper released him, and he straightened up. 'Do you think it was one of the boys here who killed Numa?'

Ormur shook his head at once, his grief-stained face resolving into certainty. 'No. No.'

'Neither do I,' said Roper. He gestured back at the crowd of mourners, most of whom had begun to drift away from the lake and up towards the school. The two of them followed, walking in silence for a time. 'You know what week it is?'

'*Hookho*,' said Ormur. The week the cuckoo begins to call.

'Good,' said Roper. 'And next week?'

'*Gurstala?*' hazarded Ormur, naming the week the bluebells flower.

'You've skipped two of them.' It seemed odd to Roper now, but he remembered being as ignorant as Ormur during his own time in the haskoli. Each Anakim week was named to reflect some seasonal event, but the mountains of the school had their own climate and their own pace, and the weeks had seemed as arbitrary to Roper at the time as they were evocative now. 'Next week is *Pipalaw*: the week rainbows bloom.'

They drew level with the score heading back up to the school. 'Take care of yourself, brother. Work hard. And stay safe. It will get better.'

Ormur looked glassily up at Roper, managed a brief nod, and turned away, following the group around the lake and towards the haskoli. Roper spotted three figures standing and waiting for him: the two Sacred Guardsmen and the Inquisitor. He went to join them and took each of their hands in turn, before staring at them in silence.

'I will find whoever did this, lord,' said Inger, smiling back at his poisonous expression. 'I always do.'

'Leave no stone unturned,' said Roper, in a low voice. 'Give him not one moment's rest. Follow him as a pack of murderous dogs and make him know ravenous fear. Pursue him onto the Winter Road and beyond if you must, and when you have him, bring me his head with two empty eye sockets.'

'It shall be as you wish, lord,' said Inger.

Roper observed them all for a moment longer. 'Good luck.'

The Anakim and the Sutherner, two of the races that inhabited Albion, did not share much. To the Sutherners, the world was filled with colour: to the Anakim, memory. The Sutherners loved to travel where the Anakim hated it, delighted in personal adornment where their neighbours scorned it, and subjected their lands to the yoke of agriculture, where the Anakim adored wilderness. Their laws were different, their customs deliberately diverse, and two fiercer enemies never existed. But revenge, at least, bound them. With either race, if you take a mother, father, sister or brother from them, no matter how complex their relationship was, you have violated family. Expect neither rest nor mercy until you have been violated in turn.

2

The Blaze

Though the air at Lake Avon carried the immaculate signature of altitude, the haskoli – the harsh school where boys were sent at the age of six to become legionaries – was set even higher, behind one of the mountains that bordered the lake. The climb to reach it took some two hours, and by the time Inger and her sacred escort had arrived, dusk was falling. The trees had shrunk and fallen away, and thick drifts of snow shone like burnished silver beneath a crescent moon.

The school was cut into the mountainside, sheer cliffs on three sides providing small protection from the elements. The buildings were completely uniform: a dozen longhouses, with timbers of straight red pine and thatch of heather, lining a central courtyard of sand, rock and drifted snow. Another, smaller lake spread before it, its icy surface rough from repeated shattering and freezing. Behind the school reared the shadow of an ancient tree which had somehow weathered the mountain winds: a single towering pine with only a dusting of needles remaining at its top. The rest of the branches were draped with hundreds of ragged raptor wings that fluttered darkly in place of leaves.

'Home, for the next while,' said Inger lightly. 'As it's dark already, I say we settle in tonight and begin our investigations first thing tomorrow.'

The guardsmen murmured their agreement, and they were led by a black-cloaked tutor into the nearest longhouse. The interior was very dark and suffused with the resinous scent of pine. They climbed a creaking flight of stairs, laid down their packs on the goatskins that bristled the floor, and emptied them in silence. Before long, Leon snatched up his sword and stalked out, saying he would sleep outside Ormur's quarters.

'Like a dog,' muttered Salbjorn, laying out his own equipment for tending, and lighting four smoky candles to guide his work. 'Do you really think the assassin is still here?' he asked, settling heavily on the floor and pulling a pot of fatty grease towards him. He began to work it bare-handed into his boots.

Inger watched him vacantly. 'What do you think?'

The guardsman's shadowed face turned towards her briefly, then back to his boots. 'He's gone. You don't kill the brother of the Black Lord and then linger at the scene of the crime.' When Inger made no reply, Salbjorn glanced at her once more. 'Do you?'

'It depends why you've killed him,' said Inger mildly.

Rain began to tap on the thatched roof and pour past the window in a fragmentary curtain. 'Do you have any suspects?'

'Many,' said Inger. 'The Black Lord has a lot of enemies, and it could be any one of them. Uvoren's two sons, Unndor and Urthr, live in disgrace or in gaol, thanks to Roper. Perhaps it is a friend of theirs. Tore, Legate of the Greyhazel, was a friend of Uvoren's from their days together at this haskoli. He commands a lot of men: maybe it was one of those, acting on his orders. The same goes for Randolph, Legate of the Blackstone. Or this might not be related to Uvoren's death at all. Never underestimate how mad the Kryptea can be, and what strange motive they can find for almost any death. Or maybe this was

Suthern work. Assassins from Suthdal, in repayment for the massacre atop Harstathur. Perhaps the Sutherners decided Roper's brothers would be more easily targeted than the man himself.' Inger fell silent, staring at a sputtering candle. 'That's just a start. There are dark forces at work in our kingdom, doing things that we do not yet understand.'

True darkness had fallen outside, and the rain drummed through the room. Salbjorn finished his boots and moved on to the rest of his equipment, adding each piece to a neat pile as he finished tending it. His cuirass bore gouges, dents and pocks, but not a speck of rust, dirt or blood. The chain mail beneath it was speckled with distorted links, but gleamed like water pouring through sunbeams. And the long sword, propped against the wall and unsheathed to allow its fresh oil coat to dry, had small chips and dinks all along its length, which was nevertheless sharpened to a pitiless edge.

'Can you smell smoke?' asked Inger suddenly, stirring from her dreamy reverie.

Salbjorn gestured towards the pot of grease. 'It's this.'

'No, I smelt that before,' said Inger, getting to her feet. She turned to the window, staring out into the school's rain-spattered courtyard. She could see nothing for a few seconds. Then her eyes accustomed to the dark outside, and she perceived the crimson glow flickering the ground in front of their longhouse. She could see no flame, but that was because it was out of sight beneath her. She turned back into the room, comprehension dawning as she registered the smoke hazing the candles. 'There's a fire,' she said, striding for the stairs. 'Beneath us.'

Salbjorn looked confused. Then he too discerned the smoke drifting across the candles, and rising up the staircase in a heavy fog. He swore, springing to his feet and hurrying after Inger. They clattered down the stairs, into the smoke, which grew dense, hot and caustic. It was obvious before they had even reached the lower storey that there was no salvation here. The pine walls flickered with the light of an already mature fire, the pair of them stopping to gape at the flames. They flowed in liquid streaks across the floor, writhed up the door and walls, and gasped black clouds that billowed over the ceiling. Inger heard Leon's voice shout suddenly from outside, yelling for help.

Salbjorn swore again, and Inger turned, pushing into him. 'Back upstairs!' she said. Choking and coughing, the pair of them staggered back the way they had come. Inger tripped over the top step and collapsed onto the upper floor, the smoke rising behind her.

'The windows!' she said, accepting Salbjorn's hand to pull herself upright, lungs convulsing at the smoke burning down her throat. The fire below was spreading rapidly: far too rapidly to have been an accident. From the look of those fiery rivers, someone had doused the floor in oil. The two of them ran to a window and leaned out over the sill and into the rain, gasping at the cold air. Beneath them, they could see the fire rising in torrents from the outer windows and beginning to consume the walls. Long-shadowed figures flitted the courtyard below, crying an alarm and marshalled towards the frozen lake by Leon's powerful silhouette. They were trying to form a bucket chain to quench the flames, but that would take too long for Inger and Salbjorn, trapped on the top floor.

'We have to jump,' said Salbjorn. His head disappeared back into the longhouse and then reappeared, heaving his precious equipment into the void where it tumbled some twenty feet to the ground, bouncing and scattering. Perhaps Salbjorn could jump: he was an athlete, young and strong. But Inger was well into middle age, and saw herself falling from the window and breaking on the stones beneath.

'I can't jump,' she said quietly.

Salbjorn, who had one foot on the windowsill, glanced at her. 'You have to.'

'No,' she shook her head, touching his arm. 'You go. I'll think of something else.'

Salbjorn searched her face for a heartbeat. 'Jump and you might be hurt,' he said. 'But if you stay here, you'll die!'

She smiled at him. 'I would prefer smoke-induced sleep to broken legs, blood loss and fever.'

They stared at one another. Shouts rang up from below, urging the two of them to take their chances and jump. Heat was billowing at Inger's back, so that she could now see the liquid shimmer it cast escaping the window above her. Sweat had begun to stand out on her brow and she could feel it trickling down her back.

'Right,' said Salbjorn abruptly. He retreated back into the room, and Inger tried to clutch at him as he turned away from the window.

'You must go!' she insisted, but she was turned back to the window by the power of the smoke. 'Don't stay—' she coughed suddenly. 'Please! I will jump if it means you will.'

'I'm going to,' said Salbjorn, reappearing with an armful of goatskins. His eyes were streaming, his face covered with sweat, and he panted at the window for a few moments, struggling to open his eyes. He hurled the goatskins down onto the ground, and then stepped up onto the windowsill. 'And so are you,' he said, lowering himself off the sill. For a moment, he clutched on by his fingertips, dangling over ground and staring down at the drop. Then he let go.

Salbjorn plunged into the dark, hitting the stones beneath and bouncing backwards with the power of his fall. Inger could hear him grunt in pain as the breath was forced from his lungs, and knew such a fall would break her legs. Even Salbjorn was getting to his feet with extreme caution, staggering on an injured ankle. He called Leon to him and the two exchanged hurried words. Behind them, the bucket-line was finally getting water onto the flames, but it was too slow, and they were achieving no more than the rain, which already pounded the courtyard. Such a lethal fire had to be by design.

A blotch of darkness was unfurled beneath Inger. Leon and Salbjorn had each taken one edge of a goatskin and stretched it between them. 'Jump!' Salbjorn called. 'Aim for the skin, it will break your fall!'

Even if the two guardsmen could meaningfully break her fall, the target looked minuscule from this height. Inger looked back into the room, and had to turn away at once from the terrible heat on her face. Her eyes began to stream and she found she could not see. By touch, she clambered up onto the windowsill. She stood, balanced on the sill, trembling, blind and hesitating, but there was nothing to wait for. Her vision would not return: not before she was in clear air.

She toppled forward.

Inger hurtled through the dark, arms flailing at the air roaring past her ears. She hit the goatskin with a *whoomp*, her momentum carrying her through and onto the stones beneath, where she jarred to a halt. Leon and Salbjorn were dragged inward by the force of her fall, collapsing on top of her. She lay panting for a moment, eyes still streaming, throat still burning and lungs still objecting to their noxious contents. She felt the two figures above her roll away, and a hand took her shoulder, turning her over so that the freezing rain splattered her face.

'Inquisitor? Are you all right?' It was Salbjorn's voice. Inger gasped lungfuls of thin mountain air, feeling her heartbeat reverberate through her limbs. She managed a nod. 'We're going to move you back from the flames. Lie still.'

She could feel the tension in the skin beneath her as the two guardsmen gripped its edges once more and dragged her across the courtyard. 'Just stay here, my lady,' came Salbjorn's voice as she came to a halt. 'We need to stop the flames spreading. We'll be back.'

Inger heard the two of them sprint away. Coughing, she sat up, wiping her eyes and forcing them open. Their longhouse, now across the courtyard, was a skeletal inferno, the outer walls a fragile façade between the night and the roaring flames behind. In front, figures scrambled to empty buckets over the flames and the neighbouring longhouse to prevent it, too, succumbing to fire. The entire scene had an eerie halo, caused by the tears still flooding her eyes. She needed water, and got stiffly to her feet and began limping to the neighbouring longhouse in search of a pail. As she approached the edge of the courtyard, a figure rounded the corner of the longhouse and thumped into her. Inger staggered backwards, too surprised to react.

Then she focused on the half-illuminated face before her. It was rough, puckered with scarring, and stared back with such menace that she took another step away. His silhouette was stocky: very much too stocky to be one of the young tutors here. And flashing at his side was a long, wicked knife.

The two of them simply stared at one another wide-eyed for a moment, each as shocked as the other. Then Inger filled her lungs.

'Intruder!' she bellowed.

Assassin.

3

When the Dead Rise

Roper and Keturah rode through a leafy arch of elm; Gray and another Sacred Guardsman, Hartvig, behind. They had descended from the mountains the previous evening, the passes still thick with enough snow to trouble the horses, and now travelled in companionable silence.

Roper did not know what was occupying Keturah's thoughts, but his were dwelling on an image. It was his dead friend Helmec. His twisted neck, his armoured chest. The filth that wrapped him, the bodies on which he rested. The image was significant, Roper knew. He did not associate it with any particular emotion. When it appeared in his head, as it did several times a day, he felt no shock or grief. It was just significant; compelling his attention. He did not hear the low noises of Pryce and Gray talking, which he knew had accompanied it, nor the smell of mud, petrichor and blood. He just remembered the image, oddly stark, and undeniably significant.

Roper felt, with just as much assurance as he knew the image was important, that he ought not to dwell on it. To be so consumed by something was possession, a cardinal sin in the Black Kingdom. So he looked at Keturah, who was staring straight ahead, wearing a slight frown.

'Your father sent me another message this morning,' he said.

'Another one? What's he complaining about now?'

'The wool shortage again.'

'Has he been going on about a wool shortage?'

'Endlessly,' said Roper. 'This is the third messenger he's sent on the subject. He seems to think I'm ignoring him.'

Keturah shrugged. 'So the women of the fortress get a brief respite from their interminable weaving,' she said acidly. 'The world will go on, what's the problem?'

'He says people don't have enough to make new summer clothes. So much has been traded to Hanover in exchange for iron that we're facing a shortfall. I gave the go-ahead for trading to begin too early and now we've exhausted our supplies.'

Keturah rolled her eyes. 'That will have upset him; my father loves detail. It's hardly the greatest crisis you've faced, though. The sheep will be rooed in, what, five weeks? And then the subjects will be able to make all the summer clothes their hearts desire.'

'I don't quite understand the problem,' admitted Roper.

Keturah glanced sidelong at him and smirked slightly.

Roper was tempted to ignore her and did for a moment. Behind them, Gray and Hartvig were swept up in conversation about which animal they would least like to encounter alone in the forest. It seemed that Gray thought bear, Hartvig aurochs. But the image of Helmec surfaced in Roper's mind once more, so he turned back to his wife. 'What?'

'You are a wartime leader, my husband,' she said shortly. 'It is the only thing that commands your attention long enough that you see it through.' Roper blinked at that. He rode in silence for a while, thinking about what she had said.

'What do you mean?' he asked at last.

'By all accounts,' said Keturah, 'and judging by what you've achieved, you are highly capable when on campaign. More than capable. Gray tells me you don't even have to think very hard: your understanding of gestures, of how your enemy thinks and your men respond, comes to you naturally. When you are at home . . .' she trailed off and then turned in her saddle to give him a corrosive smile. 'You are bored. You don't even think. You don't care enough about your trade agreements to give them a moment's thought beyond that which it takes to approve them. As a consequence, none of the plans you make in peace are coherent. This wool shortage is a perfect example. It does not inspire you like battle does, so you didn't think about it, and as a result, people will be angry.'

'I do care,' said Roper, smiling vaguely at her tirade.

'You care if it is brought to your attention,' said Keturah, her head flopping onto one shoulder in exasperation. 'But if I, or my father, keep bringing things to your attention you will get bored of that too.'

The words stung Roper, but they infiltrated each excuse he mustered in resistance.

'I don't think we're going to change that,' said Keturah, 'but let's think about your rule so far. It started with the first ever retreat of a full call-up of legionaries from battle. It was followed by our first plague in decades; a somewhat clumsy purge in which you were very obviously responsible for the death or disgrace of some highly esteemed subjects.' Here she gripped his arm, meeting his eye and giving him a very different smile to her last. She knew he had done that in defence of her. 'And finally, one of your lieutenants—'

'Your cousin,' interrupted Roper.

'Your lieutenant,' insisted Keturah, 'killed and dismembered one of the kingdom's most beloved warriors.'

Roper let out a slow breath. After the Battle of Harstathur, where they had fought and beaten the Sutherners, Pryce had taken the opportunity to kill Roper's old rival Uvoren, and obliterated his body for good measure. The act had been more than mere savagery, though Pryce was not beyond that. It had been a statement. When Catastrophe, the apocalyptic mail-clad snake, rose from the eastern deserts, the dead would rise

with her. All those with an intact skeleton would drag themselves free from the earth and stand among the ferns and the
trees, casting around with mud-filled sockets for weapons.
Those who had been honourable, noble subjects, would brave
the odds and fight against her. The greatest Anakim heroes
even had their bodies preserved in the Holy Temple so they
were armed, armoured and ready to draw swords in this last,
great conflict. They were turned to face eastwards, watching
for the moment Catastrophe would rise, ready to resist at a
heartbeat's notice.

Those who had been selfish, self-pitying, jealous or weak-
willed in life, would be seduced by Catastrophe's hissed
promises of wealth and glory, and fight on her side. When
Pryce destroyed Uvoren's body, he had made a judgement
that the captain would be one of those who fought with
Catastrophe, against the angels. It was not merely the gravest
insult that he could have administered; it also condemned
Uvoren's soul to a tortured, earthly existence. Without the
stabilising influence of his body, it could not make the journey over the Winter Road and across to the Otherworld: the
Anakim afterlife. The act had caused a public outcry. Many
had not liked Uvoren, but death absolves one's sins more
surely than redemption. The execution had martyred him.

'That seems a harsh assessment,' said Roper, in response
to Keturah's inventory of his rule.

'Set against it,' Keturah went on, 'are your not inconsider-
able martial successes. Three magnificent victories, each won
against dreadful odds. That is why your popularity is as
good as it is: our people love glory and will honour you for it.
But the longer you spend as a peacetime ruler, the more they
will remember your faults. You will get back into the Hindrunn and discover those resentful stares from people who
think you are a messy lord.'

'Has Harstathur faded from their memories already?' asked
Roper.

'That was tainted by Uvoren's death, and the rumours that

it was carried out on your orders. Husband,' she said, suddenly losing her restraint, 'you need a new campaign. You promised you would sack Lundenceaster. Our kingdom can grow rich through war again, rather than poor. Do that, and people will begin to remember how skilled you can be. They will forgive the occasional confused trade deal, or grain shortage, or civil enemy that you subdue, as long as you consolidate your reputation as someone who can bring us victories on the field. Your other option is to sit at home, watch the people get more frustrated and the Kryptea more restless.' The Kryptea were one of Roper's greatest enemies, and one whom he could not touch. They were an order of assassins, tasked with maintaining stability in the kingdom, often by executing despotic Black Lords. Originally conceived as a check against tyranny, over the centuries they had accrued power and jealousy until now their actions were utterly unpredictable. Still, people were too frightened by far to confront them.

'There are better reasons than that for invading Suthdal,' Roper replied.

'None that I can think of,' said Keturah, as though that settled the matter.

'I can think of one very good one, which I haven't heard from anyone yet,' Roper insisted. 'Do you know how many legionaries I command?'

Keturah shrugged.

'Less than seventy thousand,' said Roper. 'Do you know how many there were at the beginning of last year?'

A shake of the head.

'Ninety thousand. Twenty years before that, my grandfather led an invasion of one hundred and twenty thousand. Every year that we are at war, we have fewer legionaries. How many will there be at the end of my rule? How many left for the next generation? Defending our borders is no longer enough. The Sutherners always have more men. Agriculture means they can *infest* their land, and losing a battle does not

impact their population, like it does ours. They will always
have enough men. Every year, we will have less.'

'I don't quite see how this justifies a raid south,' said
Keturah.

'This will not be a raid,' said Roper. 'It will be an invasion.
Simply preserving our way of life here is no longer enough. I
cannot believe nobody has seen this before. Our strength
grows weaker and weaker, and our ability to subdue Suthdal –
to end this war, once and for all – is fading away. That child
you carry,' he said, glancing at the slight bulge beneath Keturah's cloak, 'may inhabit a world in which we are at the
mercy of the Sutherners. It may curse us, for not ending this
war while we had the chance and instead hoping blindly
that it lasts our own time. This war will rumble on, and in
twenty years, we will be too few to conquer Suthdal. We will
be eroded further and further until we have no choice in our
slow decline, until there is no way back. But at this moment,
we still have a choice,' he said, grimly. 'We can take this
entire island and put open ocean between us and the Sutherners. We can end this now and preserve the security of our
children. And their children. We can obliterate the nation of
Suthdal.'

Keturah was silent for a moment. 'Husband,' she said softly,
leaving the word there for a moment as an exclamation. 'When
you spoke of this after Harstathur, I did not think you were
serious. And since then the rumours have been that this will
be an avenging raid. Sow some fear, collect some loot, train
the young legionaries, make the Sutherners think twice
before they cross the Abus again . . . If our people realise you
intend to *stay* . . . To eradicate Suthdal and, what? What
then?'

'Return it to the wild,' said Roper. 'Create a new homeland
in the south.'

Keturah seemed to have so many questions she was
not sure where to start. 'And what of the Sutherners who
occupy it?'

'They'll work for us for a time and be forbidden from making weapons. But as their land returns to wilderness, they'll have to leave. There is no place for them in the wild.'

'But people will think that's insane! Spending decades south of the Abus in alien lands, how would we even do it? As you say, we have seventy thousand legionaries. That is not enough to subdue the millions inhabiting the south! People would say it's suicide, and they would have a point.'

'The alternative to what I propose,' replied Roper, 'is an even more inevitable suicide, and terrible irresponsibility. To leave an unsolvable problem for the next generation. Be complicit in the slow decline of our people. We are responsible, whether through action or inaction, and at least by action we give ourselves a chance. We should have done this years ago, in truth, but we have one last chance to roll the dice. Is this not my role? You say I don't think about the small things. Perhaps you're right. But I think about the biggest things, which others don't seem to notice beyond their focus on sheep and fresh summer clothes.'

Keturah looked incredulous and, for once, lost for words. Then she shook herself abruptly. 'But, Husband, all you say is irrelevant anyway, you don't have the authority for this. You know how people would react to the thought of being in alien lands for *decades*. The tribunes and councillors would be appalled. The legates might just about back you, though only because they love campaigning and you have a bit of a reputation with them. Some would undoubtedly think it's madness, though. The Academy would speak out against it, which would make your legionaries exceptionally nervous; the Lothbroks would love any excuse to destabilise you, and the Hindrunn women would almost certainly make life exceptionally difficult if they knew about it.'

The streets of the Black Kingdom were dominated by women. Property was shared on marriage as a reflection of the partnership that husband and wife had become, and transferred to one in the event of the other's death. Legionaries died with

such regularity that the vast majority of property and wealth
was controlled by women, leaving them a powerful and influential group, and one with whom Roper's popularity was not
high. From their perspective, removed from campaigns and
confronted with Roper's civil and domestic ineptitude, he
was not a capable leader.

'And Almighty alone knows what the Kryptea would make
of this,' Keturah added. 'You trying to subdue millions with
seventy thousand legionaries. Jokul will blow an eyeball.'

'I will find a way,' said Roper, calmly. 'It *has* to be done. It
has to. All those groups and factions you mention have to be
brought to heel, because otherwise we are doomed. We have
no choice. Do you not agree?'

It was one of those rare occasions, Roper had witnessed
just a few times, that Keturah's face bore no hint of amusement. She just stared down at the road before her, brow
furrowed. 'I find myself torn between your case for its necessity and its obvious impossibility. But I am your wife. I regret
I find you more convincing than most will.'

Roper smiled faintly.

'Who knows about this?' she asked suddenly.

'I told you and Gray weeks ago,' said Roper. 'Though it
seems you did not take me seriously. No one, other than that.'

'Right,' she said abruptly. 'Keep it that way.'

'This has to be done,' said Roper, stubbornly.

'Then keep it that way,' Keturah insisted. 'Because you will
never, ever gain the necessary support if you tell people the
truth. Are you determined to accomplish this, by any means
possible?'

'Of course.'

'Then allow people to keep believing what I believed. Let
them think this is just an avenging raid. By far the most well
disposed towards this plan will be the legates and legionaries,
because they know you on campaign. They're loyal to you, or
most of them are. Wait until we're in the south, and then tell
those who have come with you what the plan is and why. If

anyone finds out before, you will be blocked at once.' She snapped her fingers. 'You may even be deposed, or face Kryptean assassins.'

Roper thought for a moment, trying on the idea and finding it to his liking. He smiled quite involuntarily. 'Are you going to help me, my love?'

She was quiet for a time. 'Do you know, Husband, I do actually believe in you. Perhaps I have never mentioned this before . . .' She paused, frowning. 'Perhaps I have been remiss. I think you will be one of our great rulers. I cannot believe you survived last year. You have a battery of skills that I believe separate you from other occupants of the Stone Throne. Obsessively driven. An eye for the big picture. Principled to the point of madness. A problem-solver. And most of all, unyielding. I understand this. I understand why you need to do it. I suppose I had never thought about it before. But you need my help.'

Roper could hardly credit these words coming from this always cynical, often scathing woman. But he had known for a long time that her acidulous manner hid someone obsessively loyal to those close to her. She had just never expressed it so explicitly.

'My partner,' he said. 'What are you going to do?'

'I am going to work out how you subdue millions with seventy thousand legionaries,' she said. 'The Academy has all the answers. I will assemble them in one place.'

Roper looked across at her. 'So I have you with me? I thought Gray might be, but otherwise was worried I'd have to do this alone.'

'Have you never taken it seriously when I said we were a partnership?' she said, laying a hand on his arm. 'I am at your back.'

It took them a week's riding to reach the Hindrunn, where they were met with a roar of welcome from the Great Gate. It stood open already and the Black Lord's party cantered through the exposed tunnel of stone, emerging onto the cobbles of the outermost residential district. The streets crawled with memory for Roper. On his first entrance as Black Lord, he had been jeered, hissed and humiliated. On his second, the cobbles had been deserted: the subjects certain that he would gain entry with violence, which might then be turned on them. And on his last, there had finally been the peals of cheering; the bundles of bitter herbs thrown in front of the column; the hands reaching out as he passed.

There were fewer subjects than usual. Most of the auxiliary legions were out of the fortress, beginning work on Roper's grand construction project: the Great Canal. The River Abus already stretched nearly from one coast of Albion to the other, with the final unguarded portion of the island defended by a canal instead. The canal and river were to be joined, and both broadened and fortified to create a single strip of defensive water that cut the island in half, controlled by a new dam to be constructed behind the Hindrunn. The Anakim were poor swimmers, with the males unable to swim at all due to the heavy bone-armour plates beneath their skin. In the mind of an Anakim, a wall of water was near impenetrable.

The pace of those left behind was gentle. They stopped to gossip in the streets, breaking off to observe Roper intently as he passed. A herald was calling out news from atop a mounting block: four Suthern ships had been wrecked in the north-west, washing fascinating cargo ashore; two men had died in construction of the Great Canal; the melting mountain snows had brought flooding to the east; a strange blood-red rain had fallen a little north of the Hindrunn. Any who wished to hear more would trade a little food, labour or metal with the herald for the details, and he was soon surrounded by voices clamouring to hear more of the shipwrecks.

The horses were left in stables below the Central Keep, and Roper and Keturah climbed to their quarters at the top of one of the towers. Roper threw the cloak from his shoulders and Keturah shut the door behind them. The room filled with a potent silence.

'You know where I have to begin,' said Roper, after a time.

'I know where you think you have to begin,' said Keturah. Unhierea.

A land of valleys and mountains to the west of Albion, populated by a race of half-remembered giants. Somewhere no Anakim had set foot for generations, and whose inhabitants, by all accounts, treated the borderlands with Suthdal as a hunting-ground. To them, the Sutherners were just another harvest.

Keturah frowned, turning away to throw a window wide. 'I think it far more likely that you will lose your life than gain an ally if you go there.'

'It could be dangerous,' Roper admitted. 'But as we have already discussed, we are stretching the resources at our disposal to the very limits of what is possible. I just know we have to try. There were a lot of dead at Harstathur. I don't know if we're enough to subdue Suthdal as it is, and if I lose too many men while trying, then we bring about the apocalypse we're trying to avoid. We have to try.'

'But *you* don't have to go, you know,' said Keturah. 'A king, walking alone into a foreign land with nothing but his words to hide behind. We don't even know whether they speak a language we can comprehend, and if they do, whether we have enough in common with them to be able to strike a bargain of any kind. They may kill intruders on sight. They may be wholly unpredictable and untrustworthy. If you fall in Unhierea, what then happens to your grand scheme to preserve our nation?'

Roper threw down his pack and began to empty it. 'Well you'd continue it, wouldn't you? If I died, that task would be yours.' Keturah raised her eyebrows, and Roper looked away from her before going on. 'But I can't ask my men to go where I dare not. And in any case, I certainly won't be alone. I'll need help . . . someone so mindless and savage that even the

Unhieru won't intimidate them. Who won't take no for an answer, who won't back down, and who may well enrage them but will undoubtedly win their respect.'

Keturah laughed grimly. 'So Pryce, then.'

'Correct,' said Roper. 'But he'll undoubtedly anger them. Tekoa's authority would be welcome too, and he'll need some fearsome warriors with him. Vigtyr, and some others of dubious restraint.' Whoever else he sent, Roper would have insisted on Vigtyr's presence. The giant lictor had proved a valuable ally, and Roper still felt unease that he had not been able to reward him as he had intimated in their original negotiations: with a place in the Sacred Guard. Vigtyr had been gracious and effusive in his thanks for the sword and estate that Roper had granted him instead of that lofty position, but Roper wanted to bring him closer still, honouring the lictor, who was an unusually skilled and resourceful servant.

Keturah began to empty her own pack, a frown on her face. 'Vigtyr's injured, isn't he?' she said absently.

'Not badly, I hear,' said Roper. 'But time is paramount. To subdue Suthdal, we will need a full campaigning season, and must go to Unhierea at once. We can stop at the freyi on the way, Vigtyr can catch us up there.' The freyi was the girls' school, located in the wild forests west of the Hindrunn.

But Keturah did not seem to have heard this. Her face was unusually downcast, and he realised too late that he had not acknowledged his companions for this most perilous task would include her cousin and her father. He opened his mouth to say he did not know what, but was intercepted by a knock from the door. 'Messengers, messengers,' he said, moving to the door. 'If this is Tekoa complaining about the wool shortage again, I'm leaving him in Unhierea.' He tugged the door open and then stood in the doorway for a moment, completely still. In the corridor outside was a legionary holding a leash noosed around a small sheep. The animal had been shorn and stared up at him gravely.

'A present from Legate Tekoa, lord,' said the legionary, holding out the leash. Roper stared down at the sheep for a moment, and then he stepped aside so Keturah could see it.

She looked briefly from the sheep to Roper. Then, ever unable to resist a joke, she laughed like a crow.

4

The Accomplice

Inger and the assassin stared at one another for just one more heartbeat. Then the knife at his side jerked forward, flashing up beneath her ribs. Or that was where it would have gone, had Inger's hands not lurched out, palms blocking the top of his wrist and halting the blow, blade wavering perilously between her forearms. His other hand lashed out, thumping into her chest and sending her staggering back. His boot swept forward, kicking wet grit and rock up into Inger's face, and then he turned and ran. Inger toppled to the ground, hands flying to her eyes and trying to force them open. Vision blurred, she saw two dark shapes hurtle past her, swords flashing in the light of the flames. Salbjorn and Leon. 'Stop!' she gasped after them. 'Stop! One of you must stay to protect the boy! Protect the boy!' Salbjorn, the rear figure, skipped to a frustrated halt, turning back to Inger. But Leon careered onwards, pursuing the assassin around the longhouse and into the dark.

Salbjorn returned to Inger, offering a hand which she seized to pull herself upright. 'The fire was a diversion,' she said, still trying to clear her eyes. 'We must find the boy! Where does he sleep?' Salbjorn gestured to the far-left longhouse, and they broke into a run. The bucket-line had faltered as the tutors turned to stare at the scene unfolding behind them. Then the Master of the Haskoli strode into the courtyard, roaring at them to keep going and protect the neighbouring longhouse.

Together, Inquisitor and guardsman limped to Ormur's sleeping quarters. Salbjorn hauled open the door and the two of them swarmed inside. There was an audible gasp but the interior was so dark they could perceive nothing past the door. 'Where is Ormur?' demanded Inger of the darkness. 'Ormur Kynortasson?' She could just distinguish eyes, shining in the gloom, at all different heights but each one wide and alert.

'He went outside,' replied a voice. 'Just a few moments ago.'

At her back, Inger heard Salbjorn exit suddenly. 'Where? Did he say where?'

There was a pause. 'We heard the word *intruder*. I think he thought it was his brother's murderer. He went after him.'

'Stay here!' Inger commanded, turning back into the rain and casting around the courtyard. The dark shadows of the longhouses loomed before her, one of them now a flaming skeleton. The black figures of the tutors ran before it, the mountains surrounding the school leaning forward, cast in flickering light.

'Inquisitor!' howled a voice from her left. She turned and limped towards it, working her way between two buildings. There she found two struggling figures, one clutching the other, who was evidently trying to escape. 'I have him!'

It was Salbjorn and Ormur. The guardsman had one hand fastened on the boy's collar, the other around his wrist. So turbulent was Ormur's shadow that he resembled a tight column of ravens, flapping and swirling as he tried desperately to free himself. 'Let me go!' hissed the boy.

For one wild moment, Inger thought that Salbjorn would. He removed the hand from Ormur's collar, but only to strike the boy hard about the head. Ormur collapsed, stunned, and Salbjorn placed a boot on his chest to keep him down. 'Idiot,' said the guardsman, briefly. Ormur did not respond, stirring feebly. 'The assassin's up there,' Salbjorn added, giving a barely perceptible gesture up the mountainside behind them. Inger strained her eyes, but could see nothing on the mountain-side. She listened, and behind the splattering rain, the crackle of the flames and the shouts of the tutors trying to extinguish them, she discerned the clatter of rocks overhead. Suddenly, there came a roar: 'Bastard!' It must have been Leon, but the voice was so strained and so furious that it sounded more like a wounded beast. 'Bastard!'

Salbjorn crouched over Ormur, then dropped to one knee, succumbing at last to the injuries he had taken on his fall from the longhouse. 'He's lost him,' said the guardsman, quietly.

Dawn found Inquisitor and guardsmen staring at the smok-ing wreckage of their longhouse. All that remained were a few blackened timbers and a bed of grey ash, though the bucket chain had preserved its neighbour. Inger felt cold and battered. In the chaos of the night before, she had not real-ised how badly she had been jarred by her leap from the window and this morning could manage no more than a stiff limp. 'What happened then?' she asked Leon.

'He outran me.' Leon sounded furious, and then grudging. 'Whoever he is, he sprints well.' Inger made a mild noise and patted Leon's arm vaguely. He stirred irritably, taking a pace away from her.

'At least this rules out the theory that the murder was com-mitted by one of Numa's contemporaries here,' said Salbjorn.

'An absurd theory,' muttered Leon.

'Maybe,' said Inger.

There was silence for a time. 'What do you mean "maybe"?' asked Leon.

'Numa may well have been murdered by the man we saw last night. But he probably had help from inside the school.'

'What makes you say that?' asked Salbjorn.

'Oh, just a suspicion.'

'Based on what?'

Inger turned away from the wreckage of the longhouse, drifting in the direction of the mountainside where the assassin had outrun Leon the night before. The two guardsmen stared after her for a moment, and then followed. 'Based on what?' Salbjorn tried again.

Inger looked a little confused. 'Isn't it obvious?' The guardsmen observed her blankly. 'The assassin must have known Ormur was being guarded, otherwise he would certainly have just tried to move in and out without creating a scene. Instead, somehow he knew a diversion was required. Whoever torched our longhouse last night did so on purpose, lamp oil had been spilt over the walls and floor. I suspect that was partly an attempt to be rid of us, but mostly to provide a diversion, so that Leon would be drawn away from Ormur's longhouse. Now, if it was an assassin living outside the haskoli, how did he know where we were staying? How did he know we were there to investigate the murder? Someone in this school is working with the killer, and lit the fire to create enough chaos that the killer could go in and finish his task.' She looked between the two of them. 'Don't you think?'

The guardsmen looked at each other, and Salbjorn shrugged. 'Maybe.'

'I think so,' said Inger, turning back to the mountainside. 'And here we have a fresh trail,' she said, staring up the steep scree face where the assassin had escaped. 'The assassin will be waiting for another opportunity to strike at Ormur. He's somewhere in these mountains, and I want you to try and track him, Salbjorn. The trail will deteriorate fast and I hope you will begin at once. Leon, you stay here to protect Ormur when he returns.' The boy had gone running with the rest of his herd at dawn: an activity they usually undertook alone. A "herd", Inger had learned, was the derisive term used by the tutors for the groups into which the students at the school were separated. On this occasion, Inger had insisted that two spear-wielding tutors accompanied him, though privately she doubted they would be able to stop the intruder with whom she had come face to face the night before.

'The killer's going to have a lot of opportunities,' growled Leon. 'This place is very exposed, and unless we find him, the boy's dead too. I cannot be at his side night and day.'

'We will find the assassin, and until then you must do your best,' replied Inger happily.

'I will find him,' said Salbjorn, simply. He raised a hand in farewell and set off up the mountain. He had been in the Skiritai before earning a place in the Sacred Guard, and was an experienced tracker. He soon found the trail and Inger watched as he worked his way up the hillside, head scanning right and left, dropping to examine various signs with his fingers. Eventually, when he had begun to understand the path he was on, he broke into a jog, disappearing from view. Leon had already stalked back into the courtyard and Inger turned to follow him, intending to search the school.

Both guardsmen seemed lost in this role and the oblique tactics it required. A battlefield was straightforward: kill anyone not on your side. More subtlety was required here and that was what Inger had been brought to provide. She had been a Maven Inquisitor for two decades already, though was still young for the post. It was an influential role and by strict tradition only occupied by a widow, of which there was no shortage in the Black Kingdom. It began with years spent at the Academy, learning the details of a thousand crimes and the steps taken to resolve them. Decades apprenticed to a Maven Inquisitor had followed, before Inger had finally earned the right to wear the dog-headed angel over her breast. Ramnea: the angel of divine retribution.

Ramnea was a merciless figure, and though she was the Inquisitor's ultimate authority, a little harsh for Inger's liking. When investigating, she imagined another spirit watching over her shoulder and guiding her eyes. This path had been a means to escape the painful memories of her dead husband, but the further down it she walked, the closer his ghost seemed to follow. She could feel him now, at her shoulder, looking over the scene with his keen grey eyes. 'So where first, my love?'

She wandered into the courtyard, looking over the long-houses that bordered three of the sides, backed by cliffs and steep scree slopes. Leon was right: the school was terribly exposed. Keeping Ormur safe would be close to impossible. With her in the courtyard were three Black-Cloaks: teenaged tutors who had shown particular promise in the berjasti, the second stage of education in the Black Kingdom, and been seconded to teach the younger boys while receiving accelerated training in leadership.

At that moment, the students were out running over the hills, and so the Black-Cloaks were enjoying a rare moment's peace. She approached them, smiling vaguely. Boys of this age had barely seen a woman since they had first entered the haskoli at just six years and they observed her with more than a little fascination. 'A long night,' she observed, stopping before them. 'You must all be tired.'

They shared a look and nodded. 'How did the fire start?' asked one with dark eyebrows. 'Did someone spill an oil lamp?'

'Oh, maybe,' said Inger. 'I'm not sure. But then we found someone who wasn't supposed to be here.'

'Doing what?' asked another of the tutors. The question seemed a little abrupt to Inger and she stored it away, next to an image of the speaker's face.

'We didn't find out,' she said, 'but there is a good chance it's connected with the death here two weeks ago.'

'I thought that was a rival herd,' said the first speaker.

'Maybe, maybe,' she said, shrugging. 'But last night might suggest otherwise. Did any of you see anything before the fire started?'

They all shook their heads. 'No. We had all gone to bed.'

'Of course you didn't see anything,' snapped the final tutor, looking at the tutor with dark eyebrows. 'You'd lost your torch.'

The one who had lost his torch looked flatly at his companion. 'What need did I have for a torch? The entire courtyard was lit up like sunset.'

It felt as though a hand had been laid on Inger's shoulder. 'You lost your torch?' she asked.

'Must have left it somewhere.'

'And it hasn't turned up?'

The tutor shook his head.

'Have any of the rest of you seen a torch where it shouldn't have been?' They frowned at this and murmured that they had not. 'Any unexplained lights, before the fire started? Or after?' More refutation. 'Well thank you,' said Inger, smiling at them all again and offering the first half of a bow.

She turned away, surveying the upper windows of the longhouse Ormur had slept in the night before. She walked to the base of the wall and followed it round the courtyard, eyes on the ground. At the end of the longhouse, facing out onto the bleak mountains beyond, she found what she was looking for. A dark smear of ash on the stones, faint from last night's rain. She looked up and found it beneath a high unglazed window.

'That's interesting,' she noted.

Before Ormur returned from his run, Inger spent the rest of her time searching his longhouse, especially the window above that ash smear. She found nothing else to occupy her, however, and ended up waiting in the courtyard with Leon until the boy reappeared. On their return the students were encouraged to take a tooth-aching drink from a hole smashed in the frozen lake before committing to wrestling. This was the pattern of education here, Inger was noticing: intense bursts of activity one after another, followed by prolonged reflection.

Ormur hurled himself into the wrestling, his bare limbs and tunic caked in filth as he tried to throw his larger opponent. 'The boy's good,' said Leon, without looking at Inger. 'Most of the others are bigger than him and I've not seen him lose yet.'

Inger rested cool eyes on Ormur. 'He doesn't look good, though.' She meant his face; simultaneously wretched and detached.

Leon grunted. 'Found anything?'

'One of the tutors says he lost his torch last night. There aren't a lot of places to mislay things here: I think it more likely stolen. Then I found an ash smear over there. I think the killer's accomplice took that torch to signal out to the mountains from the upper window, showing where Ormur was sleeping.'

The two of them were momentarily distracted by Ormur himself. The boy had hooked his opponent's knee and was lifting it high, his opponent hopping back in an effort to dislodge himself. There was a sudden flurry of dirt as both boys crashed to the floor. The courtyard writhed with dusted figures, and another pair of boys was waiting by the longhouse for space to fight. Inger noticed they were edging closer to Leon, exchanging comments, eyes fixed on his silver bracelet: a rare Prize of Valour.

Leon turned his head very slowly towards them. 'Stand back. Or I'll put you in the lake and hold you still until you freeze in.' The boys retreated and Leon settled back to watch Ormur.

'So we have about a week,' said Inger.

'A week?' Just five days in the Black Kingdom.

'I have spoken with the Master,' she explained. 'We need Ormur close at hand so that he doesn't die before we've made any progress. He was safe this morning: the killer muddied the waters last night and will have wanted to lie still and wait for them to settle. But I don't want Ormur leaving the school again, so I negotiated with the Master for a week's lessons here. It'll be easier for you to stand guard. Then they will have the Trial, which the Master says is too sacred to be

moved. And the boys will need to start training beyond the
school again, giving the assassin quite a few opportunities to
finish his objective.' *If Ormur is the objective*, she thought. It
seemed the most likely explanation for his continued presence in these mountains, but he might be after something
else entirely.

The guardsman absorbed this news in silence. 'Five days
to catch a murderer?' he asked, after a while.

'That's what we've got, for now.'

Leon observed his young charge, now on the ground seeking advantage over his wrestling partner. 'Where do you
start?'

'The accomplice, here at the school. He is our path to the
assassin. But I fear this will not be a clean investigation.'
She smiled sadly at Ormur's efforts. 'There are already more
people involved than I had hoped, and usually that means
we are gnawing at the edge of something. Someone powerful
stands behind Numa's death. Someone who doesn't care
about trying to burn to death a Sacred Guardsman and a
Maven Inquisitor.'

'Perhaps Salbjorn will catch him today,' said Leon. 'He is a
fine tracker.'

So they waited for the guardsman, and the news he might
bring. Inger went inside and began conducting interviews
with the tutors, looking for inconsistencies that might identify the accomplice, and glancing frequently out of the large
window to observe the lessons of the boys outside. She was
struck by how they were not mere classes, but rituals. Before
they wrestled, the boys had prayed together, and then been
dusted in ash. Each student wore one white ptarmigan's claw
at their belt for every year they had been in the mountains
and, a tutor informed her, they were presented with an eagle's
talon upon successful graduation. Each day finished with
the boys ritually shaving each other's hair, which they would
only be permitted to grow when they had finished their education and reached the rank of subject. This was not just a

school, but a temple, in which these boys were initiated into the skills of war. That was why it was set high in the mountains: this was the air in which the thunderclouds soared, the birds flew, and water was born. Inger found herself at once captivated by the focus of every soul here, and a little disturbed by their single-mindedness. From the outside, this academy was an unyielding place.

Staring over the lessons also gave her an opportunity to look out for Salbjorn. She imagined seeing the blond guardsman clattering down the mountain, perhaps with the assassin bound and gagged on his back, or dragged behind him in a vice-like grip. But though the sun sank low and its burning glow began to crown the snow-capped peaks, Salbjorn did not return.

The dog star began to shine overhead, and Inger returned to the cold of the courtyard. Leon was there, huddled by the longhouse into which Ormur had retired for the night, breath steaming before him. 'No sign of Salbjorn?' asked Inger.

'None.'

They were quiet for a moment, both gazing over the jagged horizon. 'Do you think he would usually stay out after dark?'

Leon frowned at the last light in the west, giving no sign that he had heard her. 'I wouldn't have thought so,' he said at last.

Inger sat with Leon, pulling her cloak tight about her as the air grew freezing. First the stars pricked the sky above, then the clouds began to drift overhead. They shed perfect snowflakes over the pair, like an icy rain of stars, as they waited on their missing companion. When Inger had begun to tremble, she placed a hand on Leon's shoulder and got stiffly to her feet. Leon nodded brusquely, and she retired to bed, shivering into her blankets. When she awoke the next morning, the snow was still falling, and Leon just where she had left him, cloaked in white.

'Still no Salbjorn?'

He shook his head.

'I'm sure he's just lost in the chase,' she said. 'He'll come back.'

But he did not.

They waited the whole day, she questioning the tutors once more, and Leon standing guard over Ormur. They both knew now that something had happened. The snow, still falling like down, would have obliterated the trail Salbjorn had been following. When Ormur retired that evening, they took a vigil together in the courtyard once more, accompanied only by the belch of the ptarmigan and the hiss of settling snow. Again, Inger stayed until she began to shiver.

'Go inside,' said Leon. 'He'll come, or he won't. I'll find you if he does.'

'He'll come,' said Inger, placing a numb hand on Leon's shoulder.

Leon said nothing. But something else replied. A voice, faint as starlight, brittle as ice.

It said: 'Leon.'

Inquisitor and guardsmen stared wide-eyed at one another. The word had sounded straight from the Otherworld, lacking the substance of reality. If each had not been so certain from the other's face that they had heard it too, they would have dismissed it as some animal croak, or a settling of the snow-pack.

'Did you—' Leon began, but Inger hushed him. She tried to still her shivering and listen.

Then it came again.

'Help me,' it said.

5

The Stones

It was a cold stone dawn as Roper and his small party trotted clear of the Hindrunn walls. At Roper's side was Tekoa, dressed in his shimmering cloak of eagle feathers, brought to impress the Unhieru. They were backed by Pryce and two Skiritai rangers recommended by Tekoa as 'so savage they're barely capable of speech'. They certainly looked the part, with weathered faces and unremitting eyes. Their weapons and armour were lean and worn, and even their horses looked assured. Each Skiritai wore a falcon wing hanging from his hair, issued upon joining the legion, and theirs were so tattered that barely any feathers remained upon them. Bringing up the rear was a pale Keturah, riding between Uvoren's widow, Hafdis, and Gray. These three would accompany the party to the freyi, while the rest crossed the Abus into Unhierea.

They set off fast, first skirting the Hindrunn's outer wall, then plunging into a grass ocean. For a league they rode, obliterating hoar crystals and startling sheep out of their way until they came to the layers of sparse birch that marked the start of the forest. They breakfasted on the move, Roper rummaging in a saddlebag for flakes of hard salty cheese which he shared with Gray. The two of them had dropped to the back, the Skiritai leading the way. They discussed how they missed Helmec, what that image of him floating in Roper's mind might mean; the death of Numa, and whether Inger was likely to catch the killer. They agreed they were impressed by the demeanour of the two Skiritai brought by Tekoa and discussed how they might acquire such an aura themselves. Gray related the sad tale of a guardsman whose wife had just died in childbirth, and, checking the sprinter was well out of earshot, they discussed whether Pryce had been right to obliterate Uvoren's body.

'I do have some concerns about your mission, lord,' said the captain suddenly. Roper glanced at his companion in surprise. Gray's words were tailored carefully to the needs of those around him, and he would not undermine the mission to Unhierea unless he had decided there was something even more important to say. 'I do not trust Vigtyr,' he said. 'I do not like that you will be accompanied by that man on a task that is already filled with danger and uncertainty.'

Roper gave that a moment's thought. 'Surely you don't think we'd be safer without him? He is an extraordinary warrior. And highly resourceful.'

'I firmly believe you would be safer without him, lord,' said Gray. 'I do not believe fighting skill will come into your mission. There are only six of you. If the Unhieru decide that they want you dead, a good swordsman will not prevent that.' He glanced at Roper. 'Forgive me, lord.'

'Go on.'

'But someone unreliable, with their own motives, who is beyond caring what happens to the rest of you, will give cause for worry within your group as well as beyond it.' Gray was quiet for a moment. They paused as the progress of those in front slowed and were forced to drop back a little so they could continue speaking in private. 'Why are you trying to bring him close, lord?' Gray asked at last. 'Everyone has told you that you cannot trust him. He is devious, he is manipulative, and he is sick with ambition.'

'I have been told that many times,' said Roper, trying to express something he felt others did not understand intuitively. 'But people are wrong about so much! I have been told so many things that turned out not to be true. I was assured over and over again in the haskoli that the Sutherner is thoughtless, reckless and short-sighted. And then I fought Bellamus. I have met people who claimed to *know* that I had been unfaithful to Keturah, or that I had traded the eastern kingdom in exchange for the Suthern withdrawal last year: both lies invented by Uvoren. One person tells a spiteful lie, or makes an ill-informed supposition, tells a friend and through the retelling it becomes fact, until everyone knows it to be "true". I am sceptical of what I am told. Everyone who knows we are going to Unhierea has told me that it is suicide, but how would they know? I believe what I see, especially about people. Vigtyr has served me well, and has been gracious and generous. That is the best evidence I have. It is better than the rumours of people who don't know him.'

Gray looked unconvinced. 'That is a wise path, lord,' he said.

'But?'

'But look what he did to your enemies in the name of his ambition. Men died, or were imprisoned and disgraced. And is there not some instinct in you which says there is something wrong with Vigtyr? Do you not get the feeling I do when you speak to him that says: *Be careful, this man does not value you or anyone else*?'

'I do get that instinct,' said Roper. 'But maybe that is why there are so many unpleasant rumours about him. People feel uncomfortable in his presence and know how influential he is, and it drives them to spite. I shall judge his actions, not his manner. And as for your first point, he did all that on my orders. I can hardly blame him for it. It seems to me that the best way to ensure that he is disillusioned would be if I now pushed him away, having dispensed with his services. That is not how I wish to treat my allies. I will honour and value him, and hope to ensure he is a servant to us and nobody else.' Roper thought for a heartbeat longer. 'I would rather make my own mistakes, Gray, than somebody else's.'

Gray nodded. 'I see, lord, I see. You have always had assurance in your own beliefs and that is undoubtedly one of your great strengths. My service to you is and always will be without condition, but may I beg one favour from you?'

Roper blinked. 'Name it, my friend.'

'Please do not forget what I have said. You may be right and I wrong. And you convince me that it is right to give him this chance. But please remember my words when the time comes.'

'Of course,' said Roper, though he did not understand. 'Of course.'

Gray nodded, evidently unsatisfied but determined to leave it there.

Roper was deaf to Gray's warnings, and oblivious to what lay before them in Unhierea, for the forest had bewitched him. Outside these ancient trees the sun and wind blasted the hills, and everything that moved did so in straight lines. The forest was more subtle. The sunlight dripped through the leaves, the wind was a cool breath and the animals prowled and twisted. The colours were soft, the shifting of the trees was gentle, and the trunks rendered the movements of Roper's peers in subtle fragments. He could smell the new leaves and shoots bursting from walls and floor, the earth, and the musky scent of a deer couch that they passed. Each breath of this air was like a kind word in a nest of enemies. He relished the blow of the cuckoo, the flashes of movement all around as squirrels, mice, martens, birds and deer dissolved between the trunks and the leaf litter; the silver notes of a stream. It was *Gurstala*: the week the bluebells flower, and their horses cantered over a dense lilac fog. Did they really need to march south and say goodbye to all of this? Would the canal they were building not secure the north for future generations? But Roper knew those thoughts came from his stomach, and the fear knotted there.

They slept those first few nights in the forest, and by the third day, Keturah was pointing out familiar landmarks that she recognised from her own time in the freyi. There was the ravine she had fallen down on a moonless night, plunging through the dark to crash onto the stream bed below and wrench her ankle. There the gentle river overhung with willows, at which they simply must stop to collect her favourite crayfish. Although Anakim men could not swim, the women could, and Keturah had learned in that river. Ah! Did they see those ragged wingbeats? It must be the heron that had haunted this water in her own time here.

The forest was choked with mist, the trees charcoal pillars, and the day old and grey before they reached the school. You might ride right past it if you did not know to look up. There, hovering some thirty feet above the ground, was a score of treehouses. They ringed the tallest and strongest trees, supported on struts that bowed out from the trunks. The roofs were thatched in bracken, there were no rails to mark the point where security ended and the void began, and each flickered and smoked in the dying light. At the heart of the school was a house bigger than all the others, worn lightly on a mountainous hornbeam. Narrow walkways like trails of cobweb drew each treehouse to this central hub, which glowed brighter than those around it. There was a silhouetted figure standing by a flickering hearth, facing away from them and addressing an audience before her.

At the sight, Roper made a disbelieving noise and Gray spoke from his side. 'This is the freyi?'

'Far superior to your horrible mountain camp,' said Keturah. She called up to the trees, declaring their presence and that they would need lodgings for the night. After a brief delay, the silhouetted figure in the central treehouse turned towards them.

'Well? Who are you?' demanded an imperious voice.

'We are the Black Lord, the Black Lady, Legate Tekoa Uriel-son, the Captain of the Sacred Guard and our three companions,' Keturah replied mildly. She exaggerated, being lady of nothing until she had borne the child she carried. However, Keturah was never one to undersell herself, and her words seemed to satisfy the figure, who disappeared moment-arily. Huddled girls had begun to appear perilously close to the edges of all the nearby treehouses, staring down at them, until a stern voice barked out and they scrambled back from the edge.

A rope ladder unfurled from the underside of the treehouse and the woman came back into view, descending nimbly to the floor. Roper swung himself out of the saddle, the rest of the party following his example.

'There is space in this one,' the figure announced, beckon-ing to their party. The speaker was a startlingly lean, steel-haired woman whom Roper knew well: Frathi, the Chief Historian. She held the ladder steady as Keturah climbed, and Roper followed. The rungs were held in place by a central cord of twisted lime bark, and Roper found there was a tech-nique to climbing it, with hands and feet moving as a pair. He accepted Keturah's cool hand to help him onto the platform: a tightly woven mat of split willow, which squeaked and chir-ruped underfoot.

The treehouse was divided into alcoves by partitions that jutted out from the innermost wall. In each alcove was a shallow stone basin, raised slightly above the floor and cup-ping a fire that spilt light over the edges of the platform. Behind Roper, the Chief Historian had reappeared, and she crossed to into the neighbouring alcove, declaring tartly that they had interrupted her instruction.

Roper turned to look into the forest before he could be accused of anything further. Beneath him, the Skiritai were pushing the horses inside a bramble enclosure with a heavy lattice of blackthorn dragged over the entrance to seal it from the bears and wolves that teemed here. By the ancient and hard-fought pact between these beasts and the Anakim, the adults could walk the trees freely. But the girls of the freyi were a different matter, and vulnerable to attack. So they inhabited the trees, also learning fearlessness through everyday exposure to the vertiginous drop; hardiness in response to the winds that swirled through their unwalled quarters; skill with their hands to destroy and replenish the treehouses, and the organisation necessary to inhabit places of such limited space.

They ate the crayfish that Keturah had directed them to, roasted in front of the fire and accompanied by baked starchy rhizomes. Keturah kept peeling the crayfish bare-handed, straight off the fire, until Tekoa sternly instructed her to let them cool first. She still had no feeling in her fingers from the poisoning she had endured a few months before, and set her crayfish aside, tutting impatiently. It was only when Roper had finished and the forest was a deep, starlit blue that he realised one of their party was missing. 'Has anyone seen Gray?'

'He said he was going to the ring,' said Pryce, extracting a steaming crayfish from its armour.

'The ring?'

'There is a stone ring nearby,' said Keturah, directing him towards it.

Roper descended into the forest, navigating through the dark by the asymmetrical silhouettes of the trees, and came upon a clearing, bordered by a circle of upright stones. There were dozens of them, each some nine feet of worn granite, and impressed with weathered handprints.

These circles were old, Roper knew. They pre-dated the trees. They pre-dated the Academy, and even the kingdom itself. It was said that they had been built by the ancient Anakim in the days when Albion was young and still shivered and crackled with magic. They marked the points where the fabric of the world was thin and the Otherworld close. To disturb them was to invite disastrous bad luck. To count them was pointless: Roper had never tried, but was told that it was impossible to come to the same number twice. Some of them were said to move spontaneously, keeping track of the shifting seams of the earth. And it was thought that prayers said within their boundaries were particularly conspicuous. If a prayer was worthy, then there could be no more powerful place to utter it. If it displayed the remotest self-interest, jealousy or malice, it might attract more malign attention.

Roper stopped outside to observe the figure kneeling within, head bowed to the east, mouth moving silently. When Gray at last straightened up, Roper crossed into the ring and came to join him, the two sharing the silence of the forest for a moment.

'You pray a lot, my friend,' said Roper.

'I do.'

There was another pause, disturbed by a sweeping of unseen wings as something flew overhead.

'What fills your prayers?'

'I'm not sure it matters,' said Gray softly. 'When I pray, I am a quivering membrane away from the Almighty. How I appear before him is how I wish to appear before all people: as a servant. It is an exercise in being as I want to be.'

Roper had thought often about the night beside the fire, many months before, when Gray had imparted his quest to them: to transcend selfish motives and the desire for life itself, and live only as a servant. He rarely spoke of it but in his current mood, Roper wondered if he would say more. 'Is this how you seek to conquer fear? And desire? By diminishing yourself before the Almighty?'

'Partly,' said Gray. 'But I have started to believe that the state I seek gets easier with time. I have found that the more I have done; the more happy memories I have; the more contentment I feel with the life I have had, the less significant death seems to be. I have started to think that death, after a life well lived, is like sleep after a long day. It is easy.' He looked up at Roper, shrugged and smiled. 'But I have not answered your question, lord.' He looked back into the forest. 'I fear for the Black Kingdom. We have so many devious and powerful enemies. We are fewer, year on year. And Bellamus's tactics on Harstathur, and at the battle on the flood plains, show that they're finding ways to fight us. Along with my usual prayers for my loved ones, for perspective, faith, and thanksgiving for all that I have, I pray for our kingdom. I truly fear for her.'

'I do too,' said Roper. Conviction and self-doubt fought in his mind, his doubts remorselessly marshalled. Whether he had the skills to lead a campaign in foreign land. Whether he could defeat Bellamus, when his victory in their last encounter had had more than a touch of fortune to it. Whether there were enough of them to conquer Suthdal. But he had long since decided that if he feared whether or not he could do something, it was a sure sign that he should try.

'That is why we must finish this,' said Roper. 'Before they have us worked out entirely. When I spoke to you and Keturah after Harstathur, about why we are going south: did you believe me? You knew I was serious, about subduing Suthdal forever? That is why we are going to go beyond the Abus, Gray, and why we are enlisting the help of the Unhieru. If we don't finish this now, we leave that task to a generation that will have fewer soldiers with which to accomplish it, and more enemies to fight against. We are fighting to return this entire land to the wilds and secure the future of our people.' *Perhaps I am a poor peacetime ruler*, thought Roper. Speaking to Gray, it did not seem to matter. For his purpose, peacetime would have to wait.

Gray nodded. 'Yes. I knew you meant it, lord. I know this is to be a mission of conquest.'

'And you are with me?'

Gray just stared at Roper. 'How could I possibly be against you?' he said, very quietly. 'Though I fear many shall be.'

'That is why it must remain a secret for now,' said Roper.

'We will not reveal the full extent of our plans until the invasion is already underway. Until it is too late for the tribunes, councillors and historians to stop us.'

Gray smiled. 'You have developed a fine understanding of politics, Lord Roper.'

Roper was too pleased with this assumption to admit that he had developed no such understanding, and merely married someone who had.

They returned to the treehouse, where the party bade one another goodnight and retired to their separate alcoves. Roper and Keturah shared one and sat talking for a time. Roper dangled his legs off the edge of the treehouse, Keturah lying with her head in his lap, one hand flirting with the drop.

'You seem to like it here,' Keturah observed.

'It is restful,' Roper said. 'I have not felt good recently, and being here seems to have eased that.'

'Not good, how?'

Roper hesitated. 'Every morning I wake as though shocked from sleep by lightning. Even now my heart is galloping and my legs are buzzing like they're filled with wasps. It is like nothing I have felt before. But maybe it is something to do with Helmec's face, and with Numa. Or with our task in the south.'

'Is it unpleasant?' asked Keturah, frowning.

'Yes. But I don't wish to dwell on it. Not in myself, and not with you. We do not have much time left together and I'd rather spend it talking about more pleasant things.' He rested his hand on her forehead.

'It's good to tell me your troubles,' she persisted.

He smiled again. 'Do you tell me the things that truly bother you? Do you speak to me about your mother, or anything that has passed in your life?'

'No,' she said cheerfully. Roper raised his eyebrows as though no more needed saying, and they were silent until chirruping footfalls alerted them to an approaching figure. It was the Chief Historian. She stepped into their alcove and regarded them for a moment, eyes so piercing that if cold had a colour, it would have been this blue.

'Why are you here, Lord Roper?' she asked.

Roper felt Keturah's neck stiffen against his leg. 'Merely visiting the freyi, my lady,' he said mildly.

'Indeed. You, two Sacred Guardsmen, a legate, two Skiritai and your wife all came for this errand?'

Roper smiled. 'We shall be heading south tomorrow, once a final companion has joined us.'

'Where?'

Roper paused. He was conscious both that he must keep secret their plans of invasion, and that this woman, guardian of the Academy's huge store of knowledge, might have information that could help their task. 'Unhierea,' he admitted. Her blue eyes wore at him. 'I believe they could make useful allies.'

She came a little further beyond the partition, observing the pair of them steadily. 'No doubt. But do you think you are likely to survive such a mission?'

'Perhaps you could tell me,' said Roper.

'You are not,' she said.

'Explain,' Keturah commanded. 'If it please you, my lady,' she added, in response to the Chief Historian's expressionless glare.

'The Academy remembers a little of their kind, from the days when we shared Albion. We were such horrible enemies that neither of us wanted to fight the other ever again. They took the low places and the high ones: the valleys and the mountains. We had the rest, and we left one another alone. When our kind heard the howl of the Unhieru, we simply walked back the way we had come.'

'The howl?' asked Roper.

'They call their mastery over a piece of land. They say in Suthdal that sometimes you can hear it at night, far away. But no Sutherner goes near the border. The Unhieru hunt them like game.'

Foreboding settled on Roper. 'Will we be able to communicate?'

'You should have come to me at the Academy, Lord Roper. I could have directed you to the right cell, who would have more specific information,' replied the Historian. 'But certainly they talk. We know their names correspond to colours in the sky. Gogmagoc, I hear, is their word for colour at the top of the rainbow. We know they describe time as a mountain, and measure it subjectively, rather than precisely.'

'They see time as a mountain?'

'It gets thinner as you climb. That is why your life speeds up the longer you live it: you near the summit, and time grows narrow. Which raises another problem. Though they speak, even if you understand their words, they may make no sense to you.'

Keturah sat up abruptly and Roper laid a hand on her shoulder. 'Is there anything else we know?' he asked.

'Little. Even if you find the right historian, the information is thousands of years old and things may have changed considerably. Their tools are stone, or they were when we lived side by side. We know they kept sheep, and planted apple trees.' She raised her eyebrows briefly. 'If you come back, I shall be interested to hear your account. Perhaps you would report to me, when you are done?'

'I will, my lady,' said Roper.

She nodded, evidently having satisfied her purpose here. 'Good luck, Lord Roper.' She turned and squeaked out of their alcove.

Keturah sank slowly back into his lap, a frown on her face. 'Take care of yourself in Unhierea, Husband,' she said.

'I'll be safe,' said Roper, brusquely. 'Think who I'm going with.'

'Most of my precious family members,' she said. 'Take care of them too. I have faith in you all, but I'm not sure this task is worth the risk. It seems your chance of success is low. Your chance of death . . .' She trailed off.

'We just have to try.' He looked down at her. 'You are to act as regent in my absence. Your chance to show everyone the talents you often speak of. Perhaps you might take control of the kingdom when we invade as well? Almighty knows someone will need to manage the reactions of those back home when they discover our plans.'

Keturah opened her mouth to reply.

And there came the sound of galloping hooves from below. Roper looked down to see a lone rider canter through the mist, looking between the treehouses above him. 'Lord Roper!' he called. 'Lord Roper!'

'Up here,' said Roper, keeping his voice low so as not to wake the others. It was Vigtyr. He had arrived, and they would cross the river next morning.

To Unhierea.

Roper and his party left at dawn, leaving Keturah, Hafdis and Gray at the freyi. They stood beneath the central treehouse and shared a farewell. Roper gave Hafdis a kind embrace and then shared one more vehement with Gray. 'Farewell, my brother.' When he came to Keturah, he just looked at her, wearing an odd expression. His hand rested on her hip and then moved to cover her stomach, resting on the baby. They shared a look for a moment. She smiled at him, and he turned away as though he could not bear it.

Tekoa came to her next with a more expected farewell. 'Goodbye, sweet grass-snake.'

Next to her, Pryce and Gray shared an embrace, the sprinter breaking free and noticing Keturah looking wryly at him. He gave her a rare nod, 'Cousin,' and turned away. She watched as the party mounted and kicked their horses forward. Roper twisted in his saddle, sharing one last look with her before turning back to the road.

'Godspeed and good luck to you all!' she called after them.

'Goodbye, my dear friends,' came Gray's quiet voice from beside Keturah.

Keturah turned to smile at the captain. She tried to say: *They'll be back.* But found she could not. So she just turned back to watch the six companions disappear between the trees. It was not far to that dark canal, and then a narrow strip of Suthdal was all that lay between them, and the unmapped mountains of Unhierea.

Pryce let out a sudden roar and spurred out before the others. His long ponytail bounced behind him and he raised a clenched fist into the air, beginning a distant, manic declamation. 'Say goodbye to your home, men of the north! Say goodbye to friends, to comfort, music and safety; we are crossing the dark water! By this chosen company; by you, will the Unhieru know our race. Every heartsick step you take, you have ten thousand heroes standing behind you! Every word you utter will be met with a baying cheer from our watching peers in heaven! Your life will have no moment more significant than this, so take it, you bastards! Do not concede, do not relax, *do not fail*, for nothing but your best will do! To Unhierea! To Unhierea!'

6

Unhierea

'I have heard that bats sleep upside down,' said Pryce.

Tekoa, riding next to him, gave him a resigned look. 'What?'

'They sleep stuck to the ceiling, upside down.'

'No they don't, Pryce.'

'They do,' said Pryce. 'I met one of last year's refugees. She had to shelter in a cave after the Sutherners burnt her home. She said she saw the bats sleeping upside down on the ceiling.'

Tekoa laughed gleefully. 'And you believed this bullshit?'

'It's true,' insisted Pryce. 'It's because they cannot walk upright. They are not built for it.'

Tekoa turned to the Skiritai behind him. 'This is good. Are you listening? How do they give birth, then?' asked Tekoa, turning back to Pryce. 'Do they splat their offspring onto the ceiling, like a sneeze?'

'I want to know how they piss,' said Gilius, one of the Skiritai who knew Pryce from his own days as a ranger. 'Is it always on themselves?'

'They sleep upside down,' said Pryce, curtly.

Vigtyr was smiling wryly, and Tekoa quite tickled. 'Wait, wait, Pryce, we're not done,' he said in between gleeful cackles. 'What are they attached to? When they hang off the stone ceiling.'

Pryce was now staring loftily ahead.

'They have sticky feet?' suggested the Skiritai.

'But then how would they let go?' said Vigtyr.

'Do bats sometimes end up in a huge sticky ball, feet together at the centre?'

'When they fart, do they propel themselves off the ceiling?'

'And you believed this!' said Tekoa delightedly. 'It's lucky you have other skills, Pryce.'

'Maybe Pryce isn't quite as brave as we all believe,' said Vigtyr. 'He's just been oblivious, all this time.' Everyone laughed bar Pryce, whose face was now gathered into a thunderous frown.

'I won't have that from the warm grub who brought a tent, Vigtyr,' Pryce called over his shoulder, and the laughter redoubled. This was their favourite joke: Vigtyr had brought a tent with him. Aledas, the other Skiritai, professed never to have even seen a tent before. None of them, not even Tekoa, had ever used one on the trail and there had been great mirth as Vigtyr raised its canvas walls the night before.

But Pryce had not laughed. It was not funny to him. He had thought often of Vigtyr on their journey. He considered that there are some masterpieces you have to observe from far away to appreciate. A tapestry of silk, where each figure appears simple and unrefined when inspected up close, but back away and a kinetic, complementary current is revealed, sweeping from one end to the other. To Pryce, Vigtyr was the inverse of this. He made sense up close. He was wryly charming, dedicated, exceptionally skilled, physically imposing and ferociously intelligent. But when one backed away and observed from a distance, he somehow shrank to less than the sum of those things. Perhaps it was because he was so ravenously ambitious that he seemed dissatisfied with all that he had already. Or maybe it was because, in spite of his charm, Pryce had developed nothing close to a relationship with him. The tent seemed to encapsulate it: Vigtyr did not need any one of them. He would laugh with them as a group but insulate himself from them as individuals.

Up ahead, Pryce could see Roper riding with Aledas, the two of them guiding their small party. Bored of the mockery, he spurred his horse on to join them. They were riding across the narrow strip of Suthdal that separated the Black Kingdom from the mountains of Unhierea. They had crossed the Abus the previous evening, borrowing a barge from a bankside family to transport horses and weapons across the water. Now they rode fast, hoping to make it to Unhierea before word spread that there was a band of Anakim horsemen in Suthdal.

Pryce reined in beside Roper, and then tutted irritably as Tekoa cantered in next to them. 'How is everything back there?' asked Roper, glancing at the pair of them.

'The conversation was excellent,' Tekoa decreed. 'I supplied much of it.'

'How far to Unhierea?' asked Pryce.

'We don't know,' Roper admitted. 'But if we keep riding south-west, we can hardly miss it.'

'We should find out,' said Pryce, eyeing the sun sinking before them. 'If we have to spend a night in Suthdal, we'll need to find somewhere isolated.'

'Let's ask one of the locals,' said Tekoa carelessly.

The party took a small diversion, drawn over some hills and into a valley, first by the smell of fresh dung, and then the clinking of cowbells. There, they found a cowherd: a man in dirty woollen rags who stared open-mouthed as they closed in. By the time he had realised the approaching horsemen were Anakim, it was far too late to escape. He still tried, turning away from his cows and sprinting for a stream at the valley's centre, no doubt placing some desperate faith in the Suthern legend that the demonic Anakim could not cross clean water. But he did not even make the stream, Aledas

spurring after him, extricating a foot from his stirrup and
booting the cowherd to the ground. The ranger leapt off his
horse and used one hand to hold his bridle steady, the other
to drag the Sutherner upright.

The rest of the Anakim gathered round the cowherd in a
circle, staring down as the man twisted this way and that,
eyes darting from Vigtyr, to Roper, to Tekoa and back to
Roper. He seemed not to want to look at Aledas at all, leaning
as far away from the fist bunched at his collar as he could.
The Skiritai was small for an Anakim, only a few inches
taller than the cowherd, but he carried a silent and frightening aura. 'Please!' the cowherd blurted in Saxon, staring at
Roper. 'Please!'

'Calm,' said Roper, raising a hand. 'The border with Unhierea.
How far is it?'

The cowherd could not reply, mouthing the words to a
prayer.

'Unhierea,' Roper repeated. 'How far?'

'That way,' said the cowherd, jerking his head towards the
sun.

'Yes, we know,' said Roper. 'How far?'

'Five . . . five hours,' stuttered the cowherd.

'Five on foot, or with horses?'

'With horses. Please, I have children! Two little girls!'

'Five hours for him,' said Tekoa. 'What, three for us, if we
hurry?'

Aledas nodded, but the cowherd was still jabbering.

'Don't kill me, I beg, don't!'

Roper and Tekoa exchanged glances. 'Nobody must know
that we are going to Unhierea,' said Roper, switching to
Anakim and looking down at the man. Without delay, Pryce
dropped from his saddle. Aledas understood what was about
to happen and released the cowherd at once, taking a step
back as Pryce drew a sword. At the scrape of steel, the cowherd began a panicked turn and was halfway round when
Pryce struck off his head with a single back-swipe. The man's

body crumpled to the floor, his head landing on his pelvis and rolling down the valley, into the stream.

'Fixed it,' said Pryce, bending down to clean his sword on the cowherd's clothes. The Skiritai laughed.

Roper frowned, and Pryce thought he might be admonished. He did not care. This was the only way to ensure the cowherd's silence. The life of an individual was nothing when set against their task, and perhaps Roper recognised this, for he shrugged and turned his horse away. 'We can make the border before dark if we hurry.'

Pryce stayed a little to polish his sword. It was steel: one of two he wore, called Tusk and Bone, that had been forged from Marrow-Hunter, the war hammer belonging to Uvoren. The steel carried a beautiful serpentine marbling, so unlike those used by the others in their party. Their swords were Unthank-silver: an Anakim alloy which was lighter, tarnished slower and kept a better edge. But Pryce liked the weight of steel. He liked the force of a steel swing and, in any case, no longer trusted Unthank weapons. His last had shattered in combat.

He caught up with the others and they rode on, changing their course slightly whenever they smelt Suthern livestock, or saw a Suthern dwelling. These diversions were required less and less as the day wore on, the hills growing quieter and emptier. Burnt out and abandoned farmsteads dotted the land. The walls and fences fell into disrepair. And the relentless teasing, which had provided most of the entertainment so far, acquired a new and crueller edge. Fear had settled heavily on the group.

'We must be getting close,' said Roper quietly. No sooner had he observed this then the ground before them fell away. All of them had to drag their horses to a sudden halt, looking down at the vast ripple in the earth below. They were on top of a ridge, with another opposite where the lands of Unhierea and Suthdal shied away from one another. Huge cliffs layered the far side like an unending citadel, and the silence that lay over it all was dense and heavy and prickling. They observed it together for a moment. 'I wonder when one of our kind last set foot in these lands,' said Roper. 'Onwards, my brothers.' He clicked his tongue and guided his horse down the near slope, the others following.

It took some time to find their way up the other side, and they were consumed at once in a forest of strange, shrub-like trees. They looked like crab apple to Pryce's eye, though they bore no fruit on them yet. Each was tangled with mistletoe and small chattering birds, indecently loud in this place. The only creature they saw besides the birds was a squirrel, which Aledas knocked off a branch with a well-aimed sling-shot and tucked into his belt.

The sun disappeared behind the valley walls that rose sheer on either side, the ground climbed steadily, and a consistent, biting wind began to grow. 'This is katabatic,' said Gilius.

'What?'

'A katabatic wind. Probably caused by ice higher up. It will get worse.'

Pryce had brought no mittens and his fingers were growing slow and stiff. He balled them into the edge of his cloak as the sky dimmed and the wind began to howl. He noticed white fragments poking through the thin grass of the valley floor, Pryce first taking them for chalk. Then he realised they were bones: a blizzard of them. They passed ruined drystone walls, and the trees were becoming smaller, bent permanently by the wind and pointing back down the valley.

Tekoa spoke suddenly. 'Is that a settlement?' Some distant structure was appearing over the valley horizon. As they rode closer, they saw there were several of them, each a massive circular wall of stone with a roof of logs long collapsed at the centre. The walls, when they reached them, were crude, the stones that formed them enormous and lumpen, and the ruins somehow emptier still than the valley before it.

Roper stopped before the old walls, the others clustering uneasily behind. 'Hello?' he called.

Silence.

'Gogmagoc!' called Roper. 'Gogmagoc!'

There came no reply. All they could hear was the wind, moaning between the cracks in the wall.

'Deserted,' said Roper. 'But it's getting dark. We make camp here. At least the walls will shelter us from the wind.'

The Skiritai took the group's horses into an overgrown bramble enclosure by the valley wall, sealing it off with some branches, while Roper and Tekoa saw to the fire. 'What if that's seen?' asked Vigtyr, eyeing the small ball of tinder that had begun to crackle cheerfully.

'We want to be seen,' replied Roper. 'We're here to negoti-ate. And it's cold: our alternative is to freeze to death.' It sounded as though he found the second reason more convin-cing than the first.

'So where are the Unhieru?' Tekoa wondered, out loud. 'This place has been deserted for decades.'

'We will find them,' said Roper. The fire was taking hold and helping to lift the sense of unfamiliarity from these ruins. 'Some of those bones on the ride up looked fresh. They can't be too far away.'

'I can smell something,' said Aledas, in his deep, flat voice.

Roper and Tekoa look up at that, silent for a moment. 'What?'

The ranger shook his head. 'Something new. It's very faint.'

Pryce turned away and went to explore the old settlement. The bramble enclosures around the edges, which must once have been deliberately cultivated to pen livestock, had reached out and begun to consume the ruins. The old streets, if so grand a name could be applied to the uneven passageways between the walls, were nearly choked with prickling shoots. The walls towered over his head and some them had spilt across the path, so that he had to clamber over them, fighting against that growing wind. He found a crude doorway which he inspected for a while. Its top had collapsed, so he had no idea of its original height, but it must have been six feet wide.

These ruins were almost geological: in scale, in crudity, in their exceeding and obvious age.

'Look at this!' called Vigtyr's voice. It was too dark to go much further and Pryce was growing cold, so he turned back for the campsite. He arrived to find that Vigtyr had been clearing a space for his tent and unearthed a huge jawbone beneath a rock. The molars were flat, cracked and vast, and the incisors worn down to mere stumps. 'Enormous,' muttered Tekoa, he and Roper inspecting it together. 'What's happened to the front teeth?'

'Almighty knows,' said Roper, eyeing the jaw. He looked up, casting around at the walls. 'I'd suggest we fly our flag if the wind weren't so fierce. We are a delegation after all.'

He never seemed fazed, Lord Roper. The impression he gave was always one of someone who was interested but not worried. Pryce suspected that was an act, but it was one he appreciated. Emotions are contagious, and you had to be careful how you conducted yourself under pressure. The others were more obviously subdued. They conversed in murmurs and sat as though submerged in cold water, huddled and stiff.

They prepared the evening hoosh, supplementing it with the squirrel taken by Aledas, spitted and roasted. Vigtyr tried to pitch his tent, but nobody seemed willing to help him and before he could secure it, the wind tore it from his grasp. It floated down the valley, a tumbling black shadow, swallowed in moments by the dark. Vigtyr came to huddle awkwardly by the fire, where the party shared the pot of steaming hoosh, each taking a spoonful and passing it on. When Pryce tried to pass it to Aledas, he would not take it. He sat with his eyes unfocused and his head cocked, evidently listening. Pryce set the hoosh down and strained his ears into the dark.

Then he heard it.

Over the roar of the wind came a distant marine howl: a high-pitched groan that echoed plaintively through the valley. The call faded, leaving just the hollow moan of the wind. Then, very faintly, another voice replied from the dark. It was half wolf, half whale, and made the hairs on the back of Pryce's neck stand up. The eyes on the other side of the fire were wide.

'They're close,' said Roper calmly. 'Aledas, take some hoosh or send it on. I'm starving.'

Nobody slept much that night. It was too cold, though Pryce was grateful for the wind, which at least made it pointless to try listening into the dark for some guttural noise or giant footstep. As dawn showed itself behind the high valley sides, all of them sat ready by the fire. Gilius explained that the wind would likely stop as the sun warmed the valley, and so it proved. Heavy-lidded, they packed up and went to retrieve their horses.

Which were gone.

The branches that guarded the bramble enclosure had been ripped aside and there was no sign whatsoever of the beasts. The party stood and stared at the vacant enclosure in silence. 'Now do you smell it?' asked Aledas. Pryce could: there was a waft of something wild and animal. The unfamiliar, unsettling musk of the Unhieru.

'So they were here last night,' said Tekoa. 'They must have known where we were. Why didn't they come calling?'

Nobody replied, Roper simply hitching the saddlebags over his shoulder. 'Onwards,' he said. 'Let's see where this valley leads.'

They set off, Pryce stepping superstitiously between the bone fragments that protruded underfoot. He walked at the back with Aledas, who directed Pryce towards some near-invisible disturbance on the valley floor. 'We're following something,' he said.

'The Unhieru?'

'Something else,' he replied, snuffing the air.

As they walked, the dark mouth of a cave was revealed in the valley wall above them, half-hidden by more crab apple trees. 'I'll catch you up,' said Gilius, diverging from the rest of the party and trotting up the side of the valley. He had soon reached the mouth of the cave where he hesitated for a moment before disappearing from view.

They walked on for some time before Aledas pointed into the distance. 'There,' he said. 'That's what we've been following.' Ahead of them was a dark, massive shape, ambling slowly across the valley.

'What on earth?' Roper murmured. They crept towards the beast, which ignored them, grazing contentedly on the valley floor. It was not a predator, that was clear, and perhaps a little like a shaggy aurochs with a single horn in the middle of its head, rather than two on either side. They gave it a wide berth as they passed by, Tekoa admiring it speculatively.

'I believe I've heard the Academy talk of such creatures,' he said. 'A rhinoceros. They used to be common across Albion, when our ancestors arrived.'

'Where's Gilius?' asked Roper, suddenly.

'He went to look at that cave, back there,' said Pryce, jerking a thumb in the direction they had come.

The party came to an uneasy halt, observing one another. 'That was half an hour ago,' said Roper. He glanced at Aledas. 'Surely he'd have caught us up by now?'

The Skiritai did not reply by word or gesture, merely meeting Roper's eyes.

'He'll be fine,' said Tekoa. 'Doubtless he's managed to get lost in the cave and will have to grope his way out.'

'We should go and find him,' said Roper. 'Half an hour is a long time to be occupied by a cave. Maybe he's trapped.' Roper stopped there, but may as well have added: *Or worse*. That was what Pryce was thinking, and he considered that if he were worried for the ranger, the others certainly would be.

They turned back, skirting once more around the strange horned beast until they were back beneath the cave. Roper led their group up the steep sides of the valley, calling out before him: 'Gilius! Gilius!'

There came no answer.

Pryce jogged forward so that he and Roper reached the gaping mouth of the cave together. It was wide and low, and stank of the musk they had detected earlier. A feral reek of urine, which made the back of Pryce's neck prickle, as though it were being watched by invisible eyes.

'Gilius!' Roper bellowed into the cave. The only reply was a distant echo. The others gathered close, staring at the dark opening. All were still and listening for a while, as though the ranger might yet call back that he could hear and was unharmed. 'I'll go and find him,' said Roper. 'Guard the entrance for me, would you?'

'I'll go with you,' Pryce replied. Roper smiled at that, touching his shoulder briefly. Each of them rested a hand on the hilt of their sword, and they began to creep into the cave.

'Don't be long, lord,' came Tekoa's voice behind them. With every step, the light grew fainter and that animal musk stronger.

Pryce had never entered a cave before: they were sacred ground to the Anakim, and only used in times of dire need. He could not escape the feeling he was being swallowed. 'Gilius!' he called.

As the darkness grew, they slowed to a mere shuffle, Roper drawing Cold-Edge and using it to probe into the darkness. There was barely enough light to detect the dark outline of their passage. They had advanced perhaps twenty yards when the cave forked: their larger passage continuing to the left, and a narrower, shallower one joining from the right. Roper and Pryce strained their eyes into the bottomless gloom of each passageway, but could see nothing.

'My lord,' said Pryce. He was observing a patch of rock at the edge of the right-hand passage, gleaming with moisture. He took a pace towards it, reaching out a hand and wiping his fingers over the rough surface. It was slimy, and he touched the wet fingertips to his tongue. The taste of iron flooded his mouth, and he spat onto the floor. 'Blood.'

Roper and Pryce observed each other for a few heartbeats.

'We turn back here,' said Roper, quietly. 'I fear very much that Gilius is beyond our aid.' His eyes were very wide in the dark, but neither he nor Pryce moved. Pryce thought that Roper would be trying to decide if he had made the decision out of wisdom, or fear.

And something moved behind him.

In an instant, Pryce had drawn Tusk. The flash of steel caused Roper to begin a rapid turn, but he was only halfway through it when he was yanked from his feet. Cold-Edge slipped from his grasp, landing with a clang on the stone floor, and he was hoisted off the ground by an immense pale fist bunched around his ankle. Holding him was a huge shadow, which stepped forward and became a silhouette. The head was vast, the shoulders round, and one arm held Roper suspended, where he flailed and shouted. That abominable waft of urine swept over Pryce, and he stepped forward, teeth bared, blade flashing, eyes searching for where he might begin attacking this dark monster.

He was distracted by a sudden roaring behind him. Pryce did not turn, occupied by the beast holding Roper, but he could hear Tekoa's bellow, Vigtyr swearing, and knew his companions outside were being similarly assaulted. Roper was shouting in unintelligible Saxon, trying in vain to reason with his captor, to make it understand that they were here to talk.

And then the cave's last light was blotted out.

Something vast had smothered the entrance, and was advancing through the passage. Pryce could hear its heavy footsteps slapping nearer and half turned, eyes flicking between Roper and the shadow now advancing from his other side, blocking the escape. If this thing had made it past his companions outside, then they must have been overwhelmed. It shambled down the rough passageway, one hand reaching out before it, groping greedily for Pryce.

The sprinter's reflexes took command, and he dodged. This situation was new to him: never before had he been prey, rather than predator, and his instincts were not accustomed to such a role. So he did not step back, but aggressively forward, ducking beneath the reaching hand, his own snatching up towards the head of the creature, high above him in the dark. His fingertips felt matted, shaggy hair and he seized a fistful, dragging it down and raising Tusk so that its flashing tip came to rest beneath the chin of the Unhieru.

'Stop!' he howled.

The cave went still. The shouts from outside continued: feral growls and Anakim yells, but everything inside the cave had frozen. The creatures attacking them may not have understood the word, but they understood the tone, and the naked blade which Pryce twisted a little, digging it beneath his enemy's jaw. The Unhieru growled.

'Release my companion!' Pryce demanded, voice echoing through the cave. The creature did not move. Perhaps it had not understood. 'Drop him!' He jerked on the cord of hair clutched in his left hand. 'Drop him!'

The shadowed face above him uttered a few guttural words, and at Pryce's back came a heavy thump as Roper crashed to the floor. Pryce turned his head and saw the Black Lord seizing Cold-Edge and scrambling upright. He backed against the wall of the cave, holding the sword levelled before him.

'Now those outside,' Pryce demanded, jerking the matted hair in his hand towards the mouth of the cave, his sword still beneath the creature's jaw. His prisoner did not react, and Pryce began twisting and drilling the sword upwards, slowly boring into the skin. The creature began to grunt and growl, trying to jerk its head back, and Pryce gestured to the entrance of the cave once more, from which he could still hear Tekoa's voice bellowing in Saxon. Under Pryce's encouragement, the Unhieru turned its massive head towards the cave mouth and gurgled into the dark. The commotion from outside hushed.

'Now,' growled Pryce, looking up into the dark face above

him and finding the two spots of light that marked wide, wet eyes. 'Take us to Gogmagoc.' There was a slight movement in the dark as the enormous head was cocked in his direction. 'Gogmagoc!' Pryce repeated, the word bouncing again and again from the walls.

The figure before him was silent. *'Hokhmakhoc?'* it repeated at last.

'Yes, Gogmagoc,' snarled Pryce. 'Your king. Lead us to him. Gogmagoc. Now. Take us to Gogmagoc.'

It was the first word this monster had truly understood. There was silence in the cave.

And the creature began to laugh.

7

The Man in the Mountains

Salbjorn's awareness returned long before any desire to open his eyes. He could hear the whoosh and crackle of flames. He could feel their heat on his face. He could smell hot, fragrant tea. And he could smell something else too, muddy and juicy and slightly burnt.

He opened his eyes. He was lying by the hearth in the upstairs room of a longhouse, seldom lit but now roaring with flames. Above them hung a sooty kettle, and three trout were skewered beside the fire, their wounds leaking clear juices. Outside the window it was dark, and he could see white snowflakes passing by. Leon was crouched beside him, cloth in hand, removing the kettle from its hook and filling a birch-bark cup with steaming pine-tea. 'Leon?' he tried, voice emerging as a caw. 'How did I get here?'

'You crawled,' replied his mentor, without looking at him. 'We heard you yesterday evening, calling from behind the longhouse. There was a freezing trail behind you leading from the mountains.'

'Yesterday evening?' Salbjorn shifted on his nest of goat-skins and felt pins and needles burst into his limbs. He had no memory of his return, and his head swam. 'I've been asleep since then?'

'Of course. You were in a terrible state. Bruised, covered in dried blood, your lips blue. Did you find him?'

Salbjorn tried to think who Leon might mean. Then he remembered why he had been in the mountains at all. The assassin. 'No,' he said. 'I think . . .' he broke off, until Leon nudged him with his foot. 'I think I nearly did. His trail was clear right up until it crossed a cliff-face. I don't know if he took a different path to me . . .' Salbjorn paused again, frowning. 'Maybe he is just a better climber. But I tried to follow, and I fell.'

'How far?'

'Far,' said Salbjorn, suppressing the memory of that terrible plunge. 'I must have been knocked out. It was dark when I woke.' He tried to explain what it had been like, but Leon would never understand, and he was too hazy to try and make him. How he had lain in the dark, waiting for the dawn to see where he was, snow gathering on his prone form. He had lingered, the heat leaching out of him, until he heard movement in the dark.

The creak of wind-packed snow as something trod upon it. A creature passing slowly by, not twenty yards from where he shivered.

Battered, Salbjorn had propped himself upright, staring sightlessly into the black. He could hear the hiss of snow settling around him; could feel his stiff fingers and wide, wide eyes, but there was nothing to see. The footfalls were slow and heavy. It could have been anything: a wolf, a bear, a goat. A murderer. Whatever it was did not seem to notice him. It kept moving through the dark, passing beyond the range of his ears. Salbjorn stared out for a long time after the noise had passed, darkness pressing on his eyeballs, before he collapsed back, heart thumping.

'When dawn came, I started crawling back. I don't remember finding you, though,' Salbjorn concluded the garbled account. Leon did not seem to be listening. He was using a metal poker to slide two of the trout off their skewers and onto a large piece of hard flat bread. He put it down in front of Salbjorn and pushed the steaming cup towards him. 'Thank you,' he said, propping himself on an elbow and sipping the tea.

'Are you injured?' Leon asked.

Salbjorn assessed himself for a moment. He was consumed by weariness, every muscle slack and heavy, and had so many different sources of pain that it was hard to disentangle them. 'My ankle is not right. I don't know if it's broken. And I can't feel anything with my fingers.'

'They were frozen,' said Leon brusquely, helping himself to the final trout and some burnt bread. Salbjorn set down his tea and picked off a strip of trout. It was chewy and oily, and he was suddenly ravenous. For a while they feasted, tossing bones and fins into the fire. Salbjorn had consumed every morsel of fish in moments and began to eat the bread, stale but soaked in warm juices.

He thought they were both considering the same thing: an assassin who could outsprint one guardsman, then climb across a cliff-face in the dark and the rain where another guardsman was dislodged in the light. They were after no common murderer. Whoever was working against them in these mountains was skilled and ruthless.

'Where is the boy?' asked Salbjorn.

'Meditating in the longhouse. He's safe.'

Salbjorn glared at Leon for a moment. 'The assassin has an accomplice working in this school. He's not safe unless you're with him.'

'I have been looking after you,' Leon pointed out.

'The boy needs your care more than I,' said Salbjorn, though he was embarrassed.

'Well he can't rely on your care any more, can he, Salbjorn?' said Leon flatly. 'You went too far. You overreached yourself and now you will be no help until you're healed.'

'We should send for assistance,' Salbjorn muttered.

Leon paused. 'We can't,' he said. 'This snow has resealed the passes. And there's no sign of it stopping.'

Salbjorn turned to the window and the flakes floating past. Trapped, then, in these mountains with a murderer and at least one accomplice working against them. 'So it's just us.'

'For the next while. Us, and the Inquisitor.'

'Who is where?'

'Working still. She's cross-examining the tutors, trying to find that accomplice. She thinks that'll be the assassin's weak-spot.'

'I want to help too,' said Salbjorn.

'Well you're damn well not lying around here,' Leon replied. 'The Inquisitor is most suspicious of the tutors, and will leave interviewing the students to us. So that's what we'll do tomorrow, and until then, I'm going back to guard the boy.' He got to his feet, muttering on his way out, 'You'll manage now you're awake.'

Leon was an energetic soul, not used to compromising his rigid training routine for anything. Being trapped in the mountains, tethered every waking moment to a boy, was a particular struggle for such a man.

Salbjorn, aching profoundly, settled to try and rest before they began interviewing the next day.

He and Leon conducted the interrogations in the same room, so that all Salbjorn had to do was prop himself upright behind a table fetched by Leon. They began to interview witnesses for clues as to who the accomplice could be, and the morning passed without the faintest sign of progress. Leon was less than helpful, growing swiftly bored and making this clear by occasionally tutting and thrashing like a gaffed eel. Salbjorn had a cup of steaming pine-needle tea on the table, while Leon's lay empty and knocked over on the floor next to him.

'So you didn't see anything on the night the intruder was driven away?' he asked a student.

'Nothing, lord,' said the boy, his gaze unusually bright before it dropped to the floor.

'Are you all right?' asked Salbjorn, leaning forward.

The boy nodded, dislodging a tear onto his cheek. He spoke, still looking down at the floor. 'Is the intruder here to kill one of us, my lord? Everyone's saying he's trying to get Ormur, but what if he isn't? You could be protecting the wrong person.'

Salbjorn felt his heart give a slight twist. 'He's certainly not here for anything good,' he said. 'That's why you must tell us if you see anything. But there is a Maven Inquisitor and two Sacred Guardsmen here, and we will find him before he can hurt anyone. Here,' he said, rummaging in the leather bag at his side. He produced a crumbling biscuit of sedge, purple with dried sloe, and held it out. The biscuit was snatched away and crammed into the boy's mouth without a word. 'You can go,' said Salbjorn, smiling at the student and gesturing him towards the stairs at the far end of the room.

'Thank you,' said the boy thickly, getting to his feet and retreating.

'Where do you keep getting these bloody biscuits from?' asked Leon, staring flatly at the boy as he passed.

'I make them,' said Salbjorn.

'From what?'

'Whatever's in season. But these are left over from autumn.'

'Great Catastrophe,' said Leon. 'That boy isn't upset. He knows you're a trout and will give out treats to anyone who blows their nose.'

'So they want to please me,' said Salbjorn. 'And that means we get the information we want.'

'I want to question someone.'

'I'll let you question someone when I've decided they're not going to say anything and I want them punished,' said Salbjorn, without looking up.

'I'm your mentor, you can't stop me.'

'In fact I can,' said Salbjorn grandly. 'You see, I am acting as deputy Inquisitor. Who next?' He nodded his head towards the courtyard where they boys were waiting.

'Check yourself, *Inquisitor*.'

Salbjorn laughed. 'I'm injured, Leon.'

Leon thrust himself upright and poked his head through one of the small windows. Outside it was a day of hazy cloud and swirling snow. Salbjorn could hear a tutor bawling a war-hymn, the students dutifully repeating it.

> *The end has come, the sun is low, the journey's*
>   *just begun.*
> *From the mortal side of earth, to this frosted path*
>   *I've come.*
> *Walking my whole life, my shadow at my side,*
> *The wind is at my back, the stars will be my guide.*
> *In the ghostly light of the blazing silver moon,*
> *The wolves unfold as I pass and follow through*
>   *the gloom.*
> *My bones crumble as I move, my spirit set alight,*
> *Along the Winter Road I'm bound, my footsteps*
>   *cast in white.*

'You!' Leon pointed into the courtyard. 'You're next.' Leon crashed back to his seat and his target, a boy wrapped in a wretched reed cloak, hurried up the stairs into their room soon after. He took a seat before Salbjorn, the hymn floating through the window.

> *The journey is my test, my first one and my last!*
> *I shall not fear the wolf, I did not in the past.*
> *I've fought with those that loved me, and I've fought alone,*
> *I have fought through wilderness and war, I am coming*
>   *home.*

Unaccountably, this boy was plump: a significant achievement in a place where food was as restricted as the haskoli. He sat before Salbjorn with an air of anticipation, which suggested he had indeed heard tell of biscuits.

'Good morning,' said Salbjorn.

The boy looked flatly back at him and Salbjorn felt a temptation to allow Leon to conduct the interview.

'It's rude to make eye contact with a full peer, boy.' The boy dropped his eyes to the floor. 'So I imagine you know what we're about to ask. You will have heard about the circumstances under which your contemporary Numa died. Did you see anything unusual on the day it occurred?'

'No,' said the boy.

'Anything at all. Take your time. Think back to that day. Was anyone behaving unusually?'

'I didn't see anything,' said the boy. Beyond him, Leon rolled his eyes and shifted irritably in his seat. 'It's freezing in here,' added the boy, looking around as though he might see a brazier lying untended.

'Fine. You must have heard the commotion a few nights ago, when the longhouse was burnt down. We think that was caused by the same man responsible for Numa's death. Did you see anything or anyone strange on that day?'

'No. Haven't you got another cloak I can have?' The students wove their own cloaks, and this boy's was in tatters.

'It doesn't matter,' said Salbjorn. 'Forget it, you can go.'

'I heard you give out biscuits,' said the boy.

'You heard wrong,' said Salbjorn, waving a hand towards the stairs.

The boy made a noise of dissatisfaction, got up and headed for the stairs. Leon and Salbjorn were exchanging a long glance when the boy paused and turned back to them. 'Would you give me one if I told you something strange I saw yesterday?'

Salbjorn folded his hands on the table and looked up at the boy.

'There's someone living the mountains. I saw the smoke of their fire.'

The guardsmen exchanged another glance. 'Where?' asked Salbjorn.

'It was right between Skafta and Vatni,' said the boy, naming two mountains. 'Maybe two leagues away?'

'And you're sure it was smoke? It wasn't a wisp of cloud?'

The boy rolled his eyes. 'I know what smoke looks like.'

'Thank you. That is helpful.'

'Surely that's worth a biscuit?'

'You'd think so, wouldn't you?' said Salbjorn, waving the boy away again. The boy huffed and clattered down the stairs. Salbjorn turned back to Leon. 'We should tell Inger.'

'She's exhausted.'

'She'll want to know. I'll tell her.'

'Let me go. You guard the boy, I want to get out of here. I haven't left this school for a week and I'm getting feverish. I want to run.'

'I can't guard anyone at the moment,' said Salbjorn. 'You keep an eye on the boy. I should move anyway; I'll go and speak with Inger.' Privately, Salbjorn did not trust his mentor with any part of this investigation. He was terrifying in combat, fit as the wind and stubbornly unyielding. But his direct and forceful reliability was partly a result of his limitations. The same lack of imagination that left him unable to countenance retreat or a break from his training routine, left him totally unable to follow one lead to the next. He could not empathise with an assailant, envisage what they might do next or why, or identify what information might turn out to be important.

Salbjorn heaved himself upright and went to find Inger. He stepped outside, using his sheathed sword as a stick to supplement his swollen ankle, and spotted her dark figure perched on a cliff, high above the school. It was not the first time he had seen her sitting there, overlooking the haskoli, legs dangling off the edge and staring vacantly out into the void. The path to reach her was not direct, and he hobbled out of the courtyard and into the wind. Behind him was the burnt wreck of the longhouse they had occupied on the first night, half swallowed by snow.

The heather waved and bowed beneath the wind, prickling its snow blanket, and a herd of students on the slope below spotted him and hurriedly removed their crude hareskin slippers. They should have been barefoot, but Salbjorn did not care. He had done the same in his own time here. They were harvesting heather to combine with the shed wool which drifted over the mountain, and lay down as bedding. They stopped to stare as he passed above, and Salbjorn felt an embarrassing gratification to be here without Leon. The students obsessed over his mentor. They had all heard of him, heard of his sword, Silence, and stared at his Prize of Valour. Only a few of the older boys had heard of Salbjorn, who had been a guardsman for just two years.

The path passed the course for the Trial: one of the holiest and most fundamental exercises at the haskoli. Salbjorn had attempted this challenge more times than he could count and to his lasting pride, succeeded once. Most never finished it. He had not understood its purpose in his time here. It was Leon who explained it to him when he first arrived in the Sacred Guard. The Trial did not assess any particular athleticism or skill. It was just hard. You were made to try this near-impossible feat again and again, shouted on by your tutors and contemporaries who crowded round to watch, and compelled by the example of the impossible few who completed it. There was no explanation for why you were asked to do this unreasonable, unachievable thing: you just had to try, again and again and again. And ultimately, with one attempt and then another and another, it just became something Salbjorn had to do. He ceased to question why. He reached the stage where failure seemed a small thing, but conceding, even in the face of the impossible, had become unthinkable.

That was the purpose of the Trial.

It taught *asappa*, an Anakim term which translated roughly as: *You must live with it*. It implied sympathy, and was also in some way dismissive: intended to undermine any tendencies towards self-pity. It conveyed responsibility:

that this was your lot and nobody else's. Most importantly, it implied inevitability: this cannot be stopped, or run from. You must face it. It was among the most important concepts imparted at the haskoli. That was why the students faced cold-water immersion when they failed at their tasks. *Asappa*. That was why you were punished or rewarded as a group: regardless of your own performance, you might still suffer. *Asappa*. That was the purpose of this academy and of this unreasonable, arbitrary test. To develop people who did not complain, did not give up and paid no heed to their own suffering.

Salbjorn remembered the triumph of his own success, after years of trying. He remembered the disbelief he had felt a few years later when he had heard a young student, who had started just as he left, had equalled the record of completing the Trial on just his fourth attempt. He had even remembered his name: Pryce Rubenson.

He hobbled the steep path up the cliff, and arrived to find Inger sitting contentedly by the edge. She must have heard him approach, but was perfectly still, staring into the billowing snow. 'Do you enjoy sitting here?' asked Salbjorn, dropping heavily to one knee, as close to the edge as he dared.

She nodded, smiling out at the mountains. 'Yes,' she said simply.

'For any particular reason?'

'It reminds me of my days in the freyi. The treehouses are high off the ground and have no railings. And the void clarifies things, gives a little focus.' She shrugged happily, Salbjorn marvelling that within this freewheeling mind was enough insight to have achieved the esteemed rank of Maven Inquisitor.

'Any progress, then?' he asked.

She nodded. 'I think I've identified an inconsistency in a couple of the tutors' stories. I'll re-question them.'

'Good,' he said. 'One of the boys we were speaking to has

just revealed he's seen smoke coming from between two mountains a couple of leagues away.'

'Did he indeed?' She glanced at Salbjorn, smiling. 'I fear you are in no state to investigate, my tracker. And Leon needs to guard the boy.'

'I wondered if Leon might go, and take the boy with him,' Salbjorn suggested.

'Do you think that would be safe?'

Salbjorn smiled. 'There are perhaps two men in the entire kingdom who might stand a chance against Leon in a fight. I very much doubt our assassin is one of them.'

'Do you think he'd approach Leon head-on?' asked Inger, mildly. 'Do you think he's working alone?' She left a silence there which made Salbjorn shiver. 'Our little team is weakened already with your injury. Let's not send Leon and the boy off in a blizzard to pursue a phantom.'

Embarrassed and frustrated by his own weakness, Salbjorn muttered his agreement and turned to go.

'Don't let the mountains seduce you on the way back,' Inger called after him. 'They've almost got me.'

The snow lifted briefly that evening. The winds dropped. The clouds dispersed, save one to the east. It rose as a column from between two mountains: Skafta and Vatni. Salbjorn stared from his upstairs window, fixated on its origin, until darkness hid the peaks.

Though Inger's manner might suggest she was drifting absently through this investigation, she was meticulous, and it was another three days of questioning before she summoned Salbjorn to her dark interview room. He entered to find Inger seated opposite a black-cloaked tutor. Her round, pale face was fixed on him as he entered, hovering like the moon against her midnight backdrop. 'Good timing,' she said, giving a smile. 'I'm done with our friend here,' she indicated the Black-Cloak, 'would you fetch the next one? And perhaps stay with me after.'

Salbjorn stood aside so that the tutor could leave. She had never asked for company before. 'Does this mean you're about to interview your primary suspect, lady?' He did not need to call her *lady*. Sacred Guardsmen and Inquisitors were of equal status, but Salbjorn had never met a Maven Inquisitor before and could not shake the feeling that she was invested with powers he did not understand. There was the silver angel on her chest, the white raptor feathers flecking her hair and the undoubted ease with which she conducted this investigation.

Inger twinkled at him. 'I have my suspicions. For now, though, we don't know that he's done anything. It's a tutor by the name of Hagen, and we must keep an open mind and assume he's innocent until we know otherwise.'

Salbjorn bowed. 'Absolutely. I'll go and get the guilty bastard.' He left, limping through the courtyard, where it was still snowing, seeking this new adolescent to be interrogated by the kindly Inquisitor. He returned with Hagen at his side, shutting the door behind them and leaning against it. Hagen glanced nervously over his shoulder at Salbjorn. He was small, brown-haired and pale-faced. There was something frayed about him, a little frantic and a little distracted.

'You don't seem at your ease for someone who's been meditating,' observed Inger kindly. 'Relax, relax.'

Hagen tried to drop his shoulders, but his eyes still darted about the room.

'It must be an upsetting business, having this investigation occur in your home,' continued Inger. 'Confusing too, it seems.' There, she let a pause stretch, which sharpened Salbjorn's attention. The effect it had on Hagen was far more pronounced, the tutor turning to look wildly at Salbjorn, blocking his exit. Nobody Salbjorn had yet met could use pauses quite like the Inquisitor.

'Confusing?' asked Hagen, eventually.

'Yes, confusing,' said Inger, leaning forward. 'Remind me

what you were doing on the night that the assassin appeared most recently within the school?'

'I was in the storehouse,' said Hagen, miserably.

He's crumbling already, thought Salbjorn.

'Doing what?'

'Taking an inventory of the food supplies.'

'Alone?'

'Yes,' he said, voice slightly raised.

'So it must have taken you a while?'

'Yes. But it's usually done alone.'

'So did anyone walk in and find you doing this?'

There came another pause. 'No.'

'Nobody?' asked Inger, with the air that she had stumbled over this inconsistency by accident.

'No one.'

'I've just been speaking to your friend Tarla. He has confessed to entering the storehouse for birch syrup that evening.'

'He's lying,' said Hagen. 'I saw no one.'

'Well one of you is lying,' agreed Inger, her vague manner falling away. 'But it's not him, is it?'

'It's him!' said Hagen defiantly.

'Then why were you seen leaving this longhouse, just ten minutes before the fire overwhelmed ours? When you claim you were in the stores?'

Salbjorn tensed a little, waiting for what was to come.

'Who saw me?'

'You don't deny it,' observed Inger.

Hagen was silent.

'Why were you seen emerging from the opposite longhouse, earlier in the day? What business did you have there?'

Hagen still said nothing.

'You were stealing a torch,' concluded Inger. 'Which you used, first to signal to the assassin, then set the fire in our longhouse. You signalled to the assassin where Ormur was sleeping, but then Leon spoiled that by going to sleep outside. So you panicked. You set our longhouse ablaze, partly as a diversion to draw Leon away from the boy, and partly to be rid of us.'

Suddenly, Hagen moved. He sprang up with an energy that caught Salbjorn completely by surprise, and jumped at the guardsman, attempting to rip him aside from the door and run. Salbjorn did not even register Inger's cry of: 'Stop him!'. Unprepared though he might have been and still injured, he was a Sacred Guardsman, the tutor merely a half-trained teenager. Salbjorn did not even think, and it was no effort at all to hurl him to the stone floor where he landed with a crunch.

'Well done,' said Inger, who was on her feet. 'Pick him up, please.'

Salbjorn bent stiffly to seize Hagen's cloak and drag him into a seated position, while Inger crouched down in front of him. 'That was foolish,' she said. 'Now you're going to tell us everything. You will help us find the assassin.'

'I can't!' howled Hagen, tears welling over his cheeks. 'I can't! *Please!* He'll kill me!'

'Who? Who will kill you?'

'The Ellengaest!'

8

The Trials of King Gogmagoc

The Unhieru laughed. It was a slow noise of grinding rock and sand that filled the dark cave and disturbed Roper profoundly.

Pryce seemed in no mood to delay. 'Let's go,' he said, curtly, using the cord of Unhieru hair he clutched as a leash and dragging the creature towards the exit. His giant captive was forced to follow in a stoop, wary of Pryce's sword still held beneath its chin, and together they shuffled for the mouth of the cave. Roper glanced at the other Unhieru, which had seized his ankle, only able to perceive its gleaming eyes.

'After you,' he said, gesturing with Cold-Edge. The creature seemed to consider him for a moment, then he sensed its massive bulk shamble past. Roper followed, holding the sword just short of the creature's spine, not at all sure that he would be able to stop it if it chose to turn on him.

They advanced up the passage, the cave growing lighter until suddenly Roper emerged squinting into the blessed light and space of the valley. Around him sprawled Vigtyr, Tekoa and Aledas, each crumpled on the floor, and evidently only recently released by the Unhieru that stood behind each of them. Including the two that had just emerged from the cave, there were five of them, and only now that they were in the light could Roper assess these people properly.

Their skin was clouded grey, their flesh naked, and each head surrounded by a dark matted mane. Their faces were flat, intelligent, and eerily beautiful, with robust cheekbones and wide-set eyes and mouth. In composition, each was reminiscent of a bear. Not lean, but massive and so powerful they moved with a hypnotic grace. At fully nine feet tall, the one whom Pryce held captive was by far the largest, and possessed arresting eyes of a soft, honeyed gold. His mane was bigger than any other Unhieru present and stretched from brow to low back; the broad face beneath hairless, smooth-skinned and indecipherable. Roper had an idea that this captive was the leader of the Unhieru band. Though they could easily overpower the Anakim, the giants dared not act while Pryce might cut their leader's throat at any moment.

Tekoa got to his feet, rearranged the ruffled feathers of his cloak, and threw a filthy look at the Unhieru standing behind him. 'Gilius?' he asked Roper.

Roper looked pointedly at the Unhieru who had held onto him in the cave. Its fingers were stained rust red, with gore encrusting the broad, flat fingernails, and the chest streaked with blood. Tekoa followed his gaze, then looked up at the Unhieru with a look of pure spite. 'You damned *bastard*,' he said softly.

'What now?' asked Vigtyr, on his feet, sword flicking from one giant to another.

'This one takes us to Gogmagoc,' said Pryce savagely, jerking the cord of hair in his hand. 'Send the rest on their way.'

'How?' asked Vigtyr. 'We can't communicate with them.'

'Yes we can,' said Aledas, his voice flat. The attention of both Anakim and Unhieru turned to the ranger as he bent to extract the bow from his pack. Without particular urgency, he produced a twist of sinew from the side of his boot, strung the bow and fitted an arrow. Then he swung the weapon towards the blood-stained Unhieru, drawing the string back to his ear.

Roper had no time to stop him.

The bowstring snapped straight with a wicked crack and the arrow, fired point-blank, buried itself up to the fletching in the Unhieru's throat. Its great maned head snapped back, it tottered for a moment, hands flying up to the black feathers. Then it toppled backwards, landing with a crash and beginning to roll down into the valley. 'For Gilius,' said the ranger, cold as a knife. He reached for another arrow, and the other Unhieru began to scramble away. They broke into a loping trot and fled down into the valley, all except the golden-eyed leader, held fast by Pryce.

'I enjoyed that,' said Tekoa savagely.

'And now,' said Pryce, tugging on the hair he clutched in a fist, '*Gogmagoc*.'

They led their captive down into the valley, where they found the body of the Unhieru felled by Aledas. They sawed at its thick mane with swords, and used the hair to bind their captive's hands behind its back. Eyeing the enormous arms, Roper kept winding locks around the wrists until the creature had no hope of freeing itself. Then they pushed it before them, Aledas and Vigtyr standing on each side with an arrow nocked to their bowstrings as it led them up the valley.

They walked in silence for a league, the party observing the valley's edge in case the banished Unhieru should try and return. But more likely, and more disturbing too, they had gone on ahead to inform their giant king that one of their number was dead, and another captured.

Tekoa slowed a little to join Roper at the back. 'This may be the time to turn back, my lord,' he murmured. Vigtyr heard and glanced briefly at them, too slow to disguise the look of hope on his face. 'I doubt Gogmagoc will look kindly on our delegation now that we've killed one of his people. And that's if he even understands us any better than those we found in the cave. They had no interest in talking. These creatures are not our allies.'

Roper smiled at Tekoa. 'I don't know how this ends, Tekoa.

I don't know how we make Gogmagoc understand us, or convince him we're worth befriending. But we've come too far to turn back now. They know we're coming. Those others have gone before us, and doubtless reported our presence. Our horses are gone, and with them our chance of escaping before we're overhauled. We'll not escape Unhierea now until this task is done.'

Pryce had been following the conversation. He stopped to dig in his pack, and produced the Silver Wolf-Head of the Black Lord, which he fixed on his unstrung bow and held above the party as a banner.

Their captive led the party on, and soon they came upon more bramble enclosures, stoppered with long-thorned bushes and sheltering flocks of dark sheep. From some concealed source beyond the brambles rose a great column of smoke. The captive looked down at Roper, now walking at the lead of the party, and back at the smoke. '*Hokhmakhoc*,' it choked.

There came a distant, ear-splitting howl.

It echoed and re-echoed down the valley, so loud that the Anakim shrank together as one, halted dead in their tracks. To Roper's ears, it sounded like a terrible cry of pain: a shriek as might come from some stricken monster of the sea. And in response to this call, immense, ashen-skinned people began to emerge from the bushes before them. With them were shaggy, cream-coated hounds, each three feet at the shoulder and barking frenziedly as they surged out towards the Anakim.

Roper drew Cold-Edge and took a step back, holding his hand out to Pryce. 'Give me the banner, Pryce.' The sprinter obeyed, and then drew his own sword, holding its blade at their giant prisoner's throat once more.

'Gogmagoc!' Roper bellowed. The hounds were tearing towards them, fifty, forty, thirty yards distant, with a growing crowd of wild men and women swelling behind them, and baying every bit as savagely. 'Gogmagoc!'

Another drowned howl cut across them all, and the hounds slowed, no longer barking but growling. The crowd of Unhieru, of whom there were now seventy or eighty, began to slow, and Roper could see a figure pushing towards the front.

Out before the crowd stepped a giant among giants. A cauldron-bodied beast, whose dark braided mane reached down to the small of its back and was entangled with shards of bone. It had the same honey-gold eyes as their captive Unhieru, but was broader by far. It prowled towards them; the flat, eerily beautiful face fixed on Roper, eyes moving slowly between him, and the prisoner with Pryce's sword held at its throat.

'Lord King,' said Roper in Saxon, for this could only be Gogmagoc. 'We have come to negotiate.'

At Roper's words, the giant's face lost all trace of beauty. He gave a smile of horrifying breadth, revealing a black mountain range of broken teeth and some underlying insanity in the features. The creature began a growling, breathless rumble, and Roper's heart sank. It was no language he had heard before.

Then he recognised a word, and realised his mistake. The giant was speaking Saxon, but in a drowning gurgle of a voice that rendered the words near unrecognisable. 'The horse-riders,' he said. 'Foolish, dead little Suthern men.'

Tekoa replied first. 'Don't ever call me Suthern again,' he said with distaste. 'We are Anakim.'

'Ahh.' The creature hissed a mighty exhalation past its broken teeth. 'River-People.'

'You are King Gogmagoc?' Roper asked.

'I am Gogmagoc.'

'I am the Black Lord, Roper Kynortasson,' said he. 'We have come seeking an audience with you, Lord King.'

Gogmagoc looked at their captive Unhieru, then at Pryce, holding a sword beneath its chin. 'This is why you threaten my son?' he asked.

Roper felt sweat break out on his palms. So that was why the Unhieru who attacked them in the cave had stopped so quickly when Pryce threatened their hostage. He was an Unhieru prince.

'We did not know he was your son,' said Roper. 'He led a party that killed one of our number. We killed one in return, and took a hostage to ensure our safe conduct.'

Something strange happened then.

Roper was struck by a wave of dreadful, ravenous fear such as he had never experienced before. It ate at his chest, so potent he nearly retched. He could tell from the way some of his companions had suddenly staggered that they could feel it too, and Vigtyr actually dropped to one knee, the arrow clattering off his bowstring. Roper himself had to work hard to keep hold of Cold-Edge.

'Release him,' growled Gogmagoc, eyes boring into Pryce.

Roper turned and saw that the sprinter was reacting oddly to this overwhelming fear. Instead of going pale, like the rest of the Anakim, he had begun to tremble with some suppressed mania. 'I don't speak this stupid language,' he spat. 'But I am about to cut this fat bastard's throat.'

'No, Pryce!' Roper held up a placatory hand. The other Unhieru had begun to prowl restlessly, encircling their band but evidently not daring to act while their prince was held hostage. Roper addressed Gogmagoc once more. 'My companion will release your son when you agree that we can talk and walk away when we're finished.' Roper could barely see Gogmagoc any more. All his energy was going into keeping his voice steady over that fear. 'He is a difficult man to control,' Roper continued. 'If we have no assurances, I will not be able to stop him.'

'Release him,' Gogmagoc seethed. 'And we will talk.'

Roper and Tekoa looked at one another. The legate was dreadfully pale. 'We can still go back, my lord,' he murmured. 'Use the prince as a hostage, retreat to the border.

Whatever you do, do not surrender our only bargaining chip to this monster.'

'Release him,' came Gogmagoc's voice once more.

Roper looked at the giant king and saw that a slow red flush had begun to suffuse his ashen face. 'Let him go, Pryce,' said Roper. 'He says we can talk.'

'My lord, no . . .' breathed Tekoa.

Pryce searched Roper's face for a moment. Then he stepped back from their hostage, lowering his sword.

All at once, the horrible sense of dread that pervaded Roper's chest lifted. It felt as though some festering abscess had been drained, and his breathing eased. He heard an audible sigh from those around him as they too were relieved, and that red flush in Gogmagoc's face began to fade.

'Now,' said Roper, straightening up and meeting Gogmagoc's eye once more, 'we talk.'

'Do we have a plan?' hissed Vigtyr as they were led through the crowd of staring Unhieru.

'The plan is to stay calm,' said Roper, without turning around. 'Don't threaten anyone, do not be aggressive, do not touch anything, do not say anything. Don't do anything unless I've told you to. Does everybody understand?' Aledas acknowledged him, and Tekoa and Vigtyr muttered something placatory.

Tekoa turned to Pryce. 'Pryce, I believe that was largely directed at you. Do you understand what Lord Roper said?'

'I understand.'

'Will you obey?'

'Probably not.'

'Vigtyr: your job is to restrain Pryce if he tries anything stupid.'

'Absolutely, my lord,' said Vigtyr.

Pryce, wearing no discernible expression, met Vigtyr's eye. Vigtyr raised his eyebrows briefly and smiled back.

Gogmagoc led the Anakim delegation first past the

bramble hedges that penned their livestock, and then dozens
of low drystone storehouses. At any moment, Roper expected
the silent crowd to fall upon them and begin battering them
with rocks, or tearing broken-nailed at their limbs. But they
did nothing. There merely watched in eerie stillness as the
Anakim processed right to the heart of the camp: a blazing
hearth, surrounded by nests of green bracken in which more
Unhieru sat watchfully. Their feral reek was enough to make
Roper light-headed.

Gogmagoc sat by the fire, and was joined by several immense
women who seemed to be his wives. They converged on him
and began attending to his mane: skilfully unwinding the
braids, extracting vertebrae and perforated shin-bones from
his locks, tossing them into a clattering pile, and using
notched ribs to comb at the hair. 'Speak,' said Gogmagoc, gesturing a huge hand at Roper. His face was still unreadable,
and Roper had no idea how long the giant king would entertain his delegation. Three of the cream-coated hounds trotted
to the fireside and settled near the king, resting their heads
on their paws.

'I come with a gift, Lord Gogmagoc,' Roper began, reaching into a saddlebag at his side and producing a sloshing skin
of fine mead, which he held out to the giant king. Gogmagoc
took the skin one-handed, removed the bung, and took a
sniff. He directed a jet of the golden liquid into his mouth,
squeezing fully half of it past his eroded teeth before it was
passed to his wives, who shared it between them. Roper left
a pause for Gogmagoc to show some appreciation, but when
none appeared, he continued. 'It is a sign of our good faith. I
have come to propose an alliance between our two peoples.'

Gogmagoc made an impatient hand gesture. *Well?*

'The deal we offer is this. Very soon, we will take Suthdal.
We would like you to fight with us. If you help, we promise
you the return of your ancestral lands, stolen from you by
the Sutherners.'

Gogmagoc had lost interest. He was staring at something

over Roper's head, and made another hand gesture, accompanied by some choked Unhieru words. Roper turned and saw two of their lost horses – his own and Pryce's – led into the clearing. They were bucking and snorting, eyes wide and white as they leaned back from the huge hands pulling at their bridles. Behind them came the Unhieru prince whom Pryce had threatened: Gogmagoc's son, carrying a log.

Without flourish or particular effort, the Unhieru raised the log above his head, and brought it crashing down on the neck of Pryce's horse. There was a loud pop and the animal crumpled at once. There was shocking strength and brutality in that swift motion, and the surviving horse began to scream in terror. Pryce started forward, swearing at the Unhieru, but had his arm caught by Vigtyr. 'Get off me, you prick!' Pryce snarled, trying to shake his arm free, but Vigtyr seized his shoulder and enfolded him in a bear hug. Roper's horse succumbed a heartbeat later and small knives (which looked forged for Suthern hands) were used to bleed the carcasses. The three dogs ran over and began lapping greedily at the metallic splashes on the floor.

Aledas did not react, but Pryce and Vigtyr had gone still, both staring at the scene. Tekoa stood stiffly beside them, teeth bared, face the colour of crab-armour.

'My lord?' prompted Roper, looking at Gogmagoc. He had shut his eyes at the noise of the horses dying, and not watched as the scene concluded.

'You want to be friends,' the king gurgled in a voice that resembled Saxon as a rotting carcass resembles healthy flesh. His gaze rested on Roper's waist. 'I want your sword.'

'My sword is not on offer.'

'I want to see,' Gogmagoc insisted.

Roper unbuckled Cold-Edge and held it out for the king's inspection, aware of his companions' eyes on him as he relinquished his weapon. 'Built for smaller hands than yours, Lord King. But we could make weapons fit for the Unhieru.'

Gogmagoc pinched Cold-Edge's handle between thumb

and forefinger, drawing the blade carefully and casting an eye over it. 'I want this,' he said. 'Better than Suthern weapons.'

'That is mine,' said Roper, firmly. 'But if you fight beside us, we could make weapons for every Unhieru.'

Gogmagoc did not react beyond dropping Cold-Edge on the floor, making no effort to return it. He examined Roper once more, bronze glare raking him from head to toe. 'Your skin,' he said slowly. 'Your metal skin. I want that.'

Roper realised the king meant his armour. He imagined Gogmagoc dressed in steel, wielding an axe that matched his proportions. He was not sure he could ever trust such a powerful ally, let alone one who carelessly murdered his followers, and stole and butchered his horses. 'We will make you weapons, and in return you will help us invade Suthdal, and have your ancient lands returned. It is a good trade.'

Gogmagoc smiled, and that horrible insanity came over his face again. His countenance at rest was intelligent, but that smile was like the fracture in a mask, revealing something broken beneath. 'We do not need more land. We take what we want. Your offer is boring.'

Very deliberately, Roper advanced towards Gogmagoc and bent to pick up his sword. Gogmagoc made no movement at all, letting Roper take the weapon. 'What else, then?' he asked, backing away. 'What would make you join us, Lord King?'

Gogmagoc was still smiling. 'Fight us.'

'Fight?' said Roper, narrowing his eyes.

'Send us weapons. Send us metal skin. Now one of you fights one of us,' said the giant. 'We like a contest. Win, and we are friends.'

'We are not here to fight,' said Roper.

'He is,' said Gogmagoc, and he made a throwing gesture in Pryce's direction. The sprinter noticed, and met Gogmagoc's eyes.

'A fight would be boring too,' said Roper mildly, trying to

diffuse the sense of hostility growing between Pryce and Gogmagoc. Pryce was evidently furious about the death of Gilius and the slaughter of his horse, and Gogmagoc equally livid about the threat to his son. 'You are too large, it would be over in a flash. Unless, of course, we used our swords, which would be a waste of one of your fine subjects. I propose a race. My companion here,' he gestured at Pryce, 'has fearsome speed. That would be a good contest.'

Gogmagoc continued to stare at Pryce, while behind him, his wives had started braiding his mane and threading the bones back onto the locks. 'Maybe,' he gurgled. 'But he threatened my son. If he loses, he pays.'

'Pays, how?'

'I will kill him,' said Gogmagoc flatly. 'That will make your race interesting. If he loses, he dies.'

'There is no need for that,' Roper replied, still speaking calmly. 'We held your son hostage because he attacked us. It was to ensure our safety. It was no insult, merely a mark of your fearsome reputation.'

'*He* threatened my son,' snarled Gogmagoc, making that throwing gesture at Pryce once more. 'He races. If he loses, he dies. Otherwise, talking is over.'

'What is he saying?' demanded Pryce, unable to comprehend the Saxon words but aware of the golden eyes resting heavily on his person.

'He wants a contest,' said Roper, turning to the sprinter. 'I suggested a race, with you versus one of them. But he's unhappy about us threatening his son and wants to kill you if you lose.'

Pryce shrugged. 'Let's race. I'll outpace any one of these fat bastards.'

Roper raised a hand to indicate Pryce should slow down. 'Think carefully, my friend. This is not a command. If you wish to volunteer for this, it is up to you.'

'Do we have a choice?'

Roper did not reply.

'Yes, I'm sure,' said Pryce.

Roper turned back to Gogmagoc. 'We accept,' he said.

Gogmagoc slapped a flat palm on his leg, the matter settled. He leaned forward onto his feet and ambled for the
horse carcasses, which had already been skinned. 'Eating
first. Then race.' The horses were soon spitted and steaming
naked above the fire, the smell of roasting meat filling the
air.

'Come,' said Roper, leading the party to the valley wall at
the edge of the camp. 'Over here.' He wanted them to have at
least one side secure from the crowd still staring at them.
The Anakim made their own fire and toasted sedge biscuits,
and before long the separate crowd of Unhieru began to hack
apart the barely cooked horses with crashing blows of a splitting maul which they wielded like a hatchet.

'All their tools are Suthern-made,' Tekoa observed, eyes
narrowed.

'Parasites,' said Vigtyr, gazing coldly at the Unhieru. 'Why
work your own metal when it's so easy to steal it from the
people who do?'

'You could not teach these people to work metal,' said
Pryce. 'Not if you had a thousand years.'

'They're not stupid,' said Roper. 'I fear they may be far
more intelligent than they have so far shown. It's as Vigtyr
said, metal is a crop for them. The Sutherners grow it, and
they harvest it.

'I want to know whether anyone else felt that sense of
dread, earlier,' he added. 'When Gogmagoc wanted us to
release his son, I suddenly felt certain I was going to die. It
was like the world was coming to an end, and the sky going
to fall in on top of me. I've never known anything like it.'

'I felt it,' said Aledas.

'I did too,' said Tekoa. 'And at the same time, a couple of
little stones started rattling near my feet.'

None of them knew what to make of that. 'Strange,' said
Roper. 'I am certain that Gogmagoc induced it somehow. He

made us feel that way, but how, I cannot imagine. Perhaps that is how they harvest iron from the Sutherners. They terrify them into submission. Take care in your race, Pryce. Whatever game this is, I'm not sure we're following the same rules.'

Pryce seemed unconcerned by what rules the Unhieru might follow. 'What happens after I win?' he asked.

'Then Gogmagoc will join us,' said Vigtyr, still gazing over the giants swarming the dead horses.

'Is that definitely what we want?' asked Tekoa, looking fixedly at Roper. 'Undoubtedly they'd be powerful allies, but I have seen nothing in their conduct so far which leads me to believe we'd be able to campaign with them. These people are *animals*.'

'We need these animals,' said Roper, quietly. 'They do not need to be controlled. Just unleashed. But make sure you're taking this seriously, Pryce. Don't underestimate them.'

But Pryce had not heard Roper, and was instead fixated on Vigtyr. Roper followed his gaze and saw Vigtyr hurriedly look away, abashed. Something strange had passed between the two men, and Roper could not tell what. He gripped Pryce by the shoulder. 'Content?' he asked.

'It will be the easiest race I have ever run,' Pryce replied flatly, looking away from Vigtyr. 'I won't lose against an Unhieru.'

Gogmagoc soon prowled over to them, holding a dripping haunch of half-roasted horse by a bone that had sat exposed in the fire. It must have been baking hot, but his broad face wore no expression. 'Time to race.' He opened his mouth wide and tore off a strip of horseflesh, using his molars instead of his broken, eroded front teeth.

'Where do you propose?' asked Roper, getting to his feet.

'Down the valley,' said the maned king, turning away and beginning to stride from the camp. Roper gestured to his companions that they should follow. Gogmagoc led them out past the drystone storehouses, past the bramble hedges, which were now drained of sheep, and out of the camp. The dogs trotted at his heels, staring hungrily at the haunch of horseflesh swinging from his hand.

Just beyond the camp, where Roper had met Gogmagoc for the first time, they stopped. Before them was a rocky down-hill stretch that would suffice as a track, and Gogmagoc gestured with the horse-leg. 'Here.'

Pryce snorted. 'This is the track? Tell the ogre to pick his fastest subject.'

'And who is to be your champion?' Roper translated tact-fully, eyeing the track and thinking that its rough surface might favour the larger Unhieru stride.

For answer, Gogmagoc looked down at one of the dogs sit-ting obediently by his side, staring at the meat in his hand.

At first Roper did not understand. Then the true nature of this challenge dawned on him. 'The hound?' he said, looking up at Gogmagoc in horror. 'You said we would race one of you!'

'No,' said Gogmagoc. 'I said there would be a race. And if your fast one loses, he dies.'

In spite of Gogmagoc's vast size, and the enormous crowd that was beginning to gather around them, fury was build-ing in Roper. 'A new challenge, then,' he demanded. 'You have tricked us.'

'No,' said Gogmagoc again. 'No. This challenge. Or talking is over.'

This at least, Roper understood. *Talking is over* did not mean negotiations had concluded, and they could depart. *Talking is over* meant that to the Unhieru, Roper's band would occupy the same status as the horses that had just been hacked apart, or the Sutherners on whom they preyed, or poor Gilius, when he had ventured into the cave. If talking was over, then so was everything else.

Roper turned to Pryce, not sure how he could tell the sprinter of the trap he had negotiated them into. But Pryce looked back at him calmly. 'He wants me to race the dog,' he said. Though he did not speak Saxon, it seemed Pryce understood better than Roper the Unhieru language of gestures, stance and power.

Roper let out a slow breath. 'Yes. That is what he wants.'

Pryce nodded, and cast a cool eye over the dog that would be his opposition. He looked back at Gogmagoc, that strange animosity naked between them. 'Tell him I accept,' he said.

It was some way past noon, and that cold evening wind had begun to flow gently down the valley. The air was crisp, the sky spat coarse snow granules, and a crowd of Unhieru had begun to gather either side of the track. They seethed with malevolent energy, apparently kept in check only by Gogmagoc's implacable aura. If Pryce lost, Roper doubted very much that it was just the sprinter who would pay with his life. He had to beat the hound.

Pryce used a stone to dig himself a pair of starting blocks. When he was ready, Gogmagoc would hurl the bone in his hand, now gnawed milky-white, as far as he could. Whichever seized it first, the Anakim or the hound, would be declared the victor.

Whether he was so adept at hiding his emotions that none now made it past his careless exterior, or whether Pryce simply did not exist beyond the moment he was in, the sprinter showed no signs of anxiety. He finished digging his starting blocks and then went still, wrapping himself in his cloak and standing like a pillar. Roper's eyes were travelling along the track, taking in the light layer of snow over the rocks, its slight downhill slope, the hollow forty yards away where he thought the bone might come to rest.

Gogmagoc made a clicking noise and the hound skipped towards him, sitting at his feet, and alert to the long bone held low by his side. Pryce watched it too. He dropped the cloak from his shoulders and, refusing to be hurried, plodded to his starting blocks.

The dog was trembling with exuberance, dancing lightly on its feet as it waited for the bone to take flight. Pryce's energy was a focused ray of sunlight, animating exactly as he directed. Everything was still but his legs, as he kicked them into his footholds. The Unhieru watched in silence, the only sound the rattle of graupel on stone, and the crunch as Pryce dug his foot into the second starting block. He tested his footholds, straining against them briefly before he knelt back to wipe his hands on his tunic. Gogmagoc was watching from beneath his brow ridge, waiting until Pryce was ready. Finally, the sprinter leaned forward into his starting position. There he froze: low and taught.

The Anakim had gathered together, arms over each other's shoulders, watching their champion.

Gogmagoc drew back his arm.

The bone was catapulted forward, twirling through the air and, infinitely more explosive, Pryce blasted after it. Like a twisted rope, upon which more and more tension has been wrought until finally a strand snaps and unravels in a violent flurry, Pryce burst free, his boots smashing aside rock and snow to create small footholds on which he climbed upright. Each stride was small as he heaped force behind his frame, a slipstream of flying stones and earth spraying out in his wake and his long ponytail lashing behind him. His trajectory wobbled like some unstable celestial body, and then, as though he were no longer being pushed but pulled, his course straightened.

The hound's athleticism was no match in those early heartbeats. Its claws skittered on the frozen rock, and half of each long stride was hurled away across the stone. Pryce lunged ahead and built his lead by yards, then feet, then inches as the hound began to unfold itself and near his speed. It stretched out across the ground, graceful and willowy. It stretched and pulled, stretched and pulled, and as it collected its own momentum, its claws stopped slipping. Dog and man reached equilibrium, man five yards ahead, just as the bone bounced and clattered, coming to rest some eighty yards from the start line.

The Unhieru had begun to howl: a noise like a mighty wind flooding the valley. For a moment, it looked as though Pryce, veins swollen, legs driving, arms pumping, and teeth bared, might hold his lead. Then the dog began to reel him in. Its shaggy coat strained and relaxed, entire body like a single immense spring, and it took half a yard back with each stride. It was nearly level with Pryce when the sprinter's trajectory oscillated once more. He stepped, and his path veered across the dog's, knocking into its shoulder. He upset the beast's stride, it missed a landing, had to skip to stay upright, and Pryce was three yards clear again. The dog's ears were near flat along its neck, its eyes wide and greedy as it streaked after him. The sprinter seemed to have found another rung of speed, and the dog was closing less quickly than before.

But close it did. Running further apart now so that Pryce could not swerve into it, the hound laboured closer, straining every muscle and ligament to draw level. The two figures were a shaking bundle of galloping momentum and the dog stretched half a length ahead. The slipstream behind Pryce seemed to intensify, his movements become more violent, and the dog could pull away no more. The bone was fifteen, ten, five yards distant. Pryce had begun to lean forward, the hound to slow, opening its jaws wide, and Pryce dived.

He had lost not a fragment of his speed as he crashed into the ground, arm outstretched towards the bone. The dog had slowed and bent its head, and both disappeared in a burst of grit and snow. The dog's flank reappeared, tumbling over, Pryce rolling after it, and then both vanished into the filthy cloud once more. There was another heartbeat as the watchers leaned towards the scene, eyes wide, and then Pryce burst above the cloud, hurling something white and flashing up above his head.

The Anakim bellowed in triumph, raising clenched fists into the air and embracing as the bone came tumbling back to earth, where it was seized by the dog. The Unhieru fell

silent, some making small gestures of frustration and beginning to turn away. Pryce, outline pale through the snow,
wore a smile as rabid as Gogmagoc's as he held his arms up
to the sky and declaimed at the top of his voice: 'I cannot
lose! The Almighty loves me! I cannot lose!'

Tekoa was swearing over and over again, grinning and
shaking his fist in Pryce's direction. Aledas wore a small
smile, the first Roper had seen from him, and nodded slowly
at the celebrating sprinter. Only Vigtyr seemed unmoved. He
was staring at Pryce, a look on his face that was so unexpected that Roper found it hard to place. Envy, perhaps?

Pryce began to make his way back towards them along the
racetrack, holding one end of the bone and using it to tug
the hound along with him. Roper advanced to greet him.
Pryce dropped the bone, and they embraced. 'Well done, my
brother,' said Roper.

'That is a fast beast,' said Pryce. His face was covered in
grime and the left side was one broad, bleeding scrape from
his final dive for the bone. Tekoa embraced Pryce next, and
Aledas wrung the sprinter's hand and thumped his back.
Roper heard giant footfalls and turned to see Gogmagoc a
little way behind their group, standing with one of his wives,
his face still indecipherable.

Roper advanced to meet him. 'Now, Lord King,' he said,
graciously, 'we are allies.'

'No,' said Gogmagoc.

Roper froze. 'No, what?'

'No,' Gogmagoc repeated flatly. 'He cheated. He hit my
dog. He would have lost.' By Gogmagoc's side, his wife was
making a soft rumbling noise, which Roper interpreted as
laughter. She was about the same height as Aledas, the short-
est of their party, but her breadth was of a different scale. Her
body was a vast squat drum, and the root of each limb was as
thick as Roper's waist. She leered at the Anakim, who by
now had realised what Gogmagoc was saying and turned
towards him, the smiles falling from every face.

'He broke no rules you spoke of,' Roper replied firmly. 'And a man against a dog is not a fair race anyway. We have satisfied every requirement you spoke of.'

'No,' said Gogmagoc simply. 'I am not *satisfied.*' He waved an indifferent hand.

The Anakim were dismissed.

Roper continued to stare at Gogmagoc, but was shocked to hear small noises of relief uttered behind him. A hand touched his elbow, and he turned to see Tekoa standing next to him. 'We should go, lord,' said Tekoa quietly, in Anakim. 'We've done all we can, and now can leave with our lives. Frankly that is more than seemed likely. It's time to go. These people will not be our allies.'

They began to back away, all except Pryce, who was looking at Roper.

The Black Lord had not moved. He turned back to Gogmagoc, meeting those brass eyes. A cluster of other Unhieru had begun to gather around their king and queen, gazing at the Anakim.

'*No,*' said Roper, in Saxon.

A silence came over the valley like the silent rearing of a wave forced to the surface, high and smooth above the sea. Roper's jaw was set, his feet rooted to the earth and his eyes narrowed. He felt Pryce come to stand next to him. 'No,' he said again. 'We're not going anywhere.' Quietly, the rest of his group came to stand with him.

Roper was furious. They had come here for an alliance, not to be intimidated by this frustrating power imbalance. With so many Unhieru, and so far from any kind of help, Roper had no way to enforce his own will. He had to abide by Gogmagoc's whims, and the giant king was playing a different game to the Anakim. He had no interest in the alliance that Roper proposed. He merely wanted to be entertained. It was time to make Gogmagoc take them seriously. 'Another challenge,' said Roper, spikily. 'Your choice, Lord King. But we're staying here.'

Roper felt his companions stiffen at his confrontational

tone, and a tinge of that red flush suffused Gogmagoc's ashen face. But his wife was still smiling poisonously. 'Yes,' she said, almost cackling with malice. 'Another challenge will be entertaining.'

'I agree,' said Roper. 'What is your name, lady?'

'Gighath,' she replied. 'I do not need yours, little riverman. Come,' she said, clutching Gogmagoc's arm. 'Another.'

'And if we win,' said Roper, 'you will join us.'

Gogmagoc's flush was fading a little. He seemed to be deliberating. Then he gave a jerk of his head, and a slight caress of Gighath's head. 'Tomorrow, then,' he said. The sun had disappeared below the rim of the valley and the wind was picking up. 'You will have one more chance.' Gogmagoc turned away from them and stalked back to the bramble hedges.

'Come, then,' said Roper. This meant a night in the Unhieru encampment, but at least they still had a chance.

'Should we not sleep well away from the Unhieru?' Tekoa suggested.

'Oh no,' said Roper. 'It is Gogmagoc who keeps them relatively ordered. We should stay close to him.'

They turned into the wind and followed the Unhieru up the valley. It was dark and the air swirled with snow when Aledas held up a sudden hand, gesturing up at the lip of the valley. Visible against the faint lightness of the sky behind was a bulky silhouette. Roper could at first hear nothing over the gale. Then, a forlorn call was emitted to the mountains. It faded down the valley, leaving silence but for the flooding wind. Then, very faintly, another voice replied from the dark beyond the valley.

'Saying goodnight,' said Roper.

9

A Flush of Red

It was a long night in the Unhieru camp. Roper's company retired to one edge and attempted to sleep, but were kept awake by the monstrous shadows cavorting before the fire and flickering over the valley sides. Skins of what smelt like fermented milk were produced, the Unhieru drinking until the men started wrestling. Gifts were awarded to the winners; mostly Suthern-made tools, but occasionally sacks of earth with a seedling growing from the top. These appeared precious, and were placed carefully out of the way. The women sat by the sides, attending each other's hair with combs made from notched ribs and talking in a constant rumble.

Sometime after midnight, the remaining Anakim horses were led into the circle, and dispatched far less cleanly than their predecessors. They were still alive as the maned giants began wrenching at their legs. The horse, near-raw, was eaten with nets of sour crab apples, fetched from the low stone storehouses that lined the valley.

Roper took the midnight watch and observed that there seemed to be two tiers of Unhieru men. Those who wrestled were huge, with arresting eyes of honeyed gold and massive shaggy manes. But there was another tier who did not engage in the fighting at all. They were smaller, leaner, brown-eyed, and their manes were barely larger than the women. While the maned men wrestled, the others sat around edgily, eyes flicking over the contest and some creeping closer to the piles of gifts accrued by each champion. When the fighters were at the height of their engagement, these others raided their stashes, then subtly retreated. The stolen gifts were then used to curry favour among the women. This led to the most shocking moment of the evening: more so even than the live butchery of the horses.

Roper sat on watch, his companions attempting to sleep behind him, and he trying to discern the rules of a wrestling bout. As far as he could tell, it was only contact with the eyes and groin that were considered unacceptable. Choking seemed positively encouraged. Beyond the contest, one of the smaller males approached a champion's stash and attempted to remove one of the seedlings. He had hold of it and was beginning a retreat, when a hand suddenly seized his ankle. The owner had caught him in the act and dragged him, now screaming ferociously, back towards his pile. The maned Unhieru's face had changed colour and for the first time Roper could read an expression there. It flushed a deep, furious red across its cheeks, down its neck and in a maroon flash across its chest, shocking compared with the pale skin of its torso. It was the same flush that had tinged Gogmagoc on occasion.

The flushing male knelt on his smaller kin, who was still yowling and thrashing. He could not escape, however, and lay pinned to the floor as his attacker reached a huge hand towards his eye, and began to dig into the socket with long, broken nails. He extracted one eye altogether, his victim beating thunderously and fruitlessly at his attacker's chest. For the next eye, the flushing male lost the composure to remove it and set about merely flattening it with blows of his palm. The rules that had prevailed during the wrestling were revoked, for no one intervened. Roper observed Gogmagoc looking on, expressionless as ever.

The smaller male would never see again, but still his

attacker was not done. Roper did not realise what was about to happen until, with bared teeth, the flushing male lunged for his groin. Abruptly, Roper looked away. A scream, agonised and high-pitched, filled the dark valley, and Roper wished the smaller male would lose consciousness or die, but just stop that panicked yowl. At his back, he found every one of his companions awake, staring in horror at the scene before them. 'What happens in this valley, happens,' said Roper, calmly. 'Try and sleep.'

The screaming faded away, its last echoes vanishing down the valley. When he looked back, Roper saw the attack had at last been stopped by a cluster of four women, who had risen from their grooming and pushed the enraged male away. His face and chest still bore that crimson flush and he continued trying to reach his prostrate opponent, who if not already dead, soon would be.

These were strange people. Their faces, so eerily beautiful until they smiled, seemed to encapsulate their behaviour. Adoration and savagery were directed at one another with equal intensity, a hair's breadth separating the two. Madness seemed the default state, with the faculties of reason and restraint barely developed. And yet they clearly had close bonds, as Gogmagoc's immediate reaction to the threat against his son, and his deference to Gighath's wishes, had both shown. They barely had facial expressions beyond savage smiles, and the crimson flush Roper had just witnessed. And what was that feeling of terror that Gogmagoc seemed able to induce?

Watching the flushing male tear apart his own kin, Roper became terribly aware that he had kept his companions in this valley. They had had the chance to leave, but he had held them here, to try and barter with this deranged king and his brutal subjects.

Only when the Unhieru finally settled in the small hours of the morning, the fire burning low, and with it the dreadful shadows it cast on the valley walls, was Roper able to sleep. His pounding heart and the restless energy in his legs awoke him a little before the others in the morning. He pushed the feeling away and went to sit with Tekoa, who had assumed his post. The wind had died down, and they observed the heaving pile of Unhieru flesh together. 'Did you spot them giving each other apple trees?' said Tekoa.

'Is that what they were?'

Tekoa nodded. 'That is all I have seen here. Apple trees. And apart from meat, that is the only food they have consumed. We should have brought more horses. It seems the only thing we have that they value.'

'True,' said Roper. 'Do you have any more ideas? If we lose the final contest?'

'Ideas for what? To stop them eating us, or continue negotiations?'

'Well, I'd be interested in either.'

'I don't know why I asked,' said Tekoa, waving a hand. 'I've got nothing.'

'It will come when we need it,' said Roper.

Tekoa did not react for a time. 'We may disagree whether it is wise to stay here, lord, but I am glad to be with you in this place. You have a gift under pressure.'

Roper shrugged. 'It is Pryce to whom we owe our lives. We would all be dead without his actions in the cave yesterday.' Perhaps the sprinter had already been awake, or maybe he was roused by the sound of his name, but he rose at that moment and came to sit with them.

'Like poor Gilius,' said Tekoa. 'He was a superb ranger. Superb.' The three sat in silence for a time. 'If we ever escape this land, we'll have a story or two to recount,' Tekoa said quietly. He turned to look at Pryce and recoiled a little at the misshapen scar tissue on the side of his head. It had once been his right ear, claimed by Uvoren's servant Gosta. 'Your ear is awful, Nephew. Did you sleep?'

Pryce raised a hand to touch the lumpen remains. 'I slept,' he said. 'But realised too late something had taken a shit right next to my head.'

'Who wouldn't, given the chance?' said Tekoa.

Pryce ignored this, turning to examine the slumbering Unhieru. His movements always looked purposeful: there was no twitching or fidgeting, but even so he somehow boiled with energy. Roper could sense it, stirring just below the surface of this tempered spring of a man.

'Why are we here, Lord Roper?' Pryce asked. 'They are *savages*. We can't trust them. We can't fight alongside them.'

Roper was silent a while. 'I want to know that whatever happened here, we gave our very best. I fear we are doomed without their help.'

Pryce nodded. 'Gray told me this is how you would be. He warned me you would not turn back.'

Roper turned to the sprinter. 'He what?'

'He said that no matter how fruitless this became, how impossible the Unhieru seemed or how much danger we were in, you would not give up. He warned me that when faced with a challenge, you cease to question whether it is a good idea. It becomes something you have to do, because it is hard.' Pryce offered these insights flatly, without any sign that he might be revealing something Roper found uncomfortable.

Roper frowned, looking back at the slumbering Unhieru and wondering if that was right.

Tekoa cleared his throat pointedly. 'That may be accurate, lord. Look at how strong they are now. And they want weapons and armour as part of the deal. Are we to create a second enemy, even more deadly than the first? Do we *really* want these people with us?'

'Yes,' said Roper at once. But after what he had seen last night, he was not sure if he meant it.

'They are asleep,' Tekoa went on, softly. 'They drank so much last night, they won't be stirring for hours. We can go now.'

'You may go if you wish, Tekoa,' said Roper. 'I do not hold you here. If you want to leave, you should. I am staying.'

Their conversation woke Vigtyr, who did not come to join them. He stayed on his blanket with his back against a dry-stone storehouse. 'Vigtyr,' said Pryce, not looking at him. 'Did you manage to sleep without your tent?'

'I slept fine, Pryce,' said Vigtyr coldly.

They waited for the Unhieru to stir, Pryce growing bored and stepping over the slumbering bodies to collect several smoking dogends from the hearth, which he brought back to make another small fire on which they toasted biscuits. It was midday, the clouds overhead in fine shreds, before the Unhieru started to rouse. Gogmagoc was one of the last to wake, and his golden eyes travelled immediately to the Anakim, huddled together away from his people. 'Let us have our contest,' he said, pushing himself into a seat.

'And what do you propose?' asked Roper.

Gogmagoc did not answer at once, rising instead and prowling to a storehouse, from which he produced two pieces of wood. The longer one was a vast war-bow, which Gogmagoc strung with a fraying twist of sinew. Even bent, the weapon was nine feet long; the wood stiff, dark and reinforced by a sliver of horn over the belly. In his other hand he clutched a five-foot wooden streak, fletched with black feathers and tipped crudely in iron.

'The final contest is this,' Gogmagoc growled. 'You match my shot.' The giant nocked the arrow and hauled on the string, raising the bow to the sky. His huge arms trembled as the instrument bent to a perfect fragment of circle, the arrow resting an inch clear of the grip and quivering to be set free.

Gogmagoc unleashed it with a shriek like a buzzard, and the bowstring cracked straight so loudly that Roper thought the bow had snapped. The arrow was a distant splinter, climbing above the sides of the valley where it plateaued, cruising for an impossible time before plummeting back to earth. It landed pointing nearly straight down, five hundred yards down the valley, in line with a small storehouse. The distant clatter of its landing carried over the still air and

Gogmagoc turned to face them, using a palm to silence his singing bowstring.

Roper stared at the bow. It was gorgeously constructed: a weapon of such enormous size and power that it had to be made for an Unhieru, and that ingenious sliver of horn over the belly was joined with a precision that Roper struggled to imagine even an Anakim bowyer matching. It seemed that these giants were capable of great craft after all, if only given the right motivation.

Roper looked at Tekoa. 'Can we beat that shot?'

'The record for a Skiritai bowshot is a touch over four hundred yards,' said Tekoa bleakly. Even that mighty shot would have fallen well short of the monstrous arrow Gogmagoc had just unleashed. 'Aledas has come close to matching it on a number of occasions,' he added, which still rendered the Skiritai's chances of succeeding in this task next to hopeless.

'Choose,' said Gogmagoc, pointing at the Anakim.

Roper looked at Aledas. 'I suppose it's down to you, Aledas.'

The Skiritai did not reply. He merely did as Roper bade, removing the bow from his pack and stringing it with a twist of tendon taken from the side of his boot. He took this and a single arrow to Gogmagoc's mark, and gazed down the valley, chest rising and falling three times. He nocked the arrow, lifted his bow to the clouds and braced his shoulders, beginning to load the string.

'Wait!' said Roper, suddenly. 'Wait, wait, lower your bow.' Aledas eased the arrow forward, silently looking to Roper for further instructions. 'I would like you to gather your strength before you shoot,' he explained. 'Please, take a seat.'

Aledas just stared in response, the bow still held out before him. 'I do not need rest.'

Tekoa seemed to have discerned Roper's plan. 'I think you'll find you do,' he hissed, each word enunciated precisely, eyes boring into Aledas. 'Unstring your bow, you thoughtless oaf.' Under Tekoa's gaze, Aledas used a knee to bend the bow and unstring it once more, sitting down and coiling the string.

Gogmagoc stirred minutely. 'He should shoot,' said the king, looking at Roper.

'My bowman has immense mental strength,' Roper replied. 'In order to summon it, however, he must concentrate for some time. It will help him shoot further.'

Gogmagoc lost interest, turning back to a storehouse for apples.

They waited. Roper instructed his party to gather warm clothes and sit down together. The Unhieru stood restlessly around them, prowling and staring at the Anakim party. Some uttered low howls, with Aledas the focus of particular attention. 'Do not acknowledge them in any way,' said Roper.

'Vigtyr,' said Pryce, after a pause, 'how is it that you speak Saxon?'

Every head turned towards the tall legionary, who sat on the edge of the group.

'Do you?' asked Roper.

'He understood what Gogmagoc said to you yesterday,' said Pryce, lightning-blue eyes boring into Vigtyr. 'Didn't you?'

Vigtyr gave his wry smile, not looking at any of them. 'I don't, really,' he said. 'But I was raised on the banks of the Abus, and there are Saxon phrases in common use there. I picked up some bits and pieces.'

'On the banks of the Abus?' said Roper. 'Did you ever encounter Sutherners?'

'Sometimes we could see them, over the water,' said Vigtyr, sounding amused. 'We would just stop and stare at each other. Sometimes we waved. And once I found one of them, hiding out in our pigsty.'

'And what did you do?' asked Tekoa.

'I remember he made a strange gesture.' Vigtyr raised one

finger, pressing it perpendicular to his lips, his eyes narrowed as he remembered.

'What do you think it meant?'

Tekoa answered, eyes still on Vigtyr. 'It means keep your mouth shut. So what did you do?'

'I ran and told my father.'

'Who did what?'

'Killed him.' The story was related in Vigtyr's default tone. When speaking, he seemed to relish what he was saying, eyes slightly humorous throughout. When spoken to, his affect was flat, as though bored and doing a poor impression of attention. His manner kept company placated, but did not invite familiarity.

They spoke for a little longer about the Sutherners, discussing the lands they had passed through on their way here, before Pryce asked suddenly: 'What are we waiting for?'

Roper nodded up the valley. 'Look up there, Pryce.' The sprinter turned, and Roper saw the comprehension on his face as he felt the evening breeze now streaming down the valley. He looked back at Roper and gave a curt nod. Vigtyr made a soft noise of understanding. Aledas did not react or look up the valley, having either discerned the plan some time ago, or been so offended by Tekoa that he no longer cared to acknowledge them.

At that moment, Gogmagoc prowled over to the group. 'Shoot,' he said. Roper felt just the tiniest edge of that fear that the giant was able to command. It rattled in his chest for a moment, then was gone.

'Soon,' Roper replied, firmly. Behind Gogmagoc, the other Unhieru were edging closer, leaning towards the group and making snatching gestures.

'Now,' Gogmagoc demanded. The fear swamped Roper and he nearly retched. He felt his companions recoil around him, and was no longer certain whether this feeling was genuine or of Gogmagoc's design.

'No,' he replied, with all the calm he could muster. 'Soon.' He looked up into the golden eyes, and imagined that all he felt was contempt for the giant king. To win his throne the previous year, he had engaged in an immense confidence trick. The price of failure had been death. He had had to embody the role of a man who believed himself born to rule: unwavering in every situation. He had learned to control his face; become used to walking straight-backed, chin raised, stride slow and measured, so that even in a room of warriors who despised him, none raised so much as a word against him. His entire life had been spent preparing for this confrontation with Gogmagoc, and the giant king would find no weakness here.

Nor did he. All at once, the fear abated. Gogmagoc seemed to lose interest in Roper, turning away and proceeding to the cold body of the Unhieru thief killed the night before. The other giants kept their attention on Roper's band, circling them restlessly, but Roper paid them no heed. The Anakim might lack the extreme size and strength of the Unhieru. They did not have the subtlety, appetite or symbolic capacity of the Sutherners and their complex writing, which was, Roper quietly considered, impressive. But it seemed to him they possessed most a virtue that outstripped all those. Confidence.

In the face of this, some of the Unhieru were losing interest and joined Gogmagoc, who was dismembering his dead kin and spitting his limbs for roasting. 'Cannibals,' said Tekoa, eyes narrowed. The feast at least distracted the Unhieru briefly, Gogmagoc parcelling out hot flesh to a favoured minority. But when the meat was exhausted, those who had not received any returned to harassing Roper's band, more agitated than ever.

'Hold on,' Roper said. 'Keep waiting.'

In twos and threes, some of the Unhieru were beginning to advance close to the circle, minded to force Aledas to shoot, or else punish the Anakim for their delays. Pryce stood abruptly when one came too close, sweeping a sword clear of its scabbard and forcing one of the Unhieru to retreat rapidly. But it stayed just out of reach, growling rough words at him. 'Calm now,' said Roper. 'Just a bit longer.'

The wind tore the clouds apart. Behind, the sun was balanced on the edge of the valley, as though it might fall in and roll down the side. It was soon gone, taking its feeble warmth with it. They fell into shadow and, as before, the katabatic wind started to howl.

'Now?' suggested Tekoa.

'Wait,' said Roper. 'We must be certain.' The Unhieru were becoming angry and Roper instructed his comrades to stand. 'Back to back,' he said. 'Draw swords. Aledas, you stay at the centre.' More and more Unhieru were coming, emboldening the group. 'Just hold on,' Roper insisted. 'Hold on.'

It was now nearly completely dark, the pressure of the wind forcing Roper to lean forward. Clumps of moss, lichen and dried weeds tumbled away from the Anakim, and though it was no longer snowing, the spindrift streamed across the stones like high clouds. Gogmagoc finished eating, his glare turning to the Anakim. He got to his feet.

'Now,' said Roper, tapping Aledas on the shoulder. 'Quickly.'

Their circle flared slightly, swords flashing, as they gave Aledas space at the centre to string his bow. The Unhieru fell still as they saw the Skiritai readying himself. Even Gogmagoc, who had started towards them, stopped to watch, golden eyes shining through the dusk. Aledas drew his bow, aiming high above the valley, and loosed. The arrow streaked into the night and floated upwards, shrinking to a dark sliver in the evening sky. It soared down the valley, swept onwards by the wind and beyond the storehouse which marked Gogmagoc's shot. It had disappeared from sight before landing.

There were none of the roars that had followed Pryce's victory. In the bitter evening, cloaks swirling about their knees, the Anakim turned towards Gogmagoc. He had seen Aledas's shot, but not reacted. 'Wait here,' said Roper. Alone, he advanced towards Gogmagoc, making a gesture that said: *It's over.* 'We have beaten your shot, Lord King,' said Roper, stopping before the giant and staring up at him. 'As we beat your hound. We will send you weapons. We will send you armour. Now, will you join us?'

Gogmagoc stared down at Roper. Then he smiled his mad smile. 'No. I do not need to join you, river-man.'

Roper let out a long breath, deflating a little. Rage and frustration began to bubble within him at this final proof that Gogmagoc had been toying with them. He had kept them there for entertainment, no more. And now, even Roper did not believe he would turn Gogmagoc's mind. They stood facing each other in silence. 'We had a deal,' said Roper, at last.

'I do not understand your deals,' said Gogmagoc, flatly.

'But even you have rules,' Roper protested, stubbornly. 'Like the wrestling, last night. You have laws you will not break. Not unless you go red.'

Gogmagoc made a gesture like a shrug. 'Red?'

'When your kin killed the thief who stole his trophies,' said Roper. 'And he flushed bright red. All the rules were gone. Is that what this is?'

Gogmagoc gave his abrasive laugh. 'The *other-mind*? No river-man, this is not like that. If this was the *other-mind*, I would not even remember you. And you would be dead. You win your freedom. You may go. You are lucky for that, after threatening Fathochta.'

Roper was blank for a moment. Then he realised what Gogmagoc must mean. 'Your son?' Before this latest task, he would have stopped there, but he no longer cared if he inflamed Gogmagoc. 'I heard Fathochta was dead. I met the man who killed him.'

Gogmagoc froze, gaze fixed on Roper, who suddenly felt that dreadful fear once again. At the same time, he became aware that Cold-Edge had started rattling in its scabbard. 'Eoten-Draefend,' growled Gogmagoc. 'Where? Where did you see him?' As soon as the giant opened his mouth, Roper's fear faded, and Cold-Edge fell still. Perhaps it was some sound that Gogmagoc made, too deep for the Anakim to hear, but still able to elicit terror as it reverberated through their lungs.

'In my country,' said Roper. Garrett Eoten-Draefend was a hybrid whom Roper had met months before, and who had boasted of killing Fathochta in single combat. 'He came north in the invasion earlier this year.'

'He is your enemy?' pressed Gogmagoc.

'He certainly is.'

Gogmagoc was silent, watching Roper with a new expression on his face.

'So, he did kill him?' said Roper.

'The last Fathochta was killed. My eldest son. This is the new one.'

Roper remembered the Chief Historian saying that Unhieru names were colours. It seemed they were titles as well, with the name Fathochta passed to Gogmagoc's second son, after the first had been killed. He remembered Gogmagoc's rage at seeing his son threatened, and the close bond he seemed to share with his wives, and thought that perhaps he at last understood a little about these people. 'If we become friends,' said Roper, 'we could fight the Eoten-Draefend together.'

Gogmagoc did not move a muscle.

'I can promise you revenge,' said Roper. 'If you join us, the Eoten-Draefend is yours. We will help you get to him. We can kill him together.' Roper could almost feel the eyes of his companions boring into the back of his head as the longest negotiation he had yet managed with Gogmagoc played out. At last, he had the maned giant's full attention, and terrifying though it was, he held it.

'Send me the metal skin,' said Gogmagoc, slowly. 'Send me the weapons. When they come, I will join you. And I will kill the Eoten-Draefend.'

Roper licked his lips. 'So you're with us, Lord King?'

'To fight him,' said Gogmagoc. 'To avenge Fathochta. Yes, I will come for that, River-King.'

Roper did not feel the satisfaction that he had imagined. Instead, there was a strange foreboding. Since he had seen the flushing male brutalise his own kin the night before; since Pryce's words that morning, his doubt at the wisdom of what they were doing here had grown. Now that he had this powerful ally, whom they had worked so hard to recruit, he was not so sure that he wanted him.

'Good,' he said to Gogmagoc. 'Good. We'll send you what you need for the war. And then you'll come with us.'

10

The Trial

Inger shut the door of the dark room, muffling Hagen's frenzied sobs. The fierce attention which had slowly grown over her during the interrogation had subsided into her usual vague manner. 'Let's go upstairs. We won't get any more out of him for a while. Seems he's been living under pressure for a long time and that's finally broken. He needs to pull himself together.'

'What is the Ellengaest?'

Inger led the way up the stairs. 'I have no idea,' she said pleasantly.

'But that meant something to you,' Salbjorn persisted.

'Oh yes. Who that is has been a repeated question from both Ephors and Kryptea for a while now. Someone with more power than we would like, whose objectives appear to have recently diverged quite dramatically from those of the Black Kingdom.'

'A traitor?'

'I suppose so. A spy, too. The Kryptea do not often share information with us, but they believe he's been passing secrets to the Sutherners.'

'And can't they stop him?'

'He . . . but then it might not be a he . . . keeps an eye on his own tracks, and those of his Suthern masters. But all you really need to know is that it is not good news that the Ellengaest is involved in this. He has proven very hard to stop so far.'

Salbjorn felt his respect for Inger increase. Her unassuming style hid insight that was quite alien to him. The two of them sat down by the fire, untended and now just a bank of embers. Salbjorn added a little more wood, blowing to encourage the flames while Inger stared vacantly at his efforts. Leon was nowhere to be seen, and must have been guarding the boy. 'But you have his name,' he said. 'Someone must know who he is.'

'Oh, I don't think Ellengaest is a real name,' she said. 'He doesn't often deal with his agents directly. The tutor downstairs probably has no real idea of who he is, but has been threatened into helping him. We think he operates mostly through blackmail, placing people heavily in his debt and then using that to force them into acting on his behalf. He likes to use prisoners, apparently. Because he liberates them from the prison ships, they owe him everything. Prisoners also don't have responsibilities they need to fulfil, or loved ones who are expecting to see them, so they're unusually free to move and act. Sometimes we find escaped prisoners dead, probably because they've disobeyed him.

'But the Kryptea have managed to capture a few of his agents alive, and none have so far had direct contact with him. He keeps them at a distance, and controls them with a few close handlers. Who knows? Maybe Hagen will help us get to the assassin. And maybe the assassin will be one of the few who have dealt directly with the Ellengaest.' She shrugged contentedly.

Salbjorn sat back from the fire, glancing at Inger's placid face. 'Did you suspect this?'

'Yes,' said Inger. 'I was worried Numa's death was just the edge of something much bigger. Now maybe stopping the assassin won't be enough. Ormur probably won't be safe until Ellengaest is found and his viper's head has been cut from his shoulders.' She looked up at Salbjorn. 'Speaking of which, we should speak to the boy. It's the Trial tomorrow, and we'll need to put him on his guard.'

'I'll fetch him.'

Salbjorn found the boy preparing for bed and brought him up to see the Inquisitor. He had the same frayed look as Hagen, and when Inger saw him, her attention began to focus once more.

'Forgive our decadence up here,' she said, nodding at the flames. 'We have been pushing ourselves a little to try and get to the bottom of all this.' Ormur met Salbjorn's eyes and then quickly turned them to the fire. 'Please sit,' Inger said, smiling kindly. 'Are you ready for tomorrow?'

'As ready as I usually am,' said the boy, quietly, dropping onto a goatskin before the fire. Salbjorn did not sit down, leaning on his sheathed sword behind them.

'How do you feel?'

'Fine,' said the boy, dully.

Inger nodded. 'You know why we're here?'

'Because you think the man who killed my brother wants to kill me next,' said Ormur, his voice resigned.

'I'm afraid that is what we think.'

'I hope he tries,' said the boy, terribly cold. 'I want to meet him. I don't care if he kills me, I will hurt him first. I'll go for his eyes.'

Salbjorn stiffened a little at this sentiment. This was the first close contact he had had with the boy, and he had not realised how raw Ormur's grief was.

Inger looked mildly at the boy. 'You must be careful,' she said. 'Do not go looking for this man.'

'I already go looking for him,' interrupted Ormur. 'When I'm supposed to be foraging, I go and wait for him where my brother died.'

'That is exceptionally foolish,' said Inger sternly. 'That is our job. We are here to catch him and find out who sent him.

One way or another, he will die, but if he gets to you first then he gets exactly what he wants. You're playing into his hands. Swear to me that you won't go looking for him.'

The boy was stubbornly quiet and Salbjorn cuffed the back of his head.

'Answer the Inquisitor!'

Inger raised a calming hand to Salbjorn. 'Your brother would not want this killer to claim you as well. Swear, boy.'

Unlike every other student they had spoken to so far, Ormur seemed totally unconcerned by the lofty status of a Maven Inquisitor and a Sacred Guardsman. He was silent a moment, looking sullenly between the two. 'I swear.'

'On the bones of your brother,' insisted Inger. Ormur gave a jolt, staring up at the Inquisitor, who was unyielding. 'Swear it.'

'I swear on my brother's bones,' said the boy quietly.

'Very good.' Inger became suddenly hazy again. 'Be alert tomorrow. So far out of the school and with everyone distracted by the Trial, you will be vulnerable. Leon and Salbjorn will guard as much of your route as they are able, but be aware. We know this assassin sprints very well. You will have to navigate the same course as everyone else with one eye on your surroundings. Are you up to that?'

Ormur nodded.

'Then good luck,' said Inger. 'We'll be there with you.'

Salbjorn found he could not wear his armour: he moved too ponderously on his injured ankle to bear the weight. He stood on a glacier, slow and vulnerable, guarding the route of Ormur's Trial. He kept watchful eyes on the crowd gathering the route: students of all ages and tutors, invited to heckle and cheer the contestants. It was impossible to be certain they were all residents of the haskoli. And even if they were, they had already caught one traitor. There was no guarantee Hagen was the assassin's only accomplice.

Suddenly, the spectators began to bay. Ormur and the

Master were standing at the start of the course, and the Master had just drenched the boy's head in ptarmigan blood, holding a hand up in blessing. The spurt of blood was a signal that the Trial had begun, and behind Salbjorn, a jagged black flag had been raised, indicating that Ormur was now in a race against the water clock that would time his effort.

The boy broke clear of the Master and started to run. He was barefoot, sprinting fifty yards through the snow to his first obstacle: Frystir. This was a long hollow in which four feet of glacial meltwater collected, and into which chunks of glacial ice had been scattered to chill the waters still further. Ormur hurtled in, sending up a great wave and fighting his way through impeding icebergs. He raised his knees high, kicking and splashing hard as he thrashed through the pool and out, stumbling as he emerged, but managing to keep his feet and begin the two-hundred-yard dash to the glacier. Salbjorn had done this many times, and remembered well how numb his extremities had been, so that it had felt like his feet were soft bags of sand for the rock-strewn sprint.

Ormur had set off fast, but was still able to accelerate slightly for the final twenty yards. The noise from the spectators grew as they responded to this determined effort, roaring him on, and Ormur plunged into the snow on top of the glacier. He was lucky: the fall of the last few days had cushioned its sharp surface, usually exposed by this time of year. His bare feet sunk out of sight and he slowed to a wade. This was where most people failed. Their feet grew too numb and they fell into a decelerating crawl, their misery finally halted by the raising of a second flag as the water clock ran out.

Ormur stayed on his feet, lifting his knees high over the snow and sprinting up towards Salbjorn. The rage and anguish he was burning to fuel this charge were obvious in his bared teeth and thrusting jaw, and though he slowed, each step more upright and less forward, he stayed on his feet and ploughed beyond the glacier's cold grasp. Salbjorn felt a lump in his throat and a cheer escaped him as Ormur limped towards the next stage of the trial: a string of stepping stones over a deep, frozen pool. He leapt one, two, three, well balanced, and then slipped suddenly, shattering the thin layer of ice and plunging into the water.

Salbjorn let out a breath. The boy resurfaced and fought for the edge of the pool, but the Trial was over. The guardsman had quite forgotten that he was supposed to be on the lookout for an assassin and cast around suddenly. He saw nothing, and turned back to Ormur, who had emerged from the water, arms wrapped about his chest, the blood washed from his face. He ran towards a fire burning next to the water clock, where those who had made a satisfactory effort were rewarded with a cloak and cup of warm sheep's milk.

Ormur had tried hard, but was barely halfway through the Trial. Nobody, Salbjorn knew, would finish it this day. The snow on the ground made it impossibly cold, and he was astonished that Ormur had made it so far.

Salbjorn spotted Leon striding over from his post and limped to join him halfway. 'What now?' asked Salbjorn, as they drew level.

'The Master refuses to keep the boys in the school any longer,' said Leon. 'They'll be back out, running over the hills and foraging much further afield.'

'And how are we supposed to guard him then? I can't even move properly.'

Leon scowled. 'We'll find a way. The best one would be to catch the bastard who killed his brother.'

'Inger thinks that might be difficult,' said Salbjorn. 'We seem to be gnawing at the edge of something very large. Even if we catch the assassin, he may only be one of many.'

'She is an Inquisitor,' snapped Leon. 'Used to finding those responsible for crimes already committed. But we're trying to stop a crime from happening in the first place. Meticulously following the clues isn't good enough. We must be faster than that.'

Salbjorn turned a little away from Leon, silent for a

moment. He tried to remember what week it was, away from these mountains. *Svadn*, he decided. The week water goes black with tadpoles. 'I trust Inger,' he said eventually. 'She located that accomplice, and he—'

'Is now broken,' interrupted Leon. 'I heard his whimpering coming out of that room. He is too frightened of whoever controls him to tell you anything. That is a dead end.'

'I trust her, though,' said Salbjorn. 'Do you have a better plan?'

For a rare moment, Leon hesitated. 'We need the assassin. And we have the one thing the assassin wants.'

Salbjorn stared at his mentor for a long moment, Leon tapping his foot impatiently. 'The boy,' said Salbjorn, at last. 'You want to use him as a lure.'

11
The Hand

Whenever Inger walked past the dark pine room in which Hagen, the captured accomplice, was held, she felt that soft hand on her shoulder. It made her smile. 'Again, my angel? He seems broken, I'm not sure there's any more progress to be made there.' But the hand was as insistent as she had ever known it, and so she admitted herself once more to the pine-scented darkness.

Hagen, now chained to the wall in increasingly filthy conditions, no longer looked up when she entered. He had lost any interest in food and as far as she could tell, was not even drinking any more from the water pail next to him. He just sat slumped against the red-stained boards, skin pale and hair matted. As always, she came to sit down in front of him.

'How are you today, Hagen?'

There was no response. Inger studied his wretched face for a time. This broken individual would make no reply to threats or pain, as she knew Leon had confirmed. There was nothing they could do to him that equalled the terror already exerted by the Ellengaest. But he was desperate, and desperate people often responded to kindness. She could feel that hand on her shoulder once more and decided to open her mouth and see what emerged.

'Well, as we're here, I'd like to speak to you even if you don't want to speak back. My husband was a Saltcoat. He was away so often training or on the march that I didn't often get to see him. He was a good man. Not good in the way everyone here in the Black Kingdom is good,' and she smiled hazily at Hagen's cracked form. 'You know. Straightforward, upright, dynamic. He was all that, but he also cared very much. He wasn't truncated like so many legionaries become. He still had so much heart and I missed him very much when he was away. Forty years ago, he died the death we're all supposed to be grateful for: on the battlefield with honour and glory ...' She raised her eyebrows briefly. 'I tried to grieve, for a time, but really it didn't feel right. I could not accept or believe what had happened. Maybe because I spent so much time without him anyway, just the knowledge that he was dead didn't change that. It was unbelievable. I used to catch myself feeling normal and have to remind myself that my husband was dead, not just away with his trade or on campaign.

'But no matter how often I reminded myself, I seemed to feel less lonely than I had. It took me a while to realise, and to listen, but it became obvious to me that I never went anywhere alone any more. I could feel something alongside me, every moment, looking over my shoulder and watching my back. There was a new presence with me, and now I am never without him. I feel him every moment. He has been telling me that you are going to help me.'

Very slowly, Hagen's chin lifted from his chest and he turned sunken eyes on Inger. She could feel her own tears building. She smiled and they spilt onto her cheeks. 'I have never told anyone that before,' she admitted. 'But I trust that presence. And I agree with it, too. I think you're a good man who's frightened. I think you're going to help me.'

Hagen's face was wracked with despair. She looked at him hopefully, and he turned his face away. *He is responding*, she thought.

'I want to help you,' he whispered.

'Then I will help you,' she said. 'How is Ellengaest threatening you?'

But saying the name was a mistake. Hagen's face dropped and he shook his head once more. Inger repressed a sigh, getting to her feet. 'You are a good man, Hagen. I can see that.' She left him in that room, hoping those words would act in her absence. She climbed to her favourite spot on the cliffs overlooking the school and sat once more with her legs dangling over the edge.

There is a way in there, she thought. *He will help us.*

She stared out over the jagged, indifferent universe, steeped in snow and seamed with rock. 'There is something sacred here, my love. You feel closer than ever.' Her instinct that this trail might lead directly to Ellengaest solidified in the rarefied air. They might not only avenge Numa's murder, but find that villain as well. She kicked her legs, sending little stones skittering down the cliff-face, and decided that she found the degree of Hagen's fear hard to comprehend. Was a member of his family held by Ellengaest? What did he think would happen if he agreed to assist them?

The snows were coming down hard again: unseasonably so. The passes were already clogged, and now would not clear for some time. At this thought, she became aware of muffled footsteps at her back. She looked, expecting to find Salbjorn or Leon, but was confronted instead with the stiff, aged form of the Master limping towards her. 'Master,' she said, making half an effort to stand. 'I hope you haven't come all the way up here on my account.'

He smiled wearily at her, waving her back to her seat. 'Not at all, my lady. This has been a favourite place to think for many years.'

'I shall leave you to it,' said Inger, but the Master waved her down again.

'We can enjoy it together, Inquisitor.' He sat next to her, grunting a little as he arranged his stiff limbs and draped his legs over the drop. 'I find the exposure clarifies things a little, don't you?'

'I do,' she agreed.

'And is it helping with your task here?'

'I believe so. We have reached some dead ends and it seems there is only one path to the assassin. But I am hopeful. I believe the tutor we have imprisoned might one day help us. Perhaps we can persuade him to signal to the assassin, as he did on our first night here, and lure the killer into the school. Then the guardsmen can take care of him. I believe that if we have patience, Hagen will realise he has no choice but to help. And if we catch this assassin . . . he may yet lead us to an even greater prize.'

The Master cleared his throat with a crack. 'Poor Hagen. He arrived so full of confidence and pride. I've watched him crumble to pieces.'

What now, my love? 'When did that start?' asked Inger, distracted by that hand on her shoulder again.

'It was quite sudden. A few months after he arrived. His head dropped, his shoulders hunched and he fell almost completely quiet. I've never seen someone succumb to stress so completely.'

'And did it coincide with anything that you remember? A messenger coming to the school? The arrival of a new tutor here?' She brushed her shoulder gently.

The Master frowned. 'Not that I recall. But give me some time to think, more may come back to me.'

'Let me know if you remember anything.'

'And who is this greater prize, at the end of all this?'

'Perhaps you've heard of the Ellengaest?' Inger suggested, still distracted.

The Master stiffened. 'You believe that villain is involved here?'

'I do. That is who Hagen is in fear of, truly.'

There came a pause. 'I have heard much about that man,' said the Master, quietly. 'His stench even reaches up here, to

the mountains.' His voice grew fierce. 'A rabid dog. A man
with unlimited fear and ambition but no reason. If that is
where your trail leads, perhaps you should not follow it. It
cannot end well.'

Inger laughed. 'Oh no, I intend to find that maniac. He
must stand before the Ephors and answer for everything he's
done.'

'The Almighty is not mocked,' said the Master. 'Ramnea
will have him eventually, and she always exacts a fitting
punishment.'

'But after he's done how much damage to our kingdom?'
asked Inger mildly. 'After the boy Ormur is dead? I do not
just sit back and wait for the Almighty to act.' She clutched
the dog-headed angel on her tunic. 'I work with his angels. I
will pursue this to the end.'

The Master was silent for a long while. He seemed to be
sitting very close. Inger shifted a little on her perch, suddenly uncomfortable.

And that hand was on her shoulder, begging that she realise before it was too late.

12

The Great Canal

The earth was being overturned. Men sweated and swarmed over the dirt, shovels in hand, excavating great gouges in the landscape. A rattling centipede of wagons, each fair buckling beneath its load, brought mountains of clay from the north. Another carried cut stone from the west and a third tarred planks of wood from the nearby forests. Looming over all were half-finished stone towers and haughty timber cranes, depositing pallets of supplies which the men fell upon. They were stripped bare and scattered by sled. Huge boulders were tipped into the riverbed to create turbulent and unpredictable currents, making the river hard to cross in all but a few invisible locations. Tens of thousands laboured, and another dozen smaller wagon trains brought them sheep, grains, tubers, biscuits, tools, firewood and other supplies.

The Abus was being fortified and remodelled, transformed from a natural barrier into an artificially augmented one. The Great Canal.

Keturah did not like it. This felt like Suthern work. They were ordering and manipulating something wild and precious to them. It was a grotesquely vast project: a brutal exercise in terraforming that made her skin crawl. Roper had

said it was necessary, though, to defend the Black Kingdom
and all that was wild and healthy within it from the spread
of the Sutherner. It was also, he tried to persuade her, fitting
that the border between the two peoples should be a fortified
river. Half Anakim, half Sutherner. She was not sure he
believed that any more than she did.

She and Gray stood together atop a hill on the Black Kingdom side of the canal, watching over the work beneath them.
On her return to the Hindrunn, it had been she who took
command of the project, which she had found tiresomely
administrative. Today would be spent briefing the armourers, the fletchers, the smiths and the quartermasters, and she
fidgeted, tapping her foot and stretching restlessly.

'Guess what I can see,' said Gray, suddenly.

'Mud,' said Keturah.

'People,' said Gray, pointing at the horizon. On one of the
hills south of the canal stood three horsemen. Strange horsemen, who seemed unusually massive on their steeds,
watching the progress on the river. They rode over the crest
of the hill, advancing for the great construction site.

'They look odd,' said Keturah.

'Two people per horse,' said Gray.

'Sutherners?' Keturah's eyes could not discern who the
riders were at this range.

'You'll find out in a moment.' The riders were heading for
a temporary log bridge which reached over the drained riverbed some way to the right of Keturah and Gray. 'Shall we
receive them?'

'Why not, Captain.'

They arrived at the bridge's near edge just as the riders
were passing the halfway point. The horses clattered down
the logs and as the two parties met, one of the riders emitted
a roar of joy and leapt from his mount. Gray ran forward and
the two figures embraced. The other horsemen ignored this,
riding towards Keturah, who grinned up at the figure on the
lead horse.

Tekoa looked weather-beaten but in rude health: his face full of sun, his hair of wind. He waited for Aledas behind him to dismount before doing so himself, and embracing Keturah. Behind him rode Roper, who alone of the company had his own horse.

'Father,' said Keturah, beaming. 'What news?'

'In brief summary, we arrived at a valley of savage barbarians minded to murder and eat us all. Through splendid individual efforts, and a smattering of inspirational leadership, we managed to secure their friendship.'

'Are you serious?'

'That is the sum of it,' said Tekoa with a curt nod.

Keturah laughed delightedly and embraced Roper, who had come to join them. 'You must have some tales to tell,' she said, as they broke apart.

'That much is true,' said Roper. Gray and Pryce were approaching the rest of the group arm in arm, and warm handshakes were shared all round.

'What of Gilius?' asked Gray, looking over the company.

'Gilius gave his life for our task,' said Roper.

There was a silence. 'The rest of you coming back alive is frankly more than I anticipated,' Keturah said.

'At one stage that looked improbable,' Vigtyr agreed.

'Are these Suthern horses?' Keturah asked, looking the small mounts up and down.

The five travellers exchanged glances and then laughed wildly. 'There is much to tell,' said Roper. The joy at their homecoming evidently overpowered the death of one of their number.

'Then tell it,' said Keturah. 'No!' she added suddenly, holding up a hand. 'First, a fire, mutton and wine to fortify you for the tale. I should think you've earned that much.'

'And a wash, and a change of clothes,' added Tekoa.

'I could do with some pine-tea,' said Vigtyr.

'Vigtyr lost his tent, as well,' said Roper. 'We must find him a new one at once.'

'Forget all other comforts,' agreed Pryce. 'Just roll him in a bolt of canvas.'

'Canvas and tea for Vigtyr,' summarised Tekoa, before turning to the Skiritai. 'Aledas, what will you have? A baby to feast on?'

Keturah and Roper led the group away from the canal and towards their own hearth. It was *Eapea*, the week of robin song, and a trio of the birds flitted after the group as Keturah demanded wood, water, wine and meat from an aide. 'We already have tea,' she said, smiling at Vigtyr. 'And I'm sure we can reward you with a new tent, Lictor. Especially as your woman is here,' she added with a lascivious wink. Vigtyr merely looked uncomfortable in response. Lately he had been seen spending much of his time with a female companion. Rumours abounded that he was courting her, which would be Vigtyr's fourth wife, in a land where a single divorce was a scandal.

'You are back just in time, my friends,' said Gray. 'That bridge you crossed is the first of a dozen being built over the next few days to carry us south. We're ready to invade as soon as you are.'

'It seems you have some tales of your own,' said Vigtyr.

'None so significant as that,' said Keturah. 'We have been preparing for days.' She spoke coolly, leading them down an open corridor composed of bundled arrows, stacked to twelve feet on either side. 'The full strength of the Black Kingdom is ready to be unleashed on the south.' They turned into a new corridor made of bulging barrels that reeked of tar, rearing high above and far ahead. 'As soon as the Black Lord gives the order, we will march.' They emerged from the corridor and onto a grass plain, spread with thousands of campfires, a great fog of smoke rising above it. Men and women swarmed before them, wood splintered and cracked, and distant metalwork clanged. Charcoal smouldered beneath volcanic mounds, and teams of oxen dragged great limbed trees to men waiting, saws in hand, atop inches of sawdust. The scene was backed by a distant wall of hobbled horseflesh, their noses pressed to the ground and stripping the grass.

Roper broke into a trot to draw level with Keturah. 'We will be ready to march?' he asked, smiling faintly. 'You are staying to command the Black Kingdom in my absence, remember?'

She returned his smile. 'I must be blunt, Husband, the prospect of remaining in the Hindrunn while you plunder Suthdal bores me.'

'It is an honour,' said Roper, eyebrows raised. He glanced behind to check the others were out of earshot. 'And you were to manage the reaction of the Hindrunn in my absence, remember? All those who will be discontented when they discover that this is to be an occupation and not a raid. You do not want for opinions on how things might best be done and now is your chance to exercise them.'

'One of the reasons I'd rather not stay, actually,' said Keturah. 'Can you imagine the uproar when word gets back of what you're doing? This task you are undertaking is bigger than one man. We are to do this together. I have been researching in the Academy, as I said I would. I have come up with a strategy to subdue Suthdal. You shall need me, Husband.'

'While your advice would be welcome, you're also pregnant, as much as you try to pretend you aren't.' Keturah's hand flew to the small bulge at her stomach. 'You need the security of the Hindrunn and the experience of the midwives there for your first birth. What alternative would you propose?'

'That I come south with you,' she said. 'I have already spoken to the Chief Historian about it. She says I could campaign as her assistant. Making history, instead of just learning it. Exploring a new land and a new people. And assisting you.'

Gray drew level with the pair of them, evidently coming to offer reinforcements. Roper glanced at him before continuing. 'So you want to see the campaign.'

'Of course I do. I am no happier being left at home than you would be.'

Roper nodded a little at that. After a pause he replied. 'You have often said to me that we are a partnership. I have come to rely on it. Who should rule the Hindrunn in your absence?'

Keturah wore an irritable frown, not having anticipated this point. 'Being a partnership does not mean I take care of the mess you leave behind. There are many others who know the bureaucracy and organisation of the Hindrunn far better than I. Someone who sits in regularly on council meetings and wouldn't spend the first four months just learning their duties. I am still very young. I have a great deal of experience to acquire before I can be placed in charge of the Black Kingdom, as I have learned over the past few weeks.'

Roper laughed in earnest at that. 'I have never heard you speak so humbly, Wife! You are usually quite certain of your ability to resolve any situation.'

'It is wise, though,' said Gray, and Keturah beamed at his intervention.

'Just strange that this wisdom first presents itself now that the opportunity to come south has arisen,' said Roper, amused. 'This will be a long campaign. What are you to do when it is time to give birth?'

'Head north again,' said Keturah. 'I will not bear a child in alien lands. But I wish to come south. I will not be left behind with the old and the crippled.'

'And the pregnant,' said Roper.

She tutted. 'I'm not going to be joining in the battle-line, Husband,' she said acidly.

Roper looked at Gray. 'We should leave behind Skallagrim with his legion,' said the guardsman. 'He'd be more disruptive than most at discovering the true nature of the campaign, and he'd make a good peacetime ruler.'

'There,' said Keturah, flashing Gray a mischievous look behind Roper. 'It is settled.'

'I see you have discussed this already,' said Roper, facing forward again, with irritation and amusement taking his face at turns. 'I find myself outflanked and betrayed.'

Keturah laughed and took Roper's unwilling arm. 'You'll be glad to have me there, Husband,' she said sweetly.

'Which other legates can I rely on?' Roper asked.

'All of them except Tore, lord,' said Gray. 'He would rally any who were uncertain, and attempt to catalyse resistance to the invasion.' Tore had been a member of Uvoren's power-bloc and remained rebellious to Roper's command. After his actions at the Battle of Harstathur, however, when he had disobeyed Roper and taken Uvoren's orders instead, Roper had demoted him to lead the Soay Legion: an auxiliary force with much less prestige than his previous command, the Greyhazel.

'We will leave him and Skallagrim, then,' said Roper. 'There must be no reluctance in the force we take.'

They reached the fire, and while the others busied themselves preparing mutton, building up the flames with spiny oak and fetching wine, Roper rotated on the spot, a slow grin taking his face as he observed the preparations.

Keturah rose to fetch water and Roper said he would come and help, falling into step beside her. 'So tell me, Wife,' he said. 'What strategy have you come up with? How are we to rule over a nation of millions with seventy thousand?'

'Sixty thousand,' she said, looking at him wryly, 'with the two legions you're leaving behind. But I think partly we were considering this problem the wrong way. We were imagining a nation of people equivalent to our own. But my first discovery in the Academy was how disconnected the Sutherners are. Most of them just mind their own business. They tend to their own farms and flocks and trades, and are not unified by the same education and the same purpose that we are. So if we can defeat their army and their defences with the legions largely intact, ruling over them may not be impossible. It will be a confidence trick. They must be persuaded that if they accept us, life will go on. If they resist us, all hell will break loose.'

'So how?'

Keturah pursed her lips for a moment. 'Ruthlessness,' she said finally. 'If any town or city resists us, they must be utterly destroyed. The Sutherners will come to realise that resistance is not only futile, but much, much more trouble than it is worth. There are many analogous campaigns and it is effective. It will save thousands of our legionaries.'

Roper let out a slow breath. 'So any city that resists . . . and there will be many, at first. We are to kill them all?'

'I suppose so,' said Keturah. 'We are operating on a knife-edge. Lose even a small fraction of our warriors with each assault, and we will be a skeleton force by the time we reach Lundenceaster. It will be over for us. But if we can persuade the Sutherners not to resist at all, then we not only save our own soldiers but many of theirs as well. But the cities must be destroyed whether the people within survive or not. We can leave no centre where they could gather resistance.'

'Mass executions,' said Roper, bleakly. He thought of Bellamus, his great enemy from the previous campaign, and how he had found that he unexpectedly liked the spymaster on their few encounters. He thought of the babbling Suthern farmer who had directed them on their journey and had his head struck off by Pryce for his trouble.

'Have we not decided that we must do this?' asked Keturah. 'If we attempt it with techniques that we know will likely fail, it is cowardice as surely as it would be not to attempt it at all. Both are slow forms of suicide. This is our only way, Husband. We must let terror do our fighting for us. We will meet the Unhieru in the middle and carve Suthdal apart together. We will never face the threat of invasion again. We will put open sea between us and the Sutherners and return this entire island to the order of the wild. And to do that? Yes, many will die. Did you think it would be any other way?'

13

Into Suthdal

They were ready.

The legions formed up and the great river slid past, each man staring over its glistening volume to the rolling green beyond. The legates rode in front of them, flecking their soldiers with a wand made from holly leaves woven into an eye and dipped in birch sap. They called upon Almighty protection against the polluted lands into which they were about to set foot. Together the thousands knelt and prayed, and when they rose they began to sing.

Before them went the cavalry.

A thundering horde of hot, dusty flesh, rushing over the bridges and into the hills of Suthdal. The earth rumbled to the thump of their hooves and gobbets of mud leapt up behind as their path was churned dark. They spread out like a malignant vapour and descended on the landscape.

Next went the Skiritai, armed in light flexible plate and each carrying two short-swords and a bow as weaponry. Behind was the Black Lord, a cloak of lightning-riddled night fastened about his shoulders and draped over his elephantine steed. On his heels, the Sacred Guard; resplendent in heavy armour, walking, paired as mentor and protégé, relaxed and confident. Behind them were councillors, historians, master assassins, heralds and aides.

Then came the legions.

Clanking metal columns of men, six abreast, wading through the muck left by the cavalry like a prickling glacier, and moaning the 'Hymn of Advance': a staccato, wordless incantation timed to their footfalls. The femur trumpets shrieked behind, and the air overhead was thick with ghastly alien banners. Tattered wolf and bear skins. Tall, narrow flags bearing crude and disturbing Anakim pictures. Eagle wings, vulture wings, hawk wings, buzzard wings; twisting, flapping and bouncing. Just two auxiliary legions stayed north to continue the Great Canal and guard the kingdom. For six hours, the soldiers kept coming, not so much an invasion as an armed migration, vanishing between the hills.

And though the hastily constructed bridges were bending and creaking, splinters erupting from their joints, it did not stop there. The legions were followed by the baggage train: a mighty trail of wagons, oxen and sheep, twice the length of the armoured column that had preceded it and driven mostly by women.

Standing on a hilltop with a pair of companions, a dark-haired Sutherner watched this metallic advance into his homeland. He stood relaxed, and was joined now and then by a messenger, whom he invariably dispatched straight away with some new instruction or observation. He watched, unobserved, from dawn until dusk obscured the dregs of the baggage train. Then, satisfied, he nodded to his companions and turned away.

He was an upstart. An outlaw. A one-time poacher and murderer. A spymaster, a rogue and a low-born charmer, wanted as much by the Suthern king as he was by the Black Lord.

His name was Bellamus.

Part II
THE SOUTH

14

The Spymaster

Bellamus rode back into camp a satisfied man. It was called Brimstream: a transformed town where he had once hanged two of his own men, and which had become the headquarters of their small resistance. He rode its single street, past the tents that budded either side of the thatched buildings, raising a hand in acknowledgement of the greetings that followed him.

'You saw them, Master?'

'I saw them. Numbers as reported. Will, sort me a Bible with room for a message in the spine.'

'I have a message from the west, Master, reporting no signs of unusual Unhieru movement whatsoever,' said a dark, thin woman, dropping into step beside Bellamus's horse. The upstart was riding for the building which had once been the village inn, now called the Cobweb. This was partly in reflection of the thousand invisible strands of information that converged here, but also because it was apparent to every resident that if they were discovered by either side, they would be swept away.

'As expected, Aelfwynn. Reply in basic cypher that we expect nothing for at least another fortnight, until the Anakim have shipped their arms and armour.' Bellamus dismounted and handed his reins to the thin woman. He turned his back to the Cobweb and raised his arms to the street. 'Join me, my comrades! Come! Come and hear what fate has in store for us!'

People emerged from the buildings all around, converging on the spymaster. There was a special atmosphere here. So dangerous was their work that each day might be their last, which lent this town a giddy energy. To address this, and make life tolerable for his agents, Bellamus had allowed a hedonistic streak to develop. He found as much alcohol for them as he could, and cared little for the amount they consumed. So long as they could still ride and fight the next morning, he would tolerate any excess.

He beamed at the gathering crowd: soldiers who had entrusted their fortunes to him even in his state of disgrace and exile. Outlawed from Suthdal for their service to him, despised as 'Hermit-Crabs' by the Anakim, they referred to themselves as the *Thingalith*. Isolated from both sides, hand-picked and salvaged by Bellamus from campaigns and conflicts against the Anakim, they were resourceful and dependable folk, with a stubborn isolationist streak. Bellamus encouraged them to think themselves better than their fellow Sutherners, and they did. Every one of them could read. Every one had a set of Anakim bone-armour.

With them were scores of specialist spies, mostly women as they could pass across country with less suspicion, each recruited by Bellamus himself and still clutching the messages and ingeniously crafted devices that were the tools of their trade. Every face was lean and tanned, but invested with their fierce belief in their work here.

And in Bellamus himself.

Dark smudges lingered beneath his eyes, there was more grey at his temples and his most constant companion was a skin of wine. Still he grinned around with his old energy. 'My brothers and sisters, my *Thingalith*, my spies, my soldiers: the hour is upon us and the news is good. The enemy number a mere sixty thousand.' He waved a hand

dismissively and the crowd laughed. 'And we here will be
their downfall. I should ask no more of you than you have
given already. Never has a man been blessed with such dedicated and resourceful comrades. But more is what I must
ask. The Anakim must not know, but Suthdal is weak. So
weak. Our forces were stripped by the invasions last year;
our king is a cabbage,' more laughter, 'and we have neither
the strength nor the leaders to resist them on the field.' He
paused, letting his face assume the only expression that did
not take immense effort these days: weary, worn certainty.
'So we are all there is. Our resistance must be with subtler
weapons than those used by our enemy. With writing, information, misinformation, poison and disruption. We must
resist passively, infuriate and block them at every turn, make
them wallow in the homesickness that possesses the Anakim
in alien lands. And finally, when we have weakened them
enough, we will at last be able to turn them back on the field,
or send them home to think again. Believe. *Believe*, and have
faith: we can win this conflict, and tomorrow it begins. You
all know what you have to do. You are all prepared. You *must*
remember: we are all there is. We are all there is.' He let that
settle on them for a moment, and then grinned again. 'But
tonight, I want to hear you celebrating, because the waiting
is over. Get drunk, swap stories and reminisce about when
life was easy and our future certain. It starts tomorrow.' They
cheered him, and Bellamus made a modest gesture, turning
back to the Cobweb, ducking below the thatch and inside.

Within, a fire crackled in a grubby hearth and two huge
tables dominated the room. One was festooned with maps of
every scale and kind, fully half of it covered by a great tapestry of Suthdal, massed with random tokens and toys denoting
soldiers and strategic positions. The other was piled with
neat stacks of paper, weighed down by clean rocks so that
the sudden draught as he opened the door merely shivered
the corners of each pile. The huge companion who had ridden with Bellamus ducked in at his back.

'Spiced ale?' he asked, rubbing his hands together.

'Do we have milk?'

'Gallons.'

'You're a good man, Stepan.'

'Pie?'

'What kind?'

'Pork, apple, sage.'

'You're a very good man.' Bellamus removed his cloak, draping it behind a chair and settling himself at the paper-laden table. He stared down for a moment at a brooch of silver and ruby, crafted into the form of a spider – the symbol he used with his spies – which the queen had sent him. It would be valuable, but strangely he felt he could not sell it. It was a new sensation for him, being attached to a material object. However small, it was the only recognition he had received of their efforts here.

Stepan, the amber-bearded knight, brought him a pewter plate bearing a thick slice of pie, its insides glistening with jelly. 'You're slowly turning into my chef,' observed Bellamus, picking up the cold pie and taking a bite. It was salty, rich and fatty and he leaned back, savouring it.

'Easier than spying,' said Stepan, cutting himself a prodigious slice, which he set down next to Bellamus. He left it there for a time, striding back and forth across the room as he combined ale, milk and spices in a large black kettle.

'You're fond of ginger,' noted Bellamus through a mouthful of pie.

'It's the best bit,' said Stepan, transferring the kettle to a hook over the fire and giving it a vigorous stir before he came and sat with Bellamus. 'While you've got it, I'll use it.' The two had talked the whole day, and were quite happy to eat in silence. Stepan appeared more interested in food than fighting since their escape from the Black Kingdom, and Bellamus had pretended not to notice how frequently he now excused himself from raids and confrontations, pleading other outstanding duties. He sensed that the great knight was done with conflict, and seeking greater peace in his life. In time, he feared that desire would split them apart. Bellamus was still ambitious. Still hungry. They were both captivated by the Black Kingdom, but Stepan seemed increasingly reluctant to return there by any means besides reminiscing. Bellamus wanted to stand once more between the mountains and giant trees, smelling the strange musk and listening for the howls of unidentifiable beasts.

To do that, they would need to stop this invasion, and Bellamus's abilities to influence how it proceeded were limited. He was disgraced at court. If he were to send a messenger south with word of all he knew, the messenger's head would likely be sent back in a bag. The only reason his stubborn band had not yet been erased was that King Osbert had bigger problems than a miniature rebellion.

Bellamus could rely on just one ally: Queen Aramilla, and she had little formal power. She could flatter, manipulate and blackmail with the best of them, but if it was discovered that her information came from Bellamus, that would be the end of her. The upstart had been forced to grow expert in getting encrypted messages to Her Majesty. They arrived concealed in books, in eggs, the heels of shoes, the bandages of cripples that she took pity upon, sewn into new garments, and rolled into wine corks.

To defeat the Anakim, they would need to be clever. Bellamus had tried meeting them in open battle, with little success. Suthdal was weak, and they would not defeat them toe to toe. The legionaries were too good, their sense of camaraderie too potent, and they were well led by the young Black Lord. This war needed new arenas: ones where the Anakim were at a disadvantage, and Bellamus had redoubled his efforts as a spymaster. Because they did not write, it did not occur to an Anakim how valuable a written parchment might be, and they seemed unaware of the flock of messages that flitted silently through the Black Kingdom, all bound for this village. There were no Sutherners north of the

Abus, so Bellamus had to turn individual Anakim against their peers. This was a difficult feat. Having no value for physical objects, they were not usually susceptible to bribery, and they mostly hated the Sutherners and adored their people with equal fervour. But they had their weaknesses, like everyone.

Stepan finished his pie first and stood to inspect the kettle of spiced ale, the mere smell of which was a tonic. He stirred and tasted, fetched a little more milk, added it, stirred again. There came a knock at the door.

'Come!'

The door opened and a figure stooped beneath the lintel, inappropriately huge in this dingy inn.

Bellamus did not stand up, beckoning to the figure. 'Unndor, isn't it?'

The figure nodded. This was one of the Anakim messengers who sometimes visited the town, carrying word from the agents embedded within the Black Lord's army. His face was sour as he held out a scroll to Bellamus, sealed with a wax spider.

'Thank you.'

Unndor turned on his heel and left without another word, Bellamus staring after him.

He broke the wax seal over the scroll and discovered blank insides. Stepan came back to the table with two mugs of the ale, and Bellamus coughed slightly at the power of the ginger that wafted up from his mug. 'Bring me a candle, would you, Stepan?' The knight obliged before taking a seat next to Bellamus, who dragged the candle close and held the scroll over it.

'This chap again,' said Stepan, gazing at the scroll. 'His messenger doesn't seem too happy.'

'He's getting resentful,' Bellamus agreed. 'Doubtless thought he'd be doing something more interesting when he was recruited.'

Stepan watched as Bellamus moved the scroll gently back

and forth over the candle flame. 'I don't know how you read these letters, they're awful.'

'It is a struggle,' admitted Bellamus. 'Though his aptitude for letters is not bad at all for an Anakim. I should like to try teaching an Anakim child to write, and see if they are more adept. The adults mostly cannot learn at all.' Slowly, the candle singed dark, broad letters into the scroll; the lines drawn with raw sheep's milk which smouldered before the paper around it, until the hidden words were revealed in burnt brown. They were barely comprehensible. The letters were backwards and malformed, the words elided or broken at odd places, and the Saxon meanings obfuscated. 'The shipment of Unhieru armour has been accelerated,' said Bellamus, frowning at the paper. 'I think . . . I think he's saying they're reforming the chain-mail barding for their horses rather than forging it all from scratch. He thinks they'll be ready to ship out in four days.' He let the edges of the scroll spring together once more, and dropped it on the table, picking up the hot ale and taking a sip. 'We must make sure the shipment never arrives,' he said, setting down his ale and reaching for another message from a pile on the table.

Stepan fidgeted at that, and changed the subject. 'Who is supplying this information? Do we trust them?'

Bellamus frowned. 'In some ways. In others, not at all. He calls himself the Ellengaest, and he is the only one who contacted me first. We've got leverage over everyone else,' he explained, waving a hand at the stack of letters lying on the table. 'He seems to be self-motivated, which does make me a little suspicious.'

'It's more than a little suspicious,' said Stepan. 'Why on earth would he want to help us?'

'I have never met him,' said Bellamus, brow furrowed. 'Only his messengers. But I must admit he does not seem entirely normal from his letters. They often finish with tirades against the Black Lord. And he seems to envisage a future for himself in Suthdal. He's made references to earning a place at King Osbert's court as an honoured adviser, responsible for the downfall of the Anakim.' Bellamus laughed bitterly. 'If I could secure such a position, I'd reserve it for myself. But it does no harm to encourage him.'

'So he's disillusioned?'

'That's how it seems,' said Bellamus, picking up a new paper. 'And he is protected by some faction within the Black Kingdom that prevents him being uncovered. He himself is being used in some way I do not fully understand. But if you wish to know why I trust his information, it is the waft of terrible self-loathing in his messages. That convinces me as to his motives. And his information has always been right so far.'

'I'd be careful with that source,' said Stepan dubiously.

'I am as careful as I can afford to be,' Bellamus replied, without looking up.

They were silent a time longer, before Stepan spoke again. 'Did you hear they lost three hybrids this week?'

Bellamus frowned down at his paper. 'I thought they were being given less dangerous work now.' There were dozens of Suthern-Anakim hybrids in this town, used by the villagers as slaves. Bellamus had tried to improve conditions for them. At the back of his mind was the thought they might make good soldiers, if he could incentivise them properly. After all, Garrett Eoten-Draefend was a hybrid warrior of consider-able renown, and he now served Bellamus. But the change in conditions had yielded no change in their behaviour whatso-ever. They remained dangerous and unpredictable beings. Still, Bellamus flirted with the idea of using them as soldiers. They did not necessarily need to be controlled; just unleashed in the right direction.

'It wasn't the work,' said Stepan. 'Slave-Plague, I am told.'

'Slave-Plague,' repeated Bellamus, tiredly. 'Have they quarantined them?'

'They said they don't need to.'

Bellamus set down his mug and looked up from the cypher. 'What? They haven't enforced a quarantine?'

'I don't believe so.'

Bellamus cast about for a heartbeat, seeking some response from the inn's dark corners. 'For God's sake!' he declared, getting to his feet, swinging his cloak about his shoulders and heading for the door.

'I'll keep your ale warm,' said Stepan comfortably, but Bellamus was gone, prowling through the night and seeking the damned fool whose plague-ridden slaves were still permitted to wander the village.

He stalked through the dark, heading for a barn to which the Cobweb's erstwhile owner had been banished. Arranged around the barn was a score of rough kennels that housed the hybrid slaves, and Bellamus pulled his cloak over his nose as he passed them. He could sense their wakeful yellow eyes follow him through the gloom. Bellamus ignored them, hammering on the door to the barn. It was opened, after considerable delay and several additional hammerings, by a balding, braided man with the drooping face of a hound. 'I have heard there is plague,' announced Bellamus.

The balding man hated Bellamus, who could not really blame him for that. He had, after all, taken his inn and reduced him to living in a barn with a trio of oxen. The drooping face was scrunched into an expression of great sourness, and he gazed coldly through a narrow chink in the door. 'What's that to you?'

'Because your slaves are all still out here, un-quarantined,' said Bellamus, waving a hand at the kennels behind him. 'And if a single one of my men gets plague because you failed to act, then I will burn your barn down.'

'Idiot foreigner,' snapped the man. 'Plague is caused by bad air. I cannot contain the air, and it is up to God which of my slaves breathes it in.'

'No,' said Bellamus curtly. 'It is caused by close exposure

to the sick. Quarantine your slaves at once, or my men will do it.'

The man opened the door wide enough to extend an arm, poking a shrivelled finger into Bellamus's chest. 'Your men cannot catch Slave-Plague, fool. It is not the normal sort, it only spreads among the hybrids.'

Bellamus felt his rage diluted by a strange, unidentifiable hope. It gave him pause for a moment as he tried to identify its source, but being unable to find it, returned to berating the old man. 'I don't care for your opinions on infection. Quarantine them this instant.'

'What do you know?' demanded the old man, jabbing Bellamus's chest once more. 'All my life I've been dealing with hybrids. All my life! I'd have caught the plague a dozen times by now if I could have. We *cannot* catch Slave-Plague!'

Bellamus felt his anger abate a little in the face of this man's certainty, but the old innkeeper was still being careless. He removed the man's finger from his chest and tried to speak more calmly. 'I want them quarantined. Even if what you say is true, one of my warriors is a hybrid.'

'I've seen him,' hissed the old man. 'Never heard madness like that before, training a hybrid for war.'

Bellamus waved the argument away. 'Quarantine them quickly and I can pay you for it.'

'I know how reliable your offers of payment are,' grumbled the old man.

'Well believe me and hope for payment, or refuse. Either way, there will be a quarantine.' Bellamus fished in his pocket and found a penny, which he passed to the old man. It vanished into some bottomless fold of his cloak, and Bellamus found himself distracted by that odd hope that seemed to have come from nowhere. 'Sorry to disturb. But quarantine.' He nodded at the old man and turned away, ignoring the tut at his back as the barn door slammed shut.

He re-entered the Cobweb with a frown on his face, shutting the door slowly behind him.

'What did he say?' asked Stepan, clutching a second mug of ale. Bellamus looked at his friend, and became suddenly aware of the source of that hope. Once he had identified the connection, the hope he had felt became horror. He pushed it away, replying to Stepan.

'He seems pretty certain we . . . Sutherners, can't catch it.'

'That's what he said to me,' said Stepan. 'Do you think he's right?'

'I would need to test,' said Bellamus, softly.

'Oh.' Stepan chuckled. 'You have a loyal band, my captain, but good luck finding a volunteer for that. Just be cautious and have him quarantine them anyway.'

'I will, I will. But I still need to know if it affects Sutherners.'

Stepan's eyes were white in the firelight. 'Just tell me you're not going to test it yourself.'

Bellamus stayed silent.

The next morning, Bellamus was pleased to find that the kennels were empty and the slaves had been confined to the barn. He did his best to organise payment for the innkeeper, digging out a silver altar-cross and hacking off an arm. He spent the morning creating a cyphered message for the queen, detailing the Anakim invasion, their numbers and their latest location, supplied by the band of horsemen he had trailing them. He rearranged the pieces on his map of Suthdal, received a dozen messages and copied the information into a thick ledger. One was from a new and valuable informant whom Bellamus was blackmailing for information. He had arranged for one of his female agents to seduce the officer, who was married, and then threatened to expose the affair if he did not cooperate. Bellamus was proud of that: using the rigidity of Anakim society and the huge scandal the affair would have caused as a weapon. He was getting better at it. Two of the other messages were from spies who believed they were working for the Kryptea, on the side of

the Black Kingdom. Their handlers had come to them with
the sign of the cuckoo, and these loyal Anakim subjects had
been eager to obey.

Throughout his work, Bellamus was distracted, pausing
frequently and tapping the parchment with his quill. He
went to fetch a skin of wine which he drained while writing out instructions to an agent near Lincylene. He found
the cypher harder to construct than usual. When he realised he had ruined it for the third time with a speckle of
random dots, he threw down his quill. 'For heaven's sake,' he
muttered, donning his cloak and abandoning the empty
wineskin.

A moment later, he was hammering once more on the door
to the barn. The old innkeeper stormed out almost at once,
bristling and ready for a confrontation, but stopped short at
the sight of Bellamus's face. 'What now?'

'I wish to spend some time with your hybrids,' said Bellamus, not quite sure how to explain his purpose.

'Why?'

'I'd like to tend to the sick ones.'

'I tend to the sick ones,' said the old man.

'Please indulge me,' said Bellamus, producing another
penny. It was snatched away and the old man turned inside.
Bellamus followed him, shutting the door behind him.
He remembered this place. He had not set foot inside it since
hanging two of his men for stealing from the old man. The
timber crucks from which the ropes had swung met above
him, and the milking stools he had kicked from beneath
their feet were set against the wall. It smelt of dust and hay
and dung.

At the far end was a high platform on which the old man
had set up his own bed, and in a stall to his left, three oxen
were engaged in the serious business of obliterating a hay-
stack. In the far stall were three shaven-headed slaves, all
shivering in a nest of blankets. 'Where are the healthy ones?'
asked Bellamus.

'I put them up in my son's house,' said the innkeeper, opening the stall and gazing pointedly inside.

Bellamus stepped in, the stall sealed behind him. He crouched to examine the nearest slave. Because the head was shaven, it took Bellamus a moment to realise this was a woman. Her eyes were shut tight and she was moaning faintly as she shivered. There was a bluish hue to her lips and ears, her breathing was laboured, and a feeble cough rattled her thin frame. 'She will die,' said the old man, looking over the stall gate.

Slave-Plague did not seem to be plague at all; not as Bellamus recognised it. Rather it resembled an extreme version of a winter flu. He stayed in the stall for a while, the old man supplying him with a pail of mixed milk and water before departing the barn. Bellamus fed the watered milk to those who could manage it, and tried to make the unconscious woman comfortable as her cough became wretched, producing a pink foam. All the while her face acquired a bruised hue, and though he did not really have time for this, Bellamus found he could not leave. He sat in the stall with the three slaves, shackled even in their ill-health, and watched the woman fade. Her breathing grew faster and shallower. Her face gathered into a desperate frown. And then, she relaxed. Her countenance was calmed. Her chest stilled, and peace, unmistakable and unexpected, descended on the stall.

By the teaching of the church, these creatures were half-demon. She had been born irredeemably sinful, and there was only one destination for her soul. Her life had been wretched, and her death would be no better. Even so, Bellamus leaned forward, placing a hand on her cooling forehead and said a small prayer for her. Her nose was streaming onto the blanket beneath her head, and Bellamus stared at the little stream for a time. Then he wiped at it carefully with a finger, inspecting the shining fingertip for a moment. He touched a tiny cool drop of the fluid to the inside of his lip. To be certain.

Bellamus stood, marvelling at how desperate he had become, experimenting with such things in this mournful barn. He wondered, beyond being immune to it himself, what he hoped the results of his enquiries would be, and decided to think no more of it. He left, returning to the barn an hour later with two bowls of shredded rabbit soup and some hard bread for the surviving slaves.

He retired to the Cobweb for the evening, keeping his friends and the *Thingalith* at a distance and burying himself in his codes to take his mind off the foolishness of what he had done in the barn. Even Stepan was banished, Bellamus eating some of the soup alone at his table with another skin of wine. By the time the moon had risen and he had retired to bed, he had almost convinced himself that it was the end of a normal day, the notion betrayed by a ringing silence at his core. He awoke the next morning in a state of instant self-assessment. He breathed normally. He did not feel hot, or feverish. Was his heart beating a little fast? Perhaps, but the only thing to do was carry on.

15
The Empty Lands

'There it is,' said Gray, nodding to a huddle of wattle, daub and thatch, nestled between distant hills. They had smelt woodsmoke a mile before, noted the nettles on their route which always seemed to grow near Suthern villages, and so anticipated this sight. Roper, Gray and Pryce had mounted so they could keep pace with the army's outriding Skiritai, and grinned at each other as they raked back their spurs.

They lunged out before the Skiritai, thundering down a slope and towards the edge of the village. There was a woman there, hacking some weeds clear of a dyke. She looked up at the sound of their hoofbeats, and her mouth fell open. She scrambled back, abandoning her billhook and sprinting into the village, the shawl over her head slipping off and falling onto the road.

The Anakim plunged after her, into narrow streets bordered by walls of rough, crumbling daub. A man emerged from an alley to their right, a look of surprise on his face as Pryce's horse bore down on him. He had no time to react further. He was smashed flat by the charging courser, head rattling off the cobbles. The noise startled a cluster of pigeons pecking at the ground in front, which scattered before the

Anakim horsemen. Behind the flapping and the feathers, another man emerged from a barn further up the street. He saw the riders and leapt back inside, slamming the door.

Roper pointed at the door, the guardsmen shouted their agreement, and the three reined in next to the barn. Two more Sutherners emerged from a door on the other side of the street: a man and a woman holding hands, who fled out of the village. The Anakim let them go, interested in one thing only.

They dismounted and Pryce pushed at the barn door, which flexed a little but did not open. 'Barred,' he said. He and Gray linked arms and kicked at it together, synchronising their blows once, then twice. On the second kick they heard a crunching noise, and with a third the door burst inwards. The wooden arm that had sealed it cracked in the middle and was ripped from its socket. Skiritai were thundering through the street behind them, Ramnea's Own legionaries with them, and the three of them drew swords and advanced into the barn.

The man was waiting for them just behind the door, eyes wild and a pitchfork clutched in his hands. He lunged at Roper, who did not react to the blow, letting it hit his cuirass. The dull iron tips made no impression whatsoever on the steel, but one of the tines snapped off the pitchfork. 'Give me that,' said Roper, seizing the shaft and ripping it out of the man's hands. He hurled it into a corner and Pryce booted the man in the stomach. He staggered back five yards, sprawling in the hay and moaning on each breath. 'Efficient,' Roper commended.

The three of them turned their eyes away from the groaning Sutherner, and towards their real objective in this town: the barn's shadowed interior. All armies require vast quantities of food, and though the Anakim usually lived off the land when in the north, that was scarcely possible when in Suthdal. The country had been so tamed and manipulated by agriculture that most wild foods were competed out of existence. Instead, the Anakim would need to rely on the same food as the Sutherners, which meant they would have to take it from them directly. It should have been the easiest hunting they had ever done.

But the barn was empty.

'Not again,' said Gray, sniffing at the hay dust.

'Check the hay,' said Roper. The three of them ran their swords through the hay piled about the edges of the barn, but found nothing. No livestock. No concealed grain. As with every barn, granary, pastureland and homestead encountered so far, this place had been stripped of food. On the route here, they had ridden across fields of ash, with even the green crops in the fields torched. 'What are these people living off?' Pryce demanded, kicking at the hay.

'Let's ask,' said Roper. The man who had attacked him with the pitchfork was on his belly, trying to crawl back out into the street outside, which rang with screams, shouts and crashes as the legionaries ripped into the town. Roper took him by the scruff of the neck and hauled him upright. 'Your food,' he demanded in Saxon. 'Where is it?'

'Gone, lord,' wheezed the Sutherner, still fighting for breath after Pryce's kick.

'Where?'

'Taken . . . by a hybrid,' the Sutherner panted for a moment. 'With a gang of armed men. He told us you were coming . . . Said he was taking our supplies to Lincylene . . . and our good iron, so you couldn't get it. Said we should go too, if we didn't want to starve.'

Roper glanced back at Gray, eyebrows raised. 'Describe this hybrid.'

'Enormous,' said the man. 'Violent . . . A cloven nose, bright blond hair . . . He said if we did not surrender the food, he would destroy our village himself.'

'The Eoten-Draefend,' said Gray.

At the name, Pryce gave a little skip of irritation. 'What is he saying?' he demanded.

'That his food was taken by a blond hybrid with a cloven nose,' Roper translated. Garrett Eoten-Draefend, the hybrid warrior whom Gogmagoc wanted dead. Once a servant of King Osbert, he had turned his back on the king and sided with Bellamus. The long-edged sword he wielded had been made from Bright-Shock: the sword that had been Roper's father's, until he had died with it undrawn in its scabbard. Bellamus had found the body and claimed the sword. Roper still wanted that weapon back, and Garrett's head with it.

He dropped the prisoner back to the floor. 'We keep searching,' said Roper. 'Garrett can't have taken everything.'

The three of them emerged back onto the street to see smoke already billowing through the thatch of several buildings and forming a filthy column in the sky. Two feral dogs ran out of one building, barking madly and tearing down the street. The legionaries would clear away resistance. The Skiritai would search for food, and then ignite each building once they knew it was empty. In a few hours, this village would be ash. Those villagers who had not needlessly antagonised the Anakim would survive and be pushed onto the road to spread fear and herald the Anakim invasion.

One of Roper's favourite foods in the berjasti had been wood-ant larvae. To get them, he would rip apart the mound in which they lived and spread its innards over the swept forest floor, bordered by logs. Then he waited. After an hour or two, Roper would flip over each log and discover that the ants had helpfully collected and condensed the scattered larvae in the log's shadow. From there they could be scooped up at leisure, fried in fish oil and enjoyed with warm bread. This had inspired his strategy for the early part of the campaign. They had plunged into the guts of the land with the aim of creating chaos. They would burn and scatter, and inevitably, the Sutherners would gather all that was most precious to them and retreat to the nearest log: Lincylene, their great northern city. There, Roper could scoop them up. It saved his army being weighed down by baggage and prisoners before they had a place to keep them, which meant they could move fast, and take much of Suthdal before resistance had time to form. Lincylene's walls had been razed during the last Anakim invasion and their most recent information, from a raiding party the previous year, was that there were still no walls about the city.

But though Roper had expected the Sutherners to make some effort at concealing their food, he had not anticipated that it would be removed entirely. They were a week into Suthdal, and every village before this one had been similarly stripped, most of them abandoned too. The only explanation for this was that the Sutherners had known they were coming. How they had known and been so prepared, Roper could only guess.

They walked the streets, the buildings either side beginning to crackle with flames. One man lay sprawled in the mud, his guts spilling out beneath him and two silver candlesticks, which he had evidently tried to preserve, lying with him. He need not have bothered: the Anakim were not interested in silver. Some Skiritai were trying to draw water from a well at the end of the street, but the first three buckets they brought up contained sodden chicken carcasses.

'Garrett again,' said Pryce, glaring at the sopping feathers. The carcasses would have corrupted the water, but still, it would not be wasted.

The Skiritai tossed aside the disintegrating chickens and began pouring the water over the earth near the houses, under trees and beside walls. If the Sutherners had recently buried any of their food, they would have had to put them near visible markers so that they did not lose them. The water would sink faster into freshly dug earth and betray the cache, showing the Skiritai where to dig.

'Has anyone been in here?' Pryce asked a ranger emptying a water pail, indicating the house to his left. The Skiritai shrugged, and Pryce left Roper and Gray, pushing open the door to the shadowed dwelling beyond.

This seemed a prosperous village, and the house had two storeys. The ground floor was empty but for a burnt-out hearth, a filthy bed in one corner, and a flight of stairs in the other. Pryce probed the bed with one of his swords, but the rough blankets covered nothing except a straw mattress.

Something trickled onto his head.

Looking up, Pryce saw a gap between the rough wooden floorboards above him, with something dark dripping between them. He raised a hand to the wet patch in his hair, and inspected the fingertips. They were crimson.

Gripping Tusk more tightly, he crept to the stairs, climbing the ash boards as silently as he was able. He raised his head above the floorboards to see two people on the upper storey. One was a Suthern man, lying still and bleeding onto the planks of his home, the steady drip, drip of blood now sounding from the floor below. The other figure was Vigtyr. He was bent low, a bloody sword in his left hand, his right fumbling at the man's wrist. He removed something shining which rattled softly as he straightened up. Then he spotted Pryce observing him from the stairs, and gave a start.

'Oh, Pryce.' Vigtyr took a sudden breath. Then he grinned. 'Bastard tried to kill me,' he said, nudging the corpse with his foot.

Pryce just looked back at the lictor for a time, face expressionless. 'With what, Vigtyr?'

'The rope,' said Vigtyr smoothly, pointing to a length of it lying on the floor. Pryce stared at him a moment longer before turning away, creaking back down the stairs and out into the grey daylight.

In the street, he found Roper and Gray talking with Tekoa, and joined them.

'It's been the same story at every village so far,' Tekoa was saying. 'No food, water supplies tainted, most of the people gone, any metal that isn't soft and worthless removed.' He kicked irritably at the silver candlestick, which clattered over the cobbles.

'Are the Skiritai finding anything buried?'

'Nothing,' spat Tekoa.

Where Tekoa was angry, Roper seemed thoughtful. 'If the Eoten-Draefend has gathered everything valuable in the city, then he's done our early work for us,' he said. The only thing left was to harvest the larvae. 'Let's go and get it.'

The army, which had atomised over northern Suthdal, condensed that night.

Excited mutterings ran between the campfires as legionaries compared tales of what they had found in this strange land. There was a general opinion that the lack of food meant one thing: there would shortly be a battle, where they would fight the Sutherners for their supplies.

Roper ignored these rumours, and the matter of food. He had more pressing concerns.

He gathered his council together for the first time since they had crossed the Abus. There were dozens of them: legates, officers, historians and heralds, and they chattered raucously as they settled upon the great circle of logs that Roper had assembled around his hearth. Though they had found no food, the officers did not realise how long this campaign would be, and therefore how important fresh supplies would become.

'Peers,' Roper began, standing before them and raising a hand to quell the chatter. 'Peers. Tomorrow, we turn for Lincylene.' Silence fell, the orange-lit faces turning towards Roper. He felt the weight of their stares and prowled about inside the circle, eyes flicking between hearth and audience. 'As you have all found, the Sutherners somehow knew when we were coming. They have done their best to corrupt the water supplies and strip the country of food. This is nothing we can't handle. They must be living off something, and we have reason to believe they have assembled their supplies at Lincylene. When we get there, we will find food and also, dare I say it, our first battle.' The legates grinned and Roper gave a wry smile. 'I anticipate it quite as eagerly as you, I assure you. But before that, you should know why we're going at all. You should know why we're here.' Some of the faces around the fire had begun to frown. 'I will be blunt. We are not here for a raid. We are not here for plunder, or revenge. We are here to stay. This is a mission of conquest. By the end of this campaign, we will rule over the country of Suthdal, and have flattened all resistance.'

Silence, but for the crackling of the flames.

A few of the audience exchanged glances. Most just continued to frown at Roper, waiting for him to finish. 'I will tell you why,' Roper continued, a little anger spiking his words. 'And by the end, you may see whether you agree that this is the only sane option left to us. We are about to begin a task that should have started centuries ago. We have come here with nearly our full strength and number a mere sixty thousand. Legion after legion has been struck from existence as we lose the men to fill them. Our kingdom is dying. Even when we're last on the field, it is still a tiny victory for the Sutherner. We have lost another fragment of our population, while their soldiers will be replenished in a year. That must be stopped now, while we still have the strength for it. And the only way to do that, with total finality, is to subdue this country.' He glared about the circle. 'Do any of you deny this?' Whether shocked or captivated, the council made no reply. It was clear that not everyone agreed, but the force of Roper's will was undeniable.

'So our advance will be that of the locust,' Roper continued, the personable charm he so often displayed suddenly hidden as he stalked the fireside wearing the mask of the Black Lord. 'We move to Lincylene and we demand their surrender. If they agree, we take their weapons, their metal and their food, and we move on. If they defy us, we will consume them. We must preserve every soldier possible and we will sow terror and momentum, which will do the fighting before we have even arrived.

'It may be that at first the Sutherners will refuse to surrender, and many will die. So be it. What happens to them will persuade others to surrender. The death and the casualties on both sides will be at the start of this conflict. And afterwards, when they are so utterly horrified by what it means to fight the legions that they cannot bear the thought; when they have understood what resistance means; when enough men have died, and they at last realise the price of freedom is more than they can afford; this country will succumb to us.'

The flames crackled, flickering in the eyes of the assembly. Roper suspected they thought he was half-mad, but he did not care. Every eye he met dropped to the floor, until he found the dawn-blue gaze of the Chief Historian.

'You deceived us, Lord Roper,' she said, staring at him levelly. 'Why did you say nothing of this before?'

'Because I would have been stopped,' said Roper. There seemed a void in the circle of onlookers: a black absence like a missing tooth that Roper dared not look straight at. It was the space occupied by Jokul, the Master of the Kryptea. 'People would have flapped and raised problems and been conservative. A hundred different objections would have been put forward by a hundred different factions, and inertia would have defeated us with far greater certainty than the Sutherners. But the objections are insignificant, because if we do not accomplish this task, we shall fade away. Someday soon, perhaps a century or two from now, the Hindrunn will stand empty. Ivy will choke the forest roads, and the bears and wolves will wonder where the third great predator who shared their lands has gone. You here: you are the distilled few of action who stand in the way of that future.' He looked from one legate to the next. 'Is this not the very reason for our existence? To preserve our future generations? Is this not what you live for? What greater purpose could you possibly serve?'

The legates were with him, Roper could see it in their faces.

'This task is greater than we are, Lord Roper,' said the old historian. 'Never before has Suthdal been subjugated. Not since the Sutherners arrived here.'

'My lady,' said Roper, walking slowly towards her. 'Has anyone tried? We have raided and pillaged and sometimes occupied a city or two, but has this ever been attempted before?'

'Never.'

'We do not like to be away from home,' said Roper, softly. He raised a hand at the vacant landscape around them. 'We come south for a few months, are sick to our guts and decide what an appalling place this is, and how much better is our own homeland. But without our quest here, the north too shall succumb to agriculture. And if it takes a thousand years, we will make Suthdal into a new homeland. Thank the Almighty that you have lived to take up this mantle: the greatest responsibility of all. Never will an Anakim live a life so meaningful as those of us touched by this fire. Every name present will crackle through the ages in words of lightning, because you were here. Sturla Karson. Randolph Reykdalson. Meino Finnbiorson. Arslan Veeson.' Roper pointed at each of the legates in turn. 'We cannot fail, and whether you knew it or not, you have been walking down this road your entire life. We have come too far to turn back now.'

There was a strange momentum in the air. Some of the faces around the fire were appalled, but also oddly compelled, as though they could not believe they were on Roper's side.

But then Jokul's voice gusted into the circle, standing Roper's hair on end. 'What madness is this?' he said coldly. The Master of the Kryptea was small, pale and stinging-nettle lean; so unsubstantial that he might have floated here on the breeze from the west. 'You go too far, Lord Roper. You have abused your power. You cannot expect the Kryptea to stand by while you subject the entire kingdom to a deception of this scale.'

Roper was mustering a reply, when another furious voice cut in for him. 'And what will you do, Master Jokul?' It was Gray, on his feet, glaring at Jokul. 'Summon your band of cowards and assassinate my lord? Because I assure you, you would not survive that.' Roper put a hand on Gray's shoulder to calm him, but was surprised by the low growl of agreement that ran around the circle. As he was pushed back into a seat, Gray raised a hand to point at Jokul. 'Watch your back, Master. You are not the only man with killers at your command. If anything happens to Lord Roper, the Sacred Guard will make an extremely slow end of you.' That threw the fireside into silence. It was accepted that if the Master of the Kryptea thought the Black Lord had stepped out of line, he had the right to exercise vengeance. But there was an old and fierce rivalry between Sacred Guard and Kryptea, dating from the formation of the latter. And Gray, who was clearly backed by the legates, had brought it into the open for the first time.

'Defiance against the Kryptea is punishable by death,' Jokul observed.

'Are you going to kill all of us?' asked Pryce dismissively. 'Just you and your handful of mad assassins left?'

'Yes, shut up, Jokul,' snapped Tekoa. And Jokul, yielding to the grim faces directed at him from around the fireside, did shut up.

Roper looked around at his council. 'Last month, three of us about this fire undertook a secret mission to Unhierea, to recruit the giants there to our cause. They are with me for this great task. Are you? Will you follow me, once again?'

Keturah, Gray, Pryce and Tekoa got to their feet at once, as Roper had known they would. Keturah stood with one hand on her hip, as the other three drew their swords and tossed them down in a pile. 'We are with you, lord,' said Gray, eyes still on Jokul.

From the rest of the circle came silence. Several of them glanced at the four standing figures, eyebrows raised.

Then Randolph, an old ally of Uvoren's, got to his feet. He drew his sword and tossed it onto the pile. 'I am with you in this task, Lord Roper.'

Half a dozen others got to their feet just after. 'I, and the Ulpha,' declared another.

'The Greyhazel are with you.'

'And the Fair Islanders.'

In a ripple starting from the legates outwards, the audience rose unevenly. The Chief Historian was late onto her feet, glaring at Roper. 'For good or for bad,' she said, 'history will remember you, Lord Roper.'

Soon, it was only Jokul left seated. Roper did not care. He looked around the circle, aware more than ever of the responsibility on his shoulders, but strangely furious too. Nothing would turn him aside from this. Not the Kryptea, not politics, not the Sutherners and no amount of effort, regardless of how insurmountable it became. 'Tomorrow, we march for Lincylene. Now you know why.'

Drumcondra Library

Items that you have checked out

Title: The spider
ID: CCPL800003021
Due: 25/10/2022

Total items: 1
Account balance: €0.00
Checked out: 1
Overdue: 0
Hold requests: 0
Ready for collection: 0
04/10/2022

Thank you for visiting us today

ne

W hen the council was dismissed, Jokul disappeared into the evening without another word. As Roper lay down next to Keturah that night, he half expected never to wake again. Perhaps the support of the Sacred Guard and the legates had persuaded Jokul that it was not time to act, for Roper awoke to a humid day of low cloud.

They marched on, through this land that was so strange to Roper. Crossing it felt like a garden stroll. Everything was gentle and curved. The hills resembled the thatched Suthern roofs: smooth mounds unbroken by rock or peak. The landscape stood naked, free from mountain or forest. It permitted a bland and constant breeze to wear across it and made Roper feel exposed. Freed from the need to strive for the canopy above, the trees grew broad and low, studding the hills like giant mushrooms. They looked lonely to Roper. A tree should no more stand alone than should a man, and yet everywhere they were stranded above the ranks of crops that had been too immature for Garrett to bother destroying. Being able to see this waiting harvest was worst of all. Uniform plants, bred into slavery, already bowing beneath their grotesque burden of giant unripe seeds. The Sutherners adored to use iron – that temporary, rotting metal – and rust blossomed everywhere. There were many crows, but few other birds. Few deer and no predators that he had seen. No beavers, which meant the rivers were narrow, ordered affairs, flowing with none of the joy or eccentricities of those beyond the Abus. This land looked exhausted to Roper. Stripped, whipped and subjugated.

On the road to Lincylene, Roper and Tekoa made use of the time by reporting the details of their expedition to Unhierea to the Chief Historian. Roper walked like his legionaries with a pack on his back, while the other two rode next to him on coursers.

'They are a failing people,' Roper said, resisting the urge to add 'like us'. 'Much of their existence is parasitic, and relies on the Sutherners. They no longer make stone tools: they rely on stealing metal ones from Suthdal. Their apple trees, which seem to be their primary harvest, are choked by mistletoe.'

'I daresay they could expend a bit more effort if they had to,' Tekoa put in. 'The only thing they really seem to cultivate is spare time. They should perhaps groom each other a little less and spend more time tending their apple trees.'

'The grooming seemed important for bonding,' Roper observed.

'They have no need of further bonding,' declared Tekoa. 'They already adore one another as a pig loves filth. They simply roll around together given half a chance.'

'Apart from that *flush*,' said Roper, voicing what had captured him above all about the Unhieru.

The Chief Historian glanced at him, expressionless. 'The what?'

'When we were staying with them, we saw one male steal from another. The bigger male seemed to completely lose control. He flushed a deep red and killed the thief with his bare hands. He wasn't sane again for a long while after. Gogmagoc called it the *other-mind*.'

'There are stories of the *other-mind*,' said the Chief Historian, with a tiny measure of interest. 'A subconscious warrior-state which overtakes the maned males. There is a chant which suggests that once they have flushed, they do not remember any of their actions until they are back to normal.'

'That is what really worries me about fighting next to them,' said Roper. 'Whether once we have brought them to the boil, we will be able to take them off. Their intelligence too,' he added, glancing at Tekoa. 'Did you get that sense?'

Tekoa nodded.

'I believe these may be the most intelligent people I have yet encountered,' Roper went on. 'That bow Gogmagoc had. It was glorious. What holds them back from producing a great society is not lack of ability, but lack of desire. They are also the most content people I have seen. They have all the capabilities, but no *drive*.'

'A people of intelligence, power and instability,' said the Historian, raising an eyebrow. '*Can* you control them, Lord Roper?' Roper and Tekoa looked at one another.

'I do not know,' Roper admitted.

'How did you secure their help?' asked the Historian.

'We offered them weapons and armour,' said Roper. 'And Gogmagoc set us two challenges. But when we won them, he had no interest in honouring the alliance. He was only really persuaded when he discovered we would be fighting together against the man who killed his son. Garrett Eoten-Draefend. He seemed very defensive of his kin, and I think he wants revenge.'

Even the Chief Historian seemed uneasy at that. 'From everything I have heard about those people, the thought of them with metal weapons and armour is ... formidable. How many do they number?'

'Twelve thousand will come,' said Roper. It had taken a long time to convert the Unhieru number-system, which seemed to be based on pairs, to something the Anakim could understand.

'And if it came to it,' asked the Historian after a time, 'if we had to, do you think the legions could defeat that force?'

Roper and Tekoa looked at one another once more. 'I do,' said Roper, at last. 'I believe the last people standing on the field would be Anakim. But there would not be many of us.'

They found a river, and stopped to collect water. Roper had already bent down and unstoppered his water-skin before Tekoa placed a hand on his shoulder. 'Smell it?'

Roper could, now that he tried. There was a rancid waft on the breeze. Tekoa nodded upriver and Roper saw, bobbing in the flow, the bloated corpse of a cow. It must have been tethered to the riverbed somehow, for it was not flowing downstream. Roper straightened up, re-stoppering his water-skin and swearing softly. 'How has he done this?'

'When you say *he* . . .' Tekoa began.

'I mean Bellamus,' Roper finished. They knew the Eoten-Draefend was involved in the evacuations and that he worked with the spymaster. Bellamus had to be behind this.

'But they can't contaminate every water source,' said Tekoa. 'They'd destroy their own population. They must know where we're going, and poison the water in front of us. So how do we stop them?'

The Chief Historian had already begun to ride on, but turned to bark a single word back at them. 'Jokul.'

Roper and Tekoa exchanged a glance. 'Please, no,' said Roper. He had still heard nothing from the Master of the Kryptea since Gray had snarled at him by the fire, and did not wish to initiate a confrontation.

But the Historian was right. The next morning, Roper summoned Jokul, who arrived at his hearth like a cold draught. Roper stood to greet him, the two exchanging a straight-armed handshake as both men attempted to keep their distance.

'Master,' said Roper. 'Are you well?'

'Of course,' said Jokul in his thin, dry voice, neither looking well nor sounding it. He was dressed in a thick, black cloak, which he clutched irritably to his chest. 'What can I do for you, Lord Roper?'

Roper gestured to the small fire crackling beside him. 'You can sit and talk, if it please you.' Jokul sighed fastidiously and clattered to the ground like a bundle of dropped kindling. Roper ignored the sigh. 'Tea, Master?'

Jokul twitched his head. 'That would be welcome.'

Roper wrapped his cloak around his hand and pulled a pot of scalding water from the fire, pouring it over a sprig of pine needles already laid in two birch-bark cups. He passed one to Jokul and sat with him, both bewitched by the fire. 'We have had our differences, Master,' Roper began. 'And our objectives have not always aligned.'

Jokul raised a thin eyebrow. 'They should have done,' he said.

'I have done what I had to,' said Roper. 'Do we not now have the stability your organisation so adores?'

'Stability is a generous term when you cannot restrain your own officers, and you yourself seek allies we cannot control, and take drastic decisions without reference to any of the other senior offices in the kingdom.'

'I will accept that criticism as soon as you can provide me with any other means by which I could have achieved this.' Roper ploughed on before Jokul could reply. 'We are now committed to this campaign and must set aside our differences to make it as successful as we can. And so far we have encountered just one obstacle.'

'Bellamus of Safinim,' said Jokul, dryly.

'You know of his involvement?'

'It has become very apparent,' said Jokul. 'We know he has informants embedded within our force. That was less of a problem when the Sutherners invaded last year, but in familiar lands he has far more opportunity to impede our progress.'

Roper thought about that. It was as Gray had warned him, many weeks before. The Sutherners were finding ways to fight them. 'So it is him contaminating the water supply?'

'We suspect so,' said Jokul. 'But stopping him is difficult, I admit. The Sutherners have writing, which is a great advantage in this quiet war. And the Kryptea are an order of assassins, primarily, not spies. We have certainly tried to turn Sutherners to our side, but they mostly think us so vile and alien that it is hard to interact with them.

'Things have also become more difficult recently. There appears to be a faction working against the kingdom called the Ellengaest. I find it increasingly unlikely that it is a single person: more likely a group of them. But whoever he, she or they are, they have considerable resources at their disposal.' Jokul suddenly flashed a narrow glance at Roper, as though suspicious he was revealing too much. 'In any case,' he went on delicately, 'it comes down to this. Bellamus has many informants, and we have none.'

Roper knew that *gaest* was the Saxon word for demon, and he had an idea that *ellen* might convey power in some way. It was interesting that this traitor had chosen a Saxon name. 'So we find out who the informants are,' said Roper. 'Who or what Ellengaest is and put a stop to it.'

'Yes,' agreed Jokul. There was quiet for a while.

'How?' asked Roper. 'Planting false information?'

Jokul tutted and took a sip of tea. 'Without spies of our own, we would never know which information had reached Bellamus and which had not. We must simply be vigilant and tight-lipped, Lord Roper. You keep your plans to yourself until we are ready to execute them with utmost speed. Prepare as though there are multiple options you might use; seize one at the last minute and that will limit their abilities to counter them. And then we watch. We see who is behaving irregularly, and make enquiries.'

'That sounds like Kryptean business,' said Roper.

'It is,' said Jokul, crisply. 'You must leave this to us, Lord Roper. I can assure you that Bellamus's spies will become more and more reluctant to help him. On that, you have my word.'

'Will you keep me informed?'

Jokul's pale eyes found Roper's, and he took another small sip from his cup. 'I will inform you once we have made an arrest,' he allowed, at last.

'It would be useful, too, if you told me who you suspect,' Roper insisted.

'Useful for Bellamus,' said Jokul, his voice fading into his cup as he raised it for another sip.

'You don't trust me?'

'I don't *trust* anyone,' replied Jokul. 'Why would you? What foolishness. A childish desire for a confidant. If you do not resist it, you open yourself to disaster.'

Roper looked at Jokul, smiling for a moment. 'So this,' and he waved at Jokul's hunched pose, his slight frown as he addressed Roper, 'all this coldness and distance is you being professional? That is why you are as you are? The consummate Master of the Kryptea, close to no one, vulnerable to nothing, incorruptible.'

Jokul eyed Roper for a moment. 'Perhaps I just don't like you, Lord Roper.'

Roper burst into laughter. Jokul turned his head slowly back to the fire, so tight-lipped that perhaps he was resisting a smile. He had worked so hard, for so long, in a post so lonely. It must be nice, thought Roper, to have that effort recognised just once. He had never liked Jokul, whose methods lacked honour, and whose heart pumped not blood but meltwater. But for the first time, Roper felt respect for him.

'Do what you must,' said Roper, echoing words the Master had once spoken to him.

The contaminated water slowed their progress dramatically. Much of Roper's strategy for this invasion relied on using the legion's fitness and mobility to move rapidly across the landscape, catching sites of Suthern resistance unawares. Now they had to send scouts out for miles in all directions looking for clean water, which they were often unable to find.

This meant they had to spend hours gathering stacks of firewood and laboriously boil what water there was, slowing their progress to a dead crawl. Their food supplies were dwindling rapidly, and Lincylene seemed their only hope of resupplying.

Roper considered this after dark, and whenever he could banish these thoughts, he found Helmec's face before his eyes once more. He explored it, examining the scarred cheek; the pale skin; the helmet, part ripped-off. The twisted neck. There he stopped. He focused on the stars. He remembered Keturah holding her hands up to the starlight in the freyi, hoping it would heal her numbed fingers. He remembered the sense of peace he had felt there, and compared it with the rattling at his ribs that he felt here instead. Part of it was the unsettling sensation of Anakim homesickness which they called *kjardautha*. It grew worse with age, and Roper knew his experience of it would be nothing compared to what his legionaries were feeling.

On their final approach to Lincylene, Roper at last mounted Zephyr so that he could scout ahead with the Skiritai and Gray, and lay eyes on his first Suthern city. He could smell it before he saw it. It was a morning of cold diamond grass and clear spring skies, and that exhausting breeze that blew constantly across Suthdal carried wood smoke, stagnant sewage, mould, sawdust, yeast and a host of other scents that Roper could not identify. He found himself spurring Zephyr harder and harder as they climbed the final hill, pulling ahead of Gray and the Skiritai around him.

At the top, he stopped. He stared. Before him: tightly packed houses, growing towards the light; steep roofs fogged with wood smoke, the passages between the houses thronged. Above the smoke, at the centre of the city, a great timber spire emitted a strange and musical clanging. But Roper barely noticed any of this. His eyes swirled the outskirts of the city, not quite believing what he could see.

Walls.

A stout wooden palisade, studded with stone towers, atop a raised earthen bank with a ditch at its front. Roper recognised one of the smells he had been unable to identify before: cut greenwood. This wall was new. This was why Garrett had ordered the Sutherners to retreat here. The Anakim had thought the walls destroyed, and had brought no siege weapons so that they could travel lighter and faster. The Sutherners had clearly prepared long in advance, and stuffed the city with food, so they would not be easily starved out. The legions would have to enter with ladders, or battering rams, and press themselves into a tight slaughter.

'Ah,' said Gray, reining in beside Roper. 'They've rebuilt their walls.'

'So they knew exactly when we were coming,' said Roper, staring venomously at the city below. 'They evacuated, emptied the lands of food, corrupted our water supply and refortified. We have been brought to our knees already, and we haven't encountered a single enemy soldier yet. Have you ever known such a coherent resistance?'

'Never,' said Gray.

'Bloody, bloody, goddamned Bellamus.'

17

A Broken Crow

It seemed to Salbjorn that their task had become impossible. The captured accomplice, Hagen, was not speaking, though Inger seemed determined to persuade him. They had twice had a fresh trail leading to the assassin, and once lost him in the chase, once been unable to chase at all. And now, Ormur was back training miles from the school, running over the hills, fishing and hunting. Last night he had not even returned, he and his herd staying out in the mountains where Salbjorn and Leon had tried to guard him together. They took it in turns to watch, Salbjorn now returning to the school for some little sleep before he would go to relieve Leon.

It was a bitter morning, and he looked up as he approached the school to curse it. His eye caught on a dark intrusion at the base of the cliff-face: a black mass, with a single figure crouched next to it. 'Here, Guardsman, here!' It was the Master, voice stricken, standing over what seemed to be a vast crow smashed on the ground, feathers waving back and forth in the wind and wings broken beneath it. Salbjorn stopped, confused by the horror dawning on him, and then felt himself being pulled towards it.

'Inquisitor?' He was running and spitting swearwords.

'Inger!' She lay face down, one arm beneath her and legs splayed. It was a position so unnatural that he was sure she must be dead, and cast a look up the cliff from which she must have fallen. 'Master? What happened?'

'She fell!' said the old man. 'She was sitting on the edge and it crumbled off. Help me!' The Master was trying to turn her broken form over, though it seemed to Salbjorn that touching her would only make things worse. But they could hardly leave her here. They heaved her over, Salbjorn leaning close and listening for her breathing. It was there: ragged, irregular but consistent. Her lips were tinged with purple and as the Master moved her swollen wrist, her arms curled up defensively.

'Inger? Can you hear me?' There was no reply. 'We must take her inside, Master!'

Stumbling, gripping and pausing, they manoeuvred her awkwardly to the front of the longhouse and upstairs to the room where Salbjorn himself had lain injured. Salbjorn threw three goatskins down as a bed of sorts and they dragged her on top, covering her with a woollen blanket. When touched, her arms often flexed, but there had been no movement whatsoever from her legs. The two men knelt over her in silence, breathing heavily and saying nothing. The Master dropped his head in his hands. Salbjorn stared upwards and panted for a moment, then returned his attention to Inger. 'I think her pelvis is broken. Help me bind it, or she may bleed internally.'

Salbjorn had very little memory of the next few hours. They did what they could for Inger, but she did not speak and her breathing only grew louder and slower. When at last Ormur's herd returned and Leon stormed into the longhouse to demand where Salbjorn had been, he stopped abruptly at the sight of the Inquisitor, Master and guardsman kneeling on either side.

'By Almighty God, what is this?'

'She fell,' said Salbjorn, not meeting his mentor's eye.

'I don't think she's going to wake,' said the Master quietly.

Leon threw his sword and pack aside and bent to conduct his own examination. 'One of the lungs is gone,' he said brusquely. 'So's the spine. But sometimes that knocks people out for a bit and then they wake up. We'll have to see.'

'I've never seen that,' said the Master.

'You weren't at Lundenceaster,' said Leon. 'A lot of falls. And how did it happen?' he demanded. 'Did anyone see her fall?'

The Master nodded grimly. 'I saw. She was sitting on the edge of the cliff and part of it crumbled. A terrible fall.' He shuddered. 'The poor Inquisitor. When I think of the number of times I've sat where she was sitting . . .'

Salbjorn could feel tears pricking his eyes and he laid a hand on her forehead. Her silver-filamented, feather-braided hair was ragged with sweat, and she coughed suddenly.

'You don't have to stay,' said the Master kindly, eyes on Salbjorn. 'I'll take care of her. Perhaps you should be with the boy?'

'No,' said Salbjorn, waving a hand but unable to face them. 'No, I'll take care of her. Thank you, Master.'

The Master hesitated but eventually nodded. 'I'm so sorry. Tell me if she wakes.'

After he had gone, Leon and Salbjorn both slumped against the wall.

'Where is the boy?' asked Salbjorn, dully.

'Safe,' said Leon. 'Sword drill just outside.' The two lapsed into silence, before Leon shook himself abruptly. 'So what now?' he asked. 'What do we do without the Inquisitor?'

Salbjorn did not reply.

'Wake up,' said Leon, callously.

'Shut up, Leon,' he replied, low and fierce. Leon did, and Salbjorn sat thinking for a long time. 'This is all too much,' he said eventually. 'We thought we were here to assist an Inquisitor in solving a crime. But finding an assassin, who seems to be one of a network at the disposal of this monster

Ellengaest ... This is too much. We need help. Another Inquisitor, at least. More guardsmen.'

'How?' said Leon dismissively. 'The passes are shut. Nobody is coming in or out of the mountains now. Even if we weren't trapped, when was the last time a messenger came here? When will a messenger next come here? The Black Kingdom will be all but drained by now. Everyone will have gone south.'

Salbjorn almost said: *I could go.* He could try and fight through the snow to get word to the Hindrunn of what had happened here. But it was impossible. He was needed here. He could not leave Leon to hold off this assassin alone, in this place which had proved so treacherous. 'It is as you said before,' said Salbjorn. 'Our one lead is the assassin himself. If we can lure him to us, we could capture and interrogate him. We could use the boy.' There was a long silence, broken by the clack of training swords from outside the window. 'As bait,' he added.

Leon did not reply. He was staring at the Inquisitor lying on the floor before him.

Her eyes were open.

18

The Passes Are Shut

'Inquisitor?' whispered Salbjorn, leaning forward. 'Inger?' Her eyes flickered. They were horribly mismatched: one pupil huge and gaping, the other normal. She stared drunkenly at the ceiling for a time and then her head rolled towards Salbjorn. He thought she was looking at him and reached out to her shoulder. 'Inquisitor, it's Guardsman Salbjorn,' he said, not certain she could hear anything. 'You're in the haskoli, in the interrogation room. You fell off the cliff edge.'

Inger's head twisted away and she moved her right arm aimlessly.

Leon and Salbjorn exchanged a glance. 'You'll be well, Inquisitor. It was a big fall but you're doing well. You're holding on.'

Inger said something indistinct. Her head shook a little and she tried again. 'Mushed.'

'We should cool her off,' said Salbjorn. 'She's boiling.' He cleared the rough blanket covering her and she tried to speak again.

'*Mushed?*' repeated Leon, baffled.

Salbjorn had frozen. He looked down at Inger. 'I think she's trying to say "pushed".'

Inger repeated the noise, more forcefully.

'Pushed?' said Salbjorn. 'Is that what you said?'

There came an affirmative groan.

'Pushed by who?' hissed Leon.

But Inger's eyes were shut once more, and her breathing had become ragged again.

Salbjorn and Leon locked eyes. 'That doesn't take an Inquisitor, does it?' said Salbjorn. 'The Master says he saw her fall. She says she was pushed. The old man's up to his neck in this.'

'Right,' said Leon, abruptly. He stood, snatching his sword from its position against the wall and turned for the stairs.

'Where are you going?'

'To do things my way!' bellowed the guardsman, disappearing down the stairs. It was mere moments before he was back, sword glittering in one hand, the other clamped about the Master's robes. The old man was dragged bodily up the stairs, swinging like a pendulum from the garment held at Leon's chest. Face expressionless, Leon raised the Master and then hurled him against the wall. The Master's thin body fairly clattered off the wood and he crumpled at its base, looking up at Leon in disbelief. 'My way!' repeated Leon, furiously, raising his sword beneath the Master's chin. 'By Almighty God, who is Ellengaest? What is this nest of traitors you preside over?'

'Leon, calm!' Salbjorn protested, jumping to his feet.

'You have no idea . . .' gasped the Master, so winded he could barely speak, but his face still calm. 'No idea . . . who you're chasing.'

'Correct,' said Leon. 'But you're going to tell us. *You*, who were once a Sacred Guardsman.' The Master stirred at this, turning his eyes to the floor. 'Who wore the Almighty Eye, who is trusted with the education of our young, and all this time you've been facilitating the deaths of two in your charge! Two that we know of – how many others have you killed and tried to pass off as the playtime of students?'

'I haven't killed anyone,' said the Master, bitterly.

'Leon, calm,' Salbjorn urged again, holding his hands out before him, and certain his mentor was on the verge of losing control.

'What about the Maven Inquisitor?' demanded Leon, pointing at Inger's supine form. 'Do you think she's going to stand up and walk away? Don't lie, you old viper, you pushed her! You have murdered her!'

'He has my son,' said the Master calmly, turning shining eyes up at Leon. 'My boy is held by his men. What would you do?'

Salbjorn looked on in horror, but Leon was unyielding. 'You think your whelp is worth more than the twins whose deaths you're facilitating here? Than a Maven Inquisitor?'

'To me,' said the Master, hopelessly.

'Selfishness is selfishness,' said Leon, indifferently, 'whether for you or for your spawn. You disgrace the Almighty Eye. You disgrace your office.'

The Master stared up at Leon with red-rimmed eyes, shaking his head faintly. 'I know. But what would you have done?'

'Not what you did,' declared Leon.

He and the Master stared at each other. 'I am glad to be discovered,' said the Master. 'It leaves me with the course I should have taken months ago.' And he lunged forward. Leon, evidently assuming he faced an attack, misjudged his reaction and held the sword out. But exactly as he had intended, the Master was impaled on the blade, driving it six inches into his own neck. He slumped back and Leon jerked the sword aside, swearing.

'No!' roared Salbjorn, leaping forward, but the Master was dying. His worn body crumpled in the corner, visibly shrivelling as the blood leaked out of him. 'No! That was our one route to Ellengaest! To preserve the boy!'

'Coward,' spat Leon.

Salbjorn staggered back into the wall and slid down it,

head in his hands. 'What have you done? What a mess! We were trusted with this. What an appalling mess! We've butchered it! We've ruined everything.'

Leon too fell into a seat, staring with loathing at the Master's body. For a long, long while, the loudest noise in the room was Inger's ragged breathing, now approaching something close to a snore. The Master's body was pale and still, and Leon did not even move to stop the advancing tide of blood engulfing his boot.

'I'm sorry,' grumbled Leon, at last. 'I didn't think he was going to do that.'

Salbjorn did not look up. 'What now?' he asked wearily. 'Where can we possibly go from here? We need help.'

'Again,' said Leon, 'the passes are jammed with snow. And we are both needed here. Without us, the boy is doomed.'

'We could send a pair of tutors,' said Salbjorn. 'See if they can get through.'

'I do not think we can rely on the tutors' support any more,' said Leon, staring at the Master's body.

Salbjorn had not considered how this would look to those who had not been present. The Master, with a sacred position in this school, had died violently with only the two of them as witnesses. 'Then our one option is as I said before,' said Salbjorn, bleakly. 'Watch the boy, but from a distance. Use him as bait and wait for the assassin to come to us.'

'And what would Lord Roper say if he knew this was our plan?'

'He's not here,' said Salbjorn. 'And we have run out of choices. To protect him, we have to capture the assassin. And we only have one thing the assassin wants, so let's use it.'

First, however, the guardsmen had to deal with the Black-Cloaks. With as much calm as he was able, Salbjorn went outside and summoned the three tutors he found there up to the interrogation room. They laid eyes on the Master, on the pool of blood in which he lay, and then on Leon's vengeful face and crimson sword-tip. It was only the immense status invested in the Sacred Guard that prevented the tutors declaring a revolt then and there. They ignored Salbjorn's increasingly desperate explanations, backing down the stairs in silence, shock and suspicion on each face.

'Your Master was a coward and a traitor!' Leon bellowed unhelpfully after them.

The two guardsmen were frozen out. Each tutor who returned to the school was informed of what had happened, and immediately distanced themselves from Salbjorn and Leon. They would not acknowledge the guardsmen, hurrying past when Salbjorn tried to address them. They tried to win back some trust by organising a proper burial for the Master (though Leon growled more than once that the treacherous worm did not deserve such respect) but the Black-Cloaks were indifferent to their efforts.

And just as Salbjorn was feeling more isolated than ever before, Inger died. Salbjorn was watching over her when it happened, three days after her fall. Salbjorn wept for her, organising a far more heartfelt burial than the last. Even Leon went quiet at the news and briefly left Ormur unattended to drop a handful of earth over Inger's body. She was laid a little way from the school, head facing east towards the mountains. Salbjorn stayed by her grave for a while after she was buried, curling his fingers into the earth. 'Help us, Inquisitor,' he murmured.

They tried to guard Ormur from a distance and so tempt the assassin close, following the boy out of view as he went through lessons and rituals. But they were not the only ones under pressure, and Ormur's behaviour had grown steadily more reckless. The guardsmen watched from an upstairs window as he underwent a test of endurance in the freezing waters of Lake Etchachan. A fire was lit by the lake, with blankets and hot sheep's milk to tempt the boys out. There was enough milk for about three quarters of the cohort, so the longer they stayed in the freezing water, the greater the chance they would go hungry. However, stay until last of all and you were declared victor, and each member of your herd awarded a circlet of hawk-feathers. Ormur's group won this honour due to the boy's efforts. He stayed in the still waters until his shivering ceased. His eyes began to flicker and the water slid up to his chin, before a tutor seized him beneath his arms and pulled his limp body from the lake.

Ormur had shown such suicidal commitment to every challenge laid in front of him, grimly pushing himself further than any other student.

'I'm going to speak to him,' said Salbjorn, turning away from the window and going for the door.

'He doesn't look good,' said Leon.

The boy had been dragged next to the fire and had a blanket laid upon him. So long had he stayed in the waters that his compatriots had left the fireside to forage. Ormur was left recovering under the gaze of a tutor. 'I'll watch him,' said Salbjorn. The tutor, evidently not wishing to spend any time with the mistrusted guardsman, departed at once. Salbjorn sat next to the boy as the midnight blue left his lips and he roused. He sat up after a time, but kept his eyes down politely, not meeting Salbjorn's gaze. 'Look up at me, boy.'

Ormur raised his eyes as though they weighed the earth. For a heartbeat, he managed to meet Salbjorn's gaze. Then his eyes welled with tears, his head dropped and he began to weep wretchedly. Salbjorn put an arm around Ormur, who sobbed into his shoulder. 'What's happening, boy?' he asked softly.

'I don't know,' Ormur gasped, voice muffled in Salbjorn's tunic.

'Yes you do.' In response, Ormur's cries redoubled. He wept and wept.

'I can't survive this,' he choked.

'Can't survive what?'

'Numa,' gasped the boy. Every word was uttered as a spasm, followed by a hiccough or gasp, as though Ormur were drowning. 'My brother is waiting for me on the Winter

Road. He would not do it without me. I know he's waiting and will not make it to the other side unless I am there.' He turned a ravaged face up to Salbjorn. 'Release me from my oath. I have one thing left to do.'

'Absolutely not,' said Salbjorn. 'I hold you to it, boy. You have sworn not to go after the murderer, and Numa would want you to keep your word. He would want you to endure. Survive, and live for both of you.'

'I can't, release me!'

'No.'

Ormur's tears sprang forth once more. He beat twice, feebly, at Salbjorn's side, and then fell into him once more. Salbjorn held him until the boy was exhausted, his sobs dried and his spasms eased. 'We will avenge your brother together, boy. Yours is the more important part. You will survive the assassin, and frustrate him in his goals. And I will kill him in Numa's memory. Do we have an agreement?' Ormur leaned his forehead against Salbjorn's chest, silent. 'Do we have an agreement, boy?'

'All right,' Ormur breathed.

Idleness was deplored at the haskoli, and Ormur had to forage for his supper or go hungry. Leon and Salbjorn, both stiff from waiting, followed him at a distance down to Lake Avon, watching as he checked his fishing lines.

'Our plan will not work,' said Leon abruptly.

Salbjorn looked at him sourly. 'And why not?'

'Because the assassin knows we're here. He will not believe we've just left the boy to his own devices. It's obvious we're using him as bait.'

Salbjorn almost said that if Leon was pointing it out, it must indeed be obvious. But he restrained himself and said instead: 'Well then. To truly set this trap, we need to be seen leaving.'

'And just leave the boy to fend for himself?'

'Obviously not.' Salbjorn paused for a moment. 'No. I have an idea,' he said eventually. He explained to Leon, and the next day, with much unreciprocated waving towards the tutors, Leon departed the haskoli. He was dressed in the full armour of the Sacred Guard, a great pack resting on his shoulders and beside him walked another figure in guards-man's armour. But it was not Salbjorn. Had anyone been observing the departing duo closely, they would have seen the way one of the guardsmen was only able to walk at a shuffle, his shoulders hunched. They might also have noticed Leon steer him a few times with his hand gripped about the back of his neck. And had they truly known the occupants of the haskoli, they might have recognised the face of the second figure as that of Hagen, the disgraced former tutor.

Salbjorn stayed behind. While he protected Ormur, Leon would take Hagen out of the school and struggle a day through the snows. Over the next two nights, they would then use the darkness to return to the haskoli. To anyone watching the school, it would seem the two guardsmen who had protected Ormur had made a bid to escape via the snow-choked roads, perhaps in response to the assassin's continued absence. Or maybe to get help after the death of the Master and Inquisitor.

Salbjorn hoped it might be enough to tempt the assassin to return, though he was starting to wonder whether he was still in the mountains. Perhaps he had grown tired and fought his way out through the snows. Though conscious of his duty to Ormur, he felt himself relax a little.

The first day, he saw nothing. He followed Ormur from foraging to lessons, trying to keep to undergrowth and shade. At night, he slept as Leon had done, just behind the door to Ormur's quarters.

At dawn, he followed Ormur out for his run. It was hard to keep up with the boy on his injured leg, and while keeping to the undergrowth, and he lost sight of him repeatedly. He was finally forced onto the track above Ormur so that he could catch up, and was running through the snow there for some time before he was able to see the boy below him once more. He stopped, panting, and searched the scene for any sign of danger.

Something he had taken for a shadow beside the path moved. It disappeared behind a large rock. Then emerged again the other side, flickering between the trees: a dark figure, sliding close to the boy's path and then vanishing behind a bank. Salbjorn's heart thumped into life and he scrambled down the slope, making a crashing sprint between the trees to reach Ormur before he and the shadow converged.

Ormur plodded onwards, oblivious to the lethal scramble at his back and the shadow closing in on him. Salbjorn plunged recklessly down the hillside, feet navigating a rush of drops, boulders and trunks. He held the hilt of his sword steady, ignoring the stabbing pains from his weak ankle, and within heartbeats had plummeted to the lakeside, landing on the frozen gravel shore in front of Ormur. The boy started, staring at him. 'Lord?' he blurted. 'What are you doing?' Salbjorn ignored the question, staring over the boy's shoulder. Seventy yards further up the lakeside, a black, stocky figure was hurtling away.

'Back to the school, fast!' he roared, and he took off after the shadow. Before him, the figure dived up the hillside and out of sight, hidden in a narrow gully. Salbjorn plunged after him and the assassin came back into view, still running.

This time, Salbjorn knew, he would catch the figure. It was light. The snow would carry his tracks. Salbjorn wore no armour to slow him, could run in his light leather boots, and though in pain, he was a Sacred Guardsman. This was the first time in weeks that he had run in earnest, but he was damned if some common murderer would best him. By sprint or endurance, he would close this bastard down, learn all he had to tell and then cut his head from his shoulders.

He gripped his sword, and climbed.

19

Thingalith

Spring had brought balmy rain to this part of Suthdal, and the gritty track beneath Bellamus's boots was under an inch of brown water. It had been three days since he had deliberately exposed himself to Slave-Plague, and he had finally accepted he was healthy, and could resume his usual business. He called on their granary – stocked with food 'taxed' from those fleeing to Lincylene – enquired whether they had located a terrier for the rats, was pleased by the response, and passed on to the armoury. It was stuffed with weapons, rough Anakim-bone plates that had yet to be drilled and wired into armour sets, and a growing pile of loot, harvested in the chaos of this latest invasion. The Thingalith would appropriate a portion for themselves, but that did not bother Bellamus. He would have done the same in their position, and they needed compensation for this perilous existence.

A thin, dark-haired woman, muddy-eyed and grave-faced, hailed Bellamus from the end of the street. 'I was coming to find you, Master,' she called, strapping a nose-bag over her horse's head. 'The Anakim have grown tired of stumbling through empty countryside, and finally besieged Lincylene.'

Bellamus smiled at her. 'I'd heard, thank you, Aelfwynn. Do you know how they are doing for water?'

'Their progress has been exceedingly slow, but somehow they limp on, Master. I cannot imagine what they're living off.'

'I fear our enemy are more familiar with surviving in extremes than we are. You've done excellently, though. Stop here, take some food and drink, and refresh your horse. You must be careful from here on. Now they have stopped moving, they will keep an exceedingly close eye on their water.'

Aelfwynn flashed a lean smile, bowed and retreated into the house opposite, which they had transformed into the mess and was kept well stocked with hot stew and bread rolls. Bellamus stayed in the street, eyes on the western hills, vision fogged by the wine that had seen him through his three days' isolation. A distant figure swarmed closer like an ant over flesh, riding purposefully for Brimstream. The rider laboured and spurred, hair streaming out behind them, their horse stumbling twice with exhaustion. As the rider came near, Bellamus recognised her pale face and long red hair. When she had finally clattered into the street, he seized the bridle of her foaming horse and met her eye as steadily as he was able. 'I trust this is important, Marian.'

She nodded. 'Yes, Master. You said to bring word as soon as there were details of the Unhieru weapon shipment.'

'And?'

'They've been dispatched on a road north of the canal, will cross into Suthdal by the final bridge and travel directly there to the Unhieru king.'

'When did you hear of this?'

'They were dispatched yesterday morning, Master. I heard this morning.'

'Defences – do you know how the shipment is protected?'

'There was no word on that, Master,' admitted Marian.

'Never mind, there is not a moment to lose!' declared

Bellamus. 'You've done excellently, forgive me, I must ride. You'll coordinate things here until my return?'

He was gone before she could reply, darting into the mess. 'Thingalith!' he called. 'With me, if you want to save your country and your families! Weapons, armour, food, water: be ready for a four-day ride in a quarter of an hour!' The mess rattled into life, as though he had opened a door to disturb a barnful of rats. Bellamus swept out and back along the street, hammering on each door he passed. 'Thingalith! Thingalith! Ride, ride, ride; you have quarter of an hour! Four days of food, weapons and armour, prepare yourselves this instant!'

Men spilled from the houses, scattering between armoury, larder and stables. 'Where is Garrett?' Bellamus demanded of the throng.

'In the stables, Master,' reported one man.

'Make sure he's ready,' Bellamus ordered. He saw the shock on the man's face; his hesitation as he decided whether he feared Bellamus's or Garrett's wrath more. 'Go,' said Bellamus, and the man fled. 'Stepan?'

'Here, Captain,' said the knight, ducking beneath a door lintel.

'We'll need you, my friend.'

Stepan let out a breath, glancing at the distant hills. 'Where are we going?' he asked, hesitantly.

Bellamus pushed through the scattering Thingalith and into the dark space behind Stepan, beckoning the knight in after him. He turned in the shadow to face his friend. 'The Unhieru armour and weapons shipment is on the road. We have this one chance to disrupt it and delay the Unhieru from joining this war. Who knows, we may even stop them altogether.'

'It will be heavily defended,' said Stepan.

'Of course it will. That's why we need you.' Stepan twisted his head slightly, grimacing, and Bellamus reached a hand up to his shoulder. 'I know you don't want to be here, Stepan.'

'No, Captain—' Stepan began to protest but Bellamus over-rode him.

'No, it's fine,' he said. 'I understand, and you are here as a friend. But I need you now, and Suthdal needs you. Will you ride with us, one more time?'

Stepan took a deep breath. 'Of course, my captain.'

Bellamus nodded. 'Quarter of an hour.' Then he stepped out into the grey light of the street. He had near six hundred men in total and thought a little over two hundred might be available to him now, in this village. He hoped it would do. He hoped the Anakim would think the Sutherners were focused on the unfolding invasion, and that this shipment was not at particular risk, and therefore only lightly protect it to deter brigands. He hoped he could catch them before they crossed into Unhierea. He hoped they were not too late.

Bellamus found chain mail and a short-sword in his quarters and donned both. He stuffed a saddlebag with cheese, smoked pork, several loaves of stale rye, and burst back outside. Horses were clustering at the edge of Brimstream, some warriors already mounted and holding the riderless mounts steady.

Garrett was there. The huge, fever-eyed hybrid was already armoured in clattering bone plates and holding his long-bladed spear, tip sheathed in Anakim skin. Stepan mounted next to him, glittering in chain mail, saddlebags bulging with Anakim-bone plates. Bone-armoured Thingalith rose on all sides, and there was a cheer as Bellamus strode out to them. He banished the lingering nausea of the wine and beamed at them all. 'Ready, my warriors?' he called. 'There is no force as fast as you! No force this light and this powerful, who would be ready at such short notice. Great God, but I'm proud to be your captain!' He strapped his saddlebags to a horse Stepan held for him and mounted, spurring forward at once. 'Move out! We are all there is! Ride, my Thingalith, ride!'

20

Under Siege

Lincylene was surrounded.

Nothing passed through the walls in either direction, though the rams and ladders under construction would remedy this. The local trees were felled (Roper taking satisfaction in imagining the more vigorous Anakim lineages that would replace them) and shaped into clunky siege weapons, thicker than normal as they were made of greenwood.

'But there doesn't seem to be anything else to do,' he complained to Gray. He and the captain sat on the hill where they had first laid eyes on the city. The morning was in its adolescence, and a quilted grey sky hung above them. By Roper's right hand was a scatter of uprooted grass, which he fed absently.

'It is strange to hear you talk like this,' said Gray, leaning back on his hands and staring down at the city. 'You burst upon every hearth with such a sense of momentum, and understand so well how to motivate the legionaries, that I forget how new to you this is. War is mostly about waiting. Brief flurries of extreme activity, bordered by long stretches of nothing.'

'Nothing is bad,' said Roper.

'At war,' agreed Gray. 'It is important at home, as my wife

reminds me, but nobody wants time to reflect before a battle. You need a little time after, but nobody wants it before.'

'Surely nothing, either at war or at home, is time wasted.'

'You should speak to Sigrid about it,' said Gray. 'Or the Chief Historian, if she will answer your questions. That's who Sigrid took her example from. I do not understand it as well as she does, but nobody values pauses and silence more than my wife.'

Roper made a noise of interest.

'She convinces me it is a positive. But that is at home. Before an assault, silence is a terrible thing.'

'So how do we fill it?'

'For the men? With anything. Build more siege weapons than we need. Get them to stockpile firewood, or look for food or water.'

'We could have the bards sing in the evenings,' said Roper.

'Indeed,' said Gray. 'But you, lord, can devote this time to your swordsmanship.'

Roper was intrigued. 'I would like to be a better fighter,' he admitted.

'It is essential if you wish to continue your current leadership style. You place yourself in constant danger and need the skills to survive it. Find someone to tutor you with a blade.'

'I like that idea,' said Roper. 'You? Will you teach me?'

'Somebody better than me,' said Gray, firmly.

'Pryce? He defeated Uvoren one-on-one.'

'Pryce's fighting style works only for Pryce,' said Gray. 'He is a barbarian with a sword. Somebody more technically skilled.'

'But surely he is now the best fighter in the kingdom. After he beat Uvoren, I can't imagine who else might challenge him.'

'Uvoren was one of the best,' Gray agreed. 'But even he admitted Leon in anger would frighten him. And any man would fear Vigtyr's sword.'

'Could even Vigtyr kill Pryce, though?' said Roper. 'Hit him with a cannon and I believe his pieces would reassemble.'

'Bust his head open with a mace, his body would get up and gouge out your eyes,' Gray agreed.

'But if Vigtyr is so technically excellent, why don't I have him teach me?' Roper suggested.

Gray frowned. 'He is impressive,' the captain admitted. 'But not necessarily a good teacher.'

'Unless you can think of someone better . . .'

Gray considered this. 'If Vigtyr can impart a fraction of his knowledge to you, it will be time well used. I can enquire further, but he could fill the gap.'

It had not occurred to Roper that he might be able to dedicate time to self-development. When he had become Black Lord, he had been plunged into a struggle for survival. Every moment saved from assassination, from political disgrace, from Suthern invasion or losing someone close to him, had been a moment to sit and draw breath so that the ringing in his ears might fade and his heart slow. Gray's suggestion had reignited the fierce pleasure and determination that he had known during his education: that of adding to himself. Embracing failure and growth, and stretching himself into something a whit more resilient than he had been before.

When Gray left, Roper requested he summon Vigtyr. The great lictor joined him on top of the hill. Beneath the clouds, they shared a rationed lunch of dried venison and cheese, Roper informing Vigtyr that he was to tutor him in the sword.

'That would be an honour, lord,' said Vigtyr, turning grey eyes to Roper. It was what Keturah had called Vigtyr's 'lazy stare' – a gaze that did not bother to stop at the person he was looking at, but instead passed right through. It was as though he were fixated on the rock behind Roper, rather than the Black Lord himself.

'Then when we have concluded our business with this fine cheese, perhaps we might begin.'

Vigtyr chewed on a mouthful of venison, nodding slowly. His eyes lingered on the sword at Roper's side. 'May I inspect the blade you'll be using?'

Roper unsheathed Cold-Edge and offered Vigtyr its marbled handle. The lictor's precious food was forgotten at once as he took the handle, getting to his feet and testing the grip. Then he held the straight blade out before him, letting the tip drop, gather momentum, and then swing in a full arc back to horizontal. 'She's unusual, isn't she, lord?'

'Unusual?'

'A blade without taper. You would think there'd be a lot of weight at the tip but . . . it feels more balanced than I expected.' Vigtyr ran his eyes along it, not a trace of laziness in his gaze. 'This is very clever craftsmanship.' He glanced down at Roper and then reversed the blade, holding it back towards the Black Lord. 'Come then, lord,' he said. 'Let's see what you can do with it.'

Roper abandoned his lump of cheese and stood opposite Vigtyr. The lictor drew his own sword: the fine tool gifted him by Roper. 'We'll be gentle today,' said Vigtyr. 'Tomorrow, I'll bring a couple of training swords and we can finish with some sparring. First, show me your stance.'

Roper dredged up what he could remember about how to stand and settled with his feet shoulder-width apart, sword extended ahead of him, legs slightly bent and right foot perpendicular to his left. Vigtyr viewed him critically from the front and then toured Roper's stance, walking behind him the better to inspect. 'Oh dear.'

'Not good?' asked Roper.

'No, my lord, not good.' Vigtyr's blade flickered and scored a flat, cold tap first on Roper's inner wrist, then his inner knee, then beneath his shoulder. 'Your wrist is turned too far out,' he reached forward and corrected Roper's sword-hand. 'Your arm is held too far to the side of your body.' He made another adjustment. 'Your right foot is too far forward,' he kicked it back a few inches, 'and your left at too much of an angle.' He kicked Roper's left foot inwards. Then he gave Roper a shove. Roper staggered backwards, stumbling to keep his feet, Vigtyr talking before he had recovered. 'But most of all, you're much too static. Your limbs are like the roots and branches of a tree, and trees are not good swordsmen. You must buzz like a wasp.' Vigtyr raised his own sword and the tip quivered before him. 'Not too hard, not too fast. You will tire yourself. But buzz, and you will move faster and with more accuracy. Stand now, as I showed you, and buzz.'

Roper tried to mimic the posture Vigtyr had shown him, and suffered the lictor's corrections. And then he trembled the tip of his sword in imitation of his tutor.

'Too much tension, you'll be slow and exhaust yourself,' advised Vigtyr. 'Your arm should be loose in flesh, ready in nerve. More on the balls of your feet, you must be ready to move.'

Roper tried to hold all that Vigtyr had said in his mind, but invariably standing on the balls of his feet meant that he forgot the posture Vigtyr had advised. Once he had recovered it, his *buzz* had become too tense again. So it continued, Vigtyr growing steadily more impatient in his corrections of Roper. After a time, he began to show Roper with his sword why he had made a mistake, grazing his knuckles, his wrist, his forearm. Each cut drew a pale line that filled scarlet and began to weep blood. It seeped between Roper's fingers and into his palm, making his grip sticky. Vigtyr was precise in every movement, never cutting Roper more than he intended, and began to rattle off a cold inventory of Roper's abilities. 'You are fast in reaction,' he observed, 'but slow in execution. Your muscle memory is poorly trained. You think too much. Your endurance is good. But slow. Slow, slow, slow.'

Roper did not complain. He would not admit how much the cuts on his arm stung, how heavy his legs and arms were, or how turgid his thoughts had become, saturated with new information. He stayed silent, and kept trying until

Lincylene itself became a gentle source of light, alerting him to the fading sky. Vigtyr glanced after Roper's gaze and nodded to himself. 'We will resume instruction on your stance tomorrow. Only when it has stuck, will we move on. There is no sense building on weak foundations.'

Roper dropped to one knee, laying Cold-Edge on the grass and panting vacantly at the bright sweep, mirroring the sky's last light. Vigtyr offered a bow, but no words of encouragement. 'I have duties to attend, if I may, lord. The same time tomorrow?'

'Yes please, Lictor. Carry on.' Vigtyr left and Roper curled about his stinging hand, breathing heavily. He stared across the hillside, down at the city, sweat cooling his body and the pain oddly sweet. He was there for a long while before a chill breeze persuaded him to move. He stood heavily, scraping together the cold remnants of their lunch left handed, and bundling them into a cloth. There was a little blood on Cold-Edge's blade, so he kept it out of the scabbard and descended stiffly back to the camp.

'Great Almighty, what happened to you?' demanded Keturah, eyes on his red right hand. She was kneeling by their hearth, stacking freshly split wood over the embers.

'Sword training with Vigtyr,' managed Roper.

'He's shredded you!'

'They're not deep,' said Roper, dropping the cloth bundle and his sword by the hearth. He dropped after them, turning to look at Keturah. 'You're making the hoosh? Can I fetch water?'

'You can sit still,' said Keturah. 'Your hand needs treating.' Roper sat obediently as Keturah gathered water, clean linen strips and a bundle of herbs she had gathered at the freyi. She poured the water into a pot, set it to warm by the fire and added dried yarrow and betony.

'What have you been doing?' Roper asked.

Keturah shrugged. 'Assisting the Chief Historian. But I spoke to Vigtyr's new woman just now.'

'Oh, yes? She's here too, is she?'

'With the baggage train,' explained Keturah. 'Adras, she's called, and she's a brazen sort.'

'Coming from you?'

'Lewd, even,' said Keturah, with relish. 'I confess I did not entirely enjoy her company. I am baffled, Husband. She's no great beauty, and not the personality Vigtyr is usually seen with. He likes his women sickly sweet.' Keturah shuddered ostentatiously.

'That didn't seem to work for his previous wives. How did they meet?'

'They were childhood friends,' Keturah explained. 'They lived close to one another, just above the Abus.'

'So maybe their relationship was formed when they were both very different people,' said Roper.

Keturah tutted, unsatisfied with the response. 'Perhaps. When I have seen them together though, Vigtyr always looks uncomfortable.'

'That's interesting,' said Roper.

Keturah tested the temperature of the stewing herbs, first with her fingers, then she tutted at her numb extremities and dipped an elbow in. She was evidently satisfied, for she plunged Roper's hand into the hot water and scrubbed at it with a pinch of yarrow, stripping away the dried blood. Roper closed his eyes at the sting but Keturah took no notice save to tartly instruct him to open his fist. When she was done, she removed his hand, dried and wrapped it in the linen strips, securing it with a tight knot. The fire was roaring now, and Keturah went to fetch Roper's cloak, draping it around his shoulders. 'Thank you, Wife, but the guardsmen will be back soon, and I can't let them see me like this.'

'You are absurdly proud,' she said disdainfully.

'And you're not?'

She laughed delightedly, ever unable to resist a barb.

Roper began to clean and oil Cold-Edge. The sting of his hand was much reduced by the bandages and he had sheathed his sword long before the guardsmen began to return in pairs and fours. Gray arrived with Pryce and the two came to sit by Roper. 'What happened to your hand, lord?' asked Pryce.

'Training, today,' said Roper. 'Vigtyr is tutoring me in the sword.'

'And what did he do to your hand?' asked Gray.

'Just a couple of nicks.'

'Why would he do that?' asked Gray flatly.

Roper shrugged. 'To show me where I'm going wrong.'

'He can do that without incapacitating you. I will find someone else.'

'I want to keep trying with Vigtyr,' said Roper firmly.

'There is nothing you will learn from him,' said Pryce scornfully.

'He is a good enough swordsman that it is worth trying and that's an end of it,' said Roper. He had no wish to be treated like a child and would choose his own tutor. But more than this, he liked the idea of learning from one so accomplished as Vigtyr. 'Where have you two been?'

Pryce stayed silent, evidently dissatisfied with Roper's brusque tone.

'I took them running over the hills,' said Gray. He too sounded a little distant, and Roper placed a hand on his shoulder.

'A long way?'

'No. *Lung-busting*. They've earned their supper.' *Lung-busting* was the term for the legionaries' close-battle training. They would don packs, find a hill, run to the top and then wrestle each other to the ground. This was repeated again and again until the soldiers were retching, spluttering and kneeling, and still it could not replicate the exhaustion of the battle-line. Being strong and good with a sword was important in the first forty heartbeats of a fight. And after that, fitness surpassed all other virtues. A fit but limited warrior could defend until he had outlasted his opponent, and then finish him.

'We had a long run back though,' Gray finished.

'Pryce is upset because he came last,' put in another guardsman.

'I am a sprinter,' said Pryce, loftily.

Keturah laughed. 'What? You've never mentioned, Cousin.' The guardsmen around the fire laughed gleefully. Roper stayed silent. He just admired Keturah in the fire's glow, smiling to himself.

His mood was soured by Gray delivering news that he had learned on his way back through camp. 'We've had to assemble a baggage train to get fresh water, lord,' he said. 'Every stream around this campsite is corrupted.'

Roper stared into the fire. 'We will kill that man. The sooner the better. How far away is the nearest clean water source?'

'Leagues,' said Gray. 'Sturla has set up a wagon-relay to keep a supply coming in to camp. But once Bellamus realises that we're so reliant on that water source, it'll turn bad as well.'

'There's no need for that,' said Roper. He nodded to a small patch of woodland to the south. 'Alder and willow over there. And there were more north and west too. Must be lots of water below the surface. Dig some wells there and we can be assured of uncontaminated water.' The Sutherners might rely on open water sources, but they had long been uprooted from the land.

'What do you suppose they're thinking in that city?' asked one guardsman, staring at the dark walls of Lincylene. 'Do you think they're scared?'

'Of course they're scared,' said Pryce.

'Then why haven't they surrendered?'

'We haven't asked them, I suppose,' said Roper, thoughtfully. 'Maybe we should. Our case is compelling.'

'We could certainly make it so,' said Gray.

Roper nodded slowly. 'Tomorrow, then. We'll ask.'

As he lay down to sleep that night, Roper anticipated his

next lesson with Vigtyr. He was half compelled by the effort; half in dread at the inevitable pain. His limbs were still weary, his hand still throbbed and rest was an uncommonly sweet prospect. He entwined himself with Keturah, she softer in gesture than word, and was asleep almost at once.

When he awoke, Roper went to ask Lincylene for its surrender.

He rode straight for the main gate. Gray was on his right, holding a fluttering banner of ragged white silk, and Tekoa, wings affixed to his shoulders and the Wolf's Head banner of the Black Lord held over his head, on his left. Roper rode Zephyr, his immense grey destrier. The beast had been a wedding present from Tekoa and was now dressed in yards of malicious barding: steel plates dripping from the horse like ice. Astride the beast, Roper rode head and shoulders above his companions, dressed in his own bright armour and draped in a black cloak streaked with lightning. Keturah had arranged that after the Battle of Harstathur, when their forces had been delivered by a shocking ethereal bolt. Strangely it had improved Roper's reputation above any talent he had displayed. The legionaries were pious, and to them Roper was not just skilled: he was blessed.

The three horsemen stopped in front of the city gates, just beyond bowshot. Behind them Roper had ordered six legions – fully thirty thousand men – to assemble in armour, their horrid and varied banners hanging overhead. They stood in silence some two hundred yards distant, just waiting.

Roper remembered his first parlay with the enemy less than a year before. How he had sheltered behind his father's shoulder, distracted by the charismatic Captain of the Guard and in shock at the Suthern faces before him. Now he drummed his fingers on his saddle, staring impatiently at the gates before him, which had started to open. As they had for Kynortas, a huge number of Suthern knights were emerging to greet Roper, perhaps fifty riding beneath their own swirling white banner.

Nobody negotiates in negotiations. It is an exercise in intimidation.

Roper and his companions did not move, waiting for the knights and whoever it was they guarded to approach. At their centre rode a figure in fur and chain mail, a thick golden chain draped over his shoulders. As the Suthern delegation drew near, a rhythmic thumping began at Roper's back. He did not turn. It was the sound of his legionaries stamping their feet at the speed of a slow heartbeat. *Boom. Boom. Boom. Boom.*

The central figure, the furred lord, reached Roper and raised a hand in a greeting which was not returned. 'You must be the Black Lord,' he said in Saxon.

'I don't know who you are,' replied Roper in the same language.

'Almund,' replied the man. 'Mayor of Lincylene.' Almund had a freckled face surrounded by hair and beard the colour of rotting iron. His nostrils were flared and his chest rose and fell rapidly, though with fear or anger Roper could not yet tell.

'That will do,' said Roper. 'We have come to offer your city the chance to surrender, Almund. You will open your gates, pile your arms and armour outside and disgorge your fighting men to our custody. We will take what we need from the city, and your weapons of course, dismantle the walls and move on. None of your inhabitants need suffer unduly.'

Boom. Boom. Boom. Boom.

'If you resist, every single soul inside Lincylene will die.'

Almund listened to this offer with a growing smile and at the end emitted an incredulous noise, halfway between laugh and gasp. He was furious, Roper realised, but also immensely frightened. 'Ah! We were warned you would come, Lord Roper,' he replied. 'We have been stockpiling food for weeks. Our walls are fresh and strong, and infested with fighting men. And it will not be long before the Suthern army has been gathered and comes to our aid. It would be better for you by far if you turned away, crossed that vile river of yours, and returned to the nightmare forests which spawned you.'

Roper threw back his head and laughed. As though it were a signal, the legionaries at his back growled into song. Almund would not be able to understand the words, but it moaned into life like some terrible piped instrument, swelling with the evident impatience of thirty thousand wild warrior people. The thumping continued beneath it all, smashing rhythmically and regularly like the heartbeat of the earth itself.

From a land that lies in shadow
In pitch-dark and glaring light,
Where each footstep must be silent,
And each deed's in Holy Sight.
By not light but ancient custom,
Are we guided through these lands.
From a place where fear is different,
Where sole hope your comrade's hand.

It was the 'Hymn Abroad': the legions' darkly humorous response to their homesickness. The Deep Historians taught that the war-hymn was the very origin of music: a powerful incantation for unity and intimidation, and the last remnants of the magic which suffused Albion when the world was young. Though its potency had faded with the rest of the magic that the Anakim had once commanded, Roper could still feel its power. It was something the Sutherners, who approached battle in silence, seemed to have forgotten. 'That's a fine sentiment, Almund,' he said. 'But do you not have a duty of care to those in your city? Come now, if you force us to break in, we will kill you all. It will save us a lot of death in the future if your people learn now what happens to cities who resist. There are no survivors.'

Almund smiled a horrible, twisted reply to Roper. 'And

you're telling me we won't all die anyway if we let you through those gates?'

'We are coming through those gates anyway, Almund,' said Roper. 'Whether you allow us or not.'

Bid farewell to sun and daytime,
Bid farewell to stars and night,
We're the ending of your nation,
And your god who shone so bright.
The time has come for hard choices,
If you can, you must decide
What to resist, what to accept,
If to fight or step aside.

'And if I treat with you demons?' asked Almund, his voice raised over the savage chanting of the legions. 'Make a pact with you in the hope of saving my own life? How will I answer to my God?'

'You will find the words, I'm sure. Tell Him you had no choice.'

The mayor still wore his bitter smile. 'Whatever you are, whatever you can do, whoever your friends are, whatever you represent, I know this: you are my enemy. I feel that in my guts and heart and bones. Above anything else on this earth, you are worth fighting. I will take my chances in battle.'

'That is brave indeed,' said Roper, nodding down at Almund. He dug his heels into Zephyr slightly so that the beast stirred and clinked in his barding. 'And I am glad to hear you say so.' He grinned again. 'It is necessary, you know, to ask for your surrender. But these men behind me,' Roper raised a careless hand to indicate the growling legions, 'they love to fight Sutherners. I am only the handler, and I am not sure I could have held them back.' He turned Zephyr away, Tekoa and Gray falling in behind. 'I wish you good luck.'

21

The Quiet War

Queen Aramilla had discovered many years before that a life of nobility did not suit her. Her husband was a king, her father an earl, and having known nothing but extravagance all her life, it bored her. Security seemed another word for restriction, and adoration made her wish for nothing so much as solitude. One could see it in the muted expressions of her harsh and beautiful countenance; the nodding of one satin slipper, tapping at the floor; in the strings she identified and tugged in those near to her. Most of all, one could see it in the risk which she courted, a little more each day.

So it was that she sat alone in a candlelit hall, shadows cast long over the floor by a popping fire of pine logs, translating a note cyphered in the hand of an outlaw and an upstart. Over the parchment lay a fenestrated wooden frame, one of only two copies in existence. She had one, Bellamus the other, and with it she could illuminate the relevant letters among the coded ink he had sent her that morning, concealed in a book. There were sixty thousand legionaries south of the Abus, she read. Northern Suthdal was overrun, and the Anakim had turned to Lincylene. There they had discovered the walls, which she had petitioned the king to construct. The note finished with an opaque reference to a weapon that the upstart considered trialling. It showed catastrophic potential and, if effective, he was not sure whether it would be proper to use it.

That news elicited the merest flick of her eyebrows. Bellamus had never been much concerned with honour, and she could not imagine a weapon he might baulk at using. Had the sense not been so clear, she might have thought she had mistranslated the cypher. It leaked isolation and exhaustion as clearly as if the page were stained with tears.

She was just trying to decide how much she might reveal to the king, whether her fear of the Anakim outweighed her desire to see one in the flesh, when the door hiccoughed. It rebelled briefly against its latch before settling back into the frame, the fire flaring slightly with a new draught. Someone had opened the door at the end of the corridor outside. Aramilla stood suddenly, thrusting the wooden coding-frame beneath a cushion beside her, and snatching the message from the table. She strode to the fire, balling the parchment and thrusting it through an iron-linked spark-curtain and onto the flames. It landed atop a log, in such a cool part of the fire that it would take a long while to burn, but she had no time to move it, for the latch on the door behind her had started to lift. She rearranged the iron curtain and dropped her arms by her side as she heard the door swing open.

She turned her head deliberately slowly, as though she had been caught gazing vacantly into the flames, and saw her husband, King Osbert, shuffle in. He was dressed as ever in that preposterous bear fur and a gilt-rimmed helmet, his mighty eyebrows two dark blotches on his shadowed face. 'My love,' she said, giving him a short smile and turning back to the flames. The parchment had begun to unfurl, the edges smoking and the coded letters clear at its centre. She turned away, trying to regain some composure as the king dragged out a seat at the table she had occupied a moment before. It was cluttered with several goblets, a decanter, half a dozen needles and stacks of books and parchments. They were histories, philosophies and biblical readings: given to her by the king for her instruction. He hefted the decanter and filled a plum goblet for himself, taking a draught as she came to sit opposite him.

'How have you found your readings, dear woman?' he asked, goblet clunking to the table and gesturing at the books piled around them.

Aramilla gathered herself, trying to forget the note smouldering in the fire. 'I particularly enjoyed this,' she said, plucking a parchment which she had skimmed earlier that morning. 'How interesting that the Frankish once worshipped and venerated the mountain Anakim.'

'Ah,' said the king. He began a melodic instruction: 'Yes indeed. There was a time that fervour swept all Erebos, when people began to turn away from the one true God in their fascination with the Anakim. Part of their magic, I believe. Their power was stronger in the old days, and they could weave a spell to enthral whole nations of people. Only through faith in God, and by burning their feathers, are we safe from that threat.'

Aramilla nodded. 'We are fortunate to live in this more holy age.'

The king's head was bobbing sagely. 'Indeed, indeed. There is much more to be found here,' he said patting the pile of books before her. 'You must keep reading; it is a most illuminating period. I sent the same texts to your father, who was kind enough to say he was greatly fascinated.'

The only way that might be true, thought Aramilla, *is if they make a particularly unusual colour when burning.*

'This is a great secret,' continued the king, leaning in conspiratorially, 'but I have named him commander of the force that will repel the Anakim.'

'You do us all a great honour, my love,' she replied dutifully. She had known for days that Earl Seaton was to take charge of Suthdal's defence. 'I suppose there are no more generals experienced in fighting the Anakim.'

'Not since Bellamus and the Eoten-Draefend turned on me, as I was warned they would,' said the king, his head suddenly bowing. 'I am too trusting, sweet woman. Too kind. I should have listened to those who doubted them and said a hybrid and an upstart were not to be trusted.'

'When is my father to march against the Anakim?'

'He does not believe it is wise to meet them in open battle,' said Osbert. 'Instead, he will strip the land and withdraw our forces, weakening them through starvation. We have worked to fortify the towns for months now. They will have to prise open each one, and we will not face them on the field until they are nearly defeated already.'

Aramilla pretended fascination, though none of this was new to her. She and Bellamus had developed this strategy together, and she had delivered it piecemeal to her father in the form of vague musings and offhand comments. 'That sounds most wise, my love. I dare feel hopeful.'

Just then, the fire gave a loud pop, causing King Osbert to start violently. A flurry of sparks burst clear of the flames, most arrested by the iron curtain but some making it through the gap where the edges did not quite meet. And coughed out among them came the half-burnt note from Bellamus. It landed on the floor in front, surrounded by half a dozen embers, glowing like fierce chips of ruby. The king glanced at the fire, but did not immediately seem to register the paper that had been spat onto the floor.

'It is working well at Lincylene,' blurted Aramilla, trying to draw his attention away from the treacherous note lying before the fire. 'Without the walls, the Anakim would have been able to take the city and replenish their supplies.'

The king looked back at her, taking a breath which he never quite seemed to release. 'You believe the Anakim have reached Lincylene?' he asked, goblet clutched to his breast.

'What?' But she knew she had slipped. Bellamus, with his army of informants, sometimes pre-empted the Anakim movements and sent her word of what they were going to do some days before the news reached Lundenceaster. She usually kept this information back until it was more common knowledge, but distracted, she had made a mistake. She tried to think of something to say, meeting the king's narrowed gaze across the dark table.

'What is it that you've heard?' he said, after a long moment.

Aramilla still could not reply, every nerve bent towards the smouldering note lying just feet away on the floor. Above all, she must keep him away from that. 'Just that Lincylene is besieged.' she said at last. 'You didn't know? I heard tell of it this morning.'

'Where?' The words might have sounded normal from another man's lips. But he so often spoke with a tone of indulgent benevolence that its absence threatened like a roar. Her husband had been desperately paranoid ever since he had heard the news of Garrett's betrayal, and that he and Bellamus were in cahoots.

'Just some kitchen gossip I caught,' she said. 'Maybe just a rumour then,' she added. 'Maybe it isn't true.'

The king continued to observe her in silence. 'You have always known a great deal about this war,' he said, very quietly. 'A very great deal.' He got clumsily to his feet, knocking over his chair and clutching the goblet to him. He stared at Aramilla once more, and then turned his back on her, shuffling back to the door.

She dared not move, fearing that if she drew his attention back towards her, it might snag on Bellamus's message. He lifted the latch and shambled through the door, which rattled shut behind him.

She let out a breath, knowing that his trust in her had been eroded, but still relieved he had not found the note. She prayed that a formal messenger bearing news of Lincylene's siege arrived soon, and then it might just appear the kitchen gossip was faster than the official heralds, as it sometimes was. If not, she might be able to pass it off as a rumour. But whatever she did, it would be difficult to regain his trust, which she relied on now more than ever.

She stood, removing the coding-frame from its hiding place beneath the cushion and tucking it into a pocket of upholstery concealed beneath her chair. She was about to return Bellamus's note to the fire, but stopped abruptly.

The latch on the door before her had lifted once more.

The dark boards swung open, and a black figure slipped inside: the Earl Seaton.

There was barely any particular in which Aramilla resembled her father. Where she was golden-haired, lined and freckled by the sun, Seaton was black-haired, pale-faced and lean as an arrow. His joints moved altogether too freely, as though his wrists, hips, knees and elbows were fastened with string. His clothes were black and closely tailored, and his neck and fingers encrusted with gold. The only thing they shared was a look of frequent, callous amusement, which he wore now. 'Ah, Daughter, I thought I'd find you here. His Majesty seems a little perturbed,' he noted, coming to join her at the table. She hesitated, unable to resist one final glance at the note, still lying in front of the fire, before she sank back into her chair.

The earl removed the stopper from the decanter and sniffed the contents briefly. 'Heavens,' he said, wrinkling his nose and returning the stopper. He glanced up at her. 'Did you say something to upset him?'

'Just a rumour I'd heard, that the Anakim have made it to Lincylene,' she said, shrugging. 'It seemed to make him suspicious.'

Seaton tutted, sliding into a seat opposite her. 'He is always suspicious these days. Ever since Garrett and that *upstart* turned on him, he sees treachery everywhere.'

'So I'd noticed.'

'Well quite,' he said, with that look of callous amusement. 'Wrapping him around your finger must be getting increasingly difficult. I must confess, when I arranged your marriage

I didn't think I was turning our king into quite such a puppet.' He gave a tinkling laugh like an instrument of glass. 'I should probably arrest myself for treason.'

'It must be disappointing that you were not able to enslave him yourself,' said Aramilla, coldly.

He tapped his teeth thoughtfully with a fingernail. 'I daresay that would make this campaign easier. He veers so wildly between wanting to appease the Anakim and all-out assault. Do you know what he suggested to me the other day?' Aramilla tried to indicate that she did not care, but her father went on. 'That we should arm the residents of Lundenceaster and march every one of them to battle in the north.' The fire popped once more, and the earl glanced at it, spying the slight gap in the spark-curtain. 'These absurd pine logs,' he said testily. 'There should be a law against them on royal premises.' He stood and Aramilla rose abruptly opposite him, but the earl did not notice. He strode to the fire and twitched the edges of the curtain together.

Then he froze.

He bent, and plucked the singed encrypted message from the floor. He inspected it for a long while, his back to Aramilla, she standing quiet behind him. He turned to face her, black eyes boring into hers, and holding the note delicately between his fingers like the tail of a struggling rat. 'What is this?'

The silence which followed was the most corrupted and violent that Aramilla had ever known. Her heartbeat, the blood through her ears, the crackling of the fire: none of these could touch it. It shrieked around her and she stared open-mouthed at her father, but could think of no answer that would sound convincing.

'I think we'd better talk, my dear, don't you?' said the earl, stepping to the table.

'What's that?' Aramilla managed at last. The only response it drew from the earl was a grim laugh. He steered her back into the chair with cold hands and was about to take a seat himself, before thinking better of it. He circled on the spot instead and stood opposite her, gazing down at the note.

'So,' he said coldly, meeting her eye, the note shaking a little in his hand. 'So. This is his signature, isn't it? The upstart. Bellamus.' He shook the note again, more rage in his voice than she had ever heard before.

'I know nothing about that note,' she said obstinately, staring back at him. The earl could not decipher it, not unless he knew about the frame beneath her chair. 'You are getting ahead of yourself, Father.'

Seaton straightened up a little, recoiling from her with an expression on his face she had never seen before: disappointment. 'You think so, do you? I will tell you why His Majesty is so suspicious of you: because you know far more than you should. You always have. And you must know what the rumours are about the two of you. You must know what they *suspect.*' He balled up the note and thrust it into his jerkin. 'How could you not? I face those rumours every day. In court, I must suffer the knowing smiles of Lord Sutton and Bishop Widukind, telling me: "Now, now Seaton, how can you stand there so mighty when we both know your daughter is debasing herself with a commoner?" But not just any commoner: a foreign weasel, dragging himself up into the company of his betters. Our enemy. Don't lie to me.'

Despite herself, Aramilla felt her face burn. 'The note proves nothing,' she said coldly. 'You cannot decipher it.'

Seaton nodded to himself, evidently taking her words as confirmation. He stared down at her for some time, chewing on his lip. 'Oh, my daughter,' he said in a softer tone. 'I know you like your games, but I thought you had more discipline than this. I did not think you would so disgrace your family . . . I did not think you would do this to me.' He paused again, staring at her. 'And I now stand between you and the executioner's block. I must admit . . . I am tempted . . . I am tempted . . . If your ugly deception is to reach daylight, I would prefer it came from me.'

Aramilla had frozen. She had known her father would be
disgusted to learn of her relationship with Bellamus, but not
thought he would entertain her execution. 'I am your daughter,' she said, the shock in her voice real.

The earl gave an enraged laugh. 'Indeed. Do you love him?'
he asked suddenly. 'The upstart?'

'No,' she said through gritted teeth.

'Well that's something,' said the earl. 'If you are to stay
alive and our family is to survive this, our only option will
be to kill him. For now, we may as well make use of his information.' He let out a breath. 'Well, Daughter, here is how we
shall conduct this affair from now on. If I can possibly avoid
this family falling to your actions then I shall. Every message
you receive from the upstart will come directly to me and I
will use it to banish the Anakim. You will not tell him that I
have discovered your secret. And if you behave, if you can
restrain yourself, perhaps I will be able to keep this from the
king.'

'But all you have is a senseless piece of paper,' objected
Aramilla. 'I am a queen, Father. You cannot blackmail me
with that.'

'Yes,' said the earl grimly, 'I definitely can. You have noted
how exceedingly suspicious His Majesty is. An encoded
message that you have tried to destroy will be more than
enough proof for him.'

'If you—'

'Yes, yes,' said the earl, waving a hand dismissively and
turning away. 'You'll be able to make me sorry, I'm sure. I
will assume you've said all that.' He strode to the door and
turned back to her, gripping the handle. 'You have always
lacked a sense of perspective, Daughter. So subtle and sophis-
ticated, able to string men and women along as marionettes
for your whims. But for all that, you are still a child, driven
by fickle and insubstantial desires. That is why you have
compromised yourself. I have never expected much from
you. But I expected more than this.'

Aramilla blinked at that. 'We are family,' she said. 'Connected whether you like it or not. This secret will keep, and as you say, we need Bellamus.'

'I do not need *him*,' snarled the earl.

Aramilla changed tack. 'But we are connected, Father,' she said. 'What makes you think you would survive my fall?'

Amusement diluted the earl's rage. 'Look at you twist. There is no part of you that I trust not to turn on me when it suits you. I watched you grow up a vengeful snake and am fully aware that all you've managed since then is to construct a mask between you and the king. A forked tongue still passes between your lips. We will be doing things my way. Write me a report, everything Bellamus has told you in full. If at any stage I suspect you are holding something back from me, I will see to it that your husband finds this message. You must hope Bellamus keeps you well informed.' He cast her one last look of contempt and opened the door, passing into the corridor outside, his shadow slipping after him just before the door rattled shut.

'You are mistaken, Father,' said coldly to the closed door. 'I am not a child any more.' She retrieved another piece of parchment from the far side of the room, and began a message to Bellamus.

22

The Rock

It was a wolf of a day; grey and fierce. Beneath iron clouds so thick that the grass and trees were drained of colour, Bellamus lay on his stomach, peering across a valley. 'Are we ready?' By his side, Stepan gave a brief nod. Beneath them, a wagon train crawled along the valley, accompanied by eighty clanking legionaries: a fully armed and armoured century. Each wagon was dragged by a pair of massive Anakim horses and rocked and jolted over the stones in the track. The sound was of a stream: the squeak and trickle of axles and iron-rimmed wheels. Their loads were covered, but Bellamus knew that the wagons carried armour and weapons fit for giants. Thousands of them.

Across the valley was a small golden dot. It was Garrett's blond shock. Invisible from the small column below, he raised a spear, holding it horizontally over his head. He was ready.

On either side of the valley, Bellamus had positioned a hundred mounted Thingalith. Their horses' hooves were wrapped in leather to silence their approach until the last minute. Though they outnumbered these legionaries two to one, they must be swift and sudden when they attacked. Otherwise Bellamus might lose a hundred men, irreplaceable under the circumstances. They would wait until the wagon train had reached the next section of the valley, which had sides shallow enough that they could ride down them with their leather-wrapped hooves and not risk falling. Bellamus would lead a group from one side, Garrett the other, and they would smash the wagon train between them.

Sweat beaded on Bellamus's brow and ran down his back. He signalled to Garrett with a horizontal sheathed sword – *Continue* – and crawled back from the rim of the valley. He passed the sword back to Stepan, and when they had retreated far enough, rose to a hunched run, making for the band of horsemen who waited a hundred yards back from the valley's edge. Each of them wore overlapping Anakim-bone plates, a helmet with a long horsehair tail and carried a spear.

Strangely, there was a muffled pounding blossoming behind Bellamus. It grew nearer and resolved into rhythmic hoof beats. He and Stepan threw each other an aghast look as a roar like a waterfall enveloped them, and they realised what the noise must mean. 'He isn't?' said Stepan.

'He's insane,' said Bellamus.

Garrett was attacking early.

One thing to do. Bellamus turned to the horsemen before him.

'Go!' he shouted. 'Go, go, go!' The horses lunged forward, driving straight at Bellamus and for the valley rim at his back. One rider stayed behind, reserving two mounts for Bellamus and Stepan. Bellamus outstripped Stepan in his rattling bone plates, buffeted by the tawny flood thundering past, heading for the valley rim. He reached his horse and was not sure how he mounted it. One moment he was running towards it and the next he sat in its saddle, as though he had flown onto his mount. He and Stepan had agreed that when the need arose they often did things with no idea how to repeat them in calmer moments. He spurred forward, passing Stepan and pursuing the Thingalith who had begun to drop out of sight, into the valley.

Bellamus could not quite credit what Garrett had done. This was no mistake, the cloven-nosed monster simply could not resist the imminent savagery, and now their attack was a mess.

Over the lip of the valley he plunged, into the chaotic slash below. The hoof-wraps were too slippery for the gradient here and five horses stumbled as he watched, spinning, collapsing and sprawling down the valley sides; rolling over their riders and whinnying frantically. Opposite, Garrett's band had already streamed down to the valley floor and streaked through the wagon train, spears lowered like lances. Bellamus saw two legionaries hurled flat; three Suthern horses felled by Anakim long-swords and Garrett, helmetless and blond, marauding alone ahead of his men.

Then Bellamus's horse slipped.

There was a desperate, plunging sensation and images snatched through his head. The ground rushing towards him.

The sky above.

Two flailing hooves, jerking past his jaw.

The flank of his rolling horse, clods of grass flying up after it.

A hard, flat rock, rushing towards him.

It smashed into Bellamus's cheek and set his head spinning on his shoulders. Either the images ceased, or he ceased to register them, but he kept tumbling down the valley, aware of the *ooph* and impact of his chest as he bounced and rolled. There was sound too: shouts, screams, his own desperate grunting, the ring of swords, and hooves falling all about him with the force of shooting stars. The tumbling finally ceased and he sprawled somewhere flat and grassy. His mouth was full of the taste of blood and dirt, and his face pressed into the earth.

He tried to breathe, but could not. It was as though his chest was contained in a tight sheath of leather. Winded only, he prayed. He twisted onto his back and tried to haul in a breath, but still it would not come. Only then did he realise that he could not see. He scrabbled at his eyes, trying to clear them of blood, but something was wrong. The blood kept coming and whatever was beneath his left hand did not feel like an eye. It was rough, irregular, hot and soaking. But he could see with his right now, as the blood was scraped clear. There was a figure drawing towards him.

Bellamus sat up, scrambling back as the figure grew huger and huger, dark-haired and unmistakably a Black Legionary, a heavy blade grasped at its side. Bellamus clutched at his belt and realised he had no weapon. He tried to stagger to his feet, but stumbled, and twisted back to face his attacker.

Abruptly, the legionary was hurled to the floor. A horse. A careering horse had ploughed into him, smashing the warrior to the ground, and a bone-armoured hero jumped from its back. It raised a heavy two-handed sword, decapitating the legionary at his feet with a fervour that suggested it might rise supernaturally if its body retained any connection to its brain.

It was important to Bellamus, very important, even through his efforts to breathe, that he should hold a hand protectively over his left eye. He did so, staring up at his rescuer, who turned to him. 'Can you stand, Captain?'

'Stepan.'

'Can you *stand*?'

Bellamus tried to answer, but suddenly an arm was thrust over Stepan's shoulder and wrapped around his neck. The knight was dragged backwards and hurled to the floor, a Black Legionary, unarmed, dropping on top of him and clutching filthy fingers about Stepan's throat. Bellamus's heart roared in fear and he staggered upright, directing his body at the Anakim who was choking his friend. He was so unsteady that he had barely any control and he began to topple over. In one last effort, he aimed himself at the Anakim, hand still clutched at his eye, hurling himself headlong at the legionary and clashing heads. The Anakim's was like a lump of

granite and Bellamus fell aside. His intervention had changed
something though, and Stepan managed to produce a dagger
from somewhere which he plunged again and again into the
base of the Anakim's neck. Blood was spurting over the fighters and the Anakim collapsed atop the knight.

There was a whine in Bellamus's ears from the vast noise
about them, all of which he heard as though underwater.
Before him, two panicked horses were straining and straining, tipping their wagon onto one wheel and then over in a
great tumbling and clanking of metal. A Black Legionary
was caught in the steel avalanche and crushed to the ground
where his top half flailed and struggled, trying to prise himself loose.

Stepan had risen and offered Bellamus a blood-drenched
hand. 'Rise, Captain!'

Bellamus tried. It was slow, and he staggered, but Stepan
caught him. Then he surprised Bellamus by lifting him bodily into the saddle of his horse: one of those achievements he
would struggle to repeat in ordinary circumstances. But
these were not ordinary.

From the vantage point of the horse, Bellamus's uncovered
eye roved the mess this attack had become. His men could
not move their horses properly, trapped between the tight
valley walls and the wagons, and most were knotted together,
unable to escape beyond their own comrades. Some of the
Anakim fought alone, where they were surrounded and
hacked down, but two score had condensed about a pair of
wagons and resisted fiercely. They were corralled and probed
by the Thingalith but retaliated savagely, lunging in waves to
suck a horseman or two into their formation.

Stepan mounted behind Bellamus, and between them
they guided the horse towards the formation. 'Surrender!'
shouted Bellamus, voice a little slurred. 'Lay down your
arms, surrender!'

'What language is that? Not Anakim, surely,' muttered
Stepan. Bellamus had thought it was Anakim and then

realised it had been the native dialect of Safinim. He thought, and the words came.

'Surrender! Surrender! We don't want your lives, only the wagons!' If the legionaries kept fighting, the Thingalith could take catastrophic casualties. Only a few enemies heard him, turning their faces towards the cry with terrible snarling lips. One of them, countenance twisted with hate, spat a vile swear-word and then began to swarm towards Bellamus, climbing over a wagon to escape the net of Thingalith. He ran along its top, batting aside twin spear-thrusts aimed at him with a broken and bloody sword, and then jumped down to sprint for the upstart.

'Stepan!' warned Bellamus. One of the knight's great hands manoeuvred the horse sideways-on to the attacker, defending the pair of them with his great-sword. But another Thingalith got to the legionary first, blindsiding him, thrusting a lance into his armpit and dropping him to the floor. The Thingalith was then knocked from his saddle by another legionary, who had appeared as though conjured from thin air. Bellamus realised he had been hiding in the shadows beneath a wagon-bed, and Stepan spurred them closer to help his downed comrade. He swung his sword at the legionary, who blocked and parried, Bellamus holding dazedly onto the horse's mane as he leaned back to avoid the blow. Stepan had distracted the legionary long enough that the Thingalith lying at his feet had time to seize his spear, and he raised its bloody tip, jamming it between the Anakim's legs. The legionary shrieked in pain, and Stepan finished him off with a hard slash at his neck, which knocked him flat.

Bellamus's offer of surrender had only triggered a renewed frenzy of violence, and hand still clutched over his left eye, he found himself disturbed and cowed by the ferocity before him. Every Anakim movement was in brutal, abrupt jerks; the movements of the Thingalith hesitant and restrained by comparison. The Anakim were matched by Garrett, who charged into the formation with his spear, Heofonfyr, lowered and liberating a horrible swinging twist of gore above the legionaries.

The hybrid had more than a talent for killing. There was a note in him that tended towards chaos. Bellamus hated to be left alone with him. When he looked in his eyes, some deep and primitive instinct instructed Bellamus to turn away and gain some distance. He radiated a desire for disorder in all things. When he ate, every item before him was disassembled before it touched his lips. He never slept in the same location twice, invented onomatopoeic words which he was frustrated to find others did not understand, and made decisions that Bellamus would have associated with a drunkard beyond the stage of remembering his actions. At every level he was impulsive, hedonistic and destructive.

Now, he was plunging Heofonfyr left and right at the legionaries, dividing them and providing an opening for the other Thingalith. 'Leave some alive!' roared Bellamus, in Saxon. 'We need at least three, capture them! Capture, don't kill!'

Garrett had ploughed his horse right through the legionaries and out the other side. He rode clear, his mount limping and staggering, but still obedient as it turned to its master's wishes and charged once more. The Thingalith followed his example, redoubling their efforts and beginning to match the Anakim aggression with their own.

Battle, Bellamus had observed, was about mindset. Numbers, tactics and logistics could all influence the mindset of the two forces before battle was joined, but once the blades had started to ring, the lines had mashed into one, and the bodies begun to fall, it was about mindset. Were you ready, truly ready, to give all that your opponent was? How much did you mean the swing of your sword and the thrust of your spear? Were you at that rare stage, beyond intimidation and fear, where you can commit fully to combat without a backwards glance? The Anakim, though surprised and outnumbered, had the right mindset. Sheer, unyielding aggression.

The Thingalith, slightly chaotic and with too long to consider what they were about to do, had not been quite ready to match their savagery. Except Garrett. Suddenly, like sunshine beaming through the clouds above, his example made it obvious to the others that they could not shrink back or be conservative. They must attack.

Legionaries began to drop, or were dragged back, kicking and thrashing, into the ranks of the Thingalith to be subdued. A miniature charge of three horsemen dashed into the Anakim formation, transferring huge energy from body to body and knocking a dozen to the floor where they were trampled by hooves. The Anakim mindset began to suffer as their friends dropped around them and their small island was eroded. Stubbornly, they refused to yield, but their aggression faded away. The band of resisters began to flinch and hesitate. They were human after all.

The Thingalith sensed their dominance and became cruel, chiselling into the survivors and ignoring Bellamus's repeated cries to take them alive. This too, the upstart had learned: once you have pushed a man to killing, it is not easy to switch him off.

'Stepan,' said Bellamus urgently. 'I can't walk. Keep the prisoners alive. Don't let them kill all of them.' This fight was getting beyond his control. The terror of the Anakim fresh in their minds, the Thingalith were unleashing that fear on their dwindling enemy. He saw one Anakim drop his sword, fall to his knees and raise his arms in surrender to one of Bellamus's men. Bellamus saw the Thingalith, a comrade with whom he had drunk and laughed, mouth the words '*Too late, chum,*' and pin the legionary to the ground with a spear. Another friend of his was digging his spear again and again into the face of a fallen legionary, teeth gritted in hatred as he reduced it to shreds. Next to him, a pair of Thingalith had fallen atop a legionary on his knees and were trying to strangle him: both Anakim and Thingalith red-faced and quivering.

Behind Bellamus, Stepan dismounted and bullied his way

into the fray, delivering blows with the flat of his sword to awaken the Thingalith from their madness. Slowly the crowd began to emerge from its rage. The pattern of movement before Bellamus changed, from frantic hacking and stamping, reeking with violence and desperation, to something more restrained.

Then fell an odd silence, which slowly, horribly exposed the mood of the soldiers. The madness drained away, each Thingman staring at his bloody comrades, eyes wide and shocked. Some had worked the skin off their fingers with repeated punching, despite the swords they still clutched. Others had crimson teeth and blood-smeared lips. Bellamus had never, in battlefield after battlefield across Erebos, seen anything so ugly. He looked for Garrett and found the hybrid more coated with grime than any other man. His gaze lingered on the giant, quite certain it was his example that had ignited the frenzy.

'Are you all with me now?' Bellamus breached the shocking silence. 'Have you come back? Bind the prisoners.' The men obeyed at once, moving silently with faces downcast. As the surviving Anakim were trussed and piled like plunder, Bellamus inspected his band. They had taken fewer casualties than he had feared. Their skill against the Anakim was improving. Bellamus had pioneered three attacking manoeuvres for his men, aimed at the gaps between bone armour. One for the raging arteries at the neck, another for those at the groin, and a third for the bundle of nerves in the armpit, and tender organs behind.

Stepan approached Bellamus and gently grasped his left wrist, pulling it down. Bellamus, who had not realised he was still covering his eye, let it drop. 'Oh God,' murmured Stepan.

'That isn't helpful,' said Bellamus shortly. 'What's happened?'

'Your eye,' said Stepan. 'I'll get Hrothweard.'

Hrothweard was the physician who rode with the

Thingalith. He returned Bellamus to earth and sat him on the back of one of the Anakim wagons. Bellamus examined his rheumy eyes and great bushy beard, and the physician examined his eye in turn. 'How did this happen, Master?' he asked, voice soft and face serious.

'My horse stumbled. I hit a rock on the way down.'

Hrothweard reached his filthy fingers delicately for Bellamus's eye, plucking at something. 'Tell me if this hurts.'

'It hurts.'

Hrothweard ignored this.

'It really hurts.'

The physician sighed and straightened up. 'The eye is lost, Master.'

Bellamus did not feel anything particularly at this news. 'I see.'

'The rock has destroyed it completely. Our priority now is stopping it becoming infected. If it does, it may spread to the other eye and blind you completely. I will prepare a poultice.' Hrothweard turned away, leaving Bellamus staring at the floor.

'I'm sorry, Captain,' said Stepan. 'Damned unlucky.'

Bellamus swore softly to himself, the truth sinking in. He had lost an eye. He might yet lose another. 'Unlucky,' he said, after a moment. 'We didn't have to charge down that stupid incline with leather-wrapped hooves. Send me Garrett.'

'I'd give him a moment to cool off,' said Stepan, gently.

'Send him to me.'

Garrett duly appeared, his long-bladed spear balanced over one shoulder and his bright yellow hair plastered down with crumbling brown blood.

'You attacked early,' said Bellamus, fixing the hybrid with his good right eye.

Garrett heaved his shoulders, his expression blank.

'And it cost us soldiers. The incline was too steep here for leather-wrapped hooves, and men died falling down the valley. I lost an eye.'

'You should have removed your leather wraps, like we did,' said the hybrid carelessly.

'You planned to do this?' said Bellamus incredulously.

'Relax,' said Garrett. 'We would have lost a lot more men if it weren't for me. We were losing before I intervened.'

Bellamus stared dumbfounded at the hybrid and then nodded. 'Garrett Eoten-Draefend: this is the last time you command any of my Thingalith.' His voice was flat but he had spoken in rage. He suddenly became aware of how close the hybrid stood, and of the savage lance over his shoulder. He felt panic before a thought came to him. *Treat him like a dog. Show nothing but certainty.* So he stared into Garrett's yellow, sulphurous eyes, vision blurring as he tried not to blink. Inscrutable, Garrett met his gaze. Then he shrugged once more and turned away, nearly swaggering back to the site of the slaughter. He seemed to take pleasure in stepping on the bodies, both Anakim and Sutherner.

Hrothweard reappeared, washed Bellamus's eye with a squirt from a water-skin, and covered the wound with a poultice, which was cool and soothing. Hrothweard opined that an infection was likely, and Bellamus should pray.

Six Anakim had survived the frenzy alive. Bellamus gazed down at their bound forms for a moment, wondering if he would actually do with them as he had planned. He decided that he was not sure, so he might as well take them and he could decide later. They were loaded onto the wagons with the Unhieru arms and armour.

Bellamus walked, still unsteady on his feet, to the overturned wagon, which some of the Thingalith were trying to empty completely so that they could right it. The contents that had spilt from beneath the canvas covering were truly disturbing. Shirts of chain mail so large they had been rolled like sailcloth. Helmets bigger than a water pail, roughly forged from absurdly thick iron plates. Simply lifting them was a struggle and penetrating them in battle would be as good as impossible. The eyeholes were perfectly round, the mouth gaping wide. Together, the expression they gave the helmet was one of utter derangement. 'I'm glad not to be meeting you in battle,' he told the iron face, tossing its weight aside with difficulty. For weapons: axes as long as halberds, each blade dripping down its shaft and straight like a meat-cleaver.

'Bloody hell,' said Stepan, hefting one of the axes himself. 'We did some good today, Captain.'

'Worth the loss of an eye,' said Bellamus quietly.

Stepan looked up from the weapon in his hands. 'Yes, my friend. It truly was.'

With difficulty, the wagons were turned around: back up the road and towards Brimstream.

23
Silence

Climbing the hill, Cold-Edge at one side and a water-skin at the other, Roper felt light-headed with hunger. They had gone onto half-rations the previous day, and everything was harder. His legs were leaden, and the prospect of training again with Vigtyr was daunting. They would need to break into Lincylene soon, or else starve.

Vigtyr had brought practice swords with him, and set them aside carefully as Roper arrived, clearly saving them as a reward should Roper show unexpected progress. They were filling the days it took to complete the siege weapons, and this was their fifth lesson together.

Vigtyr hoped that he had not been too hard on Roper during their previous sessions. 'I thought you could take it, my lord,' he said, eyebrows raised. 'But then Captain Gray came to speak with me . . .'

'He what?'

'The captain came to speak with me. He told me I was going too hard on you and needed to back off, and that you wouldn't be able to lead or fight properly if I was taking so much of your energy. I thought that had been on your orders.'

'I see,' said Roper, frowning. 'No, don't worry about that,

Lictor. I said nothing to Gray. He saw the cuts on my arms and made his own judgement. I will speak to him.'

'We can go easier if you like, lord,' said Vigtyr, making an expression that said he did not care either way. 'But this is the best way to learn, and it seems to me you have the strength of character for it.'

'No, don't worry, Lictor,' Roper insisted. 'I am pleased with your instruction.'

'If you're certain, lord,' said Vigtyr. 'Back to where we left off yesterday? Show me your stance.'

Roper did. Vigtyr's face assumed distaste. His sword flicked out once more, a flat tap this time, rather than a cut. 'Arm in.'

Vigtyr adjusted again.

And again. And again. The adjustments grew more and more minute but Vigtyr's face grew steadily more determined. 'Do you tire of this, Lord Roper?'

'No,' he lied.

'You strike me as a man of energy. Of energy and unusual determination. Will you be happy with less than perfection?'

'No,' said Roper.

'Neither am I. That's what it takes to be the best. That pain in your hand. That endless dissatisfaction. Again.'

It must have continued for hours, though it was hard to tell how much time had passed beneath the insulating fog of cloud. Finally, Vigtyr bade Roper relax and handed him a practice sword. 'We will still begin every session that way. Again and again until you are perfect.' Roper dropped the sword and sucked greedily on his water-skin, but Vigtyr shook his head. 'You are training to fight in battle, lord. Do you think this is any harder than that will be? We must not stop.'

Roper threw the skin aside, picked up the blade and they fought. Vigtyr did not hold back. Roper rarely managed to exact a single parry from him. Vigtyr's sword would twist, gorgeously manipulated by his thick left wrist and the blunt edge would bounce into Roper's neck, or armpit, or thigh. 'Again!' Vigtyr would cry.

On the battlefield at Harstathur, where he and Bellamus had fought in a hailstorm, Roper had felt the edge of a lightning strike. Those nearer had been lifted into the air and hurled backwards, left smoking and inanimate. Roper had only felt a touch of it: a violent quivering shock to his guts and limbs that had left him dazed and sick. That was the effect that the word: *Again!* as uttered by Vigtyr, was beginning to have. He flinched at each cry of it, blinked furiously and prepared to defend himself. Each time, the result was the same. A cold, painful thump. That word. *Again!*

This, Roper was learning about Vigtyr. His fuel was endless. Within him, something fed an inexhaustible dissatisfaction. He drove on and on, growing less charming, the veneer of contentment stripping away to reveal hunger. A strange fixity came into his eyes, as though the lictor was entranced and he lunged at Roper over and over. *Again!*

Roper felt himself grow defensive. The more wildly he lunged, the more Vigtyr punished him. He would keep going as long as the lictor did, though. There could be no question of giving up. Of all the students at the haskoli, Roper had absorbed the lessons most thoroughly. Never concede. Commit. One in, all in. Serve. Serve. Serve. *Again! Again! Again!*

When Vigtyr struck Roper on the head, knocking him to the floor, Roper found he could not rise. Vigtyr stood over him hungrily and Roper could respond no further than to coil into a protective knot. Then something came over the lictor. He took a quick pace backwards and lowered his sword. 'Are you all right, my lord?' he asked.

Roper panted shallowly, and nodded.

'We will leave it there for today,' said Vigtyr. 'Do you need help, lord?'

Roper was quiet, gathering himself. 'I need . . . time, Vigtyr. Carry on.'

Vigtyr bowed low, gathered the training swords and left

Roper on top of the hill. He did not know how long he stayed lying there. In the end, it was that odd rattle in his chest, ever-present for the last few months, which forced him to sit up and fetch the water-skin. It was only when he had drained it that he noticed a pair of boots standing next to him. They were brown leather: stretched, abraded, worn and powdered with dried clay. Roper followed the boots up, to the craggy, authoritative and handsome countenance of Tekoa Urielson. He was being haunted by Jokul, who drifted round his shoulder to stare at Roper.

'You don't look well, Lord Roper,' said Tekoa. 'That is appropriate.'

Roper held out a hand and Tekoa pulled him to his feet. 'Appropriate?'

'There is bad news.'

'Well?'

'We have received word,' began Jokul, crisply, 'that the shipment of armour and weapons destined for the Unhieru was intercepted on the road.'

'Intercepted,' repeated Roper.

'By Bellamus of Safinim,' said Jokul, lingering on the final consonant of each word.

'What's he done with them?'

Jokul shrugged. 'Taken them. We don't know where. But somewhere far from the Unhieru, anyway.'

Roper looked at Tekoa, who glowered back beneath furrowed brows as though Roper were responsible. Roper folded his arms and looked down at the floor. 'And why,' he asked, after a moment, 'are Bellamus's spies so superior to our own?'

'I have told you, Lord Roper,' said Jokul, impatiently, 'we cannot match their writing, and are so othered by the Sutherners that even on pain of death, most will not help us. Rooting out every spy in this army—'

'Rooting out?' interrupted Roper. 'Vulture's guts, man; you are the Master of the Kryptea! If you want to stop a flock of carrier pigeons, do you try and intercept them one by one as they fly overhead? Or do you go to the man who is releasing them and burn his bloody house down? Forget the spies: find me Bellamus.'

Jokul went still at this. 'You still believe we are doing the right thing here, Lord Roper?' he said, very quietly. 'When we have made no progress, we are starving already, and now lost the allies you so unwisely recruited?'

'This changes nothing,' growled Roper, though he knew Jokul was not alone in looking back north and dreaming of returning home. 'We carry on. You are dismissed, Master.'

Jokul turned down the hill, pale lips drawn back in a snarl. Roper waited until he was out of earshot.

'That man is doing nearly as much to hinder us as Bellamus himself,' Roper muttered. 'You know more legionaries were found dead with a cuckoo branded into them this morning?'

'I knew,' said Tekoa. 'They were Skiritai.'

'Could they have been spies?'

'Not damned likely,' said Tekoa.

'So the bastard's killing legionaries at random to put Bellamus's spies on edge,' said Roper bitterly. 'It's mutilating our morale, and we're already starving and frustrated.'

'I've had Aledas take care of troublesome people for me in the past,' muttered Tekoa.

Roper did not smile. 'Not yet, I think. I'll deal with Jokul in my own way before I let that one off his leash. I'm more concerned with the Unhieru. Perhaps they could be persuaded to join us before the armour arrives? They'd make light work of those palisades.' He cast an eye over the walls of Lincylene.

'I fear how Gogmagoc would react if he heard that the Sutherners had stripped such valuable treasure from us,' said Tekoa. 'No doubt he'd interpret that as a sign of their dominance, and he may think better of the alliance. In any case, do you really want them here, among our men? A few legionaries killed by the Kryptea will be the least of our worries if we have to share a campsite with Gogmagoc's band.'

'We must send them another shipment,' Roper said. 'Much better protected than the last.'

Tekoa cleared his throat softly at this. 'Do you know how much the first shipment cost, Lord Roper?'

'I do not,' he admitted.

'Well don't let such details trouble you,' said Tekoa, sourly. 'But suffice it to say the debt you owe the Vidarr is already magnificent, and this war has so far yielded very little in the way of plunder. Perhaps we should leave the Unhieru in their homeland.'

'Not this again,' said Roper. 'We've already been stopped near dead. Without the Unhieru, we may as well yield to those already demanding we abandon the campaign.'

Tekoa was silent at that.

'Which we *are not* doing,' said Roper. 'We must have the Unhieru on our side. We simply must. Whatever the cost, I will make it worth the Vidarr's while.'

'So when are we going to see repayment?' asked Tekoa.

'At dawn,' said Roper. 'Damn the waiting, I'm starving, and without the supplies in that city, this army will fall apart. What we need now is momentum. We have enough siege weapons to break through. Let's flood the streets, just as we promised. Let's make Lincylene bleed.'

The two descended into the camp.

The cloud had broken, leaving great shards of rose, edged with crimson, drifting overhead. Even the sky behind was flushed, and in the west, it was a sunset of such wounded, bleeding intensity, that it looked as though it might never rise again.

Anyone might be an informant for Bellamus, so when Roper told the legates they were to assault the city with the dawn, he bade them keep it secret from their men until the last possible hour. In anticipation of renewed food supplies with the dawn, Keturah prepared some unusually fine hoosh, though Roper felt too sick to eat much.

He knew to keep himself busy. He sharpened Cold-Edge, cut fresh treads into the bases of his boots, and wrapped his palms and finger-bases in leather to shield his blisters and keep the bones securely in their sockets. He rubbed a little grease on his skin where the edges of armour and helmet would press, and drilled an extra notch into his sword-belt, which had already been loosened by this campaign. It helped him ignore the thunder in his chest and the power innervating his limbs. From the corner of his eye, he saw Keturah watch him a while.

'What were all those questions you were asking the Chief Historian about silence, the other night?' she asked, evidently trying to distract him.

'It was something Gray said about the value of silence. Apparently Sigrid and Frathi are authorities on the subject.'

Keturah looked scornful. 'Silence works for Sigrid because she's beautiful,' she decreed. 'If she were ugly, people would call her boring.'

'Boring isn't the word I'd use,' said Roper.

'What would you use?'

'Awkward.'

Keturah tutted. 'You are very wrong, Husband. She's not awkward. She is peaceful.' Keturah came to sit next to him, and as he kept facing into the fire, smiled at his cheek. 'You would be so bored if I was silent.'

'I literally cannot imagine that situation,' said Roper.

Keturah threw back her head and laughed. 'You are so sweet when you're irritated, Husband. The little sparks you let fly.' Roper smiled despite himself. 'Is my wit not what drew you to me?'

'I think you misremember the circumstances of our wedding, Wife,' said Roper, smiling faintly.

Keturah laughed again. 'It only took quarter of an hour, it

is easily forgotten. Next time we see Sigrid, I will show you she is not awkward.'

The senior legates began to return to the fire, with Gray taking a place on Roper's right. 'I hear you talked to Vigtyr,' said Roper, a little abruptly.

'I did. I told him to teach, by all means, but not to wound you, and to leave you some energy at the end of each session.'

Roper did not realise he was angry until he heard his own words. 'I am not a child, Gray. I don't need your intervention. If I feel Vigtyr is pushing me too hard then I am more than capable of saying so.'

'You would not, though, lord,' said Gray calmly, tugging off his boots. 'Your very great strength is also the thing which may lead you to overreach yourself. You commit and do not look back. You would be too compelled by the effort to ask Vigtyr to relent. You see it as a test for yourself.'

'Gray, you aren't listening to me,' said Roper vehemently. 'I do not need you fighting my battles.'

'As soon as you no longer need my service, lord, dismiss me.'

Roper gave a frustrated grunt. 'You're almost as stubborn as Pryce.'

'I admire him very much.'

Silence fell between them: the most uncomfortable that Roper had known with his friend. He stared into the fire, a little shocked by his own anger. It took him some moments to realise that he still bore the scars of Uvoren's treatment of him last year. Any hint of patronising, or control, or interference, and Roper would bristle. That and the hunger, he supposed. Everyone was snappish.

While the legates made their preparations for battle, Gray abstained from these sober tasks. He arranged himself cross-legged, a sack of fresh venison before him, and used a long knife to unroll the flesh into thin strips, which he dripped over a drying rack like wax. Presently, Sigrid came to collect his efforts, looking down at her husband. 'You don't want to try and sleep?' she asked.

'I won't sleep tonight,' he replied. 'Better to stay busy.'

Gray's wife was as strikingly beautiful as Keturah claimed, with high cheekbones, skin like pale silk, white-blonde hair and eyes the blue of daylight. She looked from Gray to Roper and Keturah, tightening the corners of her mouth and narrowing her eyes kindly in her equivalent of a smile. 'My lord and lady,' she said. 'How good to see you both.' The pair of them rose and embraced her.

'Thank you for the last time, my dear,' said Keturah, employing the fond Anakim greeting. 'I see your husband is happier with domestic duties than mine.'

Sigrid just beamed at Keturah, saying nothing. Roper made a note of this moment as evidence he could present later for Sigrid's awkwardness.

Keturah recovered the conversation. 'I fear he keeps himself busy so that we shan't have too long in each other's company. He thinks I talk too much and has been hoping you'll convince me of the benefits of silence.'

Sigrid laughed. 'I'm not sure I have any particular wisdom to bestow.'

'Tell them what you told me, my love,' said Gray, still absorbed in his task. 'There'll be a lot of silence tonight. It is as well that they appreciate it.'

'If you wish to hear,' said Sigrid, settling onto her knees.

'I'll listen to anything at the moment,' said Roper.

Sigrid looked thoughtfully into the fire. 'We might start with why we are here. I think it is to learn. To learn you must listen, and to listen you must be silent. I have tried to live my life by that, and after a while you start to see how violent words can be: even pleasant ones. Imagine a perfect moment in a forest.' Roper did. He was in the freyi, Keturah's head in his lap, the starlight piercing the leaves. 'You might remark to one another how wonderful the moment is. But by doing so, you shatter it. You restrict the experience. Words define,

enclose and categorise. You should let the silence speak. You
are sharing the experience just as much in the quiet as you
are with your words. Part of the wonder of that moment was
its silence, and the fact that you were purely in it, and not
analysing it with your companion.

'Does that make sense?' she said, looking up between
Roper and Keturah.

Roper felt his opinion of Sigrid shift somewhat. It was
true, there was nothing awkward about her steady blue gaze.
'I suppose so,' he answered her, thinking.

'Not to me,' said Keturah, bluntly. 'If everyone were to live
this way, would the result not be that everyone has less fun
talking? And that you are more likely to discover that you
are dissatisfied with your company?'

'It depends what you value in company,' said Sigrid. 'But I
am not advocating that everyone stops talking. Merely that
we should find time for silence too.'

But not now, thought Roper. *Not before battle.*

'Is there more?' asked Keturah.

'Start with that,' said Sigrid. 'And perhaps eventually you
start to realise how powerful words really are. Silence cre-
ates contrast. It is something to set against words and make
them weightier. And contrast is one of the roots of pleasure.

'But you know much of this already, Lord Roper,' she
added. 'Do you not find the same value in a battlefield? Living right at the moment; the freedom and pleasure of that.
The *contrast*, which puts your life at home in perspective
and makes the sweet moments sweeter and the moments you
might have called dull, peaceful. The flood of emotions
which battle unleashes, and the comparison of that with the
usual banality.'

Roper was intrigued. The legates had ceased their preparations to observe Sigrid, and she looked around the hearth. 'I
must return to my tasks,' she said, getting to her feet and
picking up the drying frame of venison. 'Good luck tomorrow, all of you.'

The legates murmured their thanks and good night, and Tekoa rose to excuse himself, saying he would try and sleep.

'Peers, before you go,' said Roper. 'So you know what tomorrow will be like. We will let Lincylene be an example.' His face assumed regret. 'They have resisted us and refused our demands, and they must receive no mercy whatsoever. I know it seems brutal. I know it seems almost like possession, and your honour will protest. But tomorrow we will kill every living thing within those walls. Nothing survives. Nothing.' He looked up at the cold stars for a brief moment, and then back at his commanders. 'Do you understand?'

They nodded.

'Till then.'

24

The Weapon

The last few days had been greatly disturbing for Bellamus.

It was late, and he sat by the fire in the Cobweb. He and Stepan each clutched a cup of spiced ale, rain tapping at the windows. Every time the door was opened with another message for the spymaster, a waft of cold, damp air would make the candles shudder. Their last visitor had been Hrothweard the physician, who had inspected Bellamus's ruined eye beneath the poultice and murmured his amazement that there was no sign of infection. Bellamus was not terribly surprised: fortune had always been on his side. He found that he kept missing objects as he tried to pick them up, but mostly found this amusing.

'I saw an odd figure skulking around today,' said Stepan.

'Mmm?' grunted Bellamus, with little interest.

'Very tall: too big for a Sutherner, I'd have thought. He was at the end of the street, cloak up over his head, and I shouted at him. He turned the corner, and when I followed he was gone. I couldn't see him anywhere.'

'One of our Anakim messengers,' Bellamus suggested. 'Unndor, or that other one, Urthr.' It could not be Garrett, whom Bellamus had sent out of Brimstream on a task as soon as they returned. He was furious with the hybrid, and would no longer be left alone with him.

'Behaving oddly, if it was one of them,' said Stepan. He pulled a woollen blanket about his shoulders and inspected Bellamus, clearly mystified by the lack of interest. 'What have you been up to in that barn?' he asked.

Bellamus sipped his ale. He listened to the wind moaning outside and could hear the squeal of rusty hinges that it set in motion. 'I have discovered something,' he said.

'Oh yes? This is all very mysterious,' said Stepan, comfortably. 'What is it?'

'A weapon,' said Bellamus. 'And I'm not sure whether to use it.'

'Are you going to explain?'

Bellamus took another sip. 'I suppose I am.' He nodded thoughtfully to himself and raised a hand to touch the poultice over his eye. 'You remember what our erstwhile innkeeper said about Slave-Plague? That it doesn't affect us, only the hybrids?' Stepan was nodding. 'Well he was right. I tested it myself. I went to one of the diseased hybrids, gave it every opportunity to infect me, and it didn't.'

Stepan gave a disbelieving laugh. 'Are you serious?' And when he saw that Bellamus was, he amended: 'Are you *insane*?' He gazed at his friend for a while and Bellamus would not meet his gaze. 'Why would you do that?'

'Because imagine if the part of a hybrid that is vulnerable to the plague is its Anakim part,' said Bellamus. 'I had to know. By trying to infect myself, I confirmed it wasn't the Suthern part. And after that, I just needed to test that it does infect the Anakim.'

'Great God,' said Stepan, softly. His eyes shone white in the gloom. 'That's why you wanted live Anakim prisoners. I thought you were going to try and turn them into informants, like the others. But you're experimenting on them with this plague!'

Bellamus nodded. 'Yes I am. That is what I have done.' He

stared into his cup for a time. 'And I am ashamed.' The fire
cracked loudly. 'That is not something I say very often. But I
am ashamed, because my suspicions were right. The Anakim
are vulnerable to Slave-Plague. The legionary I exposed to it
is in that barn now, dying.'

'Oh my God,' said Stepan, softly. There was a long pause.
'This is so new,' said the knight, evidently trying to find some
angle from which to approach the huge subject. 'In every way.
From you; as an idea . . . I have never heard of anything like
this before. Why did you do it?' he finally wondered. 'I've never
seen you be cruel to prisoners before. Even when you are
recruiting one of your spies . . . you have used underhanded
tactics, I know, but always obeyed your own code. I remember
you telling me about blackmail, and misdirection and outrageous deceit, but you've always drawn a line before we've come
to anything like this. Your interrogations are so civil. Never
torture, or using loved ones as leverage, effective as those
things would have been. For all people say you have no scruples, and would do anything, I've never seen the evidence of
that. Was I wrong? Or has something changed? And *why*?'

'You weren't wrong,' said Bellamus. 'I have been truthful.
I have never threatened loved ones, or used coercion or torture, though I resisted for mostly selfish reasons. The gain
seemed too small, the suffering too great, and it would have
felt unpleasant. And now this . . . This is different to me. It is
vile, what is happening to the legionary through there.' Bellamus nodded through the wall of the Cobweb, as though
they could both see the barn gleaming darkly in the rain. 'A
good man, in the wrong place at the wrong time. I pity him.
But once I'd had this thought, did I not have a responsibility
to investigate it? I knew that I might have found a weapon
that could win this war. To develop it, one of our enemies
had to die badly. Would it not have been wrong to ignore that
opportunity? Is the experiment I have done so much worse
than the scores we killed raiding that weapons shipment?'
He finished, looking hopefully at the knight.

Stepan looked away. 'It seems worse,' he said.

'I agree it seems worse, but when I think on it, there is no real reason why. He is dying badly, but no worse than someone injured in battle who gets the fever. And this is more necessary than that. Think how many people could be saved. Albion could be saved! To have shielded myself from these experiments, when I knew the difference it could make, would have been . . . cowardice.' He spoke the word bleakly into the fire and drained his mug. 'I have been searching for so long for ways that we can fight this enemy. We are so outmatched. I have developed so many weapons to try and lend us an advantage.' He gestured futilely across the room to the inventions scattered over his table. Bellamus himself was not much of a craftsman, but he had ideas, and there was no shortage of skilled manufacturers at Brimstream to execute them. He had considered how best to advantage a Sutherner against an Anakim, and settled mostly on poison.

Poison was not troubled by Anakim-bone plates, or their great size and strength, and he had developed a dozen methods of administration. On his desk lay an unusually sharp quill, which could write after a fashion (well enough, he reasoned, to convince an illiterate race), but its ink was a fast-acting poison extracted from foxgloves. Next to it lay a glove with a concealed pouch on the back, accessed by pulling a tiny thread that unleashed powder to be blown in an enemy's eyes and blind them. Beside this, an innocuous staff, the lower half of which had been wrapped with lead and expertly painted and sculpted to resemble the wood. It was slim enough that someone might be tempted to raise an arm to ward off the blow, and that arm would be folded in half. There were candles that gave off an awful eye-watering fume when burnt. Bellamus was most proud of a book, the cover of which was loaded with a spring mechanism concealed in the pages. When opened, it emitted a gout of lime-powder to corrode the eyes and mouth. As the Anakim could not read, he had even titled the book: *The Most Poison*

Pages, by Bellamus of Safinim. Subtitled: *Do not open under any circumstances.*

'These are toys,' said Bellamus dismissively. 'I may be able to arm the Thingalith to the teeth, but it will make no real difference to this war. The plague might, though. It might be devastating.'

'But what now?' asked Stepan. 'You have found this weapon – a plague that will only affect our enemies. Are you going to unleash it on them? Kill tens of thousands with disease?'

'Those Anakim have to die anyway if we are going to win this war,' said Bellamus.

'On the battlefield!' declared Stepan, as animated as Bellamus had ever seen him. 'With honour, man to man. Not cut down by this dreadful illness.'

Bellamus smiled sadly at his friend. 'You have a knight's view of conflict, my brother. I am of more humble origins. If I do not use this weapon, I cannot see how we will stop the Anakim subduing all of Suthdal. If we fight them only on the battlefield, then we will lose every time.'

'So you say, but have we not done well so far?' asked Stepan. 'Are they not growing hungrier, and wasting men and time before the walls of Lincylene? And we have just stopped the Unhieru from joining the fight, or at least delayed them. I don't see that we are losing yet. I don't think we have to resort to this.' He finished, sitting forward in his chair to stare imploringly at Bellamus.

'The Anakim are soldiering on,' said the upstart, quietly. 'I thought contaminating the water might slow them more, but our enemy is too adept at living from the land. I thought the lack of progress might make them surrender to their heart-sickness, and go back north, but some will keeps driving them onwards. We are losing, Stepan. We have not weakened that army enough, and by the time Earl Seaton gets here with his forces, he will find the Anakim army is still near unstoppable in the field.' He stood to refill his mug, offering more to

Stepan, which the knight refused. 'But I have not yet decided
what to do. In spite of all that I have said, I cannot bring
myself to unleash this on the Anakim. Not quite.'

'But you might?'

Bellamus gave a tiny heave of his shoulders. Stepan sat
back in his chair and drained the rest of his ale, staring at
the empty cup for a moment before rising to assemble a plate
of food. Bellamus picked up the pile of messages at his side,
each delivered in some ingenious way. Some concealed
inside eggs, their shells softened with vinegar, opened with
a flint blade, and then rehardened with cold water once the
message had been inserted. The one he held now was written
on silk and had been sewn into a pair of leggings. He smiled
faintly to himself as he remembered an unfamiliar cloak he
had found here the day before. He had torn it to scraps, looking for a concealed message, before one of the Thingalith had
appeared saying he thought he might have left his cloak on
the table and had Bellamus seen it? Bellamus had promised
to replace it.

Looking down at the silk he recognised Aramilla's cypher.
He glanced up at Stepan, still piling cold meat onto his plate,
and quickly produced the frame with which he could
decipher it. He had finished reading the message and hidden
the frame in the stack of papers, just as Stepan turned around
and returned to his chair. He knew he was failing to keep the
shock of what he had just read from his face, but Stepan
seemed distracted. He was not looking at Bellamus, and
spoke at last in a miserable and defeated voice.

'I want to go home, Captain.'

'Home?' asked Bellamus, distracted. 'Is it the plague?'

'No, no,' said Stepan, hurriedly. 'It is nothing you've done.
But when I went north last year, I thought it would be for a
campaign. A few months at the most. I've been away from my
wife, God bless her, and my estate for more than half a year.
I believe in the work we do here and you know I'm loyal to
you, Captain. Lord knows I wouldn't have survived our

retreat from the Black Kingdom without you, none of us would. But this isn't what I thought I was getting into. I thought there might be an end in sight long ago. I thought we would be fighting in the open, on the battlefield, not in the shadows. I miss my wife. I miss my dogs, I miss sowing the crops and I keep thinking about the apple-harvest last year, and how that was. We'd put down a dozen saplings and I want to see how they're doing. I have no word of how things are, because although I can send messages to Ede, she can't know where I am to send them back. And the Black Legions will be done with Lincylene soon, and they will move south. I want to be at home, and be with my wife and my servants when the Anakim war machine stomps over our lands.'

Bellamus listened miserably. Stepan was the closest he had to family at that moment. Crossing borders, driven by ambition and hunger, this speech made him consider for the first time what it was costing him. Then his resolve solidified a little. Stepan's idea of home sounded so romantic because he was a knight with an estate and future. Bellamus had nothing like that. He had to be here, working at his deadly trade, if he wanted hope of any such future.

'I see all that, Stepan,' he said. 'And I can't disagree, or blame you for a word of it. This is a long, bleak struggle. No doubt your life would be a good deal better in that fine home you describe, with your wife. Go, if you must. Go. I won't stop you. I owe you my life, too; you have more than paid your debt to me. All I can say in return is that I have come to rely on you.' Stepan fidgeted unhappily. 'I would miss you greatly, both for your company and your skills. You are needed here, too, where you can make a difference. But that mustn't stop you, if you feel as you have said.' Bellamus had abandoned his family when he was fourteen. He could navigate a sexual relationship with a queen without feeling any emotional investment whatsoever. And he lost so many comrades in this conflict that he rarely diverted energy into bonding with them any more. Somehow, though, he had come to rely on this knight, and he realised how alone he might feel if he were gone.

'Well ...' said Stepan. 'The Black Legions are still at Lincylene. And so far as we know, they're intending to besiege it a little while, yes?'

Bellamus nodded.

'I could stay until they have taken the city. After that ... after that, I must return to my home.'

'I am grateful for that,' said Bellamus. He raised his cup to Stepan and drank.

Bellamus needed a friend now. For the news from Aramilla was that their secret was out. Her father had discovered them, and he would have her executed unless she did exactly as dictated. *Please*, the note had said, *please, my upstart: pass me all the information you have. He will use it to fight the Anakim, and it will keep me alive.*

Bellamus stood to pour yet another cup of ale. As he busied himself at the fire, blocking it from Stepan's view, he tossed the scrap of silk on the flames.

25

Brimstream

Morning. None of those about Roper's hearth had slept. The legionaries had been spared the sleepless night, and just before dawn were finally told that they were about to assault. They rustled into life, helping each other into their armour. Keturah strapped Roper into his cuirass, sealing him tight like a clam and then planting a kiss on his breastplate. She dressed his hair, tying it into a high ponytail, which she threaded through a hole in the back of his helmet. Then she pulled it forward and Roper was transformed into a weapon of their kingdom: the man beneath hidden behind the visor. He saw to his gauntlets, she strapped on his sword-belt.

Her arms were around his waist and he placed a hand on her shoulder, nodding at the dark grey walls of Lincylene over her shoulder. Keturah turned and saw a strange thing: a column of smoke billowing above the palisade. She looked back to Roper. 'Fire?'

'But why?' he wondered. The others about the hearth, all armoured but Keturah and the Chief Historian, had turned towards it as well. Their world was calm, but some turbulence evidently churned within Lincylene.

'We should wait to see what plays out here,' said Tekoa,

observing the smoke. 'Who knows what's going on behind those walls.'

'Better yet,' said Roper, 'take advantage and get inside. If that's a real blaze they'll be distracted. We go now.' He gripped Keturah's elbows for a brief moment and then turned for the city.

'I've never understood building a settlement out of wood,' said Tekoa as the legates fell in behind Roper and trotted towards the city. They strode past the ranks of rising legionaries, ladders and rams floating with them to the edge of the encampment. The legates joined their legions, and Roper lined up with the Sacred Guard before the gate, glinting soldiers hurrying into formation with him. There were enough and Roper gestured vigorously that they should advance. Several hundred of them broke into a jog, running silently towards the walls, Roper ushering the rams and ladders to the fore. Then he held up a hand to still them, the charge faltering before it had truly started.

Something had appeared above the wall. A thing familiar to Roper, and grotesque.

'It's a head,' muttered Gray.

So it was, raised high over the wooden battlements on a pike and silhouetted against the smoke climbing fiercely behind.

And then the morning became yet more extraordinary.

The gates opened.

Without fanfare, ceremony or synchrony, the two leaves were pulled back and left yawning. Nobody tried to leave them. They just stood open, and a white flag was hoisted beside the head.

'They've surrendered?' said Gray, mystified.

'A trap,' said Tekoa assertively. 'Mayor Almund would never yield to us.'

'I don't believe Almund is in charge any more,' said Roper, staring up at the impaled head. There was a muttering running along the lines of legionaries, heads turning towards

Roper for guidance. 'Our enemy has surrendered,' he said. 'Let's occupy the city.' Concealing his trepidation, he led the legionaries towards the gates.

First, he expected a volley of arrows. And when that did not come, he anticipated a swarm of defenders as he walked through the gates. Instead, he was met with the smell of burning bread. There was nobody in view and the legions wandered inside, the cobbles deserted. 'What is going on?' muttered Gray, sword held forward.

'Hold on to that gate,' Roper commanded the guardsmen, who took up positions either side at once. The burning smell grew stronger, the smoke thicker. They drifted through the heart of the city, following the smoke and coming unresisted to its centre. There, they found a burning mountain of food. There was little flame, but smoke poured from each gap and crack in the bags of beans, corn, oats and dried meats. It was a pile that could have sustained the legions for weeks, turning to ash before their eyes and as abandoned as everything else. 'No,' Roper breathed. 'No.'

It took hours to find out what had happened, but by locating the huge central temple and posing some questions to the clergy sheltering within, they at last understood. To prevent the Anakim obtaining their food supplies, Mayor Almund had forcibly confiscated every bean he could find and piled them under guard in the city centre. If the Anakim made it past the walls, it could all be burnt together, and so prevented from falling into enemy hands. Until then, it was rationed to the occupants, but so tight-fistedly that they began to riot. It was a combination of this and the Anakim war-hymn that had persuaded the citizens of Lincylene to revolt. That night, as the legates had made their sleepless preparations for the assault, a crowd had stormed the mayor's house, overwhelming his guards and decapitating Almund himself, before advancing to the food supplies. It seemed that half the city had taken to the streets and the guards were hugely outnumbered. Their last act before being overpowered had been to ignite the food supplies. Without food or leadership, the residents surrendered to Anakim mercy.

'You wanted repayment, Tekoa,' said Roper, staring at the burning pile of food. 'We'll search the city for anything of value. Then commit it to the flames.'

The most valuable plunder within the walls was blazing before their eyes. Possessing this pile intact would have been worth the casualties of an assault, but fate had dealt them a cruel hand. 'And how do you intend to continue, lord?' asked Tekoa. 'We're already on half-rations. Without those supplies, we get weaker and weaker.'

'So be it.'

Tekoa and Gray glanced at one another. 'My lord, we will starve,' said Tekoa. 'If we cannot eat, we cannot fight. Our Unhieru weapons shipment has been lost and Bellamus is five paces ahead of us. But if we turn back now, we can take the plunder, we will have lost no men—'

'We're not turning back,' interrupted Roper. 'Not until Lundenceaster lies at our feet. That is your hunger talking, Tekoa, your hunger and *kjardautha*. We strip the houses of metal in repayment for the Vidarr and take the garrison weapons. Then we move on. Nothing else is worth the weight.'

Tekoa gritted his teeth to stop himself contradicting Roper.

'And what are we to do with the survivors, lord?' asked Gray.

'That is up to them. They can leave or burn.'

Lincylene burned.

The fire and smog vomiting from the city footprint made it look like nothing so much as a furious vent in the earth, the night sky above obscured by a column of rusted orange. Keturah sat with the Chief Historian, Sigrid, Hafdis and several other Academy members overlooking the city. A hearth

crackled between them, cheerfully competing with the
sickly light coming from Lincylene. They had been compos-
ing the record of the day's events, each of their slightly
different narratives combined under Frathi's guidance to
reach the version they thought was most accurate.

'Peers, has anyone more to add?' asked the Chief Historian, glaring at each in turn. 'Very well. It is time we descended
for tea.'

Keturah stood stiffly, linking arms with Sigrid as they
dropped off the dark hillside. Next to them walked the Battle
Historian. Hers was the only honourable position in the
Black Kingdom signified by a shaven head, as a mark of the
particular significance of her role and her commitment it.
Keturah knew she had been widowed very young and chosen
to become an Inquisitor rather than remarry, later shifting
her allegiance to the Academy. Keturah took her shoulder as
she strode past. 'My lady,' she said, 'I am curious to know
what might be happening at Lake Avon, with the Maven
Inquisitor trying to find the assassin responsible for my
brother-in-law's death.'

'Yet another avenue you are considering, Miss Keturah?'
asked the Historian, smiling shyly. Keturah had found her a
likeable figure: mild and reserved but exceedingly pleasant
and keen to please any time she was engaged.

'It would be difficult to admit a preference for a role that
requires the death of my husband,' Keturah observed. 'But it
does intrigue me.'

The Battle Historian explained to Keturah how the Inquisitor might proceed. At first Keturah listened closely, but she
soon found herself distracted by some dynamic shifting
around them: a persistent northward stream of men. 'What is
going on?' she murmured, casting about in the dark. 'You!'
she demanded imperiously of a passing Sacred Guardsman.
The man stopped abruptly, evidently caught between surprise and outrage that he had been so discourteously
addressed. 'Where are you going?'

'To see your husband,' he said.

'And why?'

'He has summoned us at once. I don't know why. Forgive me, lady,' and he turned away, scurrying into the black.

'After him,' Keturah declared, quickening her pace and making her apologies to the Battle Historian. 'Aren't you curious, my dear?' she added to Sigrid delightedly.

'I suppose so,' the darkness replied tolerantly.

Roper, when they reached him, was nearly gone. He was astride a courser, Cold-Edge strapped over his back and two large saddlebags at his side. Evidently, he was awaiting only the final dregs of the Sacred Guard before riding.

'Husband? What is this?' she demanded.

'Bellamus,' said Roper, glancing down at her. 'Jokul has found out where he is. We must fly, my love, otherwise word will reach him that we're coming. There are informants everywhere here, and we must stay ahead of them.'

'So you're riding now? At night?'

'There is some moon,' said Roper, glancing up at the withered crescent above. 'And we have no choice. This is the most important thing we have done so far. Much more important than taking Lincylene.'

'Are you going to kill him?' she asked.

But Roper was distracted. A voice crashed through the dark, declaring the Sacred Guard ready. Pryce's voice. Tekoa's bellow responded, saying five hundred eager Skiritai had been ready for a while now, and what had taken the Sacred Guard so long? The horses sensed what was coming and began to toss and whinny. 'Well then!' Roper's voice joined the fray. 'Ride now! To our enemy! After me!' And he wheeled and plunged into the night, Skiritai and Sacred Guard sweeping after him.

'Not so much as a farewell,' sighed Keturah. 'So who's in charge now?'

Sigrid gave her an odd look. 'You, of course,' she said.

*

Bellamus did not dare ask Stepan whether he had heard word of Lincylene. He suspected that the knight knew the city had fallen, and would break the news of his departure soon. For now, they worked together in silence, Bellamus with a specific feeling in his chest. There was an Anakim word for it, but no Saxon, Iberian, Safinim or Alpine tongue seemed to possess it. The Anakim called it *drondila*: the feeling that something good is drawing to a close.

The upstart tried to drown it with another skin of wine, occasionally scratching his ruined eye and encrypting a note for Aramilla. It carried news of the city's surrender, of their intercepting the Unhieru weapons shipment, and of what he had discovered in the barn. He felt extreme nausea (confided to no one) at his use of the plague. The first infected legionary had weakened, and to prevent the plague dying with him, Bellamus had been forced to infect a second prisoner. The two condemned Anakim now shared the barn. The first would not last long, the second probably had a few days.

As a boy, Bellamus had happily used hunting techniques outlawed by the nobility because there was no sport in them. They were too good, his overlords said, to be used. Bellamus scoffed at that. Efficacy should be the sole measure of whether a technique was used or not. And yet now he found himself, with surely the most effective weapon ever created against the Anakim, wavering whether to use it. But what of the two Anakim now dying in the barn? Were their lives to be wasted? What of the lives of his countrymen?

Stepan's thoughts on the matter had coloured his own and he almost left the news out of his message to Aramilla. She, he thought, would likely have no scruples on the weaponisation of plague. Neither would her father. The thought of Earl Seaton brought an involuntary curl to his lips. A vicious and supremely uncompromising man who had let his contempt for Bellamus be known on many occasions. Bellamus almost hoped the Anakim would have the better of him.

Stepan was busy by the fire, drilling a hole into the base

of a wooden queen. It was a chess piece, within which
Bellamus would conceal the scrap of silk bearing Aramilla's
message. 'Here,' said Stepan, blowing shavings off his handi-
work and tossing the piece across the room. Bellamus
caught it.

'Thank you.' He inspected the hole and set the piece down
next to its dark-stained counterpart. He picked up a pebble
from his desk, inserted it into the hole, and hefted the two
pieces. Now they were roughly the same weight. He prepared
a thin patch of leather that would cover the bottom of the
piece, lining it with sticky glue. 'Nearly ready to go,' he said,
balling up the silk message.

Stepan was silent at that. Bellamus looked up and could
see the knight's mind working. He could see his lips begin to
move, and knew what words his friend would speak. *So am
I, my captain*, he would say.

But he never did.

The door of the inn was bowled open and a thin
woman, Aelfwynn, hurtled in. 'Master, the Anakim! They're
coming!'

Bellamus was on his feet, his chair tipping over behind
him. 'What? How far away?'

'They're here! On the hills, hundreds of horsemen, they
will arrive in . . .' Her hands flailed in a gesture of extreme
urgency. 'In minutes!'

His eyes found Stepan and the two shared an aghast look.
'Flee!' shouted Bellamus. 'Take all the Thingalith you can,
and go!'

'I'm not leaving you here to fall into their hands,' said
Stepan.

Bellamus made a violent slicing gesture. 'I'm the one they
want! They won't care about the rest as long as they get me,
but if I'm with you, they'll pursue us forever and we'll all be
taken. Please, I beg you, go! Go back to your wife, and that
estate and your apple trees. Look after them all. The Anakim
were always going to find us and they will get me with you

here or without. Here, take this,' added Bellamus, thrusting the silk message at him. Secrecy did not matter any more. 'Find a way to get that to the queen. Now go.'

Stepan held the scrap of silk loosely, meeting Bellamus's gaze for one last moment. There was an understanding between the two men: a farewell; an acknowledgement that Stepan would have protested longer, had time allowed; a loving and heartfelt *good luck, my brother*. Then the knight turned and strode for the door, ducking beneath the lintel. Bellamus took two deep breaths. 'You too, Aelfwynn,' he said. 'Please leave now.' She scurried into the early light outside.

He was left alone with a sudden quiet. He looked around him at all he had prepared for an Anakim raid: his poison quill, his lead-weighted staff, the glove with blinding powder concealed inside. It all suddenly seemed so feeble against his enemy. The Anakim did not take prisoners.

'So this is how it ends,' he said to the silence. He had never thought to come so far. It had been a surprise to escape the Black Kingdom after their first invasion. An even greater one to survive Harstathur, and the king's wrath when he returned to Suthdal in disgrace. 'Chance,' he had once boasted to Stepan, the two of them drunk together after Harstathur, 'is a friend of mine.' It had certainly shown him outrageous favour so far. This reckoning did not seem unfair to him.

He could hear the panicked cries outside as his followers began to abandon Brimstream. Horses were galloping up the road and he prayed, in one of his unusual moments of faith, that they made it clear. That he was right, and he was all the Anakim would want. He was not sure about that at all, but it was the only hope he could offer his people.

All of which, he supposed, left one question.

How do I want to die? It would not affect how he was remembered, but as ever, he felt that stubborn will to resist. He had not got to where he was by giving up. Chance was no friend to those who lay down and accepted its capricious whims. He wanted to die as he had lived: on his feet, like a man. Like a Sutherner.

He donned his leather jerkin, pinned the spider brooch from the queen to his chest, put on his boots and his fine red cloak. He finished assembling the wooden queen, gluing the leather patch to her base and returning her to the empty space on the chessboard. He took a final swig from the wine-skin, put a last log on the fire, and added the wooden frame with which he encrypted his notes to Aramilla. Then he stepped outside the inn. The last of the Thingalith were riding out of the village. They had left their arms and armour behind: all but one of them, who carried an upright spear as he galloped out of the village. It was Garrett. Doubtless he would take command of those men who escaped Brimstream. Poor souls, they would not find him an easy captain.

Bellamus walked to the end of the road. It was a grey day, but he took unusual pleasure at the cold wind, the smell of the rain mixed with the grit of the road, and the feel of it beneath his boots. He stood at the edge of Brimstream, watching the dark flood of horses bear down upon him.

He laughed out loud when he saw who led them. He did not ride his vast grey destrier, presumably sacrificed in the name of speed, and no Silver Wolf-Head banner flew with him. But the upright posture, unusual height and robust countenance of Roper Kynortasson, the Black Lord himself, were unmistakable.

Roper reached him first. Cold-Edge was in his hand and he swung himself out of the saddle, holding the blade beneath Bellamus's chin as he dropped to the ground. 'Do not move,' he growled. Then he bellowed over his shoulder: 'Search the village! Keep them alive, for now.'

'A raiding party led by the Black Lord himself,' said Bellamus, proud that his voice came out as mild as he had intended. 'I am honoured.'

'It is an honour you have earned,' Roper assured him grimly. 'Do you have food here?'

'Some,' admitted Bellamus. 'Nothing like enough to satisfy your army.'

'Better than nothing,' said Roper, and Bellamus felt that instant sense, familiar with Roper, that here was a man who thought like he did. Roper gestured for Bellamus to turn around and marched him up the street. Around them, Sacred Guardsmen dismounted energetically, swords in hand, and battered down each door.

'The doors open if you lift the latch,' said Bellamus. 'And the buildings are empty. It's just me here.'

'You are the important one,' said Roper.

A Sacred Guardsman with a spray of black vulture feathers hanging from his helmet emerged from the inn before them, stepping over the shattered fragments of the door at his feet. *The Captain of the Guard*, Bellamus thought. *Gray Konrathson.*

'My lord?' said Gray, indicating that Roper should look inside.

Bellamus felt the sword-tip at his back, directing him back inside the Cobweb, and he obeyed, frowning down at the splinters of the door. Was there a need to smash his life apart like this?

Back inside his headquarters, Gray pointed Roper towards the table of weapons Bellamus had developed. Some were passed over unnoticed. The quill. The choking candles. A few books with blades hidden in their covers. But others were spotted at once for what they were. The glove with the secret poison pouch, the weighted staff, more concealed blades. Every one of them had been convincing to Bellamus, but some sign betrayed them to Anakim eyes. *Interesting*, he thought. Evidently he did not yet understand how the Anakim saw the world.

Roper left Bellamus unattended behind him and picked up the poisoned glove delicately. He inspected it at arm's length and then replaced it on the table. 'Is any of this going to hurt us?' he asked Bellamus, without turning around.

'Not if you're careful with it,' said Bellamus.

Roper picked up a chess piece: the queen Bellamus had modified to hold Aramilla's message. He hefted it, turned around and looked levelly at Bellamus. 'Now what does this do?' he asked.

Bellamus was so shocked that he almost betrayed himself. He almost asked: *But how do you know?* Instead, he just smiled. 'That is just a chess piece, my lord.'

'I doubt that,' said Roper, replacing it carefully. 'Do you play?'

'I love to play,' said Bellamus. 'But, in all modesty, I cannot often find decent opposition.'

Roper looked back at him and Bellamus felt a sudden absurd hope that he was going to be spared. Roper did not want to kill him.

The Captain of the Guard evidently sensed this too. 'There is much we could learn by keeping him alive, lord,' he said innocently.

'Agreed,' said Roper brusquely. 'Bind his hands, would you, Gray?'

Was he to be interrogated, then? Uneasily, he held out his hands for Gray to tie.

'Behind your back,' said the captain in a voice which brooked no argument, unmoved by the upstart's charming smile.

Bellamus's smile turned rueful and he showed his back to Gray, who bound his hands firmly. 'We'll take this, shall we?' said Roper, indicating the chessboard. 'See if I can offer you a game.'

'I would like that,' said Bellamus carefully, wondering what kind of game he was being offered.

'I suspect life will be very much easier with you in our custody,' said Roper. He picked a small linen bag from Bellamus's possessions and tipped the chessboard, pieces and all, inside. 'You have been making this campaign extremely difficult for us.'

Another legionary – no, an officer of some kind, with a face that was well balanced but rocky, even for an Anakim – stepped over the shattered door. He spared Bellamus a glance, both brutal and amused, and spoke to Roper. 'Good news, my lord. They have what we estimate to be about half the Unhieru arms and armour here.'

'What did you do with the rest?' asked Roper, looking at Bellamus.

'We were melting it down for our own weapons, I'm afraid,' he replied. 'Arms of that size are no good to us.' All three Anakim examined him at that, but it was the truth and Bellamus stared back, unconcerned.

The new arrival advanced on Bellamus, leaning down and peering into his face. 'What happened to your eye?' He was not particularly tall for an Anakim, but radiated a sense of authority much less subtle than that given off by Roper.

'I took a fall,' said Bellamus, shrugging. 'Hit a rock.'

'Damned careless,' said the officer happily. He looked at Roper. 'You've bound him. Is he to live, then?'

'Given the forces he mobilised against us, he's of great value to us alive,' said Roper. 'He could be very helpful in future.'

The officer smiled nastily at Bellamus. 'That is unfortunate for you,' he decreed, turning away. Roper had a truly interesting manner to him, Bellamus thought. Mild, in general, but his opinions were evidently weighty, even to the forceful newcomer.

The four of them went outside, Bellamus aware of Gray's watchful eyes on his back. 'I think we'll take the Guard, and Bellamus here, back to camp,' Roper announced to the cluster of guardsmen outside. 'Tekoa,' he said, turning to the officer. 'The Skiritai can handle things here and bring back what remains of the Unhieru arms?'

'Certainly,' said Tekoa. 'But I will rest them here before we return.'

'That would be well earned,' agreed Roper. 'We will await

your return. Burn this place, before you leave, and be careful in there,' he said, pointing back into the inn. 'Bellamus is not out of surprises just yet.'

Bellamus raised his eyebrows mischievously at Tekoa, who stared flatly back at him. 'He's a cocky bastard, isn't he?'

'Is that not what you were expecting?' asked Roper, who then seized Bellamus by the shoulders and lifted him bodily onto a horse. Bellamus found himself sitting in front of a Sacred Guardsman, bound hands uncomfortably crushed against his cuirass. A horse was brought for Roper, who mounted beside him. Bellamus twisted back to Brimstream, intending to bid his headquarters a final goodbye.

And his heart nearly lunged from his chest. A huge breath tore at his lungs, and then another, so powerful that his throat was too narrow to channel them, and he felt a painful hiccough. He looked abruptly back to the front, trying to calm himself.

He had forgotten about the infected legionaries in the barn. One of them had been led out behind him, a blanket over his shoulders. The other was being carried in his wake.

Dear God, we must leave now. Please, please, we must go now.

Before anyone observed that these captive legionaries were dreadfully sick. Before Roper asked questions, either of the legionaries themselves, or of Bellamus, as to how that had happened. Before the Anakim realised the full ramifications of what they had done. By handling the first legionary. By releasing the second. Whether Bellamus wished it or not, it had begun.

His weapon had been unleashed, and they had to go.

26

Like Locusts

Roper felt unpleasantly detached for the ride back to their encampment, as though he had drunk far too much the night before. The landscape, none of which was recognisable from their dark outward journey, was barely visible anyway through a smog of exhaustion.

He was used to being tired. Indeed, he seldom operated in any other state while on campaign. But even before Jokul had come to him with the information of where Bellamus was hidden, he had been in a state of weariness as profound as any he had known. The knowledge that they must act at once to secure the upstart, or lose their chance, furnished him with the energy to make the night-time ride. But now he could barely keep his eyes open and longed for nothing so much as that comfortable stretch of earth by his fire, wrapped in his cloak, a saddle as his pillow. His resolve had crumbled, and he told himself that just this once, he would allow his men to see him sleep. When they finally stopped, and an aide steadied his horse to let him dismount, he nearly fell from the saddle.

'Thank you,' he heard himself say. 'Gray?'

'Lord?'

'How do you feel? You must be weary.'

Roper heard the understanding in his captain's reply and blessed it. 'No, lord, I could keep going. What would you have me do?'

'Would you see to it that Bellamus is properly secured somewhere? And then rest, my friend, Almighty knows, you've earned it.'

'I will, lord.'

Roper's hearth pulled him in, and he arrived to find Sturla, legate of Ramnea's Own, and Keturah talking amiably. 'Is all well?' he asked.

'Everything's fine here, Husband,' said Keturah. 'What of your mission?'

'We got him,' said Roper.

Sturla turned away and raised a clenched fist in triumph. Keturah said: 'Dead?'

'Alive. We've brought him back. What, um . . . What . . .'

'You are exhausted, Husband,' said Keturah's voice, amused. 'Lie down. Everything is in hand here.'

Roper was not sure if the thanks he intended made it past his lips. He meant to wait until Gray was back, but his head was resting on the flattened grass, breathing in its good scent. He felt cool hands push a saddle beneath his temple, his eyes already glued shut, and he plunged into a deep, heavy sleep.

When Roper awoke, it was to voices and the gentle billow of the fire. He opened his eyes to find that it was night, and sat up, his head heavy. Several legates were talking on the far side of the hearth and Keturah was sitting next to the Chief Historian, both staring silently into the flames. Around them were the sleeping bodies of Pryce and Gray, both curled into their cloaks.

Keturah looked up at him. 'Welcome back,' she said. 'We were about to lie down, but have saved you some hoosh.'

'Thank you. Do lie down,' said Roper, sitting forward. 'I can serve to the others when they awake.' He wished he had not slept before them all, but the force of it had been irresistible. 'No sign of Tekoa?'

'None. I went to visit Bellamus, though.'

'Did you?'

'He looks like a child,' said Keturah, 'but speaks so cleverly.' Roper remembered his first interaction with the Sutherners. Their faces had disturbed him: so open, expressive and strangely endearing.

'They're all like that,' he replied.

'He *bleeds* his emotions,' said Keturah, deliciously. 'So easy to read!'

'But deceptive,' said the Chief Historian, crisply. 'Keep your wits about you. A capricious people, too easily underestimated.'

'I am not about to untie him, lady,' said Keturah.

'Not yet,' she said.

Keturah's eyes gave a swift roll, but Roper was inclined to agree with the old historian. So potent had the spymaster's reputation become that Roper's curiosity was tempered by wariness. Even here, even under guard, who knew what he was capable of?

'And what does tomorrow hold?' asked Keturah. 'We have our great enemy bound and tied to a post. We have sacked and burnt northern Suthdal's great city. What now?'

Roper prodded the fire with a stick. 'We recovered half the Unhieru armour when we found Bellamus. We will remake the rest, set it on the road, and then march.'

'Where?'

'The next source of food: Deorceaster. Losing the food here was a disaster. We'll have to struggle on as best we can until we reach the next city. They're squirrelling their food, so let's hop from one cache to another and see how they manage once we've snatched their supplies. We will consume and move on, and on again, until Lundenceaster lies at our feet.'

'Speaking of food, have some hoosh, my dear,' said Keturah comfortably, leaning forward to shuffle the pot towards him. Roper dragged it closer, hiding the disappointment at how little it contained.

Presently, Keturah and Frathi retired, followed by the legates. Roper stayed up to keep an eye on the hoosh in case
Gray and Pryce should awake and find themselves hungry.
He was still ravenous, and it was a relief when Gray awoke
and took his mind off it. 'He'll be so irritable when he wakes
up,' said Gray, looking down at his slumbering protégé. 'His
temper gets very short when he's hungry.'

'There's going to be a lot of that to endure, then,' said
Roper, examining the sleeping guardsman. 'I have great
respect for Pryce. I certainly owe him more than I could
repay. But in honesty, I have never quite understood the two
of you.' He looked up at Gray, slightly apologetic, but the captain seemed merely interested. 'How is it that you, alone,
command his respect and affection?'

'I suggest you ask him,' said Gray.

Roper grinned. 'I would never ask him. He would stare at
me and say something derisive about talking too much and
doing too little.'

'That's certainly true,' said Gray. He thought for a moment.
'He likes extremes, my protégé. I think he saw something
unusual in me; unusual commitment and energy to my
beliefs. He is the same, in his commitment to what he thinks
is important. We share that, which is crucial, and beyond it
we are complementary souls. The few things he lacks, are
the skills I have worked hard on.'

'You do yourself an injustice,' said Roper. 'You are not just
a donkey, plodding workmanlike towards your ambitions.
Some of the talents you have are innate, like Pryce's self-
assurance. You could not possibly train someone to think as
coolly under pressure as you do.'

'Oh, I'm not sure I agree,' said Gray. 'I certainly didn't used
to have much control under pressure. I think people comfort
themselves over their shortcomings by saying such things
are out of their grasp. To change your own character takes
immense effort, and people find it easier to believe that they
weren't born with a trait they desire, so they'll never have it,

than to admit it would take them a great deal of hard work and introspection to be who they want. We say: *you must be true to yourself*, and claim that is a virtue, when often it is an excuse to maintain your current habits. Because habit is all personality is. You cannot expect to behave at your best under pressure if it is not already deeply ingrained in your habits when that moment comes.

'That is why you must never surrender to possession, my lord,' he added. 'Surrender to that, and it becomes more natural to give way in future to fear, or greed, or self-interest. Surrender to nothing. Live by your principles. You are born with a character, but you can also shape it through a thousand small choices every day. You are your habits.'

Surrender to nothing, Roper thought to himself.

The two of them retired when it became clear that Pryce would sleep through the night. When Roper awoke, it was with his nose in Keturah's hair. She was still soundly asleep in front of him and he wriggled slightly closer. Her scent was so familiar now: wood smoke from the fire, and the aromatic fragrances that the Academy had imprinted on her clothes. And her own scent: sweet, and like nothing so much to Roper as the smell of comfort and darkness. *Her scent doesn't fit her*, he thought. *It should be something sour. Lemons perhaps*. He laughed.

'What are you doing back there?' she demanded waspishly.

'Nothing, sorry.' *She should smell of lemons.*

'Stop breathing into my ear,' she decreed.

He sat up, pulling his cloak from beneath him and shuddering. It was cold, and for the first time in days, the sky was clear. He kindled the fire for the others and announced he was going to try and turn Bellamus to their side. Keturah informed him where she had found him the previous night, and Roper rose too fast, so that the lack of food made him light-headed and he nearly fell down again.

Bellamus was held where Keturah had said, just a few

minutes north. Roper found him with his head leaned back against a post, around which his hands had been tied. He was trying to sleep, but whenever his unconcealed eye closed, his head tilted and slipped off the pole. He would awake for just long enough to reposition his head and then it would begin to tilt again.

Roper sat down in front of him and watched for a while. Eventually, Bellamus's head slipped forward and stayed down, facing the ground. Roper heard him utter a little sigh and he sat up, eye focusing slowly on Roper. 'Perhaps you'd like a tether,' said Roper. 'Then you could lie down.'

'And what do you want in return?' he asked, unshielded eye narrowed.

'Is there anything you'd like to tell me?' asked Roper, simply.

Bellamus blinked and there was a touch of defiance in his exhausted gaze. 'Like what?'

Interesting, thought Roper. *There is something on his mind*. 'I think you know,' he tried.

Bellamus observed him a little longer. 'I really don't.'

Roper was not convinced. There had been something hanging in the air between them. Bellamus knew what it was, but Roper did not. 'We shall find somewhere private, Spymaster. We have much to talk about.'

Bellamus licked his lips. 'Talk, where?'

'One of my officers has a tent. I'm sure he'd lend it to us for a spell.' Roper released the spymaster but kept his hands bound behind his back as he escorted him across camp to Vigtyr's brown canvas pavilion. The western side of it billowed and wafted inwards, like the sail of a ship, and the opening before them was tightly sutured.

'Vigtyr?' Roper called. 'Are you inside?'

'What is it?' bellowed a voice in return. 'I am busy!'

'It is Lord Roper,' said he, curtly.

There was a long pause. 'Lord Roper,' came Vigtyr's voice, abruptly civil. 'How may I serve you?'

'You may start by addressing me to my face, rather than through the walls of your tent. I was hoping I might make use of it for an interrogation.' To Roper's surprise, he heard whispered words exchanged inside.

'Of course, lord,' Vigtyr replied, eventually. 'My great apologies. If I might have a moment? I am not . . . presentable.'

'Whenever you're ready,' said Roper.

When, after some minutes, the stitches that held the mouth of the tent together were unfastened, Vigtyr appeared with a rueful grin. 'I am deeply sorry, lord, I was not expecting visitors.'

'That is no trouble, Lictor,' said Roper, standing aside so Vigtyr could exit. 'It is gracious of you to lend us the space.'

'Given to me by your own grace, lord,' said Vigtyr, piously. He stooped through the entrance and then cast a look back inside. And a woman walked out after him. She was small and stocky, with a pointed chin and prominent cheekbones. Most remarkable about her appearance however was the expression she wore. Open appraisal of Roper, sweeping his person from head to toe, and an evident disdain at what she saw.

Roper stared back. He had heard that Vigtyr was courting a new wife and here was the proof. Roper had had two of the lictor's previous wives pointed out to him by Keturah, and had to agree that this woman was nothing like them. They had been slender and delicate, with a superficial, and to Roper's eye, slightly immature, beauty. This woman looked rough and energetic, and even without speaking, gave off an aura of such boldness that Roper found it vaguely impertinent.

'My lord,' said Vigtyr, solemnly. 'This is Adras, who is a companion of mine.'

'Pleased to meet you, Lord Roper,' Adras added, with more of a nod than a bow.

Roper looked up at Vigtyr. 'Lictor. It is good of you to lend us this space, so we shall overlook this. However, to bring female company into your tent like this is a gross misuse of privilege. You are an elite officer. This falls well short of my expectations.'

Vigtyr bowed his head. 'I apologise, my lord. You are right and it shall certainly not happen again.'

'See that it doesn't.'

Vigtyr bowed and the reprimand persuaded Adras to offer something close to one in turn. They left Roper and his captive to the space, Roper's eyes following as they departed. Neither one had stolen so much as a glance at Bellamus. Still frowning, Roper gestured the spymaster in and followed him into the gloom.

Roper's first impression was of startling regularity. Two thick cloaks, on which Vigtyr evidently slept, lined one side like a black moat without a single crease. On the other side, Vigtyr's armour and weapons had been laid out with minute accuracy, as though dressing an invisible corpse. In a canvas sack at the head of this equipment seemed to be Vigtyr's food. Roper could tell from the way the sack was sitting that everything within was piled to similar extremes of order, and it even seemed that Vigtyr has smoothed and stretched out the sack to eliminate creases in its surface.

'Extraordinary,' said Roper, finding the space so methodical it was violent. Had the grass beneath his feet been swept too? Surely that was just a quirk of how the tent had been erected, but it did appear to have been flattened to create a smooth carpet of dark and shining green.

Roper gestured and Bellamus turned, allowing the Black Lord to untie his hands. The bindings were exceptionally snug and it took Roper a long time to wriggle the rawhide bands free. His hands released, Bellamus gave a quiet moan and dropped heavily to his knees, body wrapped around his white digits as they filled with blood and pain. Roper carried a bag over one shoulder and dropped it between them. 'There are two ways we can proceed,' he told the balled figure. 'The first will be comfortable enough for you. The second will not.

Either way, you will tell us everything we need to know. Which would you prefer?'

Bellamus was silent a while, face pressed into the grass. 'The first,' he murmured.

Roper nodded, reaching into the bag. Bellamus looked up rather suddenly, backing away on hands and heels, but when Roper's hand reappeared it was holding a white wooden queen: the chess piece he had taken from the Cobweb. He hefted it, noting that the balance was skewed too far to the base and wondering again what modification it possessed. He looked long at Bellamus, but pulled out the chessboard and laid the piece carefully upon it without saying another word. Silently, he assembled the two sides.

'We are to play?' asked Bellamus suspiciously.

'We will play, and talk,' said Roper.

'May I ask a question, then?'

'The questions will be mine,' said Roper.

'I am sure. But how did you find me? I thought I had covered my tracks well.'

Roper would not indulge Bellamus, but in this case, he did not know the answer anyway. Jokul had come to him, saying he knew where Bellamus was but that the Kryptea did not have enough men to extract him. 'How do you know this?' Roper had asked, warily.

'If I were you, Lord Roper,' had come the reply, 'I would not waste this time quizzing me. We know where he is at this instant, but as soon as he has word of that, and he will, given how riddled our army is with his spies, he will be gone. Take him now.'

Roper had permitted himself one final question. 'How many men will I need?'

The pieces were set, their two armies bristling across the battlefield once more.

'Before we play,' he said, 'there was something you feared I knew earlier, as you were tied to that post. Remember your time in our captivity can go one of two ways. So what was it?'

Bellamus paused, looking down at the board. 'I feared you knew that Garrett has taken command of the Hermit-Crabs, and would wish to hear where they are. I do not know, I am afraid.'

Roper did not believe him, but neither did he think that he would turn Bellamus through violence. His judged this was not a man who could be bullied, and he merely gestured at the board. 'Your turn first.'

The spymaster began by moving with an entire fist clamped around each piece as dexterity returned to his fingers. Roper wondered whether he was trying to make his moves appear clumsier than they were, for he was certainly nimbler in mind than digit. He began by laying two traps for Roper in quick succession, inviting him to attack and leave his king defenceless. Roper kept his face blank, pretending that he had not noticed, and laying a counter of his own.

This did not feel like a game. On a real battlefield with real soldiers, Roper had shaded their contest only because fate had intervened: an extraordinary lightning bolt, that now marbled every swirl of Roper's brain. The glare of it. The crack, which had been beyond the capacity of his ears so they had simply rung in protest. That violent thrill which had run through him. If Bellamus defeated him on this more controlled battlefield, it seemed to Roper he would have the mental advantage next time they met with real soldiers.

If we ever meet on the field again, he reminded himself. Which they surely would not. Bellamus was in his custody now and did not have the influence to command a Suthern army in any case.

But Roper was distracted, mind churning as to how he might bring Bellamus to their side.

'You must hate us with an unusual intensity, Master Bellamus,' he said carefully, eyes set on the board as though considering his next move.

Bellamus's head jerked up. 'Hate you?'

'Of all our enemies, you are our most dedicated and

resourceful. And yet the operation at your spy-hub was a small one. It must take unusual motivation to persist and cause such damage when confronted with so many obstacles.'

'Oh.' Bellamus looked down again, smiling wryly. 'No. No, I don't hate you at all, in fact.'

Their pieces wrestled for a few minutes more before Roper went on. 'Why do you do it, then?'

Bellamus made no reply for a time. In which theatre he was considering his next move, Roper had no idea. But there had been something in his wry smile at the last question that made Roper think Bellamus knew exactly what he was trying to do. 'Ambition,' he said at last.

'Is there no other way for you to satisfy your ambition?'

'For me, not really, no. You may not understand this, Lord Roper. In my world, I am one of the lowest because of my lineage. Ordinarily, there would only be so far I could rise without one of my betters putting me back down. But that does not satisfy me. Every noble in Erebos fears and despises your kind. So much that they would never seek to understand you themselves: it would make them sick in the eyes of society, and they'd be shunned. It takes an outsider, with no status to lose, to specialise in your people. And however much they're loath to admit it, that makes me invaluable to the nobility.' He glanced at Roper. 'I must admit though, I discovered that mostly by accident. When I first started to study the Anakim, it was because you fascinated me.'

'So you don't hate us.'

'Not in the least.'

'That does make you unique,' Roper observed. 'But you say you're invaluable to the nobility, and yet, at the village we found you, you seemed to be operating alone.'

'I am invaluable,' Bellamus insisted. 'But I am not immune. And the loss of our forces at Harstathur was a significant mark against me. But I hoped that in the chaos of your coming south, the king might discover once more how much he needs me, and offer a royal pardon.'

'So despite all you have done, you are still held at arm's length from Lundenceaster.' Roper smiled. 'In my country, we are treated the same from birth, regardless of parentage. And when we reach the rank of subject, we call each other "peer" to show that all is equal between us.'

'I know.'

'It has been very frustrating fighting against you. If you were one of us, you'd be a senior officer. Perhaps a legate, in command of a legion. And your own people will give you none of that, because of the circumstances of your birth?'

Bellamus looked up very slowly from the board, fixing Roper with one brown eye. His face was resolved, and amused, as if to say: *I know what you're doing, Lord Roper.* 'Indeed.'

Roper looked back at him. 'We'll need you to help us, Bellamus. It is the only way I shall be able to justify keeping you alive.'

'What do you want from me?'

'Your full cooperation,' said Roper. 'Starting by disclosing the location and extent of the Suthern forces.'

'I don't know them,' said Bellamus, with such obvious relief that Roper believed him. 'It was always a risk that I'd be captured. Everything I have done, I have done with as little knowledge as possible. Mostly I gather information on your forces and send it to Lundenceaster with suggestions of how they might use it. Little news comes back.'

'Then I want you to write a message to Lundenceaster, passing them false tidings.' But Bellamus was shaking his head.

'My messages to Lundenceaster had to be encrypted with a physical cypher, which I destroyed when I saw you approach. I can no longer send or receive messages from the south.'

'I don't believe you,' said Roper.

Bellamus shrugged. 'Whether you believe me or not does not matter. I cannot do it.' There was a fraught silence, Bellamus turning back to the board first.

The game was concluding, Roper rounding up the last of Bellamus's pieces and surrounding his king. 'Checkmate,' he announced, with as much nonchalance as he could muster.

Bellamus's good eye peered down at the board. 'Damn,' he said, with such polite dismay that Roper laughed accidentally. 'Again?'

'I have duties,' said Roper, though he suggested a game the next day, as they were still awaiting Tekoa's return. They played again the following afternoon, Roper wondering whether he could use Bellamus's ravenous ambition as a lever to turn him to their side. But though he was victorious on the board, he felt no closer to recruiting the spymaster.

He returned Bellamus to his post, and was in the act of tethering him to it when he spotted that Tekoa was back, stalking past them and glowering at the grass. 'Looking particularly confrontational, Legate,' Roper observed.

Tekoa glanced at the pair of them, and then stopped abruptly. 'One of the legionaries we found in your barn is dead, spymaster,' he said spikily. 'Another is grievously sick. And since we visited your lair, several of my own men have developed severe lethargy and pain.' He prowled towards Bellamus, almost led by his eyes, boring into the Sutherner. 'So I ask you, spy-monger. What have you done?'

27
Sickness

The nobles of Lundenceaster tended to favour litters if they wanted to travel across the city. Aramilla found them unbearably stifling and preferred to walk. While her ladies-in-waiting tried to emulate her in all things, this was too much. Their slippers were fine satin, their gowns silk, their hair piled and oiled, and all that would disintegrate within moments of contact with the filthy streets. Thus Aramilla walked at the head of a flotilla of litters, a score of royal retainers guarding every angle of her.

The cobbles heaved and bustled. Nightwater was cast down with an air of celebration, splattering knees and shins. The folk of the city (brown, Aramilla noted, always brown in hair, in garb, in shoe and in the filth on their faces) squawked and bustled like hens, carrying flour, carpets, charcoal barrows, geese. As they saw the queen and her royal guard, they hurried aside, snatching off their caps and stooping low. Or most of them did. Whores, peering from upstairs windows, called lasciviously to her, inviting her for lessons on how she might please her king. The royal couple's lack of children was a common source of gossip and wonder, but the crude shouts only made Aramilla smile, and the whores, pleased with this royal recognition, would then cry: 'God bless Her Majesty! God bless King Osbert!'

God bless King Osbert. He had not even spoken to her since their encounter in the reading room. Every time Aramilla tried to approach him in court, he had turned ostentatiously aside. An unfamiliar feeling now disturbed her: that of instability.

They reached the city walls by the barracks where Aramilla found her father. 'Ah, my dear.' He took a firm grip on her arm, steering her away from the guards as each litter opened like an oyster and disgorged a shining noble. 'And what word from your low-born charmer?' He sounded revolted.

Aramilla looked around, but no one seemed to have heard the earl's words. 'He's intercepted a shipment of weapons destined for Unhierea, without which the giants will not join the fight.'

'My, hasn't he done well?' said the earl carelessly. 'We shall go and build on his success.' All around them, the barracks were expelling men, who were heading for the gate and the huge encampment assembling before Lundenceaster. Aramilla's ladies-in-waiting climbed to the top of the wall and watched like a row of seagulls as the army to defeat the Anakim mustered. They would head north under Earl Seaton's command, gathering knights and the fyrd (a force of armed peasants) until they were ready to meet the Black Lord on the field. His forces were growing weaker through hunger, Bellamus reported, and every day their heartsickness at being abroad would increase. All the while, the Suthern forces would get stronger. Time was with them. They might lose a few northern towns and cities, but the true objective was to keep Suthdal itself. And the longer they waited, the better their chances became.

'Have you told His Majesty about Bellamus?' asked Aramilla calmly, grey eyes on the army below.

'I? No, no . . . Why, are you not well regarded at present?'

'He won't acknowledge me.'

'Your own carelessness, I'm afraid.'

Aramilla wilted at that news. The king had never been so suspicious before and she could do nothing to placate him if he would not even talk to her. She could not recall ever having felt so exposed, a feeling not helped by the lack of news from Bellamus in recent days. She looked at her father. 'I have not heard from Bellamus for some time now. There were messages I was expecting from him which haven't arrived. That is unusual.'

'Dear me, out of favour with both your lovers at once,' said the earl. 'Your powers are growing weak.'

The nobles on the battlements were applauding at the army massing below them, but to Aramilla it looked weak. It was many fewer than they had been able to muster the previous year and that force had been utterly routed by the Anakim.

'I must join the army,' said Earl Seaton. He smiled at Aramilla, giving her a delicate kiss for the benefit of the watchers on the battlement. 'Remember who our enemy is, Daughter,' he said softly. 'Remember how you'll survive this.'

Aramilla did not stay on the wall long, feeling that she needed company for the first time that she could remember. She discovered one of her ladies departing early, and ignoring this terrible etiquette, latched onto her. 'Departing so soon, Lady Cathryn?'

Cathryn, plump and dimpled, gave a sunny curtsey to the queen. 'The battlements are packed, Your Majesty. There was not much to see.'

'Perhaps I will share your litter on the way back,' said Aramilla, graciously.

Lady Cathryn waved a hand informally at the plush interior. 'As you wish, Majesty.'

I am weak indeed, she thought. For the first time in her life, she had no powerful allies. The king's displeasure weakened her own status and she became aware of the feeling of aloneness, new and leaching. She smiled at Cathryn with true gratitude and stepped into the litter.

'Me?' asked Bellamus, incredulous beneath Tekoa's glare. 'What could I have done? It sounds as though your men have fallen ill, sir.' But the spymaster's heart was thumping.

His observation was met with a corrosive stare. 'Ill? Yes, they are certainly ill. And why would that be?'

Bellamus shrugged. 'Illness happens. I do not control it.' *If the first one is dead*, he thought, *and the second unconscious, there are no witnesses to contradict me*. He stared blankly into Tekoa's livid face.

'You ask me to believe this is coincidence?' asked the legate. 'That we visit your nest, where you hold two of my men captive apart from the others, and they turn out to carry disease which has now spread through my men?'

'What are you suggesting I did?' said Bellamus, trying and almost achieving exasperation. 'Those two were separated because we had no space with the others.' That was close to true. Bellamus did not think of the consequences of this disease, or whether he wanted it to spread any further than it already had. At that moment, he merely wanted to survive this encounter. Everything else could be decided in the long hours ahead, tied to the post.

Tekoa looked to Roper. 'I think this was a trap for us. I think he wanted to be found, to introduce this disease to our army.'

That would've been the perfect way to deliver it, thought Bellamus, *if I were more self-sacrificial*.

'That seems a stretch to me,' said Roper. 'But have you quarantined the men?'

'I am not an imbecile,' snapped Tekoa. 'Of course I have quarantined them. But the two captives came into contact with scores of my men, and this does not look like plague, where physical touch is required for the illness to spread. Quarantine may not even work.'

'We must just be vigilant,' said Roper calmly. 'But as to the idea that Bellamus caused this, how would he?'

Tekoa had no answer for that. Instead he gazed between Roper and Bellamus, eyes two shining slits. 'I see he is manipulating you already, Lord Roper. Watch out for that.' He turned on his heel and swept away, cloak sliding after him like a shadow.

Bellamus took several deep breaths, trying to calm his fluttering heart. 'He seems very upset,' he said.

'No, that was fairly normal,' said Roper. He moved behind Bellamus, who felt him twisting at a leather thong, tethering him to the post at his back. 'We will speak again soon. Good morning, Master Bellamus.'

He heard Roper turn away, footsteps fading like ripples in a pond.

At first, Bellamus merely leaned back on the pole, staring straight ahead. Then he slid to the ground, knees held at his chest and took several long moments just to pant. He suspected quarantine would not work at this stage: too many had been exposed to his captives, and Slave-Plague, ill-named and not plague at all, seemed to carry well on the air. So this weapon was out, and Bellamus found himself glad for it. By most measures he could think of, releasing it would have been the right thing to do. There was a murderous, invasive force in his land: what more could he ask for than a sickness that selectively targeted his enemies? But there was no sense dwelling on this now. Even if he admitted his part in it, nothing he knew could stop this thing.

With nothing more to occupy him, Bellamus stared around the camp, thinking of the devastation that might soon overtake it. He detected an odd note of peace humming through this place of war. It smelt fresh, of grass and wood smoke and the warm air of late spring. Last night, as he had shivered at his post, he had been comforted by the amount of music in the camp. The Anakim were starving, but still sweet hymns thrummed the dark, alongside hollow, mournful piping. They always played with wind, the Anakim. Never strings, or bells. Always the ghostly and half-forgotten music of the pipes. Bellamus had dreamed of music when he was last in the north: silver and otherworldly, and he had listened closely to the tunes last night in case he recognised any of them.

He was not in the Black Kingdom, that place which so compelled and obsessed him that its name reverberated on the air long after it was spoken. But this felt like a thin layer of it. Here was an attempt to transform the Abus into a line of symmetry, with Suthdal and the Black Kingdom in perfect reflection. As much as the Black Kingdom obsessed him; as much as he longed to see those magisterial trees and the shadows that prowled beneath them, they could not have it here. As he had once said to Aramilla: *You must choose a side, and advance it with all your might.* He had chosen his side, and Slave-Plague, that rotten, harrowing sickness, was their greatest weapon.

Roper did not see Tekoa again until a few days after his confrontation with Bellamus, finding him by his fire with Keturah. Their argument was evidently not forgotten, the legate giving Roper a black look. 'What's happening to the spy-monger?' he demanded.

'I am trying to recruit him. I think he admires us a little, you know, and we may yet have his network of spies working for us.'

Tekoa narrowed his eyes at that. 'You are too soft with him already, Lord Roper. I want him gone.'

'What sort of gone?'

'The dead sort.'

'You don't think he has valuable information?'

'I do, if you're prepared to torture him. Are you?'

Roper eyed the legate. 'If it comes to it.'

'Well, well, I'd have thought it has come to it already. He has certainly earned such treatment.'

Roper wondered if Tekoa's warnings contained any truth. But then, what could the spymaster do? He was hardly in a position of power. Everyone else was fretful, Roper decided, because of his reputation.

Keturah had stripped to a light undertunic, the bulge at her stomach startlingly obvious without the folds of her cloak. She was barefoot, soon to leave with the historians on a run, thought to improve memory. 'Where are you off to husband?' she asked, observing Roper similarly stripping his outer layers.

'Training with Vigtyr. It's the first time since I disturbed him in his tent a few days ago,' said Roper, 'with his woman. What was her name? Adras?'

'Yes,' said Keturah, looking up with interest. 'Oh really? What were they up to?'

'He was evidently trying to get her out of her clothes,' said Roper.

'He must really hate her clothes,' said Tekoa, unable to resist a joke even in his dark mood.

'Father!' Keturah exclaimed, unable to withhold the appreciative cackle that followed.

'Are you sure you still want to be running, Wife? Most are struggling without food enough as it is.'

'Frathi would never let me be a historian if I missed a run,' said Keturah. 'Train well, my husband. Don't let Vigtyr take advantage of you.'

Roper left to climb the hill, a storm massing overhead. The sky rumbled like the wingbeats of a colossal bird, hidden behind clouds, which bulged and strained, leaking a gentle patter of rain. He passed legionaries attending to smoking charcoal mounds, or dragging game into camp. They could not move on to Deorceaster until the Unhieru weapons shipment had been completed, so Roper had recruited the entire army to that task. Those who were not producing charcoal were gathering iron to be transformed into giant arms and armour, or seeking what little food that had been left to them in this country.

The atmosphere was tense and resentful, and he could sense the desire of every legionary to turn around and go home. They were sick with hunger, and with the weight of *kjardautha* – the Anakim homesickness. Emotions are contagious, and the mood grew uglier every day.

Vigtyr was already pacing atop the hill when Roper arrived.

'I really must apologise for the incident in my tent, lord,' said Vigtyr. 'It won't happen again.'

'Then it is forgotten, my friend,' said Roper, raising a sword at once. 'Think no more of it.'

'You didn't . . .' Vigtyr paused. 'You didn't ask Pryce to keep an eye on me, then? To make sure it didn't happen again?'

'Pryce?' said Roper, mystified. 'Why would you think that?'

'It just seems he's been nearby a lot, recently. He always seems to be watching me. But perhaps not,' he added, in response to Roper's obvious bewilderment. 'Perhaps I was mistaken.' Vigtyr raised his blade in response to Roper, who was heartened to see the lictor now gave him a little space. He had previously been so scornful of Roper's abilities that he stood close without fear, prodding, probing and stepping, and only seldom forced into a parry. Now there was a touch of respect for Roper's skill, and they skirmished with a little footwork, each testing the other's balance.

'This is good,' said Vigtyr, appraisingly. 'Yes.' He made a sudden step forward and Roper kept the distance between them. 'And on wet ground. Your form is strong.'

That equalled the sum of praise that Vigtyr had delivered so far, and Roper tried hard to pay no attention. *Silence*, he thought. *Silence*.

And suddenly, he lunged. Vigtyr had sought to test him with another little step forward, and Roper advanced to meet him at speed, closing the gap between them like a pair of lodestones snapping together. He had not planned it and did not think about it. It simply happened, and Vigtyr retreated so fast that his foot slid over the wet grass for just a moment. That delayed him, and he was forced into a parry. Roper cut at him again, and again extracted a parry. Attack, parry; attack, parry; attack, duck. Vigtyr's blade, liberated from the task of defence, swung hard into Roper's neck. Roper staggered back, blinking, but he was pleased. He had never wrested more than two parries in a row from his tutor.

Vigtyr's face had gone very cold. 'You hid your intention well there,' he allowed. That was what the lictor had tried to teach: that Roper's countenance should be a stone mask. The Sutherners, he explained, betrayed each movement before it even began with their expressive faces. Roper's face should be blank at all times, and he must be certain that his eyes did not betray his intended target. But Roper, who had struggled with this, was coming to wonder whether there was a better way. If he had no intentions, there was nothing to hide. If he could enter that state of silence that Sigrid had spoken of: to cut out all external noise and live in the instant, there were no thoughts that could animate his face. Thoughts were slow, Roper considered. He must allow his nerves to take control, and simply act.

Vigtyr probed with one of his deceptive attacks. He did not look particularly fast, but because the movement was so economical, and because no warning preceded them, they had usually nearly reached Roper before he registered any danger at all. But this time his wrist moved of its own accord, engaging Vigtyr's weapon and deflecting it with a lunge of Roper's own. Vigtyr had barely committed and leaned away from Roper's sword, parrying the follow-up blow that he offered. Roper went forward again, attacking knee then neck. A feeling broke into his silent head, a wordless cry of triumph and incredulity as Vigtyr retreated. It plunged into Roper's focus like a thoughtless child, he struggled to reject it, and suddenly Vigtyr's sword was at his throat.

'You lost confidence,' the lictor told him.

Not quite, thought Roper. What he had lost was silence.

It did not reappear for the rest of their session. He tried too hard to find it again and it proved elusive. But as the rain began to come down more heavily, and they cleaned the water from their blades with an oiled cloth apiece, Roper was heartened. Next time, when he was fresh and the day's lessons had set, he thought he might be able to find it again. Perhaps for a little longer.

'You started very well, lord,' said Vigtyr. 'You had me pressed a few times there. Have you been practising alone?'

'A little,' said Roper, thinking that would be easier to understand than the truth, that his improvement had been due to a conversation about silence. They descended the hill together, Vigtyr graciously granting Roper the use of his tent again so he could speak once more with Bellamus. 'In the rain? Are you quite sure, Lictor? Please don't feel obliged to say yes, I shouldn't really have asked, only I have a piece of theatre planned to try and turn the spymaster.'

'No, no, lord, take it, please,' said Vigtyr, a touch of melancholy in his voice. 'I should supervise a charcoal mound in any case. What theatre have you planned?'

'Legate Randolph is going to put Almighty fear into the spymaster,' Roper said. 'And we'll see if it has any result.' They bade each other farewell, and Roper collected Bellamus, who was shivering violently in the rain.

'Chess?'

'Yes please,' he replied numbly.

Within the tent, the rain rolled comfortably off the walls, and a loud rumble of thunder passed overhead. Bellamus flared his fingers repeatedly in an attempt to restore circulation and shivered, causing Roper to glance up from assembling the board. 'I don't want to beat you because you're too cold to think.' He took one of the cloaks from Vigtyr's bed and draped it over the spymaster, who nodded gratefully.

Bellamus hugged the cloak about him, and watched as Roper took his first move. 'I hope you realise,' said the

Sutherner, 'that I am tied to a post with nothing but this board to occupy my head. You will have to be on form, Lord Roper.'

'I shall expect great things,' Roper assured him. They played in silence for a while, and Bellamus did indeed have the edge over Roper, forcing his pieces into a defensive knot about the king. But Roper was distracted, his attention focused outside the tent walls. Randolph should interrupt them at any moment. 'Why is it that you alone of the Sutherners do not hate us?' he asked, thinking to make Bellamus vulnerable.

'I think you like what you like,' replied Bellamus. 'There need be no reason . . . Though my first encounter with the Anakim was certainly a compelling one.'

'Well?'

'Many years ago – I was just a teenager – I ended up in a village beneath the mountains some way to the north of Safinim. The people there lived in terror of the Anakim who dwelt higher up. I was offered good money . . . suspiciously good, I should have realised, to keep a watch on them and raise the alarm if they came near the village. Frankly, I knew nothing about the Anakim.' He paused to make an articulate move, increasing the pressure on Roper's beleaguered huddle of defenders.

Roper looked up. 'Go on,' he prompted.

'What was I saying? Ah, I knew nothing about them, or nothing about you. We had heard of the Anakim, of course, in Safinim, but in the same way that I'd heard of elephants and woolly rhinoceroses. I hadn't the first idea what an Anakim might look like, and I was eager to find out. So I accepted the coin I was given, used it to purchase a sheepskin coat, and went into the mountains. Into their environment. You saw our army in your lands last year: you can imagine how I must have blundered and crashed about, and inevitably it was not I who kept watch on them, but they who kept watch on me.' Bellamus raised his hand, indicating the two missing fingers there.

Roper, absorbed by the story, found himself genuinely shocked when the tent flap swept open and a rain-soaked Randolph entered, his face livid and a drawn sword flashing at his side.

'Here he is!' declared the legate, advancing on Bellamus who flinched backwards. Roper stood up between them at once.

'Calm yourself, Legate!' he demanded.

'Calm myself?' Randolph's face was a deep plum, and so livid that Roper was not sure he was acting. 'While our downfall sits there, yet drawing breath? Stand aside, Lord Roper. We've never taken prisoners before, this is the last one with whom we should start!' He tried to thrust his way past Roper, who body-checked him.

'He is under my protection, Legate! Leave this tent at once before I have you disciplined!'

The two men stared at each other a while. Then Randolph began backing away. 'You won't protect him forever, Lord Roper,' he hissed. 'Not with the number of enemies that man has.' He sheathed his sword and turned abruptly, vanishing into the rain.

The entire performance had been at Roper's instruction, but still he found himself slightly shaken. Randolph took great pleasure in jokes and stories and, as Roper had hoped, had brought an equal zeal to this charade. Roper returned to his seat, Bellamus eyeing him across the board. 'As you heard,' said Roper wearily, 'it is getting difficult to justify keeping you alive. If you cannot help us, I'll struggle to keep you safe and this army together.'

Bellamus shrugged. 'It is as I've already said, Lord Roper. I'm of no use to anyone now. I'm broken, my network is scattered and I neither know any more than you, nor have the capacity to find out.' So confidently was this proclamation delivered that Roper believed him.

They played on, Bellamus increasing the pressure on Roper's pieces. Roper rather thought his opponent was overreaching himself, and so it proved. He made a mistake, lost his queen, and his strategy unravelled from there. Bellamus made a dismissive sweep. 'Damn. Damn and damn, I thought I had you.'

'Very nearly,' said Roper, rearranging the pieces. The rain was still pattering at the walls, and it was growing gloomy inside the tent. Roper appraised Bellamus, and then stepped outside the tent to request candles and a light. He thrust his head back inside swiftly, but Bellamus sat placidly. A branch of sputtering pine and two tallow candles were delivered soon afterwards, and Roper set one on either side of the board. He did not need to ask if Bellamus wanted to play again: the alternative was to return to his soaking post.

'This is like the tent I used for interviews last year,' commented Bellamus. 'It was always lit by oil-lamps. People talk more easily that way.'

'So you lost it?'

'The retreat from Githru did not afford us many luxuries,' said Bellamus dryly. After a couple of moves apiece, he said quietly: 'That really was awful.'

'The retreat?' asked Roper, scanning the board.

'Yes. Men froze to death, or lost fingers and toes. We were *hounded*. The wolves, the bears. I do not know how you live with them.'

'They don't trouble us,' said Roper. 'Not unless you're exceedingly thoughtless.'

Bellamus looked interested. 'Why don't they trouble you?'

'I don't know. They just don't, unless you're careless with your food or move as though you're weak. But if you're asking why they trouble you, I'd say it's the way you walk. I saw your army in the forests last year. You move like you're constantly lost. Aimless, uncertain meanderings. If you are not assured in our land, the predators will see that.'

'That was one of the first things I noticed about the Anakim. You have an exceptionally confident and single-minded culture.'

Roper observed the spymaster for a moment. 'Was that an insult?'

'No, no,' Bellamus assured him. 'Merely an observation. I am not claiming any way is superior. Suthern society, I think, is more prone to doubts and hand-wringing. Have we got that right? How can I show I belong to the rest, but am also different? Perhaps we should adopt this for our culture? How can we change?'

'Sounds exhausting,' said Roper. 'And divisive.'

'It is both those things,' said Bellamus. 'But it also keeps Suthern culture dynamic. We have a word you lack in Anakim: *fashion*. It is a name for something that is very briefly popular, and then slowly declines until it becomes embarrassing.'

'Sounds applicable to my rule,' Roper observed.

Bellamus raised a finger, amused. 'Not quite. I haven't given the best definition. It is usually used in relation to clothes, or hair, or pastimes. Things that your race is too austere to bother with, I think. Music,' he added, suddenly. 'You love music. Do you have songs that go in and out of general favour?'

Roper considered this. 'I . . . don't think so. Different ones are sung for different activities or at different times of year. Some songs are only for a particular annual feast, or gathering the acorn harvest. But they don't go in and out of favour at random.'

'So you do not have fashion. And perhaps it is because your society has such self-confidence. Nobody seeks to differentiate themselves from the others, because all are happy with your culture as it is. It is confident.'

Roper drummed his fingers on the board. 'What you are describing sounds to me frivolous and fickle, rather than dynamic.'

'It is all those things,' said Bellamus. 'Frivolous, fickle and dynamic. And therefore, adaptable.'

Roper raised his eyebrows at that. *Confidence versus*

adaptability, he thought. This campaign might decide which was superior. They played on, a vicious battle shuffling across the centre of the board, the exchange ending slightly in Roper's favour.

'I never finished telling you about my first encounter with the Anakim,' said Bellamus.

'No, you didn't.'

'You remember I'd gone into the mountains looking for them,' said Bellamus. 'But I heard them before I saw them. Singing, like I'd never encountered before.' There was a strange radiance to his eye: wistful and painful, and it gathered the rest of his face close in a frown. 'Unearthly noises, ringing through those snow-laden trees. It was like a cicada, and an owl, and a wolf, in eerie concert. I could feel the hairs on the back of my neck rising, and crawled into view of a fireside by which eight of them sat. Two were singing, one playing a pipe of some sort. So tall and lean and graceful, and one of them held a baby, which was almost the strangest of all because it was so quiet. I stayed until it got dark, through the night and to morning, and the baby never made a sound. But they caught me,' he said, grimacing.

'And you escaped?' asked Roper, temporarily divorced from the game. 'They wouldn't have let you live.'

'As a matter of fact, they did,' said Bellamus. He made his move before continuing. 'I had feared them capturing me, and when they did, the atmosphere was quite different from the one I had imagined. It was much, much worse. They were relaxed and light-hearted. It was not as though they were about to kill a person, but an animal of some sort that they'd snared. I thought to survive, I had to humanise myself in their eyes.'

Roper looked over the board at Bellamus, amused. 'Is that what you're doing now, spymaster?'

The tide of Bellamus's pieces was on the way out. He clawed back some pride by waging a petty war against Roper's pawns, but it was another victory to Roper. Bellamus declared his great regret, and asked if Roper might be persuaded to play again. Alas, he could not, and instead bound the Sutherner's hands and returned him to his lonely post in the rain.

When Roper squelched back to his hearth, he found it roaring, and all legates, historians and officers standing close, huddled about its warmth. All eyes were on Keturah, who was recounting an anecdote that Roper had heard before about getting lost in the Academy and having to sit through several hours chanting because she was too embarrassed to leave. Roper doubted the experience had been as boring as she described: he had once heard the Chief Historian refer to her as a 'chant-cormorant', her appetite for history insatiable. She finished to laughter, and when it died down, Tekoa took up storytelling duties. There was something a little distant about this audience, Roper thought.

He slid in beside Keturah and she glanced at him. 'Good lord, you two were holed up in there for hours. What took you?'

'Just talking,' he said.

'Charming, is he? He's very handsome, in an odd sort of way.'

'I have been seeing if he might turn to our side. But I do enjoy his company,' Roper admitted.

That confession drew Keturah's head towards him, face half-illuminated by the fire's shy touch. 'Oh? Our greatest enemy, orchestrator of a thousand disruptive plans that have slowed our progress to a crawl?'

'I know what he's done,' said Roper. 'But he is refreshing. He's so different from everyone else. I only know the kind of man that is produced by the haskoli. They are all direct, hard, confident, energetic,' Roper flapped the words away like smoke. 'And I only realise that now that I've met Bellamus. He is subtle, mild, fascinated by big questions. I can talk with him like I can with Gray, but his perspective is so different.'

Keturah was thrilled. 'Husband, this is sweet! Have you made a friend?'

'No friend, it's just illuminating. How was the run?' he put in quickly, hoping to avoid further questions. In trying to turn Bellamus to their side, all he had succeeded in doing so far was developing a fondness for the spymaster. Once or twice already, he had spotted that Bellamus was trying to manipulate him. But rather than putting him on his guard, Roper admired the intelligence behind his words. He had always rather liked Bellamus, despite everything between them. Perhaps he had known this would happen when he chose to keep him alive. When he took that chessboard.

'Oh, the run was fine but high drama here,' Keturah said, tucking a strand of hair behind her ear.

'Oh, yes?'

'There is a great sickness among the Skiritai,' she confided.

'Oh, I knew that. Let's hope the quarantine works.'

'That's what I mean,' said Keturah. 'The quarantine has failed. That's what Father says. Three score are sick, and more are being brought in every hour.'

'No.' The word uttered itself. He remembered the plague of the previous year. Trying to breathe through the smoke of the corpse fires. The barricades, the fear: streets choked with mounded bodies. His chest rattled, and he felt the tingle of disturbing energy. He looked over at Tekoa, who was staring wearily into the fire. 'No, please,' he murmured. 'Please.'

28

Hunger

Roper slid around the silhouetted audience and joined Tekoa.

'I hear the quarantine has failed,' he murmured.

Tekoa turned away from the firelight, he and Roper walking a few steps out of the circle. 'I wouldn't go quite that far,' he said in an undertone, 'but yes, it seems ineffective. What are we going to do?'

There was a slight jolt as this man, for all his irascible, forceful experience, laid responsibility on Roper's shoulders.

'Well how serious is it? Is this just an illness that people recover from, or is it worse? Does it kill?'

'It kills,' Tekoa confirmed.

'How often?'

'Both the prisoners we liberated from the spymaster's barn are now dead. It is hard to guess how far advanced the other cases are; for most the disease is still in its infancy. But there are a dozen I do not expect to survive the night. Of those infected, it seems likely that more than half will die.'

Roper gritted his teeth, turning inwards the snarl that came to his lips. If he were the sort of man who did such things, now seemed the moment to lose control. He felt an urge to snap something in half and continue tearing at it until only splinters remained; to advance to the fire and obliterate every glowing crumb. But he could not. The customs of his land marbled his flesh and encased him. All he could do was carry on.

'Tekoa,' he said. 'My brother. This can go no further.'

'Agreed,' said the legate, softly.

'*Everyone*,' said Roper, in a vehement hiss. 'Everyone exposed in any proximity at all to those two prisoners, or any of the infected, must be separated from this army. Otherwise sickness will overtake every legionary here.'

'My entire legion,' said Tekoa.

Roper stared bleakly at the two glowing spots of light that were Tekoa's eyes. He did not want to speak, but forced out four bitter words.

'And you, my friend.'

They sounded worse than he could possibly have imagined. He and Tekoa looked long at each other. Those around the fire still talked, forcing cheer and trying to raise their own spirits, while the legate and the Black Lord shared this quiet moment.

'I should go now,' said Tekoa, in the softest voice Roper had ever heard from him. 'We all should.'

He had known. He had just needed it voiced. Bravery in isolation is near impossible, and even Tekoa Urielson needed this fragmentary confirmation before condemning himself.

'I . . .' Roper began. What was there to say? That he was not sure that he could campaign without the legate's guidance and experience. That he would miss his company terribly. That Keturah would likely not forgive him for letting her father go. That without the Skiritai, the army was lost already. Even an embrace, which might have said some of that, was impossible under the circumstances. Tekoa had stayed two nights with those sick men. The part of the army for which he was responsible was rotten. They were about to cut out a great deal of good flesh to ensure they contained the disease.

'Goodbye, Lord Roper. Good luck.' The light in Tekoa's

eyes flickered, and Roper knew he had flashed a glance over his shoulder at Keturah.

'I'll tell her. We will meet again, my brother.'

'In one world or the other,' said Tekoa, with the pale gleam of a smile.

And then he had turned away, into the rain. Roper watched his cloak dissolve into the dark, and took a steadying breath. Then he returned to the fire as if nothing had happened. No one had noticed Tekoa leave, and that was how it needed to remain. If she knew, Keturah would insist she went with her father. He looked down at the bulge beneath her cloak on which she had laid her hand. He looked up at her eyes, narrowed gleefully as she delivered another anecdote. He stood there in silence, smiling whenever there was laughter, and betrayed Keturah. As he knew what to listen for, Roper could even hear the sounds of the Skiritai packing up and departing. Tekoa would likely take them to the coast, where food was more plentiful, and wait there for whatever fate delivered.

The conversation was an exertion, and an hour later was beginning to wind down, when Roper saw a phantom brush the firelight.

Jokul. Without thinking, Roper hailed him. The small man stopped, half turning his attention towards him. Roper made his excuses and jogged out of the circle, joining the stationary master. He had to know whether there was any chance that Tekoa was correct, and Bellamus had deliberately released this disease on them. 'Master. Would you tell me how you located Bellamus?'

From the slightly paler patch of dark before him, he heard an irritable tut. 'Really, Lord Roper, you do not need to concern yourself with the specifics of our work.'

'Master, please. I beg you, this is not mere curiosity, it is important. Would you tell me, in whatever way satisfies you that it does not compromise your agents?'

Jokul was silent. But Roper sensed he could not resist telling the tale. 'Very well. Prior to passing you that information, we had been trailing two suspected spies for some days. One of them realised he was being followed, and was killed to preserve our agent's identity. The other had been seen making nocturnal forays beyond the camp and leaving behind small cairns. We set a watch on these, naturally, and the night after construction, a Suthern woman was observed approaching one and digging at its base. When she retreated, she was followed, leading us right to Brimstream.'

'Brimstream? The spy-hub?'

'Quite. We investigated for some time to be certain of our discovery, before sharing the news with you. Does that satisfy you?'

'It does. I thank you, Master.' Roper returned to the fire, thinking about the account. To him, it suggested that releasing the illness had not been a deliberate act on Bellamus's part. It sounded as though it had been so difficult to find him that it had truly happened against his wishes.

Keturah did not notice Tekoa's absence until they were settling down to sleep together. 'Where's my father gone? Does anyone know?' Nobody did, of course, except Roper, who persuaded himself it was kindness, not cowardice, that she should not find out until the morning. They piled the fire high and shared a waxed linen cloak to shield the rain. Some agitation woke Roper first in the morning, two words spinning around his head, which he tried to dismiss. He revived the fire and set water to boil, dreading what was to come.

When Keturah awoke, her first glance was at the empty patch of ground where Tekoa slept. She looked at Roper. 'Did you see Father? Has he risen already?'

'No, my love,' said Roper, his voice horribly flat. 'He's gone.'

'Gone?' said Keturah, raising an eyebrow. 'Gone where?'

'We spoke about the sickness last night,' said Roper. 'It is spreading too fast, it is deadly and it seems you do not need to have touched a victim to catch it. He and the rest of the Skiritai were too closely exposed to the infected. They have left.'

Keturah leaned forward. incredulous, her mouth open. 'Left for where?'

'I do not know,' said Roper. He nearly shuttered his eyes against the expression on Keturah's face. 'Somewhere far away, to wait out the effects of the sickness, and preserve the rest of the army.'

When Keturah spoke, her voice was poison. 'You sent my father, without so much as a word of farewell, off to die with a band of infected men?'

'I hope not,' Roper said. 'He will not be careless. He'll prioritise the men according to those at greatest risk and try and preserve as much of his legion as possible. But we agreed on this,' he added desperately as Keturah stirred suddenly, getting to her feet. 'He knew that if he said farewell, you would try and stop him, or go with him, and he wanted you safe. What he did was for you, and it may have saved us all.'

Roper caught a glimpse of her derisive expression before Keturah turned away, walking from the hearth without a backward glance and stalking out into the encampment. Roper dropped his head into his hands and held it there.

'You've done the right thing, Lord Roper,' said a cool voice. Roper dragged his head upright and saw the Chief Historian sitting up, watching him levelly. 'Of terrible options, you have chosen the best.'

For some reason, that was what tipped Roper past endurance. His vision blurred, and he stood abruptly. He spared a hand in recognition of her words, and turned away to hide his tears, walking off into the camp, carefully distant from Keturah's retreating shoulders.

When Roper returned to the hearth an hour later, Keturah's things were gone. He supposed she had gone to join Sigrid and Hafdis, and did not pursue her. This army needed him and he had to carry on. So he told the full story of why Tekoa was gone to the legates, who knew most of it already from the watchmen who had reported the Skiritai's departure the previous night. 'This is just a precaution,' he told them. 'Tekoa and I are very much of the hope that he can contain it within the Skiritai and that they will soon be able to rejoin us. But there is absolutely no sense in risking the remainder of this army to sickness. From now on, we must be exceedingly vigilant. Any sign whatsoever that this sickness advanced beyond the Skiritai, please take steps to isolate the infected and inform me immediately. Tell your men this morning, as soon as we are done here.

'Otherwise, this changes nothing. Onwards. Our armourers need one more day to finish the Unhieru arms and then we send them to Gogmagoc, escorted by the Fair Islanders. We move on to Deorceaster and besiege it; assault it straight away if we get the chance. Then onwards again, to the next settlement and the next. Does anyone have any questions?'

Randolph raised a hand. 'What are we to do without the Skiritai?'

'Each remaining full legion will provide two centuries every day for scouting. The Skiritai horse have been left behind, so we still have them. We should not be badly affected.'

There was a silence after that which suggested the legates thought that as unlikely as he did. The Skiritai were the army's most specialist legion, and truly skilled at their work. They would be hard to replace.

Sturla spoke next. 'And what of food? We're starving. Half-rations for too much longer and we will barely be able to march, let alone fight.' The Skiritai were among the army's most skilled hunters, and their departure had made the food situation worse, rather than better.

Roper turned to the Chief Historian. 'My lady, are there any forests further south in which we might hunt?'

'There are,' she said. 'There is one near Deorceaster.'

'Good. Then we will devote a large portion of this army to hunting once we have besieged Deorceaster, and I hope that shall give us enough to carry on. Anything else?'

Randolph cleared his throat, glancing about the circle for

support. 'Do you think the time has come to turn back, my lord?' Roper cocked his head as though surprised at this suggestion, but Randolph, heartened by the murmur of agreement round the fire, went on. 'We have done our best, but the army is starving. We've lost our scouts. The Unhieru remain in their homeland. We've taken just one city, and to finish this we'll need to get as far south as Lundenceaster, and take that too. That city alone would be a match for this army.' He shook his head. 'We cannot subdue Suthdal. We are too few, this place too alien.' Heads were nodding fervently about the circle. 'It is time to go home.'

Roper did not raise his voice. 'Did you think this task would be easy, peers?' He gazed from one officer to the next. 'This may seem overwhelming now: that is your hunger and *kjardautha* talking. I feel that as keenly as any of you, but we do this because we must. There is no turning back, and I will not hear that suggestion again.'

Randolph narrowed his eyes at Roper, but raised no word in protest. Half a dozen other officers seemed ready to object, and Roper coldly observed each in turn until they looked away. 'Onwards.' In unhappy silence, the legates dispersed to spread orders to the legions. Roper was left alone by the hearth, his chest filled with an untraceable dread. He went to find Bellamus.

'My lord!' He was barely away from the hearth when Vigtyr fell into step with him.

'Good morning, Lictor.'

'I wanted to suggest, lord, that Bellamus should have my tent.'

Roper stopped and turned to face Vigtyr. 'An uncommonly generous offer, Lictor, what makes you say so?'

'A number of things, lord,' said Vigtyr, quietly. 'I was first thinking about what you said of the standards of behaviour expected of me. You're right, of course, I must not abuse my privileges and it doesn't seem fair that I have a tent while my men do not. But I was also thinking that as you use the tent for your interviews with the Sutherner, and his health will quickly fade tied to that pole, well. I just wanted to offer you the chance, so you didn't have to ask.'

Roper shook himself in an effort to show proper appreciation for this gesture. 'Well, that's a very thoughtful offer, Lictor. Very thoughtful indeed. I may take you up on it, if it is in earnest. I fear you're right, and the spymaster will deteriorate without some shelter.'

'I hear Sutherners dissolve in too much rain,' Vigtyr replied wryly. 'Yes of course. May I make one small request though, lord? I must admit I struggle with . . . disorder.'

'I had noticed,' said Roper, smiling. 'I've seen constellations less consistent than your tent.'

'Quite, lord. I wondered if I might keep my food in there as well. Nothing that the spymaster can use as a weapon, or to aid his escape, but I prefer things as tidy as possible, and having a separate place to put my food would help greatly with that.'

'Certainly,' said Roper, slightly nonplussed. 'It is your tent, my friend, giving you a corner of it to store some food is the least I could do.'

'I am grateful, lord.'

'Not at all. Whenever you're ready, then, I'll move Bellamus in.'

'I shall take out my possessions now, lord,' said Vigtyr.

'Thank you, Lictor,' said Roper, watching Vigtyr give a low bow and turn away. He thought again how everyone judged Vigtyr for his distant demeanour. He began walking again, wondering if he could use this development as a bargaining chip with Bellamus. But he found that with Tekoa and Keturah gone, and the whole army seemingly against him, all he wanted to do with the spymaster was talk.

Bellamus was in a forlorn state when Roper came to him. Around his post was a ring of thick mud and the spymaster, his clothes soaked and filthy, was scrunched in the middle of it like a used rag, shivering wretchedly. He opened his good

eye at Roper's approach and sat up with a tiny burst of enthusiasm. 'My lord. Time for a rematch?'

'Not quite,' said Roper. He crouched down in front of Bellamus. 'I've come to ask you some questions.'

'Oh.' Bellamus wilted.

'You heard what happened to the Skiritai?'

'I saw a legion leave last night, lord, and have caught
snatches about the sickness. They left to try and save the rest
of the army?'

'They did. I'm going to ask a particular question of you,
and I very much desire the truth. Did you deliberately infect
us with the sickness?'

'No, lord,' said the Sutherner, at once.

'Do you know anything about it?'

Bellamus shrugged. 'It sounds very much like Slave-
Plague, lord, which regularly affects hybrids below the Abus.'

'And how contagious is it? How often does it kill?'

'I truly have no idea, lord,' said Bellamus, settling wearily
against his post. 'It kills regularly, I know, but honestly, I
wasn't familiar with it before a month or so ago.'

Roper stared at him expressionless for a time. 'We were
planning to move you into the tent we play in, and out of
this,' he gestured at the mud patch Bellamus occupied. 'But
if I suspect you're lying, things will get worse, rather than
better. So I will ask you one last time. Are you quite certain
there is nothing you know about this sickness?'

'Certain, lord.'

Roper could detect no hesitation. He nodded slowly to
himself, not looking at Bellamus. 'Do you want to come to
your tent?'

'Very much.'

Roper untied him, and led him to Vigtyr's pavilion.

They moved on the next day.

The legions packed up, weariness evident in every movement. In a way that Roper would never have predicted, the

army's heart had gone with the Skiritai. Without them scanning the hills for leagues around, the army had to move slowly. Not that it would have been capable of moving faster even if the Skiritai had been there. So weary did the legionaries now seem that if they faced an ambush, Roper could not imagine his men summoning the energy to fight.

The body of their force went south, on a three-day march to Deorceaster. The Unhieru weapons shipment, whole once again, moved west, guarded by a full legion of auxiliaries.

In the evening, Roper trained with Vigtyr, near-fainting from hunger after each extended bout, and totally unable to discover the silence that he been developing over their previous sessions. He went to find Bellamus, and they talked, Roper shading their contest on the board once again. Then, unable to bear the isolation any more, he sought out Keturah.

She was at Sigrid's hearth as he had supposed. In a desperate attempt to make the landscape feel more familiar, each fire in this new campsite maintained its position relative to the others like the stars. Keturah was between Hafdis and Sigrid, trying to master the cadence of a chant. 'What is it, Husband?' she asked calmly, when he appeared.

'I wondered if we might speak alone,' said Roper.

Keturah sighed and got to her feet. 'Excuse me, sisters,' she said, striding away from the fire and leading Roper in her wake. She turned on him, arms folded, in the no man's land between three hearths.

'Will you come back?' Roper asked.

'No,' she said. 'Not yet. I daresay my fury will blow over eventually, but you have much of it to endure before then.' There was no sharp smile as she delivered these words.

'I'm sorry,' said Roper, drawing sincerity from somewhere to invest in the word. 'Truly I am.'

'Sorry that I'm angry?'

It seemed she knew from where the sincerity had come, even if he did not. He said nothing for a time, then bluntly: 'Yes. I don't believe I had a choice.'

She laughed scornfully at that. 'Oh, Husband. Always your duty will come before me, I know that. I have not dared wish for a marriage in which I was the priority. I know who you are, and it is pointless to rail against that and try to change you now. You have tried your best as Black Lord, every decision taken according to what was best for the kingdom, or what seems objectively right to you. I was an afterthought all this time; only your priority when I was the means to secure your throne. Have I ever complained? Have I ever done anything save stand by your side and support you? Have I once asked for the loyalty to me that I show to you?' The moment she left him to reply was mercifully brief. 'But when you sent my own father off to die in disease and obscurity, without allowing me so much as a word to him, you went too far. You should have trusted me, and the sense of duty I display every day. I would not have stopped him, I see why it had to be done. But I would have gone with him and that was my choice to make, and not yours. That is the very least I ask for in this marriage. To be allowed to show the loyalty I want, to those who deserve it of me. And no matter what you think, my interpretation of duty is as valid as yours. Do you have to fight at the front in every battle? Of course not, but your interpretation of duty is heroic. Mine is loving. I choose to show it most fiercely to those closest to me, and you robbed me of that, thinking it less important than the kind you display. Will my father ever know that I would have gone with him?'

'He knew,' said Roper, quietly.

'He *hoped*.'

Roper looked at her, the foundations on which he built his certainty dissolving. It was as she had said to him, months before, that war was the only thing that could command his attention long enough to see it through. *It is true*, said a quiet voice in his head. *All of it*. 'You expected me to know all of this without ever telling me?' he rejoined stubbornly. 'Given how much you keep from me, and how reluctant you are to tell me of anything important to you?'

She looked weary at that. 'No, Husband. I expected you to know far more. This is some way past the unspoken line that I thought you respected.' Roper shook his head in exasperation, Keturah overriding him angrily. 'But *here*, if I must spell it out for you. My entire life has been spent looking after my mother, who is mad. There is nothing to be done about that. It is pointless to wish that I'd had a childhood where someone was responsible for me, rather than the other way around. But now it is the only thing that really matters to me: loyalty, to my nearest. Don't ever deprive me of that again.' Her tone made Roper blink, and raised his hackles, as any hostility always had. Any antagonism and he would dig his toes in and bare his teeth. There came a long pause as she regarded him with those poison green eyes.

'I am so sorry for this situation, and the hurt it has caused you,' he said eventually. 'And I do know how much you support me. I rely on it. But I would take this choice again. I would never have let you go with Tekoa, on a suicide mission. There was nothing else to be done.'

She just laughed icily, lip curling so far back she fairly snarled at him. 'I know who you are,' she breathed. 'I know you hurt nobody but your enemies voluntarily. But you are *thoughtless*, Husband. Too blinkered by each task you sink your teeth into to consider those around you. I am so sick of drawing your attention to the collateral damage you should have considered.'

'You don't understand,' he replied, unyielding. 'I knew this would hurt you, and still I thought it was the right thing to do. I will not be blinded by your importance to me. Ever.'

Something disappeared from Keturah. Her face was set, her eyes narrowed. 'I do understand, Husband. Just leave me alone.' She turned away, walking back to the fire with a little less poise than she had shown before.

Roper turned away miserably. He had never relied on anyone before, and suddenly his happiness was entangled with that of another. He wondered whether as Black Lord, a loving relationship was an indulgence that he could not afford. He allowed himself five strides with his head low and his shoulders hunched. And then he was upright again; the weight of his heart thrust out of sight.

Onwards.

In the north, it would have been *Kartha*: the week of short shadows, which marked the end of spring and the beginning of summer. Though this land was plump and lush, every valley stuffed with verdant shrubbery as though it had tumbled in on some particularly windy night, there seemed no animals to fill it with noise. Instead, the soundscape of their march was the sick cough of crows, and the wearing breath of the west.

Two Ropers walked camp together in the evenings. Most obvious was the Black Lord: breezy, assured and energetic. He flung out bluff greetings, was always ready with a reassuring word, and doled out dauntless confidence in great helpings. He marched alongside his men, helped them set camp with a determined perfectionism, and somehow mustered the energy to train relentlessly with his sword and sweat the spymaster Bellamus every evening. In his wake he left a sense of will and energy, which his men followed numbly, ever south.

Less obvious, like an illusion only visible in certain light, was Roper. He felt always alone. His heart jumped like a caged hare, his head twitched at unexpected noises. His chest was a rattling box of flint shards, and he was often oddly vacant, distracted by the two words that flew around his head like a pair of trapped bats. Those who saw this second character were not sure how to respond. Only Gray tried hard to bring him into better focus, placing a gentle hand on his shoulder and asking how he was. The two personas merged for a moment, and the answer came that he was glad to have Gray with him.

Gray chewed his lip for a moment. 'You know, there would be no shame in leaving this campaign here, lord. We have pushed very hard.'

'No,' said Roper, before Gray could go on. 'No. Onwards.'

He tried to fill his every moment, but even in the brief interlude when he walked between training with Vigtyr and chess with Bellamus, he was hounded. By thoughts of Keturah, or of Tekoa and his dying legion, wherever they now were. Or of Helmec's face, or his dead brother up at the Lake Avon haskoli, from which he had had no word since they had left. And, most of all, whether he was destroying his people: whether everyone else was right, he wrong, and that what they were attempting was impossible.

Onwards.

On a grey day, trudging across another field of blackened crops some fifteen leagues from Deorceaster, a rider came to find Roper and request his presence at the front of the column. 'It is best you come and see this, lord,' said the man; one of the makeshift scouts they had been using in the absence of the Skiritai. Roper mounted a courser, Pryce alongside him, and followed the rider along the column, plodding hopelessly without heart or energy. Roper felt those two words in his head once more, and flapped them away.

The rider led Roper and Pryce away from the tramping legionaries, into a woodland lining one edge of their route. Not far inside the gloom of the trees, the rider dragged his horse to a halt, Roper and Pryce stopping next to him.

'What is this?' Pryce demanded.

'The feathers, lord,' said the rider, gesturing that they should look ahead.

Roper looked. Dim greens and browns, with the smell of earth and something faint and sickly that Roper could not place. Then he saw the first ragged feathers, attached to one of the tree trunks. It was a black falcon's wing; swinging and fluttering in the woodland's small breeze. Roper saw another hanging from the next trunk, and another on the next. And now that his eyes had the shape, he realised that this woodland was filled with them. Hanging from every tree, in every direction, as far as Roper could see, were black falcons' wings. Their feathers had spilt over the floor and drifted gently over the leaf litter. Each had once been issued to a Skiritai upon joining the legion, had been worn in their hair as the proud badge of membership, and now hung in this woodland. There were hundreds of them.

'Tekoa came here,' said Roper quietly. Did one of these wings represent the legate?

'Let's go,' said Pryce, curtly. 'They probably carry the infection.' But Roper rode forward, appalled, staring at the wings and leaving his two companions behind. The hundreds multiplied until every tree that he could see fluttered with one of these wings. He did not hear the hoof beats as Pryce approached, only noticing the sprinter when he had taken Roper's bridle.

'No good can come of this,' he said, dragging Roper's horse around and back out of this woodland. Roper's mouth was open, and he stared desolately about the forest. As they cleared the trees and rode back to the column, Roper tapped the messenger's shoulder. 'Does anyone else know about this?'

'I came straight to you, lord.'

'Good. Keep it to yourself.' From the corner of his eye, he saw Pryce nod curt approval. The army's morale could not cope with this news.

The next day, things began to change. They were three leagues from Deorceaster, Roper walking with Ramnea's Own Legion at the front of the column, and gossiping with a former Pendeen Legionary with whom he was vaguely acquainted. Up ahead, a swirling of men and horses became apparent, the infantry dithering, and the officers huddled conspiratorially. Roper excused himself, commandeered a horse, and rode to investigate.

They had found an army.

A league ahead, some of their makeshift outriders had encountered a band of Suthern horsemen. They had engaged them and appeared to be shading the conflict when huge numbers of Suthern reinforcements arrived. They retreated,

but very few had survived to warn Roper's forces. The Sutherners had been on fresh coursers – grain-fed, to judge by
their stamina – and the undernourished scouts had been
ridden down. Without Skiritai experience, the officers
explained in twos and threes, they had only the vaguest
sketch of where the enemy was and how many. Roper cut
through their concerns.

'Send the Cavalry Corps forward, legions advancing
double-time behind. If they have at last come to battle, it
does not matter how many of them there are. The advantage
is ours. Let's see if we can pin them down.'

He turned in a jingling flurry to the infantry. 'Battle, my
peers! Battle at last! The hour is upon us, go, go, go, go!' The
aides put their horrid femur trumpets to their lips and an
urgent ululation filled the air, like the alarm call of an alien
bird. The banners took flight and the army's heartbeat, its
drummers, thundered into life, Roper shouting over the top,
swearing at his men and bellowing them onwards. The column was propelled forward and Roper summoned Zephyr,
his vast grey destrier, which he rode alongside.

Over the next two hours, a battle seemed constantly imminent, Roper driving the legions forward, hunting after each
report of Suthern cavalry encountered in woodland, or a
glimpse of some dismounted knights, or the call of distant
trumpets. The Cavalry Corps swept ahead of the infantry,
responding to every half-credible account. Once, Roper
heard the tin clatter of distant swords, but it did not last long
and the only proof he saw was a score of Suthern bodies
cleared to the side of the road. He had the impression that
they had caught an outer edge of the army, which was flinching away from the Black Cavalry, whom Roper sent groping
after them like a murderous hand. Minor skirmishes
abounded, but from such a variety of directions that Gray
and the Chief Historian, attempting to help Roper interpret
what was happening, shrugged and threw up their hands at
each new account.

'Almighty, I wish Tekoa was with us,' said Gray.

'We are more than enough,' Roper responded.

He pushed the army right the way to Deorceaster, passing through the low Suthern forest promised by the Chief Historian. It was the first Roper had seen, and they marched nearly a league inside before he realised that it would get no denser. This was not a brush borderland between the naked hills and the true wilderness. This was it. The forest.

He and Gray looked with dismay at this refuge. The trees were stooped, cowed, and oddly lonely. Where were the creepers and climbers? Where were the wood-wasps, the gadflies and dragonflies that should have made the air by the river thrum? Where the goshawks and their phantom calls? And where was the sense of mystery, anticipation and things beyond sight that was present in the north? This was not a forest, but the skeleton of one. For generations, the Sutherners had taken the straightest and tallest trees for timber, leaving behind twisted, knotted survivors, incapable of reproducing their forebears. For all that this forest lacked, it was infested with deer, drumming between the trees like cattle. Doubtless this was another reason the trees were so mangled. There were too few predators here, but no matter. The predators were here now.

They came to the city two hours before dark. There, Roper at last allowed the infantry to rest, leaving the cavalry to continue harassing and clear some space in which they could make camp.

All they could see of Deorceaster was a closed gate, with a palisade of fresh timber spreading from either side. The walls were crowned with hundreds of silhouetted figures, who stared down at the arriving army. Roper trotted Zephyr forward to just within bowshot and bowed to the defenders. They replied with a small volley of arrows, which fell wide. Roper pointed up at them for a moment before turning away.

As the legionaries began to assume their familiar layout around the city, news trickled in that some of the Cavalry

Corps had spotted the main body of the Suthern army. Reportedly they had been too numerous to engage and were anyway in headlong retreat. Roper saw that that news was spread rapidly, hoping it would renew the army's sense of purpose. With a Suthern force in the offing, ditches and wooden stakes were assembled at the edges of the camp, with more built facing the gates of Deorceaster in case its defenders should decide to make a sally.

That evening, Roper had more energy for his training with Vigtyr than he had in weeks. They selected a clearing in the bristling forests just beyond the encampment where low trees shielded their efforts from prying eyes.

Vigtyr, struggling particularly with half-rations, had become more and more curt during Roper's lessons. On several occasions Roper witnessed his face possessed by savagery, when he would deliver truly painful strokes with the blunt training sword. Roper refused to complain. He pursued silence, that fugitive state of mind with which he only caught up for a few seconds at a time before it eluded his clutches again. But each time, he would find it again more quickly. On a number of occasions, he kept Vigtyr fighting for up to a dozen blows, and was adding a number of useful set moves to his repertoire. When they had finished, both sweat-streaked and panting in the humid air, Vigtyr nodded at Roper. 'I am impressed.' There was surprise in his words, bordering on shock, and Roper glowed. With his growing understanding of silence, he felt he knew something Vigtyr did not about the mindset in which you should fight. If he could add that to the lictor's own technical excellence, then might he one day surpass him? It was a giddying thought, though a distant one at present.

'Thank you, Lictor.'

'I can see your energy as we get closer to battle,' Vigtyr added, smiling distantly. 'You are much more motivated under stress.'

'It is true,' Roper admitted. *Some stresses*, his mind added.

Others, like the alienation of his wife hooking at his attention, or the endless doubt as to whether he might be leading his legionaries to their doom, were a constant drain on resources.

'Are we to fight soon then, lord?' Vigtyr asked as they oiled their swords and Roper saw to the small nicks he had taken. 'Will this indeed be a siege, or are we more likely to face a battle on two fronts?'

'We must assume that if the Suthern army has taken to the field then they intend to fight us at some point,' said Roper. 'I suspect they think that we have already been near-defeated by starvation, otherwise they'd have waited longer for this encounter. It suggests they are struggling without Bellamus's information.'

'How far away are they?' asked Vigtyr. 'Are we safe from them coming down on us in the night?'

'Not so far away,' said Roper. 'Two leagues, maybe. But they won't attack tonight, it'll take them a while to pluck up the courage. We were on the front foot today and they'll lick their wounds, and hope hunger weakens us further before responding. But these forests will be good hunting and we can restock our larders a little here, I think.'

'Good,' said Vigtyr sourly. 'A return to full rations would be extremely welcome.'

There was little light left to them and a faint sting of rain as they walked back to the encampment, talking about how they thought things might progress from here. Roper was confident that once they had bested the Suthern army in the field, the resolve of the Deorceaster garrison would crumble and they would surrender, rather than waiting for assault.

Vigtyr said he feared there was a great deal more to come.

29

The Earl and the Giant

Vigtyr feared very much that Pryce suspected him. Whenever he looked at the sprinter, it seemed he would move his head suddenly, as though Vigtyr had caught him watching and he had looked away hurriedly. Too often, he was nearby, and otherwise engaged in a way Vigtyr did not find convincing. He could give Pryce no more reason to be suspicious, and as he made his way towards the woodland clearing where he and Roper had trained a few hours before, he could not afford to be seen.

The weather was on his side. The drizzle had become a sweeping downpour, waterlogging the camp, splattering in the eyes of the sentries and obscuring all trace of the moon. It also drowned the noises of Vigtyr squelching and groping through the dark.

He suddenly realised that he could make out the dim silhouette of a sentry before him. He tried to veer away but the figure stirred suddenly, and Vigtyr cursed. He had been spotted. 'Who goes there?'

'Lictor Vigtyr, Ramnea's Own,' Vigtyr replied.

'Closer please, sir,' said the sentry, cautiously.

Vigtyr approached the man, smiling. 'I didn't realise I'd

drifted so far out of camp,' he said. 'A grim night to be on watch.'

He heard the sentry let out a breath as he recognised Vigtyr's huge form. 'Yes, sir. Especially with the Sutherners so close.'

Vigtyr laughed, patting the sentry on the shoulder. The man never saw the knife that Vigtyr swung up under his jaw, plunging it into his neck and twisting to unleash a hot gush. Soaking hands were suddenly scrabbling at Vigtyr's own, the nails scoring his skin, the sentry unable to make any sound but a splutter. Vigtyr held him upright by the throat as the sentry weakened and faded, slowly easing him to the floor and withdrawing his knife. He cast around for signs that they had been spotted, but could see no one in the dark. He dragged the sentry's body into the trees, and straightened up, swearing to himself. He would need to be back before the corpse was discovered, or there might be a roll-call, and his absence discovered. The Kryptea were still searching everywhere for traitors.

He had memorised as much as he could of this area in his training with Roper and knew it was not far to stumble before he could find the river running westwards through the forest. The Suthern army would surely have camped on it, and he hoped it might lead to them. In the end, it was by sound rather than sight that he discovered the water. Just enough light made it through the clouds that he could detect its rain-sparkled surface, and he followed it carefully from the bank.

He could soon see a dirty light bouncing off the sky. *Karmipp*, the Anakim called it: the light leaking from the campfires of an army and staining the cloud. Vigtyr broke into a trot, following the light out of the woods and onto a broad field, sown with shadows. On the far side of this, were the campfires of an army. There were dark figures guarding them and Vigtyr made directly for one of them. 'Stop!' cried a Saxon voice, half in fear. 'Who goes there?'

'An Anakim informant. I am here to see Earl Seaton,' Vigtyr called back, in Saxon.

The sentry shouted for a companion and three more men converged on him and Vigtyr. 'Get down on your knees!' demanded one of the new arrivals, levelling a black polearm at him. 'Hold your hands out.'

Vigtyr tossed down his knife. 'I am unarmed,' he said, unmoving and impatient. 'I am an informant. Take me to Earl Seaton.'

One of the sentries laughed. 'The earl, is it?' he said. 'And who after? His Majesty the king?' His fellows did not join in the joke, eyeing Vigtyr's huge shadow.

'I have a letter he will wish to see,' said Vigtyr spikily. 'I can assure you that if I do not see him and he discovers you turned me away, none of you will survive tomorrow.' That seemed to carry some weight, but the man with the polearm insisted.

'You go nowhere without bound hands.'

Vigtyr held his hands out before him and they were roughly tied with one of the sentry's bootlaces. Then he was dragged into the camp. Figures rose dramatically from the dark as Vigtyr was spotted, a low hiss and muttering following him as men woke their fellows and gesticulated at his form.

They reached an officer and there was a brief consultation. Evidently the officer found the situation ridiculous. 'Just kill him.' Vigtyr made a few points, well chosen, and the officer lost his certainty. Eventually, he was led on. *This is all taking too long*, thought Vigtyr, glancing to the east for signs of light. He was running out of time to get back.

Through the dark before him solidified the squat mass of a pavilion, billowing in the small breeze and guarded by six plate-armoured retainers. The suggestion that this Anakim prisoner might see the earl was met with incredulity. 'His lordship has been long asleep,' whispered one violently. 'On no account will I wake him.'

'I think it is better not to take the chance, in this case,' said the officer who had arrived with Vigtyr, not troubling to keep his own voice low.

'It is not you who will deal with the consequences if his lordship is displeased,' hissed the bodyguard, stubbornly.

An imperious voice spoke from within the pavilion, invading the conversation. 'What in God's name is occurring out there?' The figures outside the tent observed one another in silence. 'Answer at once,' the voice decreed.

'Forgive me, my lord,' replied the bodyguard, 'there is an Anakim here who claims to be an informant and says he needs to see you.'

'Well execute him and dump him in the river,' came the voice, impatiently.

Vigtyr stirred suddenly, jerking forward. 'I bring word from Bellamus of Safinim!' he blurted.

Silence.

The sentry who had been holding Vigtyr tried to jerk him back, but Vigtyr resisted. The flap in the tent opened and Vigtyr came face to face with Earl Seaton. His lean frame supported a cotton nightshirt as a mast wears a sail, and he looked Vigtyr up and down for a moment. 'I'm not surprised you brought him to me,' he said to the retinue that trailed Vigtyr. 'I'd have done what he said too. What a bruiser.' Nervous laughter took flight around Vigtyr, as though this were an audience brought in to add atmosphere to some entertainment. 'You had better come inside,' said the earl, who then turned to a bodyguard. 'All of you, keep your eyes on him, eh? Galbert, lights and candles at once.'

The earl disappeared into the canvas mountain and Vigtyr was invited after him by something sharp resting at his back. He had to stoop low beneath the flap, and in the dark interior he could feel the canvas roof resting on his head. Nothing was visible within: there was only the soft clank of armour as other bodies pressed into the room. The walls smelt of damp and wax, and Vigtyr wondered where in this great soup of darkness the earl might be.

After a moment, a glowing face and hands appeared at the doorway, sheltering a small flame. This was applied to various points around the room, leaving behind growing fragments of light. The candles stood upon black iron sticks, and by their glow was summoned the tent's interior, including Earl Seaton. First his eyes, then his hands and face, the black robe he had pulled on over his nightshirt and the powerful chair in which he sat.

Earl Seaton seemed content to regard Vigtyr silently as more candles were brought and lit. 'Not the brazier,' he snapped, as Galbert attempted to light it. 'We won't be here long.' Galbert took this as a dismissal and scurried out of range. The earl sat forward on his chair, snapping his fingers at Vigtyr. 'You, giant; kneel.'

Vigtyr knelt.

'If you bring word from Bellamus of Safinim, it will surprise you to learn that he is dead.'

'What? No lord,' said Vigtyr. 'He lives.'

'This is tiresome,' said the earl. 'I have witnesses, dozens of them, who saw him seized by Anakim forces. Your race does not take prisoners, and we have not heard from the upstart in weeks. He is dead, as surely as you will be soon. You are here to plant false information. What is it then? Speak.'

'He was captured, lord,' said Vigtyr quickly, stumbling over the Saxon words in his haste. There was some laughter from the watching soldiers and Vigtyr felt a drop of rage added to his fear. Perhaps he had been gulled by his civil dealings with Bellamus, but he had at least expected to be taken seriously. 'But the Black Lord kept him alive,' he continued. 'He thought that as a spymaster, Bellamus might have information the Anakim could use. I come with a letter from him as proof.'

'Where?'

Vigtyr did not know the Saxon word for pocket and indicated his right thigh with a pat of his bound hands. Earl Seaton nodded at an armour-plated guard, who thrust a hand into Vigtyr's pocket and retrieved a scrap of linen. Seaton unfolded it, gazed down and gave a dismissive snort. He held it out to show his audience. Written in an untidy hand in thick lines of charcoal were the words:

Alive

Bellamus of Safinim

'Strangely,' said the earl, 'Bellamus now writes roughly as well as you speak Saxon.' There was another round of mocking laughter. 'Though I suppose he was rather late in learning his letters.'

Vigtyr's anger grew a little. The note was real, and had been hard to acquire. By offering his tent for Bellamus, Vigtyr had secured a private place to meet the spymaster. Leaving his food inside had given him an excuse to enter. Thus, he and Bellamus had been able to conduct an exceedingly brief audience the previous evening. 'The note is real,' he said stiffly. 'We Anakim cannot write. That is his own hand.'

Seaton gazed at it a little more closely. 'You,' he said, pointing at one of the audience. 'Bring me that knight, the one close to the upstart.' There was the sound of flapping canvas behind Vigtyr as someone exited the pavilion. 'We shall find out the truth of this,' said the earl.

They waited in silence for a time, Vigtyr's panic building. Even if he did leave this pavilion alive, he was surely out of time to get back to the Anakim camp before dawn, or before a roll-call highlighted his absence. 'If you do not listen to me soon, lord,' said Vigtyr, 'it will be too late.' That was met with the dismissive gesture, as though the earl were trying to flick water from his fingertips. Presently, the canvas at Vigtyr's back opened once more.

'Ah, Sir Stepan,' said the earl, eyes fixed at a point above Vigtyr's shoulder. 'We could do with your assistance.'

'As my lord requires,' said a voice at Vigtyr's back. Into view strode a Sutherner of unusual height and breadth, his beard amber, and his long hair tied back in a tail.

'This one,' said the earl, pointing a finger at Vigtyr and giving the lictor a roguish smile as though he had caught him misbehaving, 'tells me Bellamus is still alive, and that this,' he wafted the note before Stepan, 'is his own hand. Could you confirm?'

Stepan took the note with a small bow and studied it. 'It is hard to tell,' he said. 'The letters are so large because the lines are so thick.' Vigtyr stirred, staring desperately up at the new arrival. 'But . . . there are familiar elements to it. It would not surprise me at all if this was in his own hand.' Stepan's eyes had widened as he spoke. He looked imploringly at Vigtyr, who tried to make it clear from his face that he spoke the truth.

'Very interesting,' said the earl, holding out a hand for the note, studying it in turn, and balling it up to toss delicately at the cold brazier. 'You may leave us, Sir Stepan.'

'Could I stay, my lord?' asked Stepan. 'I should like to hear what comes of this.'

'If you wish. So,' Seaton turned back to Vigtyr, 'if this is true . . . I cannot deny I would prefer him not to be in the hands of the Black Lord. But why would you help the upstart?'

'I have been an informant for months,' said Vigtyr. 'I have a personal grievance with the Black Lord. I want him toppled, and Bellamus is helping with that.'

'What is your grievance?' pressed Seaton.

Vigtyr hesitated. 'I served him well last year. He promised me a reward that I have very long desired, and then refused it. He used me to gain his throne, and then tossed me aside.'

'And what are you imagining I'll do with this information?' asked the earl. He was relentless. Perhaps it was simply his style, or maybe he was still suspicious of Vigtyr, and trying to press him into making a mistake.

'I thought you might conduct a raid to free him,' said Vigtyr. He detected a sudden movement as Stepan's head turned towards Seaton, but Vigtyr kept his eyes on the earl.

'I find my suspicion reignited,' said Seaton. 'It is more than plausible you're trying to lure us into a trap. I have no assurances that you are indeed working for the upstart, save that unconvincing scrap of linen. It seems equally likely to me that you are working for the Black Lord and were sent here to trick us.'

'I believe him, my lord,' said Stepan, before Vigtyr could reply. 'I believe that to be Bellamus's handwriting.'

Seaton eyed him suspiciously. 'More like you want to believe. I find myself suspicious of you too, Sir Stepan, and that your allegiance lies more with this low-born spymaster than with your king.'

'Bellamus is certainly a friend of mine, lord,' said Stepan, mildly.

'Can you have a friendship with a man like that?' asked Seaton, the malice in his voice naked at last.

'I believe so,' said Stepan, meeting the earl's gaze calmly.

'Well, you are blinded by it,' said Seaton, dismissively. 'A delegation to get him would most likely end in torture and death at the hands of the Black Lord.'

'I would go,' said Stepan, at once. 'As would the thirty men I arrived with. If you can create a diversion, lord, and help drain the legionaries from their camp, I could go and get Bellamus.'

Seaton tapped his teeth with a fingernail, looking not at Stepan, but Vigtyr. 'Tell us about the work you have done for the upstart in the past,' he said.

'I would send him information, lord,' said Vigtyr, sensing a vague hope, which he clung to desperately. Getting back to camp before dawn had become a distant concern. For now, he must survive this tent.

'How?'

'I would write messages in sheep's milk.'

'Write how? The Anakim cannot write, you said so yourself.'

'I have been taught, lord,' said Vigtyr, with a touch of pride. 'Bellamus sent one of his Anakim agents north with me, a woman named Adras. She has been teaching me Saxon words and letters.'

'By God,' said Stepan softly. 'He speaks the truth, lord. Bellamus had one Anakim informant who could write, close to the Black Lord. His messages would arrive in invisible ink, and Bellamus would singe them to read the letters. I saw it myself.'

Seaton raised his eyebrows and Vigtyr tried to look earnest, scarce daring to believe his fortune.

'Well, well, well,' said the earl, slowly. 'The upstart lives indeed, does he? That ability of his to survive is quite exceptional. If we are to find him, he will need to be somewhere obvious.'

'I have moved him to the only tent in the encampment, lord,' said Vigtyr. 'Right in the middle, in front of the gates of Deorceaster.'

'Indeed?' said the earl, looking strangely at Vigtyr. He could not tell whether Seaton was genuinely impressed, or mocking at his eagerness to help. 'And how are we to reward your service?'

'I thought that perhaps I might join you, lord?' said Vigtyr, in a rush. Earl Seaton's eyes widened in astonishment and Vigtyr went on swiftly. 'I've supplied a great deal of valuable information, at personal risk. I admire your kind, lord, and had hoped that there might be a position of status for me, one day.'

Seaton's mouth was open. Then he burst into cruel laughter, those around him taking up the chorus as well. Vigtyr looked down and cursed himself silently. *Idiot*. He should have waited for when Bellamus had been freed. He would be able to testify for Vigtyr.

Seaton was wiping tears from his eyes. 'Give this extraordinary creature some gold,' he said, nodding to a servant. The man produced a leather purse from a chest by one wall and dropped it clinking into Vigtyr's pocket.

Gold, thought Vigtyr, dully. The weight of it would once

have delighted him, but on campaign that weight was simply a burden. He was also coming to wonder if he should not be a bit more like Pryce, who seemed so satisfied, and so disdained material things and personal adornment.

'Escort him to the edge of the encampment and cut him loose,' said the earl, talking over Vigtyr's shoulder once more. 'And we shall decide how to proceed with this new information.'

30

The Spymaster Unleashed

Keturah awoke with a jolt, and found the Chief Historian standing above her. There were half a dozen acolytes in her wake, lightly dressed and shivering in the dawn. Frathi herself wore only a short tunic but evidently had no time for cold. 'Come!' she called. 'The sun is high.' The sun was barely visible: a bloody conflagration consuming the tattered grey in the east, and tinting Vigtyr's nearby pavilion, in which Bellamus was now imprisoned. The others around the hearth were stirring feebly, and Keturah stood to strip her cloak. The Chief Historian eyed Keturah's pregnant belly. 'You are doing well, Tekoasdottir, on such short rations. You must be weary.'

'I battle on, my lady,' said Keturah, gravely. She was weary. So weary and sick she felt she could barely stand, let alone join a morning run, but habit compelled her.

There was no warning or stretching. The Chief Historian broke into a trot across the camp, the train of acolytes falling in behind her. Soon their little band was among the dripping shade of the forest, Frathi setting a pace that Keturah could match – for now. Frathi was not fast, being nearly one hundred and seventy years old, but she left the camp and arrived back at exactly the same pace, her lean arms and legs moving in the same mechanical swings, her face the same jagged and impassive blank.

Pigeons cooed throatily from the branches, and once Keturah caught the abrupt percussion of a woodpecker. The mud squelched between her toes and at one point she found herself slipping down a bank and splashing heavily into the cold stream below. Frathi threw a glance over her shoulder, saw she was unharmed and carried on. Someone dropped into the water beside her and Keturah felt two hands beneath her arms trying to help her rise. 'Thank you, my dear,' she said, turning and expecting to find Sigrid, but confronted instead with Hafdis. Uvoren's widow had so far demonstrated energy for no more than lagging behind the main group. Yet here she was, using precious reserves to help Keturah to her feet. Keturah gave her a smile, realising belatedly it was slightly incredulous, and led Hafdis on after the retreating runners.

This morning was harder for Keturah than usual. She found the main train drawing away from her and laboured after them, feeling nauseous and feeble. Her mind conjured reasons for her weakness: it was her pregnancy, and the short rations, and maybe the lingering effects of that poison she had taken on Uvoren's orders. She did not think she had felt quite the same since, though it was hard to remember. Perhaps she just noticed her weariness more now. Whatever the cause, she tutted and expostulated under her breath as she watched her compatriots, led by the rangy figure of the Chief Historian, pull away through the trees. Eventually she was left alone in the forest, following the footprints left behind. Keturah had so longed to explore this land, but all she felt was heartsickness for her northern home.

The path looped back to camp, the trees began to thin, and unsettling noises reached her ears. Something discordant, chaotic and energetic that she could not identify.

She emerged from the trees to see glittering figures seething across the campsite, like the tide retreating from an estuary. Every man was encased in armour and a white rattle of noise filled the air, as though this tide had dragged with it a million scrambling pebbles. There had been no march scheduled today, and the legionaries she could see were only taking their arms and armour, leaving packs and food behind. The Sutherners must have attacked.

Distantly, one figure towered over the others on a steel-grey horse, gesticulating and marshalling the currents around him. She could sense his force of will from here in the strange and beautiful symmetry obeyed by the soldiers nearest him. She gave a small smile and felt a little burst of pride in her husband, before remembering to be angry. She managed to twist the smile into a scowl, and began to trot towards her hearth, hoping to find Sigrid, Hafdis and gossip.

She weaved between the onrushing soldiers, dispensing sentiments of good luck, godspeed, let them have it and take no prisoners. The hearth, when she came to it, was fully populated by her friends, on their feet in excitement and each taking a spoonful from a communal porridge pot before passing it on. 'We saved you some, my love,' said Sigrid, passing Keturah a separate helping crammed into a cup.

'This is overgenerous,' said Keturah, seizing the pot as it passed and returning a dollop to it.

'You are pregnant,' said Sigrid.

'Never mind that, what's going on?'

'A Suthern assault, I gather,' said Sigrid, taking a spoonful of the circulating porridge. 'They've attacked our western flank in great numbers. Fortunately, they ran into Ramnea's Own, who put up a terrific resistance and now we're going into full attack. I hear your husband is saying we must take this chance and break them now, and we're planning to drag them into a full engagement.'

'Well, what stirring news!' said Keturah. 'Good luck, peers! Finish them now! Onwards!' There were not many legionaries left nearby, most of them having already swept towards the western horizon, but Keturah dispensed hearty wishes until the last of them were gone, before turning her attention to the cup of porridge. 'Almighty, I hope they catch them,' she said to her companions. 'If we can destroy their army it would be our first real progress for weeks. This has been dreadfully frustrating.'

'I hope we can beat them,' said one of the acolytes. 'I've never heard of a Black Army trying to fight so weakened.'

'And Lord Roper *still* thinks we can take Lundenceaster,' said another. 'Fresh armies of one hundred thousand have failed there.'

Keturah shot the acolyte a poisonous look, but Sigrid saved her having to reply. 'Lord Roper understands how to fight,' she said. 'If anyone can defeat this army, it's him.'

'We should go hunting while they're gone,' declared Keturah. 'I'd certainly welcome some meat, and it's preferable to fretting here until they return.' This was met with general approval and bows were unwrapped carefully from oiled cloth, twists of gut-string produced from pouches of essentials, and knives whetted briefly. They divided into small groups, Keturah going with Sigrid and Hafdis. The latter had no bow with her, but preferred not to be left alone. She still contrived to be the last ready, fussing over which clothes to wear and how cold it had been in the forest. By the time they were ready to leave, the other hunters had long dispersed.

Keturah began to stride for the forest, but sensing reluctance, turned to see Sigrid standing by the fire, frowning into the east. 'Ready, my dear?' Keturah asked.

'Yes, yes, I'm ready,' said Sigrid, distractedly. 'Look over there,' and she pointed to the furthermost rim of Deorceaster's palisade wall. The land beyond had begun to stir darkly.

'They look like horses,' said Keturah. 'That's where the Cavalry Corps was camping, wasn't it? They're a bit behind.'

'The cavalry has gone already,' said Sigrid. 'They went past before you arrived.'

Keturah frowned too. There was suddenly a terrible stillness in the air. The distant mass churned and marshalled, drawing unmistakably in their direction, a low noise creeping before them like a distant, endless rumble of thunder.

'Almighty God,' said Hafdis, breathlessly. 'My God, they're knights! The trees! Run, run!'

'Too far!' cried Keturah. 'They'll cut us down long before we get there.' She cast around, eyes alighting on Vigtyr's tent just as Sigrid pointed in the same direction.

'To the pavilion!'

It offered feeble cover, but the alternative was being caught in the open. All thought banished, they turned and ran for the tent. Keturah cast her bow by the fire, praying it would survive whatever the Sutherners had in mind for their camp. The thunder rolled on and on, Keturah's weariness replaced by a horrible energy. They hurtled past cooling embers, scattered pots and cloaks and sacks, while behind and beyond their destination, the dark wave of cavalry rumbled closer. They would reach the tent barely in front of the knights.

There aren't so many, thought Keturah, *a few hundred at most*, and she almost laughed. They stood no chance. There were three of them, and between them they had Sigrid's hunting bow and two knives. They reached the tent and tore at the stitches that held the entrance shut, aware every second of the enemy bearing down upon them. They managed to open a slit about three feet off the ground and plunged through the gap like rabbits to a warren.

Inside, Bellamus was tied with his hands behind the central pole, his teeth bared and in such a state of dishevelment that it was obvious their sudden arrival had disturbed his frantic efforts to free himself. The rag over his eye had come loose, revealing a white-scarred orb beneath. The only other contents of the tent were a sack in one corner, and a low wooden table before the spymaster, bearing a few candles and a chessboard.

There was a sudden hush as Sutherner and Anakim regarded each other. *We should kill him*, thought Keturah. When the knights searched the tent, as they undoubtedly would, they would free Bellamus. With his tricks unleashed once more, this army was doomed. He could not fall back into Suthern hands.

Keturah held her knife low at her side, but she did nothing. It did not seem right to execute a man tied to a pole, even a Sutherner. Even this Sutherner. They were not soldiers. All three had hunted from their early years and had an entrenched respect for their quarry. If they were to encounter a hare or a deer so trussed, its eyes wild with fear, they would have released it. If it was not won by their own efforts then killing it seemed against the unspoken rules of the game. And this was not an animal. This was a man, staring up at them beseechingly, quite certain these three women, with their drawn knives, had come to finish him.

The time for thought had ended, for individual hoof beats were emerging from the rumble, along with snorting and whinnying, and the calls and shouts of knights as they saw the pavilion and closed in. Sigrid had an arrow on her string, and turned to gaze steadily at the gap through which they had entered. Hafdis was panting in terror and uttering low moans, holding her knife two-handed. Keturah moved away from the entrance and backed against the canvas, thrusting the knife into her belt and upsetting the low table in front of Bellamus. She held it in front of her stomach as a shield, all thoughts of killing the spymaster gone. Somehow, they all felt like refugees in the tent. It was the people outside who were the enemy.

'You should go,' said Bellamus, from the floor. 'Please. You obviously cannot win this.'

'Shut up,' said Keturah, imperiously.

There was a jingle of harnesses and the hoof beats beyond the canvas ceased. Then a clanking and a thumping as their enemies dismounted. And next, worst of all, the scrape of a sword being unsheathed.

Ashen light fell through the parted base of the entrance and Keturah imagined it blotted out as a figure crawled

through. An armoured man, whom they would have to try
and kill. She swore at herself for abandoning her bow, so
that now she would have to batter at whoever appeared with
this table.

Then, with a sweeping noise, a slice of light materialised
in the fabric before them. A great-sword had slashed into the
canvas, its edge stopped by one of the cords that held the
door-flaps together. A foot of murderous steel rested within
the tent for less than a heartbeat before Sigrid unleashed her
arrow through the gap. There was a shriek of pain and the
sword retreated, quite gently, from the opening slash, as
something thumped to the ground outside. There came a
single-word exclamation in unintelligible Saxon and Sigrid
nocked another arrow to her string as a second sword-slash
cleaved the entrance open altogether.

A man, steel-plated and clutching a blade, advanced into
the tent. His eyes were covered by a plumed helmet, the only
flesh on show his snarling mouth. That was where Sigrid
planted her second arrow in a pop of shattered teeth. The
man stood frozen for a moment before he was tipped forward
by a thrust at his back and another knight stormed the tent,
a sword flashing before him.

The knight saw Sigrid scrambling for another arrow and
went for her, raising his blade. Keturah had no time to think,
raising the table between them. She caught the sword on its
edge, a violent shock running through her arms and knocking her back. The sword was jammed in the planks and she
yanked it with her, determined to keep its edge away from
Sigrid. The table jumped and rattled in her hands as the
knight tried to free his sword, but she clutched it tight. A
second knight was in the tent, war hammer in hand, and a
third behind him. The war hammer was swung at Hafdis,
who screamed and ducked. Keturah grimly kept her attacker
busy and stumbled into a corner, pulling the knight with her
and losing sight of Hafdis. From the corner of her eye she

could see Sigrid loose another arrow. There was a crash and Sigrid screamed terribly, dropping her bow and lunging forward with her knife.

Keturah had no time to wonder what was happening as the table jumped in her hands, the tip of the sword quivering above her shoulder. She gripped tighter and tighter. Her opponent might be a man of war; she untrained, pregnant and desperate. But she was an Anakim: a wild and forceful being so unlike this Sutherner, his lineage long abandoned by the natural order. So she gripped the legs of the table, gritted her teeth and swore again and again that nothing, *nothing* would make her let go.

The light at the entrance was blotted out once more as another figure, a startlingly tall silhouette, stooped through the slash. It walked with unnerving calm, a splitting-axe held in one hand. Then it was past Keturah's field of view. She heard a sound like a thump on a steel drum, and then again. The jerking on the table died abruptly, but Keturah would not let go. She pushed the table forward, crying out until a voice of pure command snapped at her. 'Drop the table, Tekoasdottir. There is more to come.'

Keturah released the legs and the table fell to the floor, tipping onto one side with the weight of the sword still lodged in its planks. Revealed before her was the angular visage of the Chief Historian. Low in one hand was a blood-drenched axe and her other was held out towards Keturah, quite steady. Keturah seized it and allowed herself to be pulled from her corner, over the body of the knight who had attacked her. Then she saw Sigrid, kneeling in the opposite corner. Her shoulders were heaving, a bloody knife was abandoned by her side, and beneath her lay Hafdis.

She was dead. She lay half-concealed beneath the body of a knight. He had a bloody wound in his neck; she a smashed and flattened chest. 'Almighty help us,' whispered Keturah, raising her hands to her face.

'There is no time for despair,' declared Frathi. She strode to Sigrid and pulled her upright. 'Prepare your bow, there is more to come.'

Keturah could not absorb what had happened. Everything she felt was crowded out by the noises of destruction swirling around the tent. Bellamus still sat tied to the pole, but his face too was in shock, for there was a sword embedded in the pole beside his neck, forcing his head into an unnatural angle against its edge. Someone had tried to decapitate the spymaster, who had evidently moved just fast enough to be saved by the post to which he was tied. Keturah stared dumbly at the Sutherner.

'Release me!' he bellowed. 'Release me, and I'll fight with you! They're here to kill me, not rescue me!'

Numbly, Keturah moved to obey, but an iron hand gripped her wrist. 'Fool!' cried the Chief Historian. 'Don't touch that serpent. Arm yourself!'

Sigrid scrambled for a dropped sword and Keturah wrenched free the blade that had been meant for Bellamus. She took up its appalling weight and stood shoulder to shoulder with Sigrid and the Chief Historian, who still held her maroon-headed axe. Beyond the canvas walls was the din of chaos, but nobody seemed to suspect that the men sent to kill Bellamus were now all dead themselves. They would doubtless find out soon, though: alerted by their unclaimed horses.

Keturah stooped suddenly and dragged the table in front of the opening. As she did so, she heard a cry from outside. There were senseless words, and Bellamus looked up at her steadily. 'They are coming,' he said bleakly. 'Let me go.'

'Don't,' commanded the Chief Historian, with eyes for nothing but the entrance. Keturah backed away. They had weapons now and somehow Frathi's implacable resolution had brought a sense of control to the tent. She would not allow her gaze to stray to Hafdis, lying in the corner. She blocked it out with thoughts of what more could be done to prepare. One thing, it seemed to her.

She waited a heartbeat by the central pole and then manoeuvred the heavy sword above Bellamus's rawhide tether. It fell away beneath the edge and Bellamus suddenly stirred, stretching his arms and letting out a cry of satisfaction.

'Fool!' screeched Frathi, but she did not move. Bellamus was on his feet. He wrenched the sword from the table with a squeak, and then stretched his arms, blade held aloft and free, finally.

'At last!' he roared. 'At last!'

31

Reciprocity

'Where are the attackers?' Keturah demanded. 'You said there were more coming!'

'I lied,' said Bellamus. 'Forgive me, it seemed the only way to secure release.' He stood before them, sword held low.

'Spymaster,' said the Chief Historian, 'if that is not the last of your treachery, I will make certain you know a worse end than decapitation.'

'We all stand a better chance of survival with me holding a sword,' said Bellamus. 'I will not fight against you.'

'You owe us your life,' said Sigrid, voice quivering. 'Do not forget it.'

Bellamus smiled wryly. 'Not yet, I don't. My life very much hangs in the balance. Now!' he said, eye blowing open, 'there are more coming! I hear them!'

He turned to the entrance and backed towards Sigrid, who had propped her sword against the canvas and nocked another arrow to her bow. The four of them waited together, Keturah glancing constantly over her shoulder in case someone should try and slash through the fabric at their backs. But the attack came from the entrance again.

The first man through the slash flinched abruptly at the

sight of Sigrid's drawn bow, and the arrow that had been aimed for his throat hit the top of his breastplate with a clang and tumbled off. Keturah stepped forward and was aware of the three figures flanking her doing the same. The knight tried to thrust his halberd at Bellamus, but he parried with the sword and at the same moment Frathi's axe hit his helmet, Keturah jabbing at his breastplate. Her blow was turned aside by the slippery armour, but Frathi had more luck and the knight crumpled to the floor.

With a clanking and a thrusting, another three knights, one after the other, surged through the entrance. The first went for Frathi with a mace; she stepping back from Keturah's view. The second took a mighty sweep across both Keturah and Bellamus, succeeding in driving them back. But then a feathered shaft appeared in his eye, his head snapping back before he fell like a tree. The third swerved from behind his toppling comrade and went for Bellamus with a halberd. The spymaster ducked. Sigrid had snatched up her sword and tried to strike a blow, but it was tentative and the knight turned it aside with a gauntleted forearm.

Keturah had to leave them and help Frathi, who was backed into a corner by her assailant. The Historian was managing to block over and over by a hair's breadth, and Keturah raised the sword high and heaved it down onto the knight. Through the handle came an awful feedback as steel, bone and brain gave way beneath the edge, which carved halfway into the helmet. Unaccountably the knight did not fall. He no longer attacked, just swayed, sword embedded in his head, until Frathi poleaxed him with a side-swipe of the hatchet.

Keturah nearly retched at what she had done but Frathi did not let her, thrusting her shoulder around to face the knight behind them. Bellamus had pinioned his arms, weapon forgotten, and Sigrid planted a perfect arrow over the spymaster's shoulder, into the knight's neck. He fell, but more were stepping through the slash and Keturah cried out, realising she had dropped her sword.

One attacker went for Frathi, another for Keturah. It was all she could do to retreat from the halberd thrust at her breast and she nearly lost her footing. Her eyes jumped for a weapon, but though the floor was littered with them, she would not have time to pick one up before being impaled by the halberd, which was heaved back for another thrust. She twisted aside desperately and seized the halberd before it could be withdrawn, her fingers half on the shaft and half on the blade. The knight wrenched it back savagely but Keturah held on. Blood leaked between her fingers but she felt no pain in her numbed hands and held on grimly, refusing to give the knight another chance to strike. He looked horrified at her bloody hands, and then up into her face as she refused to let go.

That was the expression he wore as he died. Abruptly, he staggered forward, gasping, and Bellamus delivered a second desperate blow to his back, dropping him to the floor. Keturah felt an absurd need to thank the spymaster, but there was another knight behind him and she cried out a warning instead. But the knight fell, one of Sigrid's arrows knocking him flat. More knights were coming and Keturah snatched up the dropped halberd in her bloody hands, desperately aware that the four of them were hanging on by fingertips.

At her back came a violent, tearing shriek and daylight suddenly splashed over the bloody interior. Then came a roar like a pride of lions and tall Anakim figures surged among their beleaguered band, armoured in the black cuirass of the Sacred Guard. Keturah recognised Gray's mouth beneath the visor of his helmet, the captain slashing violently at the knight attacking Frathi and giving the Historian time to bury her hatchet into a breastplate. Then came another figure, not bothering with his sword and simply bowling two knights over with his armoured chest.

Roper. Her Roper, screaming a vulture's cry and cutting the head clean off an opponent. The swing was so wild that it came perilously close to Sigrid, but the buffeting current of guardsmen was relentless and purged the tent of knights. The Sutherners stumbled and were knocked back, outnumbered now. Keturah felt a scream of triumph come unbidden to her throat, and charged forward with her halberd lowered. The knights were in retreat, but she followed the guardsmen out of the tent and into the bright lands beyond. But there was no one to strike at. Every Sutherner she could see was on horseback, fleeing the scene as Sacred Guardsmen prowled after them.

A hand gripped her shoulder hard and she found Roper beside her, his eyes searching her for injury. 'Wife?' was all he said, voice trembling and gaze fixed on her face.

Tears suddenly flooded her eyes. She dropped the halberd, brought her hands up to her face and howled, as Roper too dropped his sword and enfolded her. There they stood, the fury between them forgotten at last, she sobbing wretchedly into his shoulder, and he making odd keening noises. 'Hafdis!' she cried.

'I know,' murmured Roper. 'I saw.'

Men were still dying around them, but the Sacred Guard had such tight control over the situation that it did not seem to matter. A violent shivering overtook Keturah as she remembered with horror the feeling of that sword in her hands, splitting the knight's helmet open. And then the sight of Hafdis, crushed in the corner, Sigrid leaning over her. She retched.

'I am sorry,' Roper was saying. 'I am so sorry. None of this will ever happen again. None of it. I was stupid. So stupid.'

'What are you doing here?' Keturah demanded, voice emerging furious, though she had not felt that as one of the emotions crowding her.

'There is no time, my love,' and he pushed her gently away. 'I must go. We can do this. We can finish them here!' Roper was suddenly manic. 'We only came back for you, but the army is still advancing. Sturla's in charge, but they need me.'

'I will not be left here again!' she declared.

'No, come with me, now, now! We will get you a horse, but

we must hurry. We can finish this now! They're over-committed and I have them.'

Gray had arrived, leading Zephyr with one hand and a courser with another. He and Roper helped Keturah, who had never felt so weak, into the saddle. Roper mounted on Zephyr beside her and Sacred Guardsmen reared up around them. She saw Bellamus, hands bound once more, heaved onto a horse, Pryce climbing up to occupy the saddle behind him. Sigrid and Gray shared another mount and the Chief Historian, imperious on a black stallion, swept past straight-backed. Abruptly, Keturah reached out. 'My lady!'

Frathi turned towards her, eagle-like in her poise and fierce gaze.

'Thank you. You saved me. And Sigrid.'

'It was you who stopped them, Tekoasdottir. But it is not over yet. Come, now! We must ride!'

The band of riders swept forward like a flock of geese, Roper at the head of the V, the figures in his wake riding like the possessed.

The battle that followed was not like any that Keturah had heard of. There were no infantry lines, sustained engage-ments or war-hymns bellowed across the plain. It was fought in a great swirl around the city; through the fields and trees. The Sutherners drew back, pursued by the legions, who seemed too weary to catch their enemy, until Roper appeared. Then he would bawl at his men, riding just ahead of them and dragging them on, on, so that they pursued and man-aged to pin first one part of the Suthern army, and then another. If the legions would not keep up, then Roper would spur ahead with the Sacred Guard and attack the retreating Sutherners with their tiny band, holding them and inviting his legionaries to come and save them before they were over-whelmed. They always responded, finding the energy to reinforce the Guard just before they were surrounded. They would crush one group, then Roper would drive on, seeking the next.

At one point, mounted Sutherners came hurtling from their left in their thousands, heading straight for the Sacred Guard. They were intercepted within moments by the Black Cavalry and the two forces swarmed angrily together like wasps against bees. The formations passed through one another as colliding constellations, surprisingly few falling from either side as they galloped and clashed.

Roper and the Guard kept moving, tearing around the city in a game of cat and mouse, which might have been farcical had so many bodies not strewed the grass. Arrows spat from the defenders on the walls and the Sutherners stayed close to them, and the pitiful shelter that they offered.

Once, the gates of the city were heaved open and defenders sallied out behind the Sacred Guard, evidently hoping to catch them unawares. It seemed Roper had expected this, for an entire legion had been concealed in the forests, and roared forth in reaction, turning the attack upon its head. Chaos reigned, no part of this mêlée clear without the Skiritai, but Roper, gesticulating with Cold-Edge like a baton, was so relentless that the chaos seemed not to matter. By the end of the day, Zephyr was foaming and tossing, as tired as any of the legionaries and refusing to do more than trot at his master's command.

It was supposed later that Earl Seaton had only planned to distract the legions, giving his knights time to ruin the pitiful Anakim food supplies and kill the spymaster. But he had underestimated how fast even exhausted legionaries could move over rough ground. His forces were overcommitted from the start and he showed no desire to engage in a conflict that he was certain to lose. He retreated, sacrificing piece after piece of his army to the Wolf, which worried at him, and preserving the most valuable of his soldiers. The rest were dragged down, engaged and surrendered in hopeless fragments.

The legions took no prisoners.

By the time it was over, the sun hung low and bleeding

over the trees. The evening was balmy and still, so that the legionaries traipsed back into a camp hazy with wood smoke. They crashed to the floor without strength to unbuckle helmet or breastplate, heaving and gasping into the crushed grass. Roper saw Keturah, trembling still and furious with her body for this betrayal, to the remnants of their hearth, and then left with Gray to collect water for his spent warriors. The camp followers, who had fled to the trees when the knights had attacked, began to emerge in wonder at this atmosphere of unexpected peace: an army crumbled to ruin by its endeavours. They could have asked for no better ratio of men killed to men lost, but still this did not feel like a victory. They had weakened Earl Seaton's army, perhaps fatally, but this battle was tactically insignificant. They finished the day where they had started, Deorceaster still standing, their victory divided into fifty tiny pieces.

Sigrid joined Keturah at her hearth, the two of them sharing a look and a quick embrace before they sat down together. Keturah felt empty: so empty that she would not have been surprised if she had shrivelled, her skin wrinkled and creased as she collapsed in on her hollow core. But she was also proud, in some battered way. They had survived. They had foiled the attack on their camp by preserving the spymaster. Usually so quick with a joke and some cynical observation, Keturah had never felt humour so far from her mind. For a moment, she just had to be still, in this silence, with her friend.

After a time, she found she could not bear the thought of Hafdis lying alone in that tent. She glanced at Sigrid, who nodded, and together they ventured back to the tattered mound of canvas. Keturah ignored the dim, scarlet-stained walls and stepped over the armoured corpses, eyes only on Hafdis. Together, she and Sigrid dragged her body out from beneath the knight who had killed her and began to clean it. They fetched water, washing blood from her lips, dressing her hair and closing her eyes. Sigrid stripped some hawk-feather fragments from her arrow fletching and they wove them into a necklace, fastening it about her neck and turning her towards the east, before Keturah shrouded her in a cloak.

Keturah wanted to bury her, but was trembling so violently that Sigrid took her hands, staring down at the jagged wounds inflicted by the halberd she had snared. 'We can do that later,' she said, guiding Keturah back to the hearth, where they drank pine-tea and wept together.

Roper returned to the hearth soon after. He shook hands quietly with his legates and the Chief Historian, thanking them for their part in the victory that day. 'It does not feel a great step, but it is. This had to be done. This *had* to be done, and it was a triumph.' Then he came to Sigrid, whom he embraced warmly. 'I am very glad Keturah had you in that tent with her, my lady,' he said. Sigrid's smile was bleak and weary.

And last, Roper came to his wife. She sat still on the floor, looking up with tear-stained eyes as he crouched down before her. Gently, he placed his hands on her cheeks and they leaned together, touching foreheads.

For the first time that she had seen in months, he was calm.

It was dark before Roper came to the shreds of Vigtyr's tent. Front and back gaped like ragged curtains. The air was cooling without the cloud cover of the previous weeks and for the first time that Roper could remember since they had crossed the Abus, the stars had come out. It eased the homesickness that twisted the camp. The steel points still shone in their familiar patterns. The Bear and the Dying Hunter. The Winter Road and the Dark Birds that flew above it.

The two Sacred Guardsmen sitting outside the tent heaved themselves upright as they saw Roper. He waved for them to relax, shaking each by the hand and asking about their day. 'I am exhausted, lord,' confessed one. 'That was tough.'

'A huge effort,' Roper agreed. 'But incredible will from the legionaries. The Sutherners weren't expecting that much energy, and we've given ourselves some breathing room. We'll hunt tomorrow, get as much food as we can. Once we've managed that, our position is a good one.'

They acknowledged this wearily, but Roper could tell they did not believe their hunger would be lifted any time soon. He saw them sit back down before he passed inside the shadow of the tent. He had ordered the bodies cleared out earlier, but could see nothing within. He spoke to the void. 'I do hope you're still in here.'

There was a soft laugh. 'I'm afraid so.'

Roper rattled his tinder-box and, after a little fumbling on the floor, managed to light the corner of a linen spill. By the small yellow glow, he lit three candles set on the low table before Bellamus, now deeply notched from Keturah's use of it as a shield. The spymaster's face came into view.

Roper closed his tinder-box and fell back onto the floor, hugging his knees. They looked at each other for a time. 'I'm sorry,' said Bellamus, gesturing at the stained walls, his hand lingering at the corner where Hafdis had died. 'Sorry for what happened here.'

'I am too,' said Roper. He was so exhausted as to be entirely numb, completely unable to absorb the death and violence of the day. 'Why is your own side trying to kill you?' he asked.

Bellamus sighed, lips twisted by the roots of a smile. 'Mostly, I would think, because Earl Seaton is no great supporter of mine. That was always true, and will be even more so with some . . . news that recently came to his attention.'

'What news?'

'It doesn't really matter,' said Bellamus, shrugging. 'But also, killing me would have been easier than extracting me. He probably thinks I know things which would be exceedingly helpful to you.'

'I expect you do,' said Roper, mildly. The two shared a look for a moment longer. Then Roper spoke in a quiet voice. 'Keturah tells me you saved her life.'

Bellamus snorted. 'Far less surely than she saved mine.'

Roper picked up one of the chess pieces on the table before Bellamus, his hands considering its rough surface. 'Well, spymaster. It gives me an excuse to admit that I am sorry we are enemies.'

Bellamus shrugged. 'I knew that. I'm sorry about it too.'

Roper felt almost as though the next words came without his consent. 'I'm not sure I can keep captive a man who fought beside my wife and unborn child.'

Bellamus looked incredulous.

'The only point of all this; keeping you alive, coming to speak with you, was to press you for information. I know I won't do that any more.'

'So you're going to let me go, then?' said Bellamus hopefully.

Roper laughed. 'Well now that you voice it out loud, it does seem absurd. But I think that may be what I'm about to do.' They stared at each other for a moment.

'One last game?' Bellamus nodded at the piece in Roper's hands.

'I would like that very much,' said Roper. He untied the spymaster and the two sat opposite each other once more. Roper took the first move. 'How was it?' he asked, gesturing about at the ruined tent. 'In here.'

'Desperate,' said Bellamus, bleakly. 'We were so far outmatched. Every one of us was hanging on by spider-silk. If you had not arrived when you did . . . Why did you arrive?' he asked suddenly.

'We should never have let it happen in the first place,' said Roper, taking a move. 'As you know, we lost the Skiritai – our scouts – to that sickness. We should have known that raid was coming, but the scouts we did have were inexperienced, and knew nothing about it until it was too late. One of them came to find me belatedly, and fortunately we'd already mounted the Guard so they were more mobile for the chase. Almighty, that was a close-run thing.'

Bellamus was getting the better of the early exchanges on the board, and Roper frowned and began to concentrate. His pieces and the spymaster's scraped into menacing positions, full of bluster but seldom making good on their threats.

'And what are you going to do with your freedom?' asked Roper.

'Trying to distract me, Lord Roper?' said Bellamus, smiling. 'You could let me win, just this once.'

'I'd rather know,' said Roper. 'I suspect there's not much you can do to stop us now, but I'd rather know what I'm about to unleash upon myself.'

Bellamus raised his eyebrows. 'As you say, there's not much I can do to you now. My spy network is broken. You scattered it when you arrived at Brimstream, and it will take me years to reassemble that secretive band of men and women. They'll all think me dead, and move on with their lives. They'll go back to their homes; my favours and threats will expire.' He shrugged. 'I am broken. I am a commoner once more, without the leverage I once had over my betters.' He brooded. Then he looked up and grinned. 'Perhaps the time has come to find a woman. I had a friend, in Brimstream. He reminded me of what a life of peace could look like. A good woman, a small farm, some dogs and fruit trees and hunting. A life where my duties and the things I find satisfying coincide. As a spymaster I was constantly threatened and running, and the things I did rarely came off, or had any discernible effect. I just had to keep trying. Perhaps the time has come to find something more consistently rewarding.' He smiled to himself. 'Imagine that.'

Roper smiled back. 'That sounds a good life. That's what I want. That's why we're here. Security. If I were to go and live that life now, it would be my children who had to do this, or my grandchildren. And they would have fewer men with which to accomplish it. This war never ends. It will wear us down, until quite suddenly, the moment will arrive when we do not have the strength to finish it comprehensively. And then they will curse their ancestors, who lived in this semi-security and frittered away the time and strength to grasp it. We can leave them with a better life than we have enjoyed.'

'And what are you going to do with the Sutherners when you have taken this land?' asked Bellamus.

'Subdue them,' said Roper. 'They can stay, but they will not be allowed weapons, or to train at war. And eventually, whether in a hundred years or a thousand, they will have to migrate to Erebos. This island is returning to the law of the wild, and the Sutherner does not belong there.'

Bellamus looked very long at Roper. Shadows fluttered on the walls as moths crowded the candlelight. Then he nodded slowly to himself, looking back at the board. The spymaster's pieces were shuffling back, retreating beneath Roper's renewed onslaught. Roper advanced, twisting and grappling to get to Bellamus's king. The way was not quite clear, but Bellamus's pieces were hopelessly scattered.

Until they closed in around Roper. A counter-attack began, Bellamus unravelling Roper's formation from back to front. At first it seemed isolated: one lost bishop. Then came a knight, and his queen. It was too late by the time Roper realised the rot that had set in. Bellamus drew his attention and then took his pieces one by one, until Roper's king was left naked. From there, the tussle was exceedingly brief, and wooden pincers enclosed his king.

Roper blinked down at the board. Then he laughed. 'Damn! I wanted to preserve my record. That improvement was by an order of magnitude. That was genius. How did you do that?' He frowned, a sudden suspicion creeping over his face.

Bellamus sat placidly, a small smile in place. 'You over-reached yourself, Lord Roper. You've become complacent!'

Roper smiled and shook his head. 'Did I? I suppose I did.' But still he looked at Bellamus, the spymaster returning his gaze until something uncomfortable had formed between them. 'Well,' said Roper, holding out his hand. 'Congratulations. Well played.' They shook. 'I can't believe I'll leave it at a loss,' he said, dismayed.

Bellamus laughed. 'You surely aren't reconsidering my release based on losing our final chess game?'

'You do have a way of phrasing my thoughts that makes them seem absurd,' Roper allowed. 'Come, then. I'll see you past the sentries.'

There was still disbelief on Bellamus's face as Roper stood, and held out a hand to pull him up. The spymaster's knees cracked as he got to his feet, and he hunched over for a time, looking frail.

Together, they left the tent. Bellamus had nothing to take with him, so they simply strode out into the camp, Roper dismissing the astonished guardsmen. They moved away from the dim glow of Deorceaster, and towards the trees Vigtyr had fled into just the previous night. The outer sentries examined Roper incredulously, confirming his intentions as if they could not believe he knew what he was saying. Finally, they let them past and the two reached the trees. Roper took off his cloak and handed it to Bellamus. It would trail behind the spymaster like a shadow, but keep him warm until he could reach shelter. 'Do you swear you will not act against us?' asked Roper. 'That you'll go off and find that woman and that farm of yours? That you won't make me regret this?'

'I swear,' said Bellamus. 'I'm exhausted by all this, and it's fruitless now. I'm going to go and enjoy myself, at last. Thank you, Lord Roper. I hope we meet again.'

Roper's teeth flashed in the dark. 'I rather hope we don't. Farewell, Bellamus.'

'Farewell.'

Roper turned away, calling out his return to the sentry.

He did not believe Bellamus. Not really. A man could not change his nature, or at least not with a single decision. It takes toil and strife, and eventually, if you have tried long enough the change can become habit. Bellamus was a spy-master. A wildly ambitious upstart, driven obsessively for glory. He would never be happy with those fine things he had described, even if he did briefly seek them out. He might even find them before realising it was not enough for him. But he had lost his web of spies, and would have to scuttle off somewhere and spend many years weaving before he was the centre of so many imperceptible strands once more, and was once more a threat to their campaign.

In one of their games Roper had spoken of responsibility to the spymaster. Told him it was what made life worth liv-ing, and there was great truth in that. It gave Roper purpose, but if he had been true to his responsibilities this evening, he would have executed Bellamus, or tortured him to see if he knew anything that might aid their cause. But he liked the spymaster and felt a vague debt to him now that Keturah and he had fought side by side. He had been true to his responsibilities at the cost of everything else in his life for so long, that just once, to ignore it was a relief. There was an unmistakable lightness as he walked back into camp. For once, he was not acting out of duty or necessity. That was for him. And for Keturah.

32

Help Me

In the dark, just beyond the camp, Bellamus stood and watched as Roper strolled away.

There had been no guilt at deceiving him. Bellamus could empathise with those dreams of women and farms, but not afford them himself. Not when he could be trampled at any moment by some lord demanding higher rent or taxes. Or worse, by some Anakim master, oblivious to the need to sow wheat, clear the dykes and trim the hedgerows. He had almost talked himself out of this conflict before Roper had explained what would happen to Suthdal when this was all over. Complete evisceration. A vast terraforming project that would remove all traces of Suthern influence on this land. Certainly nothing that Bellamus could live with, in peace.

He could go back to Safinim, or to Iberia, but what did those places have for him? Nothing. Long-forgotten relationships, stale landscapes and lifestyles. Obscurity. And here, he had the ear of a queen, if he could only get word to her. His web was not completely gone. He still had Vigtyr, almost alone of his informants in being self-motivated, rather than moving at Bellamus's direction. There was much he could do with his aid. This was not over. He was not done.

When Roper got back to the chessboard, he would find one

piece missing. The queen with the sealed compartment inside. Bellamus was already planning how he might use that.

There were very few things unique to all humans, the spymaster considered. They all shared fire, language and laughter but most other things varied. Numbers were inconsistent. So were morals, language-structures, tastes, time and values. They were taught, or imprinted by whatever strange, invisible, and unmistakably unique code distinguished the brain of the Anakim and the Sutherner. But there was something new that Bellamus had started to notice only in the past few years. A universal instinct which transcended all of that: a powerful obligation that could not be reversed or swayed by culture, duty or education, and he had used to secure his release.

Reciprocity.

The cloak of the Black Lord about his shoulders, he turned and disappeared into the dark. This was not over yet.

Roper fed the fire, aware of Keturah's eyes resting on him. 'Where have you been, Husband?' He nodded his head to the dark. She held out her hands towards him and he stared down at her tattered palms in horror. 'It doesn't hurt,' she said calmly. 'It is a strange world. I would be dead now without Uvoren's poisoning.' She jerked her hands impatiently and he used her wrists to pull her upright.

'Those wounds need cleaning as fast as possible.'

Keturah shrugged. 'First, I must bury Hafdis.'

'Where is she?'

Keturah gestured towards Deorceaster. 'Over there. We covered her with a shroud.'

They walked in silence for a time. When they were a little way beyond the glow of the flames, he turned to her. 'I have just released Bellamus.'

She smiled faintly in return. 'That's no surprise. You've liked him for weeks.'

He could not return her smile. He stared at her, unsure where to begin with what he knew he must say. 'I will be honest with you. I can't think with you here. All my attention should be on this campaign and this army, and my thoughts turn to you, again and again.' He paused, trying to make her understand. 'Your presence makes me feel weak.' He held out a hand to the side of her cheek, and she leaned her head into it. 'I intend to surrender to that vulnerability fully, one day. I will let it reduce me to nothing and live stupefied by your side, somewhere in the wild. We'll exist among the forests, hunt for our food and build our own shelter and see to our own fires. We will raise our children, and each day will be lived only for its own sake. And we'll be able to have that because of what we do here. Because of the future we'll secure. But we must finish that task. For now, my life does not belong to me. I have responsibilities. Things I must finish.'

She spoke suddenly. 'It's all right, Husband.' She laid a hand over her belly. 'It is time I went north, in any case. These are no lands to bear an Anakim child. Not yet. Though I know you will make them into that, one day.' That reply nearly broke Roper. Where was her stubborn and acidulous retort? Her tart observation of how he was wrong, and why? He could do no more than embrace her silently. When they broke apart, she looked at him closely. 'There have been so many strange moments where you are distracted. When we lie together at night, I can feel your heart straining. What has been on your mind? I am not the only draw on your attention.'

He gripped her elbows and hesitated, feeling the pressure of the two destructive words that had circled in his head for so long. 'I have had . . .' he took a breath to fortify himself. 'Two words going around my head for months now.' He gripped her arms even tighter. He took a breath, nearly able to say them, but they were too big. He could not get his mouth around them. He tried again, and choked them out. 'Help me.' Her face blurred before him and tears splattered down his cheeks.

'My love,' she said, horror in her voice. 'How? How can I?'

'I don't know,' said Roper, shaking his head. 'But I'm not sure I can hold on any more. All I have felt for months is a rising dread. It is constantly like I have to retch. I can't stop it, I can't live with it, I can't carry it alone. Help me.'

Her hand found his chest, covering his galloping heart. 'All right,' she said, with such authority that it stilled him. 'It's all right my love. I know how.'

He waited.

'I am amazed you have held on for this long. First, you must accept the way you feel. *Asappa*. Live with it. It will pass, like everything else. This is the price you have paid for taking on the greatest responsibility I have ever heard of. You have shouldered a problem that was immense to start with, but has become harder and harder with each setback. And you can handle near anything with the right company, but you carry that alone, because you alone do not wish to turn back. You have been this army's will and energy for so long, it has isolated you.'

It seemed she understood something that Roper had not. His efforts had been so convincing that he himself had fallen victim to them. No one thought to reassure him of the raised spirits and sense of momentum he left in his wake, because his energy seemed so natural. Her words steadied him a little, but always there was that doubt gnawing at him. 'And you?' he asked, steeling himself for her reply. 'Even Gray has suggested it. Everyone thinks we're beaten. Would you turn back?'

She met his eyes. 'We spoke about this before, my love. We decided. There is no turning back. We must finish this.'

He clasped her hand, and leaned his forehead into hers, breathing deeply.

'So here is what you must do.' Her hand spread over his heart. 'Take Lundenceaster.' He could see her smile into him. 'Finish this. But you will have to do it alone. You are right; there is too much turbulence for you to focus. I am going

north, and before our child is born, you will have Suthdal on
its knees, and have lifted the responsibility from yourself.
And then we will go to that wilderness, beyond our dark
river, and heal.' She broke away from him. 'Will you promise
me that?'

Roper nodded.

'Keep yourself healthy until you can do that. Find something to distract yourself. Find that silence. Pray with Gray.
Training with Vigtyr should help too, you always come back
more focused. Throw yourself into it, until the Suthern capital has fallen and King Osbert lies at your feet.'

Now he was recovering, he felt disturbed by his loss of
control. He had bent every nerve towards being the person
this army needed for so long that admitting all this to Keturah, even she, was a betrayal of that. Already, his walls were
reassembling. Keturah let him compose himself, one arm at
his waist, observing him wryly.

'Shall we return?'

Roper nodded, holding his hand briefly at her cheek once
more before moving back to the hearth. He did not wait for
any questions from the legates. 'I've just been to see Bellamus. I released him.'

'You what?' said Randolph, abruptly. Every face about the
fire turned towards him, horror evident in many.

'I released him!' said Roper, tipping back his head and
glaring at them all. 'His power is broken! We've swept away
his web, and in any case, what are we? Well?' he demanded,
casting about. 'What are we? A spider is no threat to a
wolf!' No one had replied, but suddenly Roper was prowling
around the fire, meeting every eye turned towards him. 'He
is irrelevant, forget him. Forget the Sutherners and their
plans. This is our plan: we will gather food from the forests
here for a few days. We will assemble supplies for one final
push. At all times, we will make it look as though we have no
thoughts other than staying here and continuing the siege.
But this city is worthless. We destroyed its garrison today;

Deorceaster is neither a threat to us, nor of any value. Earl Seaton and his men will retreat to Lundenceaster. When they're inside, we'll force-march south and trap the whole rotten lot inside the city, king and all.' The legates and historians listened in silence as Roper paced before them, possessed once more by a manic energy. 'Keep your silence on this. Do not utter it to a soul not touched by the light of this fire. Make your preparations to depart in utmost secrecy, and we will catch them by surprise.' He turned towards them all, gaze flashing like a torch over the group. 'Does anyone have anything to say?'

Nobody did.

'Now you know,' finished Roper. He made to turn away, but then caught himself. 'I have one more thing to say. If any of you want to go home, then do so.' He pointed north, staring at each one of them. 'The road is straight and smooth. And may history have mercy on your decision.' He glared at them all, and then nodded curtly. 'If anyone needs me, I'm going to train with Vigtyr.'

He stalked into the dark. Vigtyr, when Roper found him, was sitting by a hearth he had kindled alone. He was reluctant to train. It was late, they had fought to exhaustion a few hours before, and one of them might be injured in the dark. But Roper could not be still and eventually the lictor relented.

That evening, whether because he did not have Roper's stamina, or because of the dark, or simply because Roper was possessed with such a corrosive energy, Vigtyr could not match his lord. They piled the fire with resinous pine branches, and in the surrounding flutter of shadows, Roper forced his retreat again and again. He battered his defences aside, his attention relentlessly focused on the dark flash of Vigtyr's sword; sometimes visible, sometimes not. For the first time ever, Roper struck Vigtyr a blow with his blunted blade. And then again. And again. Vigtyr's teeth were unveiled in the dark, and between them issued grunts and growls as he tried to match Roper's aggression. But his own energy was far less focused and that was to Roper's advantage.

Roper was stopped, eventually, not by satisfaction, or fatigue, but guilt. It took him some time through his possession, but at last he detected Vigtyr's mood. He was afraid. Roper was not harming him physically in their training, but peeling back the layers of his character. Beyond the catty and distant façade, past the bared teeth, Roper caught flashes of something small and frightened, flinching in the darkness. Vigtyr's identity as a swordsman, which for decades he had used for validation by comparing his skills favourably with others, was suddenly pulled aside. Roper was not a match for him: in daylight, both men refreshed, he would struggle as surely as ever to land a hit on the lictor. But through the dark and exhaustion, all that mattered was energy. Roper had it. Vigtyr did not.

Roper pulled back suddenly. Vigtyr, grateful for the reprieve, shied slightly out of the firelight. 'I'm sorry, Vigtyr,' said Roper. 'This isn't fair. Not fair at all. You deserve rest after today.'

Vigtyr panted and then jerked his head, curtly.

'Thank you for putting up with me.'

'You are improving, lord,' Vigtyr mumbled. 'That would have been hard to resist under any circumstances.'

Roper held out his hand and shook Vigtyr's. 'There will be no duties for you tomorrow. You have earned a rest.' Vigtyr seemed shocked and Roper, not possessing the subtlety to rectify it at that moment, left him, feeling distantly ashamed of himself. He was so preoccupied that he stumbled into a legionary, hastening in the opposite direction. 'Beg pardon,' said Roper.

'My fault, lord,' said the legionary. He seemed extremely young to Roper, though he could barely be a year Roper's junior. Indeed, now Roper looked at him, he was not a legionary at all, but a *nemandi*: an apprentice. 'If I may, lord, it's you I was looking for. I have a message.'

'Oh?' Roper's first thoughts were of Tekoa, sending word that he had vanquished the sickness. 'Come to my hearth, we'll have tea. Have you come far?'

'A long way, lord,' said the messenger, falling into step with Roper. 'From the Lake Avon haskoli.'

Roper faltered at that. He had been completely distracted from the Inquisitor and her two guardsmen in the north, and their quest to uncover his brother's killer. 'Almighty, yes. Yes, of course. What's the word?'

'It's your Inquisitor, lord,' said the messenger. 'I'm sorry to report that she's dead. And Guardsman Salbjorn has gone missing.'

Roper supplied the messenger with tea, beckoned Keturah and Gray close to hear, and then bade him report fully.

'I'm afraid there was treachery in the haskoli, lord,' said the messenger. 'Guardsman Leon has been there alone for a long time now. Months.'

'Months?' asked Roper. 'Were you delayed?'

'No, lord, I made it south as fast as I could have done. The delay was in anyone coming to the haskoli. The mountains have had unseasonable snow this year, and your Inquisitor and guardsmen were trapped inside. I was sent from the ber-jasti to see how many tutors Lake Avon would require this year, and found the snows only just melted enough to allow me through. When I arrived, Guardsman Leon told me of the dead Inquisitor and his missing protégé, and bade me bring word south to you as fast as I could. He himself dared not leave your brother's side.'

'Ormur is well?'

'Yes, lord, I saw him. In grief still, but well physically.'

'What happened to the Inquisitor?'

The messenger hesitated. 'Guardsman Leon said that she was killed by the Master of the haskoli himself, lord. Pushed off a cliff edge. She survived just long enough to condemn him.'

Roper was stunned. 'The Master?' he repeated. 'He *killed* her?'

'Leon says he was a traitor, lord. Working for the Ellengaest.'

'And what about Salbjorn?' asked Gray.

'He was guarding the boy alone,' said the messenger. 'According to Leon, he apprehended the assassin trying to reach your brother. Salbjorn pursued and was not seen again. Guardsman Leon now believes that the assassin showed himself deliberately so that Salbjorn could be lured into a pursuit and killed alone. Leon has not left Ormur's side since.'

'Almighty God,' said Gray, softly. 'Poor Salbjorn. So, missing for months, and almost certainly dead too.'

The messenger nodded. 'I fear so, sir.'

'There's a good soul gone. And Inger,' said Roper. 'She seemed a good woman.' Nobody spoke for a time, each head slightly bowed.

'My lord,' said Gray, dropping heavily into a seat. 'Leon will need assistance. If he has been guarding the boy alone, then it will have been relentless; day and night. Ormur will be completely safe, and Leon totally unable to capture the killer. Even if he had the freedom to pursue, he is not an imaginative man. His only chance of catching him would be if he stumbled into the assassin on a dark night.'

Roper turned back to the messenger, who was gulping down mouthfuls of hot tea. 'Had they made any progress in identifying the killer, or any suspects, before you left?'

'They had imprisoned an accomplice of the killer's,' said the messenger. 'A tutor at the haskoli. But Leon says he is broken and knows nothing about the assassin, nor the Ellengaest, who he claimed was directing him.'

Roper thought of this obscure enemy, so desperately seeking the death of his brother. For months, the Ellengaest's assassin in the north had shown frightening persistence, and someday, regardless of how careful Leon was, the assassin must succeed. Even a man as disciplined as the guardsman would tire, and his opponent needed but an instant. 'So Leon needs somebody more imaginative in the north to help find this killer,' he said, looking at Gray. 'Any good candidates?'

Gray furrowed his brow and looked down. Before he could reply, Keturah spoke. 'Send me.'

Nobody replied, Roper just looking to Gray.

'I mean it,' she persisted. 'If I'm working with Leon, I'll be perfectly safe. I need to return beyond the Abus anyway, and I fancy I could add the dimension that Leon is missing.' Her tone was acidulous once more.

'I'm not sending you, heavily pregnant, to hunt down an assassin,' said Roper. 'Fine job of it though you would no doubt make.'

'Really,' she said, exasperated. 'Then who will you send?'

Again, there was no reply.

'You need your warriors,' she went on. 'Anyone sufficiently skilled and imaginative to hunt down the murderer is also needed here. I am not. Your options are to send me north and have me thrashing bored in the Hindrunn, or use me to help catch this killer. I have been speaking with the Battle Historian about the methods of inquisition, you *know* I'd be good. Come now.' She laid a hand on Roper's shoulder. 'This works perfectly. Indeed, you cannot stop me. When I go north, I will take a tour of the haskoli. I was so taken with those mountains.'

Roper shook his head. 'I don't think so,' he said. 'An Inquisitor and a guardsman dead already. I am not risking you.'

Keturah glanced at Gray. 'I can usually rely on you as an ally, Captain,' she prompted.

'Not this time, Miss Keturah,' said Gray. 'Lord Roper is right. That haskoli has proven a perilous place indeed.'

Keturah sat back, dissatisfied and leaning on her palms. 'Let me see to those,' said Roper, twisting aside to produce his medical roll. She held out her hands and Roper cleaned them, one eye on his work and another on her face to check he was not hurting her. She merely looked weary and he finished by winding boiled linen strips around the palm, knotting it firmly. 'Thank you,' she said. 'Now I must bury Hafdis.'

'I will come and help,' said Roper, rising with her, Sigrid also getting to her feet.

'No, my love. We were with her. We'll do this.' Keturah and Sigrid disappeared into the dark, picks in hand, going to bury their friend.

The next morning, as the legionaries and camp followers prepared themselves for a hunt through the forests, Roper assembled horses for Keturah and the messenger to take back north. They would go to the Hindrunn and tell Skallagrim, who was ruling in Roper's absence, that another Inquisitor, another Master and a dozen legionaries were required in the haskoli.

Anticipating an increase in their food supplies, Roper crammed their saddlebags with oats, cheese, fruit leather and dried mutton. When he was done, Keturah observed that the poor horse would barely be able to stagger past Deorceaster, let alone make it to the Hindrunn. 'The horse will manage,' said Roper.

'As will I,' said Keturah, raising a leg imperiously for Roper to help her mount. The young messenger hauled himself up on another horse. Keturah was checking bridle and reins, but Roper gripped her hand. 'You will take care?'

'I will, if you send me word at once should you hear from my father.'

Roper nodded. 'Of course. By the time I see you next, we'll have taken Lundenceaster.'

'And you may be a father,' she observed.

'I hope that pleasure will wait for the conclusion of our duties here,' said Roper. 'Ride safe, my dear. Look well to your road.'

'Farewell, my love.'

Roper grasped her hands swiftly in his own, and then she turned away, coaxing the horse north. The messenger fell in behind her, and Roper stood watching them go, wondering if she would turn back.

The next three days were spent hunting, but it was a joyless task. The legions operated as a vast brush, combing the forest and flushing all manner of quarry before them. Before long, a wave of deer, rabbits, hares, squirrels, foxes and even a few badgers scrambled between the trees and out onto the fields, flanked and trimmed by outlying cavalry. They were driven towards crescent gouges, manned by camp followers sporting bows and spears. As the frantic animals flooded into the trenches, or shied away from the fall, the spears and bows pinioned the earth. It was monstrously efficient, and before long the trenches were crammed with ragged fur. The sweeter game: the hares, rabbits and deer, were taken at once for salting, drying or smoking. The foxes, squirrels and badgers, scarcely palatable even when fresh, were roasted and eaten to sustain the processing. Vile work though it was, after three days they had rations to last them two weeks. That should be enough, Roper thought.

They took a day of rest, so unusual that the legionaries were instantly suspicious. It brought them to the conclusion that they were due to assault Deorceaster, and that night the rasp of whetstones filled the dark.

But it was long before dawn that Roper sent the first jolt through the army's nervous system. He roused the legates, they rallied their primary captains, these the secondary captains, and finally the lictors. The legions were to prepare, in silence, for a long march.

When dawn came, and the defenders of Deorceaster looked out over the ramparts, it was upon an empty field, strewn with ladders that would be too short for the walls of Lundenceaster.

The legions were on the road.

33

The Incantation

The play was utterly interminable.

Aramilla fairly seethed upon her plump cushion. Next to her, Earl Seaton's carefully arranged face could not disguise his amusement. King Osbert was capering across stage, clanking in the costume of a chivalrous knight to the indulgent claps and cries of the audience.

Some time ago, His Majesty had professed his desire for a new adventure story to take his people's minds off the Anakim threat to the north. He assembled the finest playwrights, briefing them as to what he required, and then rejecting each response. The king informed them as kindly as he was able that they lacked true imagination, or were out of touch with the people, and eventually, each playwright was relegated to the position of scribe. The king had dictated every word of the rousing speech he now delivered to the audience, the pained belief in his own words clear on his face as he gestured and strode.

The tyrannical king to whom he ostensibly delivered these words; a man with proportions even more pigeon-like than Osbert himself, sat bored and forgotten on a throne at the back of the stage. By popular acclaim from the audience, who had been advised they were playing the part of courtiers, he would soon be replaced by the worthy King Osbert.

Reportedly, there was more to come. Osbert had been so inspired by his work on this play that he had begun another. Not that he confided such things to Aramilla any more. He had only grown more distant from her, which might have been a relief, had she not found his eyes, narrowed to wet slits, resting so regularly on her face. He suspected her in some way, though of what was unclear.

There came a triumphant cry from the audience as Osbert at last succeeded in rolling the tyrant off his throne and sat there himself. Earl Seaton sprang to his feet, applauding wildly. Aramilla rose with the rest of the audience and dutifully banged her hands together.

In the great shuffling and scraping of wooden heels on stone, Aramilla almost missed the herald pressing towards them. Even through his contortions around the festooned nobility, he showed unmistakable anxiety. So she leaned close as he drew near her father and hissed in his ear.

She was able to detect three things over the applause, and they were enough to powerfully intrigue her. The first two were words: 'Anakim' and 'outside'. The third was the gesture with which Earl Seaton responded; a slow and incredulous turn of his head. He whispered something back and the herald shook his head vehemently. '*No*, my lord. I *assure* you.'

Earl Seaton swept from the room, leaving a wake of ruffled finery. The play was not yet over, but Aramilla had heard the final act consisted mostly of Osbert ruling wisely and this applause would be her best chance to escape unnoticed before then. She hastened after her father, through the crowds and out into the evening. After the dark of the playhouse, the last remnants of light in the west were somehow unexpected. Striding down an otherwise deserted street, four retainers clanking into position around him, was Earl Seaton. He made for a canopied litter, the bearers jumping to their feet. She ran after him, disdainful of her rustling silk skirts, and

walls, which had resolved into a fathomless incantation; a horrid hybrid of song and chant.

As she topped the wall, she could at last see over the battlements and onto the fields surrounding the city, and she staggered back as though struck by an arrow.

Beneath her, just out of bowshot from the wall, a metallic noose had encircled the city. It stretched as far as she could see: ranks of armoured men, glinting in the sun's last rays. Suspended above was a cloud of ragged banners in forms grotesque and alien, bouncing and swaying in step. It was as though an armoured hand had stretched forth from the wilds, reaching out to grasp the city. There came a blare of trumpets, the sound filthy and corrupted compared to the clean howl of brass.

And reverberating around her was that incantation, growling through the very stonework of the city. It was like ringing in her ears, or the roar of blood, or a cold sweat. It spoke the primal language of the body: that of a wolf's growl, a whale's cry and a lightning crack. She had to turn away, holding her hands over her ears. She was not alone. Many of the soldiers around her had done the same or clutched onto each other as this Anakim battle-hymn reached a crescendo.

Earl Seaton was staring dumbfounded at this besieging army, his mouth agape. Aramilla darted to him. 'You said they were miles north, starving at Deorceaster!'

'They were.' He could not drag his eyes away from the prowling figures below. 'They were.'

The Anakim had come to Lundenceaster.

They were trapped.

Part III
LUNDENCEASTER

34

The Smell of Blood

'They're enormous.'

'Bigger than I remembered,' agreed Gray.

'I didn't know Sutherners could build such things.'

Roper had heard much about Lundenceaster's fearsome walls, but still could not believe what he saw before him. They were immense, the lower half covered in a layer of green moss like felt, and for the first time Roper understood why there had been such trepidation at coming here. Almost as bad as the walls was the knowledge that the best of Earl Seaton's army had retreated here to reinforce the garrison. The vast majority of Suthdal's forces were now concentrated in Lundenceaster, guarded by the fiercest walls in Albion, save those around the Hindrunn.

At least we're all here, thought Roper. *At least, one way or another, it's nearly over.* At last, the legions, and all his enemies had arrived at the same place. If they could take the city, they would destroy Suthdal's king, her capital and her army. If they could take the city, Suthdal would succumb to them. Out loud, he said: 'So how do we get inside?'

'Well usually you'd starve them out,' said Gray.

'I have no doubt all the food that was absent from our march has already been drawn into the city. We will starve long before they do. Not only do we need to get over the walls, we need to get over them fast. Otherwise we're done for.'

'I've tried ladders here before,' said Gray. 'It was a disaster. Climbing so high, with men above and a drop below, you are almost defeated before you have reached the defenders. We used a ram, too, which made no impression on the gates whatsoever. With our men as they are, ladders and rams are impossible.'

'Quite. So what else can we do?'

'We should consult the Historian. She may have a few precedents for us.'

Together, Roper and Gray went to seek out the Battle Historian. Hers was one of the most senior positions within the Academy, beneath only the Chief Historian, her deputy, and the Deep Historians. Instead of being devoted to a particular time-period, as most of the others were, her job was to study war of every kind.

She listened to Roper and Gray's requirements with interest. 'Siege weapons might be fastest,' she said. The last of the day was fading, leaving the walls just a blotch in the dark, which they examined together. 'Of which trebuchets are by far the simplest. The disadvantage of that, though, is that once you have created a breach in the walls, the defenders know exactly where you will attack. A breach, if the enemy has time to prepare, can be even bloodier than ladders.'

'We won't survive that,' said Roper. 'Anything else?'

She considered for a while. 'Sapping has been used before, at such times,' she noted. 'Though it takes time.'

'I've never seen it done,' said Gray. 'What is the process?'

'You dig trenches, as usual, around the walls,' said the Historian. 'It looks as though you are just preparing for a siege, but in one of them, you begin a tunnel that runs towards the wall, aiming usually for a corner or a tower. When you are beneath the wall, you undermine it, removing the foundations and replacing them with wooden stakes. When the walls are left standing on nothing but the stakes, a fire is set, which burns away the supports and makes the wall collapse. If you're ready to attack when that happens, you can rush the breach and outflank the defences altogether.'

There was a pause as Roper and Gray considered this. 'It sounds excellent,' said Roper. 'Though it is at the borderline of what we have time for. Our supplies might just see us through. We would have to start straight away.'

'That would be wise,' agreed the Historian.

'And what of the Unhieru, lord?' asked Gray. 'Shall we wait for them, for the assault?'

Roper shrugged. 'If they are here by the time we've finished the tunnel, then we shall use them. But we can wait no longer. We have to take this city before starvation takes us.'

'And still no word from Tekoa?'

Roper was silent for a while, remembering the forest of shivering falcon wings that they had passed on the march. Gray knew nothing of what they had found, and nor did the rest of the army. It was between Roper, Pryce, and the messenger they had sworn to secrecy. 'Nothing,' he said, very quietly.

But one of the Skiritai reappeared later that night. Roper could not sleep, kept awake by his rotten heart, and so, by chance, was standing with a sentry, talking quietly and staring out into the star-pricked darkness. 'I see lights, lord,' said the sentry, suddenly. They stood on a hill at the camp perimeter, and on the field spread below them, three ghostly lights flickered nearer. 'Do you see?'

'I see,' said Roper. Whoever carried them, they did not mind being seen, and the torches quickly grew larger and brighter. Roper realised from their movement that they must be held by men on horseback, and rested a hand on Cold-Edge. 'I think they're Sutherners,' he said softly. 'Prepare your bow.'

The sentry nocked an arrow to his bowstring, shouting out a challenge as the horses entered the light of the brazier. They were Sutherners: armoured in the Anakim-bone plates, worn by Bellamus's Hermit-Crabs. The sentry drew his bow, and the Hermit-Crabs came to a halt, looking on with shadowed faces.

'Are you here to talk?' Roper asked, calmly.

For answer, one of the riders ejected something from his horse, which hit the ground with a heavy thump. Then they turned around and galloped back into the night, taking their fiery torches with them. The object that they had hurled to the ground rested full-length before sentry and Black Lord.

Roper began to move towards it, but unexpectedly the shape coughed. He froze, throwing out a hand to hold back the sentry. Laboured breathing was coming from the dark, and then the shape groaned softly. 'Who's there?' Roper asked of the shape.

It made no reply beyond another disintegrating cough. 'He needs help,' said the sentry, starting forward, but Roper gripped his shoulder.

'No. Do not go near that man.'

The two of them listened as the rasping grew heavier and heavier. Whatever this figure was, Roper had the impression it was gathering strength for something. And then, two words were choked from the dark. 'Stay . . . back.' The laboured rasping went on a few breaths more, followed by a final word, barely distinguishable, which chilled Roper to his marrow. 'Plague.'

Roper tapped the sentry's arm. 'Give me your bow.' It was handed over in silence. Roper drew the string, aiming briefly for the source of the rasping. When he released, the arrow whipped into the dark. There was a brief splutter, a few heartbeats of choking, and then silence. Roper handed the bow back to the sentry. 'We cannot let that infection back into the army,' he said.

'So what do we do with the body?'

'Find some oil. Cover your face. Douse the corpse and burn it.' Evidently the Hermit-Crabs had not disbanded, and were commanded by someone in Bellamus's absence. Roper could not imagine where they had found an infected Skiritai, but where there was one, there had surely been others. 'We need bowmen on the perimeter this night. I doubt this will be the only time this happens.'

Roper was right. He strode back into camp to spread word of what they had seen, only to find three messengers converging on him at once, each with a similar tale of sick Skiritai being dumped at the perimeter. 'Distribute bowmen around the camp,' Roper decreed. 'No watchwords tonight. Kill anyone who tries to come near.'

It transpired that in one case, a sentry had handled the infected Skiritai before realising his mistake. He was now apparently waiting at the edge of camp for Roper's decision on what was to be done with him. 'Take me to him,' said Roper. He was led half an hour across the fire-lit camp, thinking all the while what he would do with this man when he arrived. He insisted on a small detour to his own hearth, where he collected his bow and half a dozen arrows. When they reached the sentry, Roper found him hovering near the infected Skiritai body, ten yards clear of the brazier that was his post. Roper stopped at the brazier, staring out at the sentry. 'I'm sorry this lot has fallen to you, my friend,' he said.

'A bad night, lord,' the sentry replied. There came a sudden snoring rasp from the infected Skiritai, lying a few feet from him.

'He's still alive?' Roper asked.

'Yes, lord.'

Roper was silent, looking into the flames of the brazier. 'Do you love your peers?' he asked eventually, looking back at the sentry.

'Yes, lord.'

'You love your home? Your family?'

'I do, lord.'

Roper nodded, staring at him. 'So you know what you have to do?'

The sentry replied in a rush. 'As the Skiritai did, lord. Leave.'

'Yes, I am afraid that is what you must do,' Roper agreed. 'But . . . don't let yourself become like him,' he added, indicating the snoring Skiritai. 'Don't let them use you against your loved ones. Will you promise me that?'

'They'll not take me alive, my lord,' came the voice from the dark.

'You are a good man. Godspeed. I hope you come back to us some day.'

The sentry bowed deeply to Roper. 'Until then, my lord.'

Roper smiled, and the sentry smiled back before turning away into the dark. He was singing softly under his breath as he faded into the night. Roper waited until he was out of sight, and then fitted an arrow to his bowstring. Relieved that he was not going to use it on the sentry, he turned it on the dying Skiritai. It took a second arrow before he was quiet. Roper turned to the messenger who had brought him to this place. 'Make sure you cover your face when you burn the body,' he said. 'Don't touch it.'

Dawn found the legions stripped to their labouring fatigues and dividing their time between digging, and muttering about the infected Skiritai of the night before. It did not take long to excavate huge trenches around the city; banked earth piled behind them, and sharpened stakes thick in front. All this was visible to the anxious defenders looking out from the walls. Invisible to them was the tunnel, begun in the base of the eastern trench, and reaching out towards the city walls like the roots of a destructive fungus. It was only appropriate, Roper thought, that they would undermine the walls from the east. In Anakim religion, that was the direction of the apocalypse, and it seemed fitting that the Sutherners should know a similar dread when they looked to the rising sun.

Roper joined his men digging in the tunnel, spending a cramped and exhausting morning in increasing dark before he emerged, filthy and squinting, into the daylight. There was news: more infected Skiritai had been left near the rivers and brooks that were being used for water. 'Shoot them,' said Roper, bleakly. 'There's nothing we can do for those men, and if that sickness gets back into the army it will be the death of us all.' Privately, he thought it would be a miracle if one of their number did not contract the illness. He walked the camp, finding himself terribly distracted by each cough, each sneeze, each man who looked a little pale. But there was no shortage of pale, exhausted men.

Vigtyr had been excused from digging so that he would be ready to train with Roper that afternoon, and when the two finally clashed, something had changed between them. Vigtyr was more hesitant, Roper emboldened, and able to find that silence so much more easily than before. Though Vigtyr still won more often than not, on three occasions Roper struck him a blow that might have been fatal with a real sword.

Roper had not suddenly surpassed his opponent's skill with the blade. Though he was improving rapidly, the biggest change was between them. They were growing used to each other's style and somehow, it was Roper who was developing a mental edge. He watched Vigtyr grow at turns angry and fearful before him, and though it was a piteous sight, he could not help the compelling pleasure that began to overtake him. That of overwhelming something previously feared, and of having taken on a challenge and found himself up to the task.

But there was also the thrill of something a little more disturbing, which translated less well into words, yet familiar to Roper from his experiences as a hunter. Whatever this feeling was, it came from the wild side of Roper's character, untouched by the discipline insisted on by the Black Kingdom. Lacking words with which to describe it, Roper settled on another sensation to liken it to.

It was the smell of blood.

35
The Tunnel

The Anakim had been outside the city for more than a week. At first, the streets had been deserted, but it was not long before that threat had been partially forgotten, and business had resumed as best as possible. The granaries were full to bursting and there was a general opinion that the Anakim could not get through the walls. The barbarians did not know how, and hunger would finish them before the city was in real danger.

No, the real danger was within the city itself, because King Osbert had lost his mind.

Aramilla and her father had gone to the king with news of what they had seen beyond the city walls, and the response had been disturbing.

They knelt before His Majesty, backstage at the playhouse, and surrounded by the smell of fresh paint and sawn wood. The king, still dressed in his shining armour from the stage, seemed barely to hear their words. He looked down at his feet, and then began rummaging through a pile of props, selecting a bow and contentedly testing its flex.

Earl Seaton and Aramilla exchanged a glance. 'Your Majesty?' enquired Earl Seaton. 'Majesty, have you heard what I have said?'

King Osbert still did not reply, but his head began to shake as he examined the bow in his hands. An involuntary exclamation escaped his lips, almost a moan. Still, he said nothing.

Earl Seaton elbowed Aramilla, and she opened her mouth. 'Majesty,' she said gently.

'Oh! She speaks!' King Osbert looked up suddenly at Aramilla, his face crimson and quivering. 'You dare? You dare at this time!' He dropped the bow and pointed a shaking finger at her. 'She who conspires against me, she who drew them here! Admit it, confess! You are with *them*!'

This accusation was so absurd that Aramilla saw no need to defend herself. She almost laughed. But her father evidently did not agree. He stood suddenly, seized her arm, and dragged her from the chamber. Stumbling back, Aramilla was followed by the deranged king's howls of 'Treachery! Treachery!'

'Do not go near him,' snapped the earl, eventually releasing Aramilla in a corridor, his advice never needed less.

Aramilla had spent the days since spent mostly shut inside one of her father's halls, half-expecting to be arrested. The king was always at his most fearful at night, and each morning that she awoke in her own bed, free from the grip of royal guards, seemed too good to last. She reasoned that the king's disintegration was too complete for him to bother with her. There had been rumours that he was equal to no more than sitting silently on his throne, banishing all servants and slowly wasting away. But she could not convince herself. As surely as leaves fall in autumn, the king would rouse himself, and Aramilla would find herself rounded up for a sham trial, ending in a public decapitation.

Occasionally she thought of escape, but that seemed as plausible as the hope that the Anakim might just have come to see King Osbert's play.

On the eleventh morning of the siege, Aramilla awoke to a sense that something had changed. Her door creaked as a maid entered the room, wordlessly setting and lighting a fire in the hearth before departing. Aramilla ignored her, lying draped in light silks, listening to the sounds of the household stirring. Someone was scolding a servant for carelessness on the floor below. Another pattered down the corridor outside her chamber, carrying something heavy from the weight of their tread. All sounded as it should, but still there was that sense of change. She turned over and at once, her eye stumbled over something new.

On her bedside table was a carved wooden chess piece. A yew-wood queen, facing her, which had certainly not been present when she had gone to sleep. Aramilla sat up and glanced at the door: the maid had gone. She reached for the queen and examined it. It was roughly carved, and out of place in a manner that she had come to recognise as Bellamus's signature. No part of it yielded to a tug or a twist. The only join that she could see was between the wood and the leather oval on which the piece sat. This did not respond to casual investigation, and she cast around the room for something she might use to prise it off. By the fire was a knife, which the maid had used to carve off some wood curls for tinder. Aramilla retrieved it before returning to her bed. Using its edge, she was able to lift a flap from the leather patch and then tug off the base altogether.

Beneath, there was a hole.

The piece was hollow, and she upended it onto the bed. After a vigorous shake, a small stone dropped onto the covers, wrapped tightly in parchment. With another glance at the door, she unfurled it and read the message it bore.

My Queen – The Anakim are undermining the city walls. Proceed to the east side of the city, where you will find two planted flags revealing the extent of the tunnelling. This area must be defended. Tell your father TODAY, and await further instruction tonight. Be ready to leave. In haste, B

Aramilla turned the parchment over, without expecting to find any more. She thrust a finger into the chess piece, but felt only the rough wooden interior. Finally, she turned her attention back to the note.

It looked like Bellamus's hand, but it could not possibly be from the upstart. How he could have delivered this message was beyond her, and in any case, it was not in his usual cypher. It seemed more likely that this was a trap, laid by King Osbert, the purpose of which was to confirm her guilt. If she were to pass this information on, even to her father, it might be taken as proof of her treachery. Perhaps Earl Seaton had struck a deal with the king to preserve his own status by submitting her as a sacrifice. That would not surprise Aramilla. The more she thought, the more likely that seemed.

And yet, if she remained in this city she would be killed, either by her husband or, if she believed the note, the Anakim. And if Bellamus had got inside to deliver it, then there might be a plausible means of escape.

There was only one thing to do. She dressed swiftly, not bothering to call for her maids. She thrust the chess piece into the fire, balled the note into her skirt and strode to the kitchens downstairs. She found it steamy and frenetic, readying a breakfast of rye bread, porridge and fish. 'Cathryn? Is Cathryn here?' A curtsey rippled through the room.

'She's fetching water, Majesty,' called the cook, a great pink oval of a woman, sweating liberally by the fire. 'She'll be back soon.' Cathryn joined the fray moments later from a door by the hearth, balancing two huge pails, which she set on the floor by the cook. 'Not here!' snapped the cook. 'I'll trip over them, take them somewhere else.'

'Come with me, Cathryn,' called Aramilla imperiously. 'I have a task for you.'

Cathryn freed herself from the cook's aproned gravity and ducked through the press to Aramilla. The queen took her hand and led her outside into a throng of people, which they battled against to turn east. Aramilla wore her plainest skirts, hoping to pass by unharassed. Cathryn, in yards of dark cloth fit for the kitchen, was less conspicuous still.

'Where are we going?' asked Cathryn.

'To the walls,' replied the queen. 'There's something I want to see.' Aramilla had never needed company before. That was something that had come with her newly precarious position.

'We're not going to stare at the Anakim again, are we?'

'Not this time.'

'Wherever we go, it's better than that kitchen. Cook is so greasy that I fear for her next to that open hearth.' Aramilla did not respond, but Cathryn needed little encouragement from an audience. 'She's very unhappy with me,' she continued. 'I climbed onto the roasting spit yesterday and she came in while I was revolving over the hearth.'

Aramilla stayed aloof for the remainder of Cathryn's stories, her exploits at turns clumsy and mischievous. Though high-born, Cathryn's usually indulgent father had grown exasperated by her frivolous behaviour and sent her to the kitchens in a belated attempt to school her in responsibility.

They reached the north-eastern edge of the city, and Aramilla led them south, around the inside of the walls. She thought about the note tucked into her skirt, wondering what form the flags might take and whether they existed at all.

When she encountered the first, it was obvious.

A staff, some twelve feet tall with a tattered black cloth hanging from it, had been planted in the ground. Above this was an eye: the evil eye of the Anakim, woven from holly leaves. This little slice of Anakim art was out of place here among the timber and thatch. She pointed it out to Cathryn, who observed it sunnily. 'A little barbaric, isn't it?'

'That's what we've come to see,' said Aramilla. 'There should be another one further along.' There was; three hundred yards past the first. Aramilla looked back along the wall in horror. 'There is a tunnel,' she said to Cathryn, 'underneath the walls between these two flags.' So transfixed

was she by the thought of those wild and unearthly folk min-
ing the very earth beneath her feet, that she did not notice
how she had already started to believe the note.

'A tunnel? What for?'

'Dug by the Anakim, to bring down our walls.'

'Are they burrowing creatures, then?' Cathryn did not
seem to have absorbed the magnitude of this news.

Can this be true? If it was, how had Bellamus got word into
the city? And it was not in his own cypher: that was suspicious above all. At that moment, she decided she could not
risk telling her father. It still seemed most likely that this was
a trap laid by him and the king together. Its promise of escape
from Lundenceaster was simply too good to be true.

She and Cathryn walked back to her father's hall and Aramilla explained where she had learned of the tunnel. Cathryn
frowned at the news. 'Do you really think this is a trap? If the
king is determined to have you arrested, he won't need proof.
He'll just do it, and nobody would question him. Not in his
current state.'

'Why else would this message be uncyphered?' demanded
Aramilla. 'He has never sent me unobscured details before,
still less something this important.'

Cathryn had no answer for that, and when they were back
in the hall, Aramilla led her to her own chambers and summoned food for the pair of them. They chewed on bread and
salty cheese, Aramilla too distracted to taste anything.

Be ready to leave.

She packed a warm cloak, two loaves of bread and some of
the cheese in a leather bag. Anything else might seem silly,
as though she really was about to leave the city. But still, she
encouraged Cathryn to do the same and once she had
returned with her bag, the two passed the day in Aramilla's
room. Cathryn read and talked, Aramilla did nothing in particular. She just waited. Several times she took out a quill,
ink and parchment, and pored over a note, but she could not
get past the first word: *Father.*

The houses beyond the window dissolved into darkness and Cathryn, mystified by Aramilla's inactivity, summoned candles. By their sputtering light, the room filled with shadow and conspiracy. If Bellamus did send another note, was this where it would arrive? Might it be near the flags they had inspected that morning? Cathryn peppered her with questions as to what their plan was, and Aramilla largely ignored them, for she had no idea. She just waited.

When a nearby church bell struck midnight, Cathryn glanced at the window and said she should go to bed. 'Cook will have me up before dawn to help with the breakfast.' Aramilla held the note crumpled in her hand and did not look up at Cathryn as she stood. 'Let me know if you hear anything, Majesty,' she added, the end of the sentence lost in a yawn. With a perfunctory curtsey, Cathryn picked up her packed bag and shuffled to the door. Aramilla did not look up, hearing only the click and creak as the door was unlatched and opened.

Then there came a pause. 'Majesty?'

Aramilla stood at once. 'What is it?'

Cathryn was standing in the doorway, staring down at something near her feet. Aramilla near elbowed her friend aside and saw that lying on the floor beyond the door was a glittering brooch. It was a spider: the same she had sent to Bellamus months before as a token of favour. Between the pin and the spider's ornate body was stuffed a scrap of paper. Heart sinking at the crudity of this delivery, Aramilla removed the message and unfurled it, scanning the scrawled lines within.

My Queen – Proceed to the flags by the eastern wall.
At midnight, I will get you out of the city.
*   B*

Still uncyphered, with a cruder messaging system than she had ever received from Bellamus before, but it was his brooch. It must be from him, and her choices were to believe or die. 'Come!' she said, springing to her feet. 'We're late already.' She was out of the door and halfway down the corridor, Cathryn on her heels, before she froze. She battled for just a moment and then turned back. 'Wait here.' She hurried back to her room and flew to the desk, scrawling a passage of liquid night for her father. The Anakim were undermining the walls to the east, marked by two banners. The information came from Bellamus

He might find it in time. It might give the city a chance.

She left the note, spattered with black constellations, and rushed back to join Cathryn. Together, they exited onto the deserted cobbles beyond the hall. The night was close and they sweated as they ran, Aramilla holding her bag in one hand and the front of her skirts in the other. Her calves were soon burning and the plump Cathryn was labouring to keep pace with her, but as far as she knew, they might have already missed the rendezvous with Bellamus. Around them, all was still but for the occasional scrabbling of a rat. One window they passed was illuminated by a candle, the light seeping between twin shutters.

The bulk of the wall grew in the darkness and when she reached it, she cast about wildly, sweating and panting. This place seemed as deserted as the rest of the sleeping city. She could hear Cathryn clattering nearer, and swore, once, twice, three times, because she had had a chance and missed it. If only they had checked outside the door earlier.

Cathryn reached her, wheezing and coughing. 'Where . . . is he?' she managed.

'We've missed him,' said Aramilla, bitterly. It was at least half past the hour and Bellamus was wanted by the crown. He would not linger here.

Then Cathryn screamed.

It was a piercing alarm, which sent a jolt through Aramilla the instant before she saw what had triggered it. An enormous figure; shadowed, powerful, and unmistakably other, had stepped from an alley. It spoke a word, which might have been an attempt at 'Silence,' but so heavily accented as to be near incomprehensible.

Aramilla flinched backwards, but the apparition did not pursue her. Cathryn had seized her forearm and they stared at the figure for a moment. It raised a hand, beckoning them closer. 'With me,' it said.

Cathryn screamed again and Aramilla clapped a hand over her mouth. 'Shut up, shut up!' She scanned the walls behind the figure but could see no guards. The battlements were still, the streets deserted and covered in the faintest film of moonlight. She looked at the figure. 'Are you an Anakim?' she demanded.

'With me,' the figure repeated in a growl.

It was like being confronted by a bear. In the street, this thing looked totally out of place. Perhaps it was his stance, which seemed braced and confident at the same time. He radiated sensory awareness, every piece of his attention on her and their environment. He did not wait for her response and turned away, back towards the wall. She had never seen a stride so purposeful. Each step was deliberate and focused in a way that made her consider her own walk. She felt suddenly silly and ungainly, like a puppy rushing for milk. This wild man exuded a composure which she had summoned only in her most dedicated moments. 'We must follow,' she breathed, dragging Cathryn forward.

'No! Leave me!'

'Fool!' hissed Aramilla, her grip unyielding. 'This is our only escape. He will be an informant for Bellamus.' She dragged Cathryn after the giant, who had rounded a corner onto the street that ran along the inside of the wall. By the time they caught sight of him again, he had crouched down over a cobble that protruded slightly above its fellows. He removed it, and then those that surrounded it, eventually excavating an opening roughly a yard square. He reached into it and pulled out a wooden frame, on which the cobbles seemed to have rested. Then he looked up at the two women, still standing ten yards distant.

'Inside,' he said, pointing into the hole.

'No!' shrieked Cathryn, trying to break free again. 'Release me, I won't follow that thing into its pit!'

Aramilla seized her shoulders. 'Look at my face!' she demanded, but Cathryn still flailed. 'Look at me!' She managed to hold Cathryn's eyes for a moment. 'We are surrounded, and you have proof before you that they have undermined the walls. They will break through. Leave now, or die.'

'I will not go into that hole!' she cried.

'You *have to*. We both do.'

Cathryn paused for just a heartbeat and Aramilla took it. 'Come!' she insisted, dragging her companion towards the hole and ignoring the moan it elicited. 'I'll go first.' She met the eyes of the Anakim briefly, who was just staring at them steadily.

'I can't, I can't, I can't,' chanted Cathryn hysterically, staring down at the hole.

'Go in,' said the Anakim. Those words, in that voice, at last silenced Cathryn.

Aramilla dropped her bag into the hole, darkness swallowing it at once. She lowered herself down after it, trying not to think at all. Within, she could not see so much as an outline. She reached forward with a trembling hand, feeling walls of rough earth, which crumbled to her touch, and panting at the sense of dread that closed around her. The tunnel was perhaps four feet high, and she shuffled a little way in, pushing her bag before her. The passage seemed to be angled downwards, sloping deeper into the earth. She heard a thump and a moan as Cathryn dropped in behind her. 'Milly!' she cried.

'I'm here,' said Aramilla. 'Just keep going. Follow my voice, that's all.'

There came another thump at Aramilla's back. 'He's behind me!' cried Cathryn.

'Of course,' replied Aramilla, supressing her own fear at this thought. She had expected a thrill at first meeting one of his kind, but all she felt was unease at this thing that was so crudely like her, but so different. 'He's helping us out.'

'Silence!' came that alien voice. The two women fell quiet, and Aramilla's experience of the world focused to her groping fingertips.

She pressed on, starting slightly when Cathryn's hand seized her ankle, using her as a guide through the dark. She even suffered her to remain, glad of any sort of companionship. 'You're doing well, Cat,' she whispered. 'Just keep going. We're escaping, think of that.'

Aramilla wondered whether she could see light ahead of her. Her knees pressed uncomfortably on small stones and lumpen clods, and she found herself scrambling faster, hunting the yellow light she now perceived on the wooden stakes bracing the walls. The tunnel levelled off and she let out a small cry of relief as she emerged from what seemed to be a small side-tunnel into a much larger chamber. This was illuminated by a thickly smoking torch, held by an Anakim even larger than the one behind them. 'Bellamus sent us,' said the torchbearer, in an accent hardly more comprehensible than his fellow. 'We will get you out.'

Aramilla nodded and stood gingerly. The tunnel was high enough to accommodate her with room to spare. Cathryn emerged from the tunnel behind, starting visibly at the sight of the torchbearer. The light he held revealed a subterranean chamber stretching to either side, its roof supported by regularly spaced wooden stakes. Against many of the stakes lay bundled twigs, and looking up at the ceiling, some six feet from the floor in this larger tunnel, she was shocked to see flat, carved stone. She felt the enormous weight of the wall above them, supported only by these thin stakes.

And then she realised the purpose of the bundled twigs: they were going to burn the tunnel down. They would collapse a great stretch of the wall and then flood through onto the streets. Even if her father found the note she had left, she could not think how he would be able to stop this.

The Anakim were nearly ready.

A few rough words at her back made her turn, and she saw the first Anakim emerging from their tunnel and turning to push a mound of earth in behind him. He steadily concealed the entrance until the way they had come was indistinguishable from the bare earth to either side. It seemed that even the Anakim command did not know about the tunnel through which she had just left the city. They would certainly not facilitate the escape of the Suthern queen, and with that came the knowledge that the worst of the danger was not behind her, but just beginning. These two would need to smuggle her out of their camp.

'Come,' said the torchbearer. He turned away, so vast he had to stoop even while on his knees, and shuffled away, leaving them in darkness. Aramilla took Cathryn's hand and followed, the first Anakim bringing up the rear.

The torch provided a measure of light by which they could now move, and they shuffled on for what seemed to be miles. The torch began to dim, its flame growing blue and feeble, and when it finally smoked out altogether, to be discarded by the side of the passage, even Aramilla groaned. She fumbled on, moving as fast as she dared but still able to hear the Anakim ahead growing steadily more distant

'Hurry!' The word hissed down the tunnel and Aramilla broke into a trot, hands scrabbling desperately along the walls until she thought she could see light up ahead once more. But not the yellow, dirty light of a sputtering torch or candle. Light of silver and midnight blue; the aura of moon and stars.

She emerged gasping into the night, taking greedy lungfuls of the free air. She found herself in a trench, one side bordered by an earthen bank that bristled with savage wood. 'Lie down,' commanded the tall Anakim, gesturing at a filthy wooden tray lying in the trench. A frame tethered it to a pair

of ponies, and beneath the torchbearer's gaze, Aramilla pros-
trated herself on the tray's hard surface. She felt Cathryn
squeeze in beside her, breathing raggedly. There was a creaking of leather as the Anakim bent down, and then his voice
spoke next to her head. 'We will cover you in earth. Keep air
in front of your face. Do not move until you're uncovered, or
you die. Make no noise, or you die. There is only one horse.
You will have to share. Ride west, as far as you can tonight.
Bellamus will meet you at Wiltun.' Aramilla did not understand much of this, but dared ask no questions. She nodded
into the board and the figure went on. 'I am a friend to the
Sutherners, whenever you need. You may have heard my
name: Vigtyr.' There came a pause, the Anakim perhaps
expecting some recognition, but Aramilla just waited for
whatever was to come.

There was an aged crack as some stiff canvas was unfurled
and then thrown over the pair of them.

Keep air in front of your face.

Aramilla raised herself up slightly to create an air-pocket
beneath the canvas, but almost dropped back onto the tray as
the first mass of earth was deposited on top of them. Next to
her, Cathryn screamed again. 'No! No, no, no stop, this is too
much!'

'Silence!'

'Cat, we can't turn back now,' said Aramilla, though her
own voice was quaking. More earth was heaped on the canvas, and more and more until Aramilla was sure that the
Anakim themselves had stood on top of her. She was crushed
into her forearms beneath her, straining desperately for air
and aware at the same time how little of it there must be
beneath this canvas. The weight above reached the point
where she felt she could barely fill her lungs, and kept building. Beside her, she felt a sudden flurry as Cathryn's panic
overwhelmed her and she tried to fight her way free. But she
could not: they were both crushed against the board, her
nose squashed into the wood.

She felt a jerk as the board was dragged along the trench. Already the air seemed to be running out, each breath satisfying less than the last. Nothing in her life had prepared her for this: the huge pressure bearing down on her and trapping her in this place, the fear that she might be discovered and executed by the Anakim, the requirement to stay calm so that she did not consume precious air with struggling and panting.

She reached for memories as a distraction, and seized on the drips of ink that she had left on the note to her father, now sitting in her room. Next, the feel of the chess piece's rough interior when she had inserted a finger to check for more than the note that had led her to this place. Then the feeling of her nose and lips pressed into the board before her, forehead crushed into her immobilised forearm, the building heat. Each distracted her a little, so that she did not have to look that terror in the face. Cathryn had fallen silent, and no matter how hard she tried, Aramilla was dogged by panic. *Please, please stop now. Unearth me.* But the board slid and scraped onwards. She hauled in hot, precious air, counting her heartbeats.

Aramilla was not sure what happened to the rest of the journey. She suddenly became aware of the load above her lessening and she began to fight upwards. There was some give in the earth and she heaved against the canvas, determined to escape this stifling atmosphere whether she was discovered or not. Suddenly the pressure was gone, she flailed, and the canvas was ripped aside. The cool air rushed to her face and she cried out, flopping off the board and feeling the grass between her fingers. There came weak sobs and a hiss of 'Quiet!' behind her as Cathryn was unearthed, but Aramilla could do no more than lie and pant, feeling how easily her ribs moved, utterly quenched by the night air.

A boot nudged her and she turned onto her side to see the first Anakim looking down at her. There was a tree behind him, a horse tied by the reins around its trunk. 'West,' he said. Then he turned away, leading the ponies and emptied tray back the way they had come.

Cathryn still lay weeping quietly into the earth, and Aramilla felt a sudden urgency. There were two of them, and just one horse. She scrambled upright, going for the reins and making a mess of untying them. She fumbled at the leather, loosing them at last and hauling herself into the saddle. She kicked the horse forward, throwing one last glance back at Cathryn, who had not moved. She was just staring after Aramilla in confusion.

The queen brought her horse to a halt. She turned back to Cathryn, still lying on the ground, staring after her. 'Come on, Cat.'

'Were you going to leave me?'

'I'll leave yet if you don't hurry.'

It took some moments of scrambling before Cathryn was seated behind Aramilla. Before them: leagues of unenclosed night. At their back: a besieged city, surrounded by a wild army, and ruled by a madman.

They went west.

36

Ellengaest

'What's your name?' Keturah asked the messenger she travelled with. It was another grey day, and they were travelling off-road to avoid detection until they had made it back into the Black Kingdom.

The messenger, a black-haired, small-framed adolescent, gave Keturah a shy smile. 'Gero, my lady.'

'Do you like the mountains, Gero?'

'Yes, my lady.'

'That is lucky indeed,' said Keturah agreeably. 'It seems to me that we might take a tour there before returning to the Hindrunn.'

'My lady?'

'I was so taken with the haskoli that I wish to see it one more time, and to give my greetings in person to Guardsman Leon.'

Gero looked unhappy. 'I thought we were returning to the Hindrunn, my lady, to take them news of the help that is needed at the Lake Avon haskoli.'

'I shall know much better what help is required if I visit myself,' declared Keturah. 'Come now, we shall enjoy the journey.'

They did, passing through Suthdal and crossing the Abus

into *Kossi*, the week of glow-worm light. They were not long into the Black Kingdom when they came upon a stone circle. It was the same that they had encountered near the freyi, all those months ago. The sacred border of the Otherworld, built by the ancient Anakim and invested with immense power. That time Keturah had stayed respectfully distant, but these rings were said to move, after all, and encountering it twice seemed unlikely to be coincidence. She left Gero outside the circle, advancing onto the grass within; dense and green, as though the deer dared not graze here. It felt cold between the stones, and she knelt at the centre of the circle. She prayed for the power to find Numa's murderer, and the perspective to see what was beyond her. Then she stood, bowing her head respectfully and turning back to her horse. Gero said not a word, and Keturah merely nodded back to the path, and north.

Gero turned out to be unexpectedly good company, and Keturah teased him throughout their journey. On one occasion, she convinced him that she was a *teetir*: a spirit that occupied the space beneath the hanging fronds of a willow. Amused by his terror, she wound him yet tighter with every wild legend that she could half remember. Had he heard of the *vesihest*: horses with coats of rattling shells, that inhabited foaming waters and fed on people? Had he seen that stag with pine branches for antlers? It was, after all, a sure sign that the Otherworld was near and at any time they might expect to be swallowed in unnatural fog, emerging to find a land painted in shades of pearl, where the air simmered like broth, and words and song prickled with ancient power.

So time passed, and they came to the mountains. They climbed past Lake Avon, past the fading trees and into the haskoli. It did not seem to be summer among the peaks, but spring, the slopes still scattered with snow-bones.

Keturah had devoted much of the journey to the Battle Historian's advice, thinking how she might proceed once they arrived. She led Gero straight into the haskoli courtyard, where they were observed curiously by the Black-Cloaks. She demanded directions to Guardsman Leon, who turned out to be beneath the Feather-Tree with Ormur. They found him standing outside a circle of a dozen boys and paused, waiting as the students finished their lesson. A tutor was instructing them in the uses of a birch fungus. It was a cool day, fresh and breezy, and Keturah dismounted, very content to lean against her horse's warm bulk and wait until Ormur was done.

Leon spotted Keturah just as the class was dismissed, offering a weary bow. The students stood and left in silence, forming a column two abreast and descending towards Avon to forage. Keturah watched them go, slightly taken aback by the discipline of boys so young. 'Miss Keturah,' said Leon, taking a pace towards her. 'The Black Lord sent you?'

'Indeed,' said Keturah, ignoring Gero's panicked start at the lie. 'I'm here for a bit more information and to assist you in finding Numa's killer, if I can.' Keturah expected surprise on Leon's part and was disappointed by its lack.

'Good,' he said simply. 'Where do you want to start?'

'I hear you have a prisoner named Hagen,' said Keturah.

Leon scowled. 'That worm,' he growled. 'Totally broken. Too enthralled by fear of Ellengaest to help in any way at all.'

'Nevertheless, I hope to interrogate him.'

Leon shrugged. 'He's this way. Boy? With me.' Ormur looked rebellious, but fell into step as they walked to the longhouse where Hagen was held. Gero followed behind, leading their two horses.

Leon led them to a door in one of the longhouses, producing a key from a chain around his neck and scraping the lock open. He pushed the door in and the first thing that greeted Keturah was a dark and rancid waft. She wrinkled her nose and stepped into the shadows. 'Grim conditions to live in,' she announced to the void. There came a soft clinking of chains as somebody moved in the room. The floor was scattered with hay and by the light now streaming through the door, she could see a teenager slumped against the wall, squinting up at her silhouette. His arms were tied behind his back and he made no reply to her pronouncement. Beside the prisoner was a pail of water, nearly empty, and a small wooden plate adorned with a few strands of hay.

Keturah crouched down to Hagen's eye level, keeping her face blank over the sweet smell of urine that rose from him. His hair was dishevelled, his face pinched, gaunt and pale, and heavy pockets hung beneath his eyes. 'You'll have seen better days,' she commented, looking him up and down. She could hear Leon behind her, tapping a foot with impatience. 'What's your name?' The captive looked away from Keturah, eyes resting on the floor. 'Mine is Keturah. It would be rude not to reply,' she said mildly.

He whispered something, shook his head and cleared his throat. 'Hagen,' he tried again, a little stronger.

'A handsome name,' declared Keturah, reaching forward a finger and tilting his chin towards her. Hagen met her eyes for a moment, his own filled with hurt and suspicion, and beneath all that, a vulnerable glint of hope.

'How long have you been here?'

'I . . .' He stopped to clear his throat again. 'I don't know.'

'Well it won't be much longer, if you can help me,' said Keturah. The captive rested his head wearily against the wall behind him. He closed his eyes, squeezing a tear between the lids and out onto his cheek. She reached forward and rested her hand on his shoulder. 'Hagen? What's the matter?'

He moaned hopelessly.

'I'm going to help,' she said kindly. 'Poor man, you've been here long enough. But I need something from you first.'

'I can't help,' whispered Hagen, hoarsely.

'Your situation cannot get worse than it is now,' said Keturah, squeezing his shoulder. 'You are doomed if you won't speak. But if you will, I can release you.' Keturah had no authority to deliver any of what she promised, but was not greatly concerned. Her duty was to Ormur, and to Roper, and Numa's memory, rather than the ruined traitor before her.

'You can't release me.'

'In fact I can; I have inquisitorial powers,' she lied. 'I am in charge here.'

'The Master . . .' said Hagen, faintly.

'Is dead,' finished Keturah, and Hagen looked up suddenly, showing some energy for the first time.

'Dead?'

'Suicide,' said Keturah, looking at the captive with interest. 'He was a traitor, and killed himself when discovered.'

'When?' breathed Hagen. 'You're sure?' He was suddenly sitting straighter, seeming to inflate slowly as though a weight had been taken off him.

'Of course I'm sure. It was months ago, you hadn't heard?'

'I . . .' Hagen glanced over her shoulder and she knew he was looking at Leon, standing in the doorway. 'Nobody has spoken to me for some time.'

'Well he's dead. I have the power to release you if you please me enough.'

The captive was staring around the room as though seeing it for the first time. Then he shook his head. 'What do you want?'

'I know you can summon the assassin,' said Keturah. 'You've done it before. You have a signal that he'll respond to.' She and Hagen stared at one another. 'Summon him tonight. Let us take care of him. In return, I'll get you a better room, somewhere safe. You'll have light, and better food, and won't be tied up.'

'What will you do, when he comes?' breathed Hagen.

'We'll ask him some questions,' said Keturah, 'and he may lead us to Ellengaest.' She saw Hagen pale at the name and went on. 'But nobody need know that you helped us. As far as anyone will be aware, the assassin will just have made a mistake. One for which Leon,' she gestured over her shoulder at the fiend barring the doorway, 'will make him pay.'

Hagen seemed unequal to a reply.

'Seems to me this is a chance you must take,' said

Keturah, scarcely daring to believe he might be capitulating. 'If you don't, you will be executed for aiding the death of an heir to the Stone Throne. Your options are to help me, do the right thing, and gain the rewards; or face certain death, in squalor and disgrace. Of course there's a tiny risk from Ellengaest if you help, but I'd sooner take a small risk with honour, than a big one with disgrace. I suspect you would too.' She squeezed his shoulder and his eyes disengaged from hers. 'Hagen? Look at me. What do you say? Will you summon him for us?'

He stared at her hopelessly. 'He won't trust my signal any more,' he said hoarsely. 'I haven't been able to contact him for . . .' He shook his head, staring up at Leon.

'Months,' supplied the guardsman, dispassionately.

'Only months,' said Hagen, bitterly. 'But he'll have been waiting to hear from me for that time . . . He'll be suspicious.'

'Nevertheless,' said Keturah, 'will you try for me?' He said nothing, but she could see he was wavering. 'Please,' she said, squeezing his shoulder again.

He flinched slightly at her touch. Then his head slumped in a wobbly, hopeless nod.

'That is the right choice,' said Keturah, patting the centre of his chest. She looked over her shoulder to the guardsman. 'Would you untie him Leon? I believe he has earned some food, and somewhere better to wait for the evening.'

Leon duly untied the captive. Keturah felt no fear, for the man was so wretched that he no longer seemed capable of independent effort. She and Gero helped him upstairs to the room where he had first signalled to the assassin. Keturah sent for food and Hagen ate ravenously.

'We'll do it tonight,' said Keturah. 'We will have Leon with us,' and there she paused, for Hagen had flinched violently at the guardsman's name. 'And Ormur, so that we know he's somewhere safe. Then you will signal, and we'll see if anything comes of it.'

'And if he responds?'

'Then Leon will be waiting for him. We'll capture him and see if he knows who Ellengaest is.'

'And then?'

Keturah shrugged. 'And then he'll die.'

'So explain to me one more time,' said Leon.

Keturah almost clapped a palm over her face. 'All you need to know is that you wait downstairs, and if the murderer comes through the door in front of you, then capture him.'

Leon nodded, satisfied by this.

'There's one thing I've been thinking,' she said, after a pause. 'After the assassin drew Salbjorn away, Ormur was undefended for the whole day until you got back. Why wasn't he killed?'

'I had wondered,' said Leon. 'All I can think is that whatever happened to Salbjorn, he managed to keep the assassin busy for a long time. When he was finally finished, there wasn't time to go back to the boy. Maybe Salbjorn injured the assassin. Maybe they killed each other.'

The two were silent, thinking of Salbjorn fighting alone during his last hours, perhaps knowing that the longer he resisted, the greater the chance Ormur would survive. 'At least that suggests the assassin is now working alone,' said Keturah. 'He should be the final piece of this.'

Behind Leon was Ormur, looking everywhere but at Keturah. She was struck by how withered he looked.

'Ormur?'

His gaze met hers briefly and then fell back to the floor.

'You will stay up here with us.' She indicated Gero, who now held a stout staff so that he could stand guard over Hagen. 'You'll be completely safe, and we'll see if Leon can at last capture this assassin.' The boy made no reply and Keturah prayed that they could bring some measure of closure to his ordeal. *If we don't, this grief will kill him*, she thought.

Through the window, it was dusk. The sun hung just above the mountaintops, and the boys and tutors scurrying in the courtyard below trailed silken shadows. Gero suggested they light the fire in the room and make tea, but Keturah forbade it. There must be nothing out of the ordinary. But there were apparently good supplies of birch sap, and Keturah went to fetch a container, which they shared between them. They waited in silence, every now and then taking a draught of the sap, which was fresh and woody. Ormur lay listless by a wall. Gero fidgeted. Hagen looked dead.

Shadows consumed the courtyard outside. The slow moon rose. The snow-bones were burnished silver. The steel points of stars pricked the dark.

'You may begin, Hagen,' said Keturah, nodding at their captive. 'Leon? Please go downstairs now.' Leon crept out of the room, and Keturah passed Hagen a tinder-box and a torch that reeked of pitch. The torch sputtered into life and Hagen kept it carefully low, proceeding to the window, which faced out towards the lake. 'If he comes,' whispered Keturah, causing Hagen to pause, 'you will be rewarded.'

Hagen hesitated, torch in hand. He glanced back at Keturah and then out at the mountains once more. He bounced the torch six times over the windowsill. He waited a moment, then repeated it five times. Then four and finally three. He held the torch away from the window, putting it head down in an iron brazier to puff and sputter.

'So what did you tell him?' asked Keturah.

'That was the signal,' said Hagen, hoarsely, 'that the Master said I was to give above the spot where the boy slept unguarded. I will repeat it through the night, and if the assassin still trusts it, he will come in below us.'

'The Master?' whispered Keturah, not having genuinely credited his involvement in this. She began to understand that it was less her powers of persuasion, and more the death of Hagen's chief tormentor that had gained his help at last.

They waited. Keturah stayed back from the window, watching the moonlit courtyard from her shadowed corner. All was still, and just as the torch resting in the brazier was beginning to fade, Hagen repeated his signal.

The room stayed silent, the courtyard stayed empty, and the five of them waited. At what she supposed was about midnight, Keturah finally detected movement outside. She put a finger to her lips and crept a little closer to the window, looking out into the pearly courtyard. There was a creature staring right back at her, fairly irradiated by the moon.

A wolf.

It shone as though steel-plated and looked directly into her hiding place with gilded eyes. Then it passed on, moving through the courtyard like a wisp of smoke. Keturah felt herself smiling and crept back to her corner.

Some time later, she suggested to Gero that he should go and check that Leon was awake. Gero nodded and crept downstairs. Presently, there came the sound of a thump. Gero reappeared soon after, looking ruffled. 'He's awake,' he muttered.

Hagen lit a second torch and signalled again. The mountains yielded no reply. 'He isn't watching tonight,' whispered Hagen.

'Keep trying,' Keturah decreed. But the torch burnt out and still, there came no sign. They must have been only a couple of hours from dawn when she felt Hagen's eyes turn to her. 'Light the final torch,' she said.

'He suspects,' Hagen whispered, 'or he's dead himself.'

'Then it will do no harm,' said Keturah. 'Light the torch.'

Hagen did, and signalled for the fifth time that night.

And then the sixth.

The moon had gone and there was a smoky tinge to the east. Keturah let out a long breath. 'Damn,' she said, very softly. She stood and stretched. Ormur, who seemed to have been snoozing in the corner, stirred suddenly, glancing about the room, before settling back against the wall.

There came a soft clatter from the courtyard. Gero, still standing over Hagen, blinked. 'Did you hear that?'

'It's nearly dawn,' said Keturah, with a shrug. 'Some of the tutors will be getting up.' She wondered what to do now, and whether Salbjorn really might have killed the assassin. Perhaps they would try again the following night. Or perhaps Hagen had been too fearful to give him the right signal. She glanced at him once more, and screamed.

Crouched on the windowsill behind him was a dark, stocky figure. The assassin, silhouetted against the first light of dawn, a knife clamped between his teeth. Keturah could just make out his eyes, searching this room, which he had clearly not expected to be so full. The figure leapt from the windowsill, lunging with his knife at Gero, who was just able to parry with his staff.

'Leon!' Keturah howled.

Hagen scrambled back and into a corner, eyes bulging as Gero and the assassin grappled, Gero conceding one step after another until he had been forced back onto the low sill of another window. The assassin drove him back further until he was on the verge of toppling over and tumbling into the courtyard. Gero clutched onto the frame, but to do so he had to release his staff, which had been holding back that wicked knife. The blade was suddenly free and the assassin drew it back to strike his opponent.

Then Ormur charged out of nowhere, screaming in his high boy's voice and seizing the assassin's knife-hand. Keturah jumped after him, grabbing the hand with Ormur and wrenching at it, trying to prise the fingers open and free the knife. The assassin was immensely strong, and even the two of them combined were pulled this way and that by his right hand. His left had clamped about Gero's throat and was forcing him back, back, so that he leaned further out of the window, nearly overbalancing.

There were footsteps thumping up the stairs behind Keturah, whose grip on the assassin's knife-hand was weakening.

'Hagen, help us!' she called, but Hagen had huddled into the corner, hands covering his mouth as his nightmare appeared in this room. The assassin gave a brutal heave which threw Keturah back, her grip torn loose. Ormur still clutched onto the assassin's wrist, teeth bared, as he was lifted bodily from the ground by the strength of his brother's murderer. He too must lose his grip soon, and Gero, purple in the face and choking, teetered on the window ledge.

Crash.

Something smashed so hard into the assassin that Keturah felt the impact reverberate through the floorboards. The assassin was bowled over, Ormur spinning aside, the knife dislodged to land on a goatskin, and Gero just snatching the frame of the window before he tumbled backwards.

The assassin had been flattened and now lay yowling and hissing like a trapped animal as Leon bore down on him, a shining blade thrust through his leg, pinning him to the floor. The skewered figure was spitting, swearing and aiming wild kicks at Leon with his free leg, but the guardsman was indomitable. He kept him there, and kept him there, and kept him there.

And suddenly, the assassin fell still. He lay panting and grunting, that sword still through his leg and black blood flooding the floor beneath him.

'You bastards.' He spoke in a hiss like quenched steel. 'You poisonous bastards. Release me.' He twisted slightly onto one side to alleviate the pain of Leon's sword in his thigh.

'I promise you,' said Leon, 'you will never move under your own power again.'

The assassin's appearance had been so sudden that only now did Keturah wonder what had brought him to this room. He must have been suspicious of Hagen's signal coming after such a delay, and so had avoided the main entrance, somehow swarming up the outer wall and bypassing their ambush altogether.

Now he coughed and gasped, glaring at the sword through his thigh. 'Months,' he rasped. If Keturah had to imagine the voice of a snake, it would sound like this man. 'Freezing, insect-bitten months in those bloody mountains, and I didn't even get the boy. Knew it was too good to be true. Stupid. Stupid, stupid, stupid.'

'So you murdered Numa?' demanded Keturah, stepping forward. 'And Guardsman Salbjorn? Well done, Leon,' she added to the guardsman.

'Of course.' The assassin gasped suddenly as Leon twisted his sword. Another surge of black blood pumped out beneath the shadow.

'I think you've hit an artery,' said Keturah to Leon.

'I'm sure of it,' replied the guardsman.

'We need him alive! Take out the sword, I will bind the wound.' She prepared to tear strips from her cloak but Leon was shaking his head.

'He's done for.'

'I am,' agreed the assassin, gritted teeth shining from the floor. 'What a stupid way to spend your final months.' His gaze strayed to Ormur, and Keturah saw the hunger there. 'And so close,' he said wistfully, smiling at the boy. Ormur was pale, but stared back defiantly.

'Who are you?' asked Keturah, imploring Leon to keep his sword still with a hand on his elbow. She felt terrible fear and responsibility that this man might die without yielding the information they needed. If her interference destroyed the only lead they had, she was not sure she would be able to look Roper in the eye again. Though he would be generous, she knew. He would not blame her.

'Endre,' replied the man.

'And who sent you here, Endre?'

Endre just grunted. It might have been a sound of amusement. It certainly indicated that he planned to say no more.

'I know you work for Ellengaest,' said Keturah. 'Why would you show loyalty to a man who sent you here to die?'

'Ellengaest freed me from prison,' said Endre. 'I'd have been rotting on one of those hulks without him. Mountain-time has been better than that. Anything is better than that. So yes, I have more loyalty to him than the bastards who have me pinned to the floor.'

'Ellengaest is working to bring down the Black Kingdom,' said Keturah. 'Did you know that?'

Endre raised an apathetic hand. 'Yes.' The pool of blood beneath him was expanding and he lay his head on the floor suddenly. 'Get this over with,' he breathed.

'Very well,' said Keturah, speaking calmly, though she could feel time slipping away. 'As a servant to Ellengaest, once you are finished, we will obliterate your body.'

His gritted teeth flashed once more. 'No. Not for this.'

Keturah laughed. She was so practised at it that it came out genuinely delighted. 'Of course for this! You lie dying and unrepentant; a murderer and servant of the man trying to destroy our kingdom. Give me his name, his real name, and I will save your body from obliteration.'

The only response was a laboured panting.

'What do you owe him?' said Keturah, mystification in her voice. 'He freed you but only to transform you into a slave. Into his dog.'

'I am no man's dog,' seethed the voice abruptly, words slightly slurred.

'You are fully domesticated,' said Keturah, mercilessly. 'But that's irrelevant. Unless you give us your master's name, we will destroy your body. The screaming fragments of your soul will travel the world like a cloud of misery. That is all that will survive for eternity.'

Endre's cheek was lying in the tide of blood. He shook his head. 'Vigtyr,' he named. 'Vigtyr Forraederson. Vigtyr the Quick.'

Keturah stepped backwards.

At last.

At last they had the name, and her first thought was of Roper, working so closely with that giant, that traitor. He was in terrible danger.

Her attention snapped to Endre once more, and she leaned over him, speaking urgently. 'What is his plan? What will he do?'

The assassin's eyes were closed, and Keturah feared he could say no more. Then he began to speak, words so slurred they were hard to distinguish. 'The army is full of his informants,' he mumbled. 'People in his debt. He sends their information to the Suthern spymaster, to help him defeat Roper . . . As Roper's campaign fails, Vigtyr believes he will be executed by the Kryptea. And that he will win the gratitude of the Sutherners, and earn a place at their royal court.' Endre's face was deathly pale, and he was panting harder. 'That's what he wants,' he said. 'There. I told you. That's all I know. Save my body.'

Keturah glared down at him. 'I thank you for your help, Endre. It has been invaluable. Your body will be blown to smithereens.'

'No!' shouted the figure, eyes flying open.

Leon leaned forward on his sword and glowered down at the assassin. 'For Salbjorn,' he said, giving his sword a twist. A fresh black surge flooded out beneath Endre, whose frantic scrabbling faded in a few heartbeats.

'Vigtyr,' breathed Keturah. 'Vigtyr.' The white mountaintops through the window were capped in orange light. 'Leon, ride. Take my horse and ride now. Warn them. If you arrive before they assault Lundenceaster, you could save thousands. Bellamus is broken. Vigtyr is all that's left: you must stop him.'

'I have a duty to protect you and the boy,' said Leon, pulling his sword free of Endre's leg.

Keturah stamped her foot. 'Irrelevant! Go! Go! Go! Go, now!' Leon backed towards the stairs, and Keturah pursued him. 'Ride now, as fast you that horse will take you! To Lundenceaster! For Vigtyr; kill Vigtyr! Go!'

37

The Walls of Lundenceaster

'We're ready, my lord,' said Gray.

'Ready?' asked Roper. 'We could burn the tunnels?'

'And the wall would come crashing down. Or so the engineers say.'

Another clouded day. Roper, Gray and Pryce lined one of the eastern trenches, surveying the walls. Everything about Roper felt damp. His feet were wet from wading through the water that was now up to his ankles. His fingers were cold and wrinkled, and he felt constantly on the verge of shivering. And gnawing at him as surely as his hunger, was the seemingly insurmountable task which lay before them. 'I know I said we would not delay,' he said. 'Almighty knows I want this over, one way or another. But I do not think we can take this city, as we are. The defences are too potent. There are too many defenders. We have been too weak, and too heartsick, for too long, and our resolve is too fragile. We need the Unhieru to finish this task.'

'How far away are they?' asked Gray.

'Not far,' said Roper. 'I had word that they'll be here in two days with the Fair Islanders.'

'And what if they're delayed by another two days beyond

that?' said Gray. 'With our rations so meagre, this force may simply disintegrate.'

'I know,' said Roper. 'I know. But it's a chance we have to take, and the scouts are confident they'll be here.'

'The word of our scouts is worth considerably less these days,' Pryce observed.

'Nevertheless. We wait for them.'

'And at least the Skiritai are no longer being dumped at the edge of the camp,' said Gray. Each night for a week, torches had bobbed at the outskirts of the camp as Hermit-Crabs attempted to feed them Skiritai bodies, and each night they had been driven back by volleys of arrows. From what-ever source the infected Skiritai derived, it seemed to have dried up. Roper dared hope they might yet resist that perish-ing disease, but the risk of it had nevertheless made foraging for food, fetching water and firewood very hard. Every time they ventured away from the safety of their archers and defences, it was the worst fear of every man that they would encounter waiting Hermit-Crabs or infected Skiritai bodies, and be forced to make that lonely and self-sacrifical march into this alien land. The exhaustion of this army was so con-suming that even with the Unhieru, Roper was not sure his troops had the morale to take on Lundenceaster.

They talked for a time longer, Gray enquiring after Roper's lessons with Vigtyr.

'I had another this morning,' said Roper. 'It feels as though I'm making a lot of progress.'

'Vigtyr doesn't enjoy the lessons any more,' said Pryce. 'A sure sign that you're progressing.'

'That is the impression I get,' Roper admitted. 'He doesn't actually like it when I get better.'

'I heard him describe you as exceptional, the other day,' said Gray. 'He thinks you could be a master.'

Roper was astonished, and desperately wanted to enquire further, but they were interrupted by a staccato trumpet burst from the north. *Soldiers Coming*. The three men exchanged glances. 'More infected?'

'Let's find out,' said Roper. They clambered out of the trench, each smearing their front with mud as they wriggled away from the edge. From this distance, Roper could see a large mass of men, moving through the trees beyond them. For an instant, he forgot how small the trees in Suthdal were, and he grossly overestimated the size of these figures and supposed the Unhieru had arrived early. But as he drew closer, he recognised the banner held overhead: a swirl of ragged falcon wings. 'I don't believe it,' he said. 'I don't believe it!'

Before this stream of weary men trudging into the camp, a lone figure rode straight-backed. The rider spotted Roper and curbed his horse towards him, Roper breaking into a run, a grin spreading over his face.

He stopped before the rider and beamed. 'Legate Tekoa,' he said. 'Come to join us for the last dance?'

'Such as we are,' said Tekoa.

'The plague?'

'Has surrendered. Two weeks since our last case.'

Roper stepped closer and held up a hand to Tekoa. The two shook, and Gray was next in line. Pryce stayed where he was. 'You're back,' he said.

'Yes, Nephew. I'm back.'

'How many Skiritai survived?' asked Pryce artlessly.

Tekoa's voice was very even as he replied. 'There are fifteen hundred of us left.'

'Fifteen hundred more than I'd dared hope,' said Roper. 'And that you are among them is even better.'

'There's no need to start gushing, Lord Roper,' said Tekoa.

'And tell me,' said Pryce, voice still flat. 'How is it that the Hermit-Crabs were able to harvest so many of your infected?'

There was a pause, Tekoa examining his nephew. 'I had not heard that,' he said, at last.

'That is fortunate for you,' Pryce replied. 'Meanwhile, we've had to deal with your sick men being dumped—'

'It's done,' Roper interrupted. 'The Skiritai here are healthy. There is no more that—'

'You have had to deal with my sick men?' Tekoa overrode Roper, staring icily at Pryce. 'Do tell me what that must have felt like, Nephew. I cannot imagine.'

Pryce narrowed his eyes, starting forward but Roper thumped a hand into his chest. 'Enough, both of you! Nothing can be gained from this, it is done. It is the hunger making you argue. We have one thing left to do.' Roper jabbed a finger at Lundenceaster's towering walls. 'And if you do not give it every scrap of energy you possess, then all we have done so far will be for nought. Emotions are contagious and you must both watch yours.'

Tekoa and Pryce were still staring furiously at one another, until Gray took Pryce by the arm. 'We're on trenches soon, Pryce. Let's get ready.' The two of them retreated, Pryce throwing one last disgusted look at his uncle before he allowed himself to be drawn away. Roper looked back to Tekoa, and found that behind the anger lay an unexpected vulnerability.

'Nothing came of the infected Skiritai left by the Hermit-Crabs, Legate,' he said. 'Once we'd realised what they were trying to do, we drove them off with arrows.'

Tekoa nodded curtly and then raised a hand to his face, covering it briefly. He was silent a while, Roper taking a pace closer. 'I'm ... I'm sorry, Lord Roper. I did not think that would happen.'

'Put it from your mind,' said Roper. 'The assault is the only thing that matters now.'

Tekoa nodded, passing a hand over his face again. 'Where is my daughter?'

'She went north to have the child. She should be back in the Hindrunn by now.' There came another pause, and Roper beamed, knowing what a boost this arrival would give his men. 'I am exceptionally glad to have you back, Legate.'

Tekoa nodded, not looking at Roper fully. His eyes were like marble; his joking forgotten. There was no real joy in his words, just the compulsion to continue. 'Let's finish this,' he said.

Tekoa never spoke to Roper about how it had been to wait in isolation while sickness ate through his legion. Roper heard stories from other Skiritai of the brutal quarantine he had imposed, with the legion divided into *Definitely Sick*, *Maybe Sick* and *Definitely Well*. These last were preserved at all costs. As soon as he had left camp, Tekoa gathered his men and told them bluntly that the time had come to lay down their lives for their peers and their kingdom. Should anyone suspect themselves of sickness, they should join the *Maybe Sick*. Should it be confirmed, the preferable course for this most contagious of diseases was walk off into the woods somewhere and wait for it to take its course. If you survived, you would be permitted to rejoin the *Maybe Sick*. Healthy men could not be risked tending to the infected, and Tekoa had twice placed himself in the *Maybe Sick*, and twice survived.

Hearing this, Roper realised that it must be the *Definitely Sick* who had wandered into the woods and been captured by the Hermit-Crabs. Tekoa must have realised the same, but never spoke of it, and Roper did not press him. The legate was darker now and his humour more caustic, but Roper was very glad to have him and his rangers back. Especially when the Unhieru arrived.

They came from the west.

Roper, Tekoa, Gray and Pryce stood together when the burst for *Soldiers Coming* sounded once more. 'That'll be the Unhurried,' said Tekoa.

Roper had thought he was too weary for fear, but at the trumpet he felt sweat prickle his palms. 'Onwards,' he said, without thinking. The four broke into a trot, heading for where the trumpet sound had issued.

'Is there anything I should know before meeting these people?' asked Gray.

'It is the same as anything,' said Tekoa. 'Don't back down under any circumstances.'

Roper had expected to see the Unhieru towering from a distance, but the first sign that they were drawing near was a still crowd of legionaries, all facing into the trees. Beneath the canopy of the forest, Roper could detect massive, shadowed movements. He pushed into the gathered soldiers, who opened a channel rapidly once they registered him. There was evidently considerable enthusiasm that he should take command, and Roper smelt on the air that feral reek of urine.

As the legionaries stepped aside, Roper saw Gighath: the brown-eyed female who had laughed so poisonously at their delegation. She was advancing towards a captain who stood before the crowd and yielded to her, footstep for footstep. Roper could see the earth beneath her bare feet sliding out of the way under the pressure she exerted. He placed a hand on the retreating captain's shoulder. Relieved, the man ducked behind Roper, who strode forward to meet Gighath. Emerging from the trees behind her were more Unhieru, both men and women moving with the gracious prowl of bears.

Roper gave Gighath a courteous bow, exposing the back of his neck to her for much longer than felt natural. 'An honour to have you here, my lady. Tell me, do you know where Gogmagoc is? I wish to greet him.'

'This is that poisonous wretch, Gighath isn't it?' came Pryce's voice from behind Roper.

In response, Gighath bared her broken teeth, but spoke no words. Roper found his attention drawn away and to the right, as though there were a hook in his ear. There was a gentle clinking of something slow and armoured moving through the trees. As he looked into the gloom, Roper spied something enormous and shining, shifting from side to side as it walked. Gighath, following Roper's gaze, choked a word. *'Hokhmakhok.'*

Roper nodded, bidding Gighath a polite goodbye that he did not feel she had earned. He strode forward, calling out: 'Gogmagoc! Gogmagoc!' High above, a horrifying metal face was turned towards Roper. Alone of the Unhieru, Gogmagoc had worn his armour for the occasion. Being unfamiliar with Unhieru faces, the armourers had allowed a margin for error by creating eye and mouth holes much larger than usual. The resultant piece worn by Gogmagoc was like a vast, upturned steel bucket; mad, pitch-black and perfectly round eyeholes perforated its front, above a tall alcove for the mouth. Beneath this, chain mail cascaded down his front, already spattered with rusted links and so shapeless that the newcomer resembled a vast iron phantom. In one hand, he clutched the head of an enormous axe, its shaft dragging along the ground behind like a plough.

Roper felt his peers backing away from the giant king, and he could not help but imagine what it would take to stop this creature, so armed and armoured. A cannon might do it, or a fire-thrower. But in the field, with bladed weapons moved by muscle-power alone, Roper could not see how to penetrate the chain mail, even if you survived coming within range of his axe. He thought of Gilius, of the horses, of the *other-mind*, and Gogmagoc's aura of insanity, and was less certain than ever of the wisdom of having these people here.

The metal apparition had gone still; wide, mad eyeholes gaping at Roper. He offered another bow, sensing the feral intelligence surveying him beneath that shocking helmet, making judgements in some code Roper could not understand. 'Welcome to our army, my lord Gogmagoc. You have arrived just in time.'

'In time for what?' growled the apparition.

'For a good competition,' said Roper.

Gogmagoc laughed. That slow grinding noise, which made the hairs on the back of Roper's neck stand up.

'Come and share my fire, lord king, and we shall talk.'

Gogmagoc made an expressive gesture with his

hand – *Continue* – but said no more. Roper turned away and led the king back to his hearth, the crowds around them parting in silence. After Roper and the giant king came Gray, Pryce, Tekoa and a whole procession of Unhieru: first scores, then hundreds pouring from the trees. They kept their distance from the legionaries, each side eyeing the other and communicating past one another.

At his fire, Roper set fresh wood and two pots of pine-tea on the flames. Gogmagoc pulled off his helmet and rattled his bone-fastened mane, falling into a seat. Gray and Tekoa stood around the fire, eyeing the giant as the tea brewed, but Pryce simply dropped next to him and began tearing at the grass. 'How was your journey, Lord Gogmagoc?' Roper enquired.

The king just shrugged. 'Complete. Where is Eoten-Draefend?'

'We do not know for sure,' Roper admitted. 'But the vast majority of the Suthern forces are behind those walls.'

Gogmagoc inspected Lundenceaster. 'So we cannot get him,' he growled.

As Roper had hoped, Gogmagoc assumed Garrett might be inside too, and under no circumstances would Roper dissuade him of that notion. 'Leave the walls to us,' he said. 'But there are a great number of defenders, which we will need to fight together.'

'Many defenders, but not enough,' Gogmagoc declared. 'We will enter first.'

Roper smiled. 'I was going to suggest just that, lord. With your armour, I suspect our enemy shall struggle against you. We will create a breach – a hole – in the wall tonight. Perhaps you should pick one thousand of your number to be first inside. Any more and you may run out of room to move.' *And we'll probably lose control of you*, he thought.

'Yes,' Gogmagoc agreed.

'Good,' said Roper, eyeing his guest. 'Good. When darkness falls, we shall begin.' *At last.*

'It is decided,' said Gogmagoc. He picked up the scalding bucket of tea and drained it in one swallow. Roper looked aghast at the king, who lumbered upright. Without another word, he prowled away, helmet gripped loosely at his side.

Darkness fell.

Roper walked the camp, breathing through his mouth to avoid the unsettling musk of the Unhieru. He had never known an army so silent. He could almost see the weight of what they were about to attempt pressing down on the legionaries. He had ordered that they eat the last of their rations to give them strength to fight – whether they won or lost, they would not be needed tomorrow – but though all were starving, most just stared mutely at the food.

Roper had forced down his own rations, but knew how his men felt. In a quiet moment when it was just he and Gray left by the fire, he turned to the captain. 'I don't feel good.'

Gray gave an encouraging smile. 'In what way, lord?'

'Sick. Weak.' Roper paused. 'Afraid.'

Gray nodded, his face looking old in the shadows of the fire. 'I feel the same, my lord. Lundenceaster has a reputation. These walls are where armies come to die, and now it is not just our own lives we are fighting for. It the very future of the Anakim. The men feel that.'

'I do too,' said Roper, quietly. He looked at the dark mass of the city walls. 'I would only say this to you, my brother. I have never wanted to do anything less in my entire life.'

Gray nodded. 'I know, my lord. I don't much want to either.' They were quiet for a moment, before Roper looked back at Gray.

'But it's at least simple, isn't it? Turn back from here, and we starve. But take those walls, those streets, and we secure our future. We must do it. For our loved ones in the north, and those generations yet unborn.'

Gray put an arm over Roper's shoulder. 'And here we are at

last, lord. Just getting this army here is achievement enough that the Academy shall remember you forever.'

'I shall reward myself with the honour of being the first Anakim over the breach,' said Roper.

'My lord,' said Gray, withdrawing his arm. 'You cannot.'

'I can.'

'No,' Gray said vehemently. 'You must trust me. It is this simple: those who begin an assault do not survive it. You are needed. Without you, this army falls apart, and you will not survive being first into that breach. Believe me now, you cannot go.'

Roper was silent. Privately, he felt so unsettled that he was not sure he could bear to wait beyond the walls. Better to be active and in danger, both of which would mask the unnatural churning of his heart. That was truly what drove him on, but Gray was also right. His first duty was to the army. 'All right, Gray. I will wait.'

Other officers began to gather at Roper's hearth to wait for the assault. Pryce appeared and Vigtyr. The Chief Historian, Tekoa, Sturla and half a dozen other legates, sheltering in the fire's glow from the distant howls of the Unhieru. The giants had made the camp feel very unfamiliar.

Roper and Gray talked aimlessly, their only purpose to distract their companions and prevent them getting lost in their own thoughts. 'I've been thinking about one of the conversations I had with Bellamus,' Roper began.

'Tell me,' said Gray, sharpening his sword in the firelight.

'It was about choice,' said Roper. 'And I've trying to work out if he was telling the truth, or if everything he did and said in that tent was some kind of performance.'

'What makes you think he was performing?'

'The chess,' said Roper, thoughtfully. 'I beat him at every single game, except the last. In that one, he outclassed me. I was left . . . I was left with the feeling that he'd been letting me win, and only played me properly that last time.'

Gray frowned. 'Why would he?'

'I don't know, but he is an unusually committed and resourceful man. And that makes me wonder if I can trust any of what he told me. Or if it was all to mislead me in ways I do not currently understand.'

'So what did he say about choice?'

'He claimed,' said Roper slowly, 'that for those in Suthdal, choice is considered a great positive. They love it. They think if you have the freedom to choose, you will make yourself happier.'

'A child's philosophy,' said Pryce scathingly. 'Which is happier, the man who accepts what he has and makes the best of it, or the one always glancing over his shoulder, wondering if he should have chosen another path? Choice is a terrible burden.'

'It can be welcome sometimes, in small things,' Gray allowed. 'What to do with an evening, what to eat ... But I must agree. Imagine having to choose what to do with your life. Imagine having to choose your own name, or even your own sword. You should grow around your circumstances, rather than trying to change them.'

'Yes, yes,' said Roper. 'I said all this. I asked how he lives with the uncertainty, constantly wondering what might have been. And he said that it is an opportunity to exercise his personality. He thinks to himself before each decision: "What choice would the man I would like to be make?" Each choice is a way of getting closer to who he would like to be. That, he said, was liberating.'

Silence followed this report. 'That is interesting,' said Gray, stowing his whetstone in a pouch and sitting back to ponder, sword still resting in his lap. 'I don't think you need doubt everything he said. I believe a man could be convinced by that.'

'A one-eyed man,' Pryce observed.

'I don't think you're in a position to be criticising people missing sensory organs, Pryce,' said Tekoa, and the company laughed. Pryce ignored the comment.

'I believe I've only seen Pryce laugh once in my entire life,' said Roper, observing the sprinter. 'That night by the fire before Githru, when Uvoren's four guardsmen lured me away and attacked me. Pryce followed us. Before he attacked, Asger said there was a thought going through his mind, and I said it must mean someone else had put it there.' The group chuckled again. 'And Pryce laughed. I don't believe I've seen that since.'

'Amusing as that is, I'd imagine you were probably a little nervous as well, Nephew,' said Tekoa. 'You must have known you were about to try and kill four Sacred Guardsmen.'

Pryce was quiet a moment. 'I was not nervous,' he said. He fidgeted with his long ponytail, winding it briefly about his fingers, and then looked up at Tekoa. 'Until Lord Roper said that, I didn't think I was going to try and kill anyone.'

As Pryce spoke these words, Gray's head sank into his hands. There was a long silence as the party absorbed this news. Tekoa was looking incredulously at his nephew. 'You cannot mean to say ... Are you seriously confessing that Lord Roper making that joke was what made you decide to protect him?'

Pryce shrugged.

'That otherwise, you'd have let Uvoren's men murder him?' Tekoa clarified.

'Yes,' said Pryce, simply.

There was a stunned silence. 'What say you to this, Lord Roper?' said Tekoa, clearly struggling to comprehend what his nephew was admitting to.

Roper smiled at Pryce. 'I knew it already,' he said lightly. 'It was obvious to me, when Pryce made his choice.'

'It is one I would make again,' said Pryce, curtly. 'No matter how many times you asked.'

Roper blinked and looked away suddenly. Gray saved his having to make a reply. 'That must be choice at its most valuable,' said the captain. 'Being able to reward those we think deserve it.' Roper thought of Keturah, and her desire to follow Tekoa when he had been exiled from the army. Tekoa himself was clearly dwelling on other matters.

'It's all very touching,' he said acidly. 'But are we going to brush over the fact that Pryce decided to take on four guardsmen single-handed, based on a joke that he liked?'

It seemed Pryce was going to maintain a haughty silence, but then he shrugged again. 'It was not the joke. It was watching a man who refused to kneel, even when he was about to die.'

'You should have seen what came next,' said Roper, and he recounted how Pryce had defeated his four esteemed opponents. Somehow, that night, the absurdity of the story made it funny. Pryce did not contribute, looking bored at the attention as he was quizzed on whose stroke had taken his ear, whose created the white scars on his forearm, and who had died easiest.

Among the laughter, one question was blurted in earnest. 'Does everything come easily to you, Pryce?' It was a voice of naked envy and admiration; so exposed that several of the officers looked down, as though they had witnessed something indecent. Roper looked, and was astonished to find that it was Vigtyr who had spoken. He was staring wistfully at Pryce, who eyed Vigtyr in return.

'Everything I care about.'

Vigtyr dropped his eyes at that, staring into the hearth. Roper was filled with sudden pity.

There was a very long silence, broken only by the delicate tinkling of the cooling embers. Roper looked at the faces, glowing red about the fire, and found nearly every eye resting on him. He met them all and nodded to himself for a few moments. 'My friends. It is time.'

In the blackness, the figures around the fire got to their feet.

Anakim and Unhieru gathered together before Lundenceaster's moss-covered walls. While the legates rode in front of their legions, blessing them with an eye of woven holly, the soldiers watched the smoke. From three vents in the earth, three columns billowed, the base of each illuminated dark crimson by the flames burning underground. It was too dark to see if there were any defenders on the wall, but the Sutherners would surely have realised what the smoke indicated, and have abandoned that stretch of their defences.

The Unhieru waited in the trenches; a line of them, drenched in chain mail and watching through their ghastly helmets. Behind them were the legions, dressed in their own plate armour and deathly still beneath the banners.

The moment, when it came, was not one moment at all but a long string of them.

First there came a mighty crack.

A fine puff of mortar issued from one of the towers embedded in the wall, illuminated by the faint glow from the city and hanging in the air. Then the earth in front of the tower slumped oddly, eliciting a great black gust and three licks of flame from the smoke vents. In that flare of light, two dark cracks flashed across the wall, one either side of the tower.

Then a long moment of silence.

The smoke began to die, and Roper feared the sapping had failed and they had only weakened the wall. He had issued the Unhieru with ropes and grapples to haul on should this happen and, standing in the trench above Gogmagoc, Roper prepared to order their advance.

He was stopped by another broken crack from the wall. And then another.

And then, impossibly slowly, hard to distinguish through the dark but ultimately unmistakable, the tower began to tip forward. Like a toppling tree it gathered momentum exponentially: almost gentle and abruptly breathtaking. It landed in a thunderous crash, which Roper felt through his boots as a physical shock in the earth. A huge cloud of dust roared from the sides and rubble cascaded from the wall behind, slumping into a high breach.

The breach.

It was still thirty feet of uneven rubble up which the Unhieru would have to climb, overlooked by the walls on either side that the Sutherners would fill with bowmen, making the passage lethal. But it was there. It was time. Suthdal was within their grasp. They simply had to climb that breach, and take the city behind.

Roper laid a hand on Gogmagoc's armoured back and spoke into the dark.

'Good luck, everyone.'

38

The Breach

The drumming began; profound waves of it, thrashed out by the thousands at Roper's back. Lundenceaster knew what was coming and it was time to appal it into submission. With an energy that caught Roper by surprise, Gogmagoc launched himself from the trench, chain mail jingling about his knees and long-bladed axe clutched at his side. He released an ear-splitting exclamation: a drowned marine howl which rang from the dark walls and brought the other Unhieru clambering out of the trenches after him. Led by their giant king, they began to lope for the breach.

Roper watched with the Sacred Guard at his back, Ramnea's Own behind them. Beyond the Unhieru, fire began to drip from the walls that still stood either side of the breach as the defenders tossed down burning hay-bundles. They were lighting the battleground so that their bowmen would have clear targets, turning the breach into a smouldering mouth, scattered with blazing teeth.

The Unhieru were three hundred yards ahead, their roaring a distant, stag-like bellow, when Gray came to stand next to him. Dread prowled through Roper; his heartbeat indistinguishable from the profound drumming that filled the air.

He turned to smile at Gray, placing a hand over his chest. 'Whatever lies behind that breach, it's better than this.'

Gray smiled back. 'Foolish, lord.'

Roper drew Cold-Edge and turned to the Sacred Guard behind him, looking from one man to the next. 'Are you with me?' Three hundred swords were pulled from their scabbards. 'Then let's finish this!' Roper turned for the breach, running over the wooden bridges spanning each trench, the guard labouring after him.

They flooded the dark no man's land before the walls, the top of which had begun to glow with the light of hundreds of torches as defenders packed the battlements. The bone trumpets blared, and Ramnea's Own started after them, boots tramping in eerie synchrony and ragged banners swaying like fragments of the night itself. The legion droned into life, beginning the 'Hymn of Advance', and giving a cheer that Roper had not expected, which carried him forward.

Three waves now marched for the wall; two big and one small. First came a thousand Unhieru, led by Gogmagoc: shock-troops, whom Roper hoped would overwhelm the initial defences and crush Suthern morale. Next the smallest wave: Roper and his Sacred Guardsmen. They would follow Gogmagoc into the breach and direct the attack, choosing their interventions carefully and coordinating the efforts of the third wave, who followed a few hundred yards behind. Ramnea's Own Legion: the best of the Black Kingdom. Mostly proven veterans, seasoned with absurdly talented youngsters looking to make a name for themselves, and earn a spot in the Sacred Guard.

They might be few, hungry, heartsick and exhausted, but they had energy for one final effort. Between them, they would seize control of the breach. Once it was secured, they could use it as a doorway into Lundenceaster. The legions would be pumped inside, interspersed with bands of Unhieru, and street by street, building by building, they would overwhelm this city. That was the task of these first

few waves: secure the breach. Manage that, and Lundenceaster would fall.

Far ahead, there came a whistling and a dry crackle as the
Unhieru were spattered with longbow shafts. Roper quick-
ened his pace, wanting to get as close as possible while the
Unhieru drew all the fire. The night was filled with panting,
the clank and bounce of armour and the thump of boots. A
fog of shattered stone and smoke lay over their path, drying
Roper's mouth and stinging his throat.

Gogmagoc had reached the stones of the breach and led
his band swarming up the face, dodging the blazing hay-
bundles on their path, arrows tumbling off their mail. The
first of them were silhouetted at the top, against the dust that
lingered overhead, stained a rusted orange by the fires. The
Unhieru seemed to totter there, shadows frozen at the summit, before a dozen were hurled backwards. They spilt back
down the breach in a trail of rock dust and rolled to a halt at
the base, lying motionless. Roper faltered, staring at the dead
giants. There was something terrible behind that breach.
Something powerful enough to stop an armoured Unhieru.

Whatever it was, Gogmagoc had ignored it and led the rest
of his band on, over the crest of the breach and out of sight.
Roper pursued him, the ground now prickled with arrow-
shafts, but the bowmen on the walls still ignoring them.
They were clearly too fearful of the Unhieru to bother with
Roper and his guardsmen, who had reached the base of the
breach. The giants were now hidden from view, and Roper
set his hands on the shattered stone before him.

He climbed.

The Unhieru had managed to scale this steep face of
unfastened rock, but they were enormous and powerful, and
this first barrier was formidable. Each foothold slumped
beneath his boots and unleashed a cascade of rubble, Roper
making it five feet from the ground before his section of the
face subsided entirely and he slid backwards. He landed on
an Unhieru body lying face down, chain mail pooled about

its bulk. He stood to try again, this time making it twelve, fifteen, eighteen feet hand over hand, before the stones slipped again and he tumbled back to the base. His limbs were heavy from prolonged hunger, and he took a moment to sit and pant. Guardsmen were swarming forward around him, meeting with equally limited success, one tumbling onto Roper as he tried to rise and knocking him back to a seat.

And the arrows began to focus on them at last. Spitting, whipping and shrieking from the intact walls either side of the breach, they cracked off the stone and rang from their armour. Roper answered with aggression. He stood once more, gathered his strength and launched himself at the stones. He made it ten feet before the rubble began to slide beneath his boots once more, but now had enough momentum to climb free of the miniature landslide and on, skirting the blazing heat of one of the hay-bundles dropped from the wall above. His legs were leaden, and he was barely halfway up the breach. He was panting, his throat prickling, the dry taste of rock dust thick in his mouth, but he heaved on, outstripping all guardsmen save Pryce. The sprinter had adopted the same mad aggression and they laboured up, up together; heavy armour bouncing, thighs and calves burning, arrows cartwheeling through the air, neck and neck as they staggered to the top.

They slowed together. For the first time, Lundenceaster was revealed beneath them: streets crammed with dark timber, wattle and daub. Mossy roofs slumped far beyond like a forest canopy. But it was the ground directly beneath Roper that drew his eye: a wide gap between the breach's inside slope and the nearest of the city's houses. It had been lit with a hundred blazing hay-bundles, casting frightful shadows from the swarming Unhieru. In that flickering light Roper could see that the nearest houses had been modified. Every high window had been expanded and now heaved with men crewing siege bows; each like an enormous crossbow

mounted on a timber frame, spitting iron bolts into the grotesquely churning silhouettes below. Any space not occupied
by siege bows was crowded with longbowmen who added
their own rolling volleys to the deluge.

Roper stood still, Pryce at his side, the two staring down
at this scene. The Sutherners had known where the breach
would be, and fortified and transformed these houses into
miniature watchtowers. Between these and the bowmen on
the walls above, arrows fell into this killing ground like hail.
More guardsmen joined them on the crest, dust-stained,
panting and staring down at the Unhieru bodies, scattered
everywhere like burnt-out hay-bundles.

Onwards, Roper.

'With me!' he called, jumping forward. He clattered onto
the rubble of the breach and began to slide down, accelerat-
ing out of control. An arrow bounced off his breastplate with
a thump that knocked the breath from him. Another seared
past his cheek, opening up a stinging cut. He was still plummeting, the skin of his palms scored and torn as he tried to
slow his fall. The ground was rushing up to meet him and
when he finally hit it, his legs crumpled beneath him in a
cloud of dust, pitching Roper forward to land on his front.

That saved his life. Just as he was getting to his feet, a bolt
from a siege bow shrieked overhead and hurled back a
guardsman staggering up behind Roper, punching right
through his armoured torso and out the other side. The man's
body rippled with the shockwave, and he collapsed. For one
moment, Roper thought it was Pryce, but then he saw the
sprinter on his right, helping Gray to his feet.

Caked with dust; aware of every inch of his unarmoured
skin as arrows hurtled down around him, Roper tried to
stand again. There came a deafening crash and a blast of
energy swept over him, rattling chips of stone off his armour.
A boulder, dislodged from the wall above by a defender, had
smashed onto the slope of the breach, bounced and rolled to
a halt less than a yard away. Two guardsmen were trapped

beneath it; one by his leg, another his arm, both pulling furiously to try and free themselves.

There was nothing Roper could do for them. He called Gray and Pryce to his side and ran forward with a little stream of guardsmen. They had to escape the exposed ground beyond the breach, which for some reason was still choked with Unhieru. Ahead of them was an alleyway between two of the fortified houses, which might offer some shelter. They weaved between burning hay-bundles and stampeding Unhieru, the air hot with fumes and thick with dust.

Reaching the alley's welcome dark, Roper cast left and right for an entrance. If they could get into one of the houses, they could kill the bowmen firing out of those high upstairs windows. He spotted a door and kicked at it, but it was unyielding; the other side evidently barricaded.

He abandoned the door, limping on down the narrow street with his trail of guardsmen, and seeking only to get as far as possible from that breach. They turned a corner and halted suddenly. Before them was a flat shadow: a fresh palisade wall, blocking the street completely. Its top was lined with yet more longbowmen, and a volley of arrows swept into them. Roper was hit in the stomach, the blow knocking the breath from him. He turned back, scrambling around the corner with the rest of the guardsmen, but three were left behind. Two were dead, and another had fallen with them, each leg punctured by an arrow. Gray plunged back for him and was knocked flat by a second volley. Miraculously he stood again, preserved by his armour, and dragged the wounded guardsman back around the corner. Roper groaned on each breath, trying to get the air back into his lungs, and Gray laid a hand on his shoulder. 'All right, lord?'

'While you're here,' Roper managed, straightening up. 'No way through. Another street,' he gasped.

They tried again, running back the way they had come and into the flickering ground before the breach. It was still crammed with Unhieru, and now some of Ramnea's Own were tumbling down the inside of the breach to join the throng. As they ran, a guardsman beside Roper dropped with a shocked grunt, poleaxed by the feathered shaft protruding from the nape of his neck. Then another fell without a sound, struck in the eye. 'Move!' Roper shouted, head low and arms raised against this ceaseless rain. He led his party left, passing one house before plunging into the next dark street. But this too was blocked after just a few yards by another fresh palisade, lined again with longbowmen.

They suffered another volley and reeled back, out of the street and into the sickly light before the breach, where Roper was appalled by the sheer mass of bodies and arrow-shafts bristling the ground. 'Another street!' he demanded.

But it was blocked.

'Another!'

Blocked.

Roper re-emerged into the space before the breach and ground to a halt, staring left and right. The Sutherners had transformed this part of the city into a huge net. Each street was blocked with a new palisade wall, penning the attackers into the space between Lundenceaster's stone wall and the fortified houses. Arrows rained from their windows, and the inside of the high exterior walls, turning the net into a killing floor.

They were trapped.

Ramnea's Own Legion were making the problem worse as they continued to pour down the breach, but able to advance no further. They pressed each other closer and closer until some could hardly move, creating a superlative target for arrows, siege bolts and rocks forced down from the walls above. But still they did what legionaries do, and obeyed.

The attack was disintegrating, with even the uninjured now cowering behind whatever scraps of shelter this place afforded. What frightened Roper above all else was that he could see no faces turned towards him, begging for the solution. Their heads were down, covered by their arms. They seemed to have accepted that this was where their great quest to secure the north ended. In this arrow-smashed acre, where the only solution remaining to these exhausted soldiers was to stand and die.

A siege bolt streaked into Roper's group, picking one guardsman off his feet altogether and hurling him into two companions, bowling them over. 'Get down!' Roper shouted. 'Down, down!' He dropped behind an Unhieru corpse, pressing himself against its chain-mail side as a feeble respite from the arrows. Two guardsmen piled in beside him, huddled as tight as possible into the mailed flesh. One of them was hurled flat on his face, a siege bolt sprouting from the back of his helmet in a crimson spurt. His companion barely reacted beyond drawing himself tighter behind his feeble shelter.

Now that he was behind the meagre protection of this corpse, Roper was not sure he could leave it again. His eyes travelled up the inside of the breach, wondering if they could survive retracing their steps, but it seemed so steep and was anyway still filled with advancing legionaries. They needed to signal back to the army that no further men should advance, but how, Roper could not think. To move was to die. The singing of Ramnea's Own had ceased, but outside the walls the drums still rolled on and on, like monstrous barrels over stone cobbles.

'What do we do, lord?' asked the guardsman next to him. 'What do we do now?' Roper did not know. He could not see Pryce, or Gray. He could not see Gogmagoc. All he could see were crouching, cowering men; flames roaring above them; shadows licking over everything. It was like his very first battle. He was responsible for everyone here, and there was no good option to be taken. He raised his hands to his ears, trying to think, to shut out the roar of drumming, the arrow-strikes, the flames, the Unhieru.

It was only after a dozen heartbeats had thumped past that he realised everything had gone quiet. The breach was still.

Roper raised his head. Arrows still flickered across his vision, but they had lost their sting. The cries of his legionaries and the heaving Unhieru made no impact on Roper.

Silence.

After months of struggling, it was a tool he could use as easily as the sword clutched by his side. It was just as Gray had said: *You are your habits.*

Roper saw clearly across the breach, gaze settling on the grappling hook dangling off the belt of the Unhieru body he crouched against. He took the grapple and stood.

It was like trying to advance into a storm-driven sea: battered and bludgeoned at once by wave after wave of projectiles. Chips of stone stung his cheeks, and he could barely see, so tightly screwed were his eyes. 'Follow me!' he shouted over the crack of arrows. 'Follow me! With me, if you can move! With me!'

He could no longer feel his rattling heart or the dread in his chest, both sealed out by silence. He was still weary to his bones, but he had to advance into these arrows, and he did, wooden shafts splintering beneath his boots and two hitting his armour obliquely, making him stagger and leaving deep gouges in the steel.

Around him, men began to crawl and stumble to his voice, rising against the horror. 'Grapples!' Roper called. 'Bring grapples!' They were snatched from dead Unhieru, and Gray arrived at Roper's side, carrying one in his right hand, his left forearm impaled with an arrow. He rapped his fist on Roper's shoulder, and Roper seized his hand fiercely. 'I'm glad I have you, brother,' he said.

'As long as I am possibly able, lord,' said Gray. Together, a crouching, flinching shamble of guardsmen and legionaries in their wake, they crowded down the nearest street.

'You!' Roper roared at two Unhieru cowering beneath the walls of a fortified house. 'With us!' They swung upright, reinforcing their band.

An arrow found the back of Roper's elbow and he gasped

at the shooting pain that swept up his arm, making him drop the grapple. A figure had scooped it up for him in an instant. It straightened, and Roper recognised Pryce's haughty jaw-line beneath the visor. More men: legionaries, guardsmen and Unhieru, came to join their band, even as those march-ing with them dropped beneath the burden of multiple arrows. Roper drove them on, unaware of the words he had started bawling. 'With me, with me! On your feet! It's not over yet! Not here! This is not over, and we will not stop until it is!'

They advanced down a street Roper had already tried, leaving the firelight behind and rounding a corner into another pounding volley. Roper was struck twice, but the blows seemed so distant he could not tell if they had hit armour or flesh. 'Kill!' he was bellowing. 'Kill! Kill! Kill!'

They were within six feet of the palisade, the gritted teeth of the bowmen shining white above as they drew and loosed point-blank at this band of attackers. 'Throw the grapples! Grapples, up the wall!'

Grapples were tossed onto the palisade, some of the legion-aries hauling on the ropes and trying to climb them hand over hand. 'Down, down!' Roper shouted, pointing instead at the Unhieru. 'Pull it down!' he ordered. 'Pull down the wall!' Many of the grapples were unhooked and hurled back down by the longbowmen, but a few legionaries had pulled hard on their ropes, digging the grapples' sharp edges into the palisade.

One Unhieru seized a rope and began to pull. A bowman by the grapple drew his knife and began sawing at the cord, which snapped under pressure. But more grapples were being hurled upwards, the Unhieru ready to pull as soon as they bit into the palisade. Under the power of six, eight, ten ropes, the wall began to sag outwards. The earth at its base started to warp and Roper stepped back to avoid being crushed. The air twanged as the ropes snapped beneath knife and pressure, some of the Unhieru stumbling backwards as the resistance on their ropes vanished. But still half a dozen hauled trembling at their lines, and with a groan and a crack, a great section of the logs making up the wall was pulled forward.

Those Unhieru without ropes suddenly had an edge they could grip onto. They began to tear at it bare-handed: hauling, wrenching and widening. The movement dislodged several longbowmen from the firestep and they tumbled down into the waiting arms of the Anakim, who were suddenly possessed by a feral energy. They seethed and massed like churning locusts, vicious fury spreading and crackling from them. Roper was screaming over the top of the din as the wall began to shake and buckle: 'Yes, onwards! Onwards my brothers, my peers, my animals! They cannot stop us!' Arrows still spattered their band, but the longbowmen seemed to be aiming mostly at the Unhieru, their shafts bouncing ineffectually off the thick chain mail.

The gap in the wall was wide enough for an Anakim to squeeze through but Pryce, nearest to the hole, turned to Gray. 'Lift me!' he commanded. Gray lent Pryce a boost, Roper assisting with his uninjured right arm, and they propelled the lictor upwards, where he seized onto a splintered palisade support. Pryce clamped his sword between his teeth and began to swarm up the exposed edge of the wall. He was spotted by a defender, who turned a longbow on Pryce's head at a range of less than a yard. Roper shouted a pointless warning; there was nothing Pryce could do. Then Gray's sword cartwheeled out of nowhere, spinning lethally at the bowman and forcing him to stagger onto the wooden battlement. It was all Pryce needed. He seized the bowman's boot and dragged him flailing and swearing from the wall.

Then he was on the firestep, dwarfing the defenders he faced, sheathed in steel and a shocking strip of it clutched in his hand. The longbowmen could only face him one at a time on the narrow firestep, armed only with bows and knives, and armoured in leather.

They disintegrated before him.

Pryce's sword swung in momentous arcs, spitting body-parts down off the wall. Three arrows smashed into his chest, one after another, doing no more than staggering the sprinter before he launched himself back at the bowmen.

Behind Pryce, the wall buckled further until with a cracking and a groaning, a section some eight yards across was dragged flat. Three Unhieru flooded through at once, unleashed on the city and completely beyond Roper's control. He seized Gray's wrist. 'Take the Guard through the gap and hold on to it at all costs! This is our only way into the city and we *must* preserve it! I'm going back to show everyone the way.'

Gray nodded, casting a final glance at Pryce, whose work on the palisade was done. The blood-spattered, arrow-stuck guardsman now walked lazily across the deserted firestep, kicking prone bowmen out of his way.

Roper turned back, pushing against the press of invaders trying to go through the hole they had made, and forcing his way back towards the breach. It glowed from behind the houses like the landing site of a star. He stepped out from the shelter of the street, into the light of the killing ground once more, where a sea of men still cowered from the arrows and siege bolts spinning overhead. 'Here!' Roper roared, shifting slightly so that an arrow met his armour at an angle rather than head-on. It streaked off into the ground. 'This way if you want to live! This way to finish what we've started! Advance! Advance! Advance!'

Anakim and Unhieru began to pick themselves up, emerging from behind boulders, houses and corpses, and staggering towards Roper. Without warning, he was knocked off his feet by the force of an arrow, slamming him into the cobbles. His armour preserved him once again, but surely his luck could not hold for much longer. He spat dust from his mouth and pushed himself upright, something soft beneath his fingers. He looked down and realised he had his hand on the face of a dead legionary.

He staggered away, and was instantly distracted by a mass of splintered wood being ejected from a window above him. It crashed to the floor, and it took several moments for Roper to realise that it was the remnants of a siege bow. There came a panicked scream from the window, and then the siege bow's three crew members were hurled after it, one after another. The first crashed into a burning hay-bundle in a gust of sparks, where he flailed, trying to drag himself out of the flames. Another landed on his head, and did not move again. The third landed legs first and emitted an agonised scream as they buckled beneath him. Still he rolled onto his belly, and tried to crawl away from whatever was in that house.

It was Gogmagoc. His mailed bulk squeezed through the window, tearing the frame wider and crashing to the ground after his victims. Axe in hand, indifferent to the arrows that whistled about him, he prowled to the next house. The crew within spotted the threat and turned a siege bow on him at point-blank range, the great engine jumping violently as the trigger was released. Roper did not see the bolt: it was too fast and the breach too dark, but he saw where the chain mail on Gogmagoc's back twitched as the bolt punched straight through his body and out the other side. He saw the dark cloud of blood that spurted after it, and the puff of shattered stone as it streaked on and hit a cobble behind the giant king. Roper noticed, but Gogmagoc did not. He reached the house and in two swings of his axe, chopped through a corner beam. The house began to lean to one side, the siege bow crew reeling back from the windows as the whole structure teetered. Gogmagoc heaved at the building, and it buckled and collapsed in a cloud of dust and a great heap of splinters. Muffled voices cried from the wreckage and the giant king stood above; a shining outline with the two mad, perfectly circular eyes of his helmet staring across the breach.

A hand gripped Roper's shoulder and he turned to see a filthy legionary. 'My lord, Suthern soldiers in the streets! Hundreds of knights trying to seal off our path into the city.'

Roper did not reply, turning away to cast an eye over the men flooding towards them. He spotted half a dozen Unhieru and shouted that they should join him. They obeyed, wading through the legionaries.

'My lord?' repeated the messenger. 'The knights.'

'I heard you,' said Roper. 'They're dead.' He looked up at the Unhieru who crowded about him, staring back through those awful round-eyed helmets. 'Follow me,' he said, turning his back to the breach.

They passed from the flickering light of the hay-bundles and into the street once more. Roper could see nothing but bodies and dark passageways; up ahead were screams, crashes and clangs, and growing over all that, a battle-hymn was chanted by that knot of feral men who had broken through the wall with him. Somewhere out of sight, the Sacred Guard had found some energy and were fighting like starving dogs.

Roper struggled towards the gap they had made in the palisade wall, joining a press of men trying to force their way through. The press dispersed rapidly when they saw the trail of Unhieru who followed Roper, each man standing back to allow the Black Lord and his giant allies passage. Roper passed through the wall, and was immediately called left: 'My lord!' In the dark, he could detect knights swarming through an alleyway that led onto their street, attempting to flank his forces. He commanded that the Unhieru should take the knights, who faltered as their passage was suddenly filled with immense chain-mail figures and staring helmets.

Roper left them behind, rounding another corner to find that Gray had assembled the Sacred Guard into a battle-line that was rebuffing a company of knights. These had evidently come to try and stopper the gap that was the only escape from the trap enclosing the breach.

The Guard were growling the 'Hymn Abroad' as Roper broke into a sprint, bellowing his presence to the guardsmen,

Cold-Edge flashing at his side. Some of the rearmost guardsmen turned and cheered as they saw him pelting for the line.
'Move!' he roared. 'Move! Move!' With yards to spare, four
guardsmen scrambled aside and the enemy line was exposed
to Roper. He dropped his shoulder and crashed into the
them, transferring the full energy of his charge to the stationary knights. Three were knocked to the ground and
Roper staggered, stumbling over them, pushing another
away with his elbow and lurching right through the line. He
turned, sword raised, to see guardsmen scrapping their way
into the gap he had left behind. Another four knights were
knocked down in quick succession, rattling off the cobbles.
What happened to those four was so fierce that their comrades faltered. They seemed to decide in that instant that
here was not where they would stop the Anakim after all.
That point would come further into the city, and weakened
by that thought, the line disintegrated. The knights backed
off faster and faster until they turned away completely, running back the way they had come. One tried a sly lunge at
Roper's neck as he passed. After his lessons with Vigtyr, it
was pure reaction, Roper turning the attack aside and skew-
ering his opponent's armpit in the same motion. The man
howled and dropped onto the street, where Roper finished
him with a downward hack.

    The guardsmen were pursuing the knights down the
street into the dark city, but Roper summoned them to him.
'Here! Here, here, here! I need you here!' Gray responded
first, a few dozen guardsmen behind him. 'Help me,' Roper
said to Gray, holding out his arrow-shot arm, as their little
band clustered together. Gray gripped the base of the arrow
shaft protruding from Roper's elbow and began cutting the
bulk of it off so that it would not snag as Roper fought. The
head would need to be extracted later.

    'Gather close and listen,' said Roper, teeth gritted as Gray
finished his work. Roper began to perform the same crude
operation on Gray's forearm, still talking. 'We need to get

onto the outer walls and clear off the longbowmen.' The panting guardsmen were following his example, hastily tying scraps of linen around crimson wounds, or stabilising loose joints with strips of leather. Each face was covered with dust from the breach, and streaked with sweat. 'We must do this as swiftly as possible. Every second they are allowed to remain, more legionaries die coming over the breach, and getting stuck in that killing pen. Before anything else, and before this assault can progress, we here must reach the outer wall. With me, now!' He turned down another dark street lined with timber houses, guessing the direction of the walls, and beckoning his men to follow.

The night was filled with Anakim incantations, the barking of dogs and human roars of every kind. The residents, doubtless having heard what the Anakim planned for cities that resisted, leaned from upstairs windows and hurled down tables, crockery and shutters; some unleashing hunting arrows that pelted Roper and his band. Roper was struck by the corner of a table and then a pot crashed over his helmet, making his head ring. He lost control, turning and kicking in the door behind him. The interior flitted with shadows and he stilled them abruptly with Cold-Edge. Back on the street, their band staggered on, emerging into the relative light of a market square. The buildings did not crowd so close here, and over the houses Roper could see their objective: the walls.

'This way!' He led them towards another street branching off the square. But as they drew near, the passage began to fill with a roaring and flickering light. A band of men burst into view, rounding the far corner into the street, torches bouncing as they ran. They were city watchmen, dressed in chain mail, carrying large square shields and spears, and charging against Roper's small advance. Roper roared, his guardsmen howled, and the two formations crashed together. The guardsmen were outnumbered, but there was a reason Anakim did not carry shields. The mindset of a warrior with a shield is conservative, and better than their opponents, the Anakim understood the power of shock.

Roper ran over his first enemy, battering into the shield raised against him, knocking him down and stumbling over his body into the next man. He parried the spear-thrust aimed for his groin, and with his free left hand seized his enemy's throat. He dragged him close, flinching at the jolt of pain from his injured elbow, so that his spear was useless, and tried to choke him as he used Cold-Edge to fend off another watchman. But his left hand was weak, and the watchman ripped himself free. He drew back his spear, but then the tip of a blade burst out of the chain mail on his chest and he dropped like a stone, Gray removing his sword calmly from the body and then swinging it into a raised shield.

'Shit, behind! 'ware behind!' shouted a guardsman. Roper kicked an enemy back to buy a heartbeat, and stole a glance over his shoulder.

Knights.

Forty of them, shining and rattling, burst into the square behind Roper's band and charged them. 'Back!' Roper shouted. 'Back, here!' They had already been outnumbered, and now found themselves assaulted on two sides. Roper broke free of the fighting and ran to the corner of the square, so that at least there was only one direction from which the enemy could come at them.

As soon as the first of the guardsmen ran to join him, he realised his mistake. Better by far that they had run for one of the empty streets leading off the square, but that had been too much like retreat to occur to Roper. This corner might be a little easier to defend, but there was no hope of escaping it. He had trapped them.

Even as he turned to watch, two guardsmen running towards him were hacked down and butchered. The rest barely had time to form a rough line before the knights and watchmen smashed into them. Roper parried a sword, then a spear. He wanted to strike back, but so many were the blows coming at him, so thick the flush wall of shields, that all he could do was defend. He felt a shockwave reverberate through his chest as a sword-thrust broke through his plate armour, stopped by the bone underneath. In anger, he tried to strike back but only succeeded in opening himself to two further blows: one a spear-thrust that grated into his belly, another a mace that grazed his chin and nearly broke his jaw. He wafted Cold-Edge in reply and stumbled backwards, just as the guardsmen around him were doing.

Roper had doomed them.

In a thoughtless instant, he had trapped them in this corner as they were assaulted by fully three times their number. Watchmen and knights were sharing shields, and so many men reached forward to chop at the guardsmen that it was impossible to strike back without opening oneself up to another attack. Roper just had to defend as a guardsman to his left: a peer called Yaddur, with whom Roper had laughed and eaten, took a spear to his neck. He raised his free left hand, as though to keep the furious blood within his body, and held his feet for just another heartbeat before crumbling. This exposed the guardsman on Yaddur's shoulder, who took a slash across his face, knocking his head back and opening the underside of his chin to a spear that went through his jaw. Three teeth were knocked free from his lips and the guardsman was dead at once.

Back, back; the guardsmen crowded into the corner. Now the man on Roper's right was Gray, and he was terrified that he was about to see the captain fall. He and Roper worked shoulder to shoulder, Roper's eyes trying to shut themselves at the sharp points bristling and jabbing before him. He took some on his sword, some on his armour and some were saved by Gray, who seemed to have stopped defending himself and was edging in front of Roper. He pushed the captain back to his side with a heave of one weighty arm, movements growing slow, so slow as he tired and his chest heaved. 'I'm sorry!' he gasped at Gray, but the guardsman had no breath for reply.

Roper could see only his gritted teeth and the sweat dripping off his chin as he batted away another attack.

A wave of profound dread hit Roper so hard that he nearly vomited. He staggered, panting, and did not realise at first that he suddenly had a little space. The Sutherners were backing off. Their aggression had lifted, the rain of blows thinning abruptly. They felt the same fear as Roper. In the pause, he had time to look up, over the heads of the Sutherners, and see what they had all felt.

There was a monster in the square with them.

One of the Unhieru, punctured and dented, covered in a paste of dust and blood, lurched across the cobbles, advancing towards the rear of the Suthern band. It was not Gogmagoc: there was no hole in his back or chest, but this fiend was nearly as vast. The enormous battle axe by his side clinked as it dragged over the cobbles, and it was this sound that caused the rearmost Sutherners to turn around. They had time to look up into the insane helmeted face: wide circular eye holes gaping blankly back at them, before the giant axe swept into the formation. Three men were knocked halfway across the square, shields and spears scattering over the cobbles, and one watchman landing in two halves, joined only by a thin scrap of flesh. Only then did most of the Sutherners realise what was happening behind them, turning just as the Unhieru began to advance, trampling into the Sutherners.

'Attack!' Roper shouted. Their enemy was distracted, and they had been given a chance. Together he and Gray led a wedge into the formation, most of the Sutherners too preoccupied to respond, their attention on the clinking, clockwork pillar of war that exuded dread like a poisonous fume. The guardsmen renewed their attack, Roper not attempting to kill but lead a wedge through the enemy ranks, and out from that suffocating corner.

Before them, one knight had led a small charge against the Unhieru, thrusting a halberd into his chest. It made no impression at all on the thick chain mail, and the knight was catapulted across the square with a backhand. Still the Sutherners stood and died, Roper stupefied by their bravery. As the giant trampled into their formation, the uninjured Sutherners he left behind assaulted him from the rear. One knight thrust his sword into the chain-mailed back, heaving and twisting the blade two-handed until at last it broke through, sinking eight inches into flesh.

He had the Unhieru's attention.

The giant turned its nightmare face on the knight. It tried to strike back with its axe, but for some reason its arm was now too weak to raise the weapon. It still managed to seize the knight's helmeted head with a left paw, jerking it again and again so that the knight's body left the ground and cracked like a whip; horribly flaccid as joint after joint dislocated beneath a wave of energy. But the Sutherners had sensed the weakness in their terrible enemy and swarmed upon it, thrusting madly with every weapon they had.

Roper and Gray finally battled through the Suthern formation and back into clear square. 'Go!' Roper shouted. 'We must get to those walls! Go, go, go!' He held open the passage through the Sutherners as the surviving guardsmen pelted past him, streaming for the street that led to the walls. The Unhieru was howling, spinning around and at one point managing to shake the mass of Sutherners off it completely. But it had just a few heartbeats of respite before they hurled themselves forward once more, hacking and stabbing and tearing and chopping. A quarter of its broad chain-mail shirt fell away completely, blood sheeting beneath, and the giant's right arm swinging uselessly by its side. Weapons dug into the vulnerable flesh and finally, the giant toppled, flattening another pair of watchmen.

Roper stayed just long enough to salute the dying giant, before Gray seized his arm and dragged him away.

They left the square, the shouts and screams of the Sutherners, the final grunts of the Unhieru, and staggered back into the dark. Roper's chest was heaving, his throat so tight it felt bruised, but still he and Gray shuffled on, leaving behind that narrow escape, eyes on the shadow of the walls rising ahead of them. From the upper windows, the rain of projectiles began once more. 'Just keep going!' Roper gasped, raising his arms over his head and staggering as a pot shattered on arm guards, showering him in china shards.

He swerved to avoid a table that smashed onto the cobbles in front of him, and quite suddenly, the barking he had heard throughout the night swelled into a feral baying. Roper felt himself slowing as the noise grew louder, and then a pack of howling dogs tore around the corner before them: twenty, thirty, forty of the beasts, teeth bared and chains of saliva swinging from snarling lips. Roper heard Gray's voice calling: 'Dogs! Dogs coming!'

Roper stopped and raised his sword, just as a fire-screen came down on his shoulder from a window above. He staggered a little, his sword dropped, and the first snarling dog had its teeth in his left wrist. It wrenched its head left and right, Roper trying to keep it at a distance while aiming a huge kick at the next dog, pelting towards him. He caught the animal beneath its neck, lifting it upright and cartwheeling it onto its back. But another had leapt over its supine companion and into Roper's chest, knocking him to the floor. The first dog still had its teeth in his wrist and pulled at his flesh, while the other opened its jaws and went for Roper's face. On pure instinct, Roper managed to get Cold-Edge across his body, jamming the blade between the dog's teeth and holding it back. He could smell its hot breath, teeth held open just inches from his lips. Then he sliced the sword violently and the animal's jaw was separated from its head. The dog collapsed, dead at once. Still the barking was deafening; the night filled with snarling fur and dripping teeth. He could feel another mouth fastened into the leather of his boot and worrying back and forth, while the guardsmen behind him swore and hacked.

Roper lunged at the dog with its teeth still fastened on his wrist, hacking Cold-Edge down on its back. The animal dropped, but another had launched itself at Roper, teeth bared in a snarl. He was saved by a guardsman standing above him, who caught the dog on the point of his sword and pinned it to the cobbles. Roper dragged himself upright, trying to haul his foot away from the dog that still held his boot and swung its head back and forth as though he were a rabbit it was trying to still. He lashed out with his sword, and then when the animal would not let go, he tried again, cutting off its head. 'Shit,' he swore. 'Shit!'

His hand was bleeding badly, and still crockery, pottery, lamps and furniture rained from the upstairs windows. One lamp survived the fall to the cobbles with its wick still lit, and a great pool of flame suddenly lit the street. The remaining dogs yelped and leapt back, Roper trying to leap after them but finding he was too weary. Instead he staggered right through the pool of burning oil, his boots flaming for a few heartbeats after he was past. 'We *must* . . . get to those walls!' He could barely speak for coughing. The guardsmen tottered through the fire behind him, following the retreating shadows of the hounds, their arms raised against stools, pokers, buckets and pans.

At the end of the street, at last, was the dark shadow of Lundenceaster's outer wall. Roper wanted air so badly that each breath was a groan, but still he stumbled for a tower set into the wall and overlooking the breach. In the tower would be stairs, which they could use to finally get onto the battlements and clear off the longbowmen. With every moment they delayed, arrows poured into the enclosure that the Sutherners had created around the breach and legionaries died.

At the base of the tower, three men stood on guard. They saw Roper's band, and turned into the tower behind them, disappearing through the door at its base. By the time Roper arrived, the door, solid oak and riveted with iron, had been slammed shut and bolted. He tried first his shoulder and then a boot, but found it unyielding. For just a moment, he leaned forward, resting his hands on his knees and gasping for breath. The guardsmen reached him, several of them leaning against the tower and sliding to the ground, chests heaving. 'We need a ram,' Roper managed, hardly able to get the words out through the pressure from his lungs.

Gray nodded, sweat streaking the blood on his face and dripping off his nose. For a moment, the score of them that remained just breathed. Roper cast around for sign of more enemies, but the streets were empty. That was as well: their band was in a wretched state. Each man was covered in bites, grazes, bruises, and the filth from the breach. Gray, Roper and three other guardsmen had arrow-shafts protruding from their flesh. Two guardsmen had lost their helmets, one of them with the hair rubbed off his scalp in a huge bloody bald patch. Roper's savaged hand was throbbing and did not move easily, and between that and his shot elbow, his left arm was good for very little.

'There was a bench that might do for a ram,' Gray panted at last. 'Thrown down in the street back there.' He and two guardsmen hobbled back the way they had come, soon reappearing holding a heavy oak bench between them.

'Let's go,' Roper said, tucking Cold-Edge into his belt so that its filthy blade would not contaminate the sheath, and taking one edge of the bench.

'You are relentless, Lord Roper,' said Gray, a grin parting his filthy face. One of his teeth had broken in half. He took up the other side of the bench, two others behind them and a fifth guardsmen standing at the back. They retreated five yards, and then surged towards the tower door, Roper and Gray angling the bench towards the handle. The shock of the impact wrenched Roper's shoulder, but the door burst open. Roper bounced off the stonework of the doorway, while Gray and two others stumbled to the floor.

Head spinning, Roper seized Cold-Edge from his belt once

more, and stepped over the bench, into the tower. There was a man waiting for him behind the door, who lunged with a flashing blade. Roper, stunned from his collision with the doorway, completely missed his parry and the sword grated into his armour, breaking through its pocked surface and stopped once more by the bone. He staggered back and nearly tripped on the bench behind, kept upright only by a steadying hand at his back. Then he raised Cold-Edge, bringing the pommel down on the man's head. Something gave way beneath that blow, and his opponent crumpled at once. Roper stepped over his body, onto the first stone step of the spiral staircase immediately behind the door.

Another man waited in the dark above him and hacked at Roper with a sword. The staircase was appallingly cramped for an Anakim, and holding Cold-Edge right handed, Roper found his ability to parry was badly impeded by the central support of the staircase. He and Vigtyr had worked on fighting left handed and right, but with his palm savaged by the dog, Roper could not grip his weapon. But they had to progress up this staircase, and Roper began to climb, holding out his gauntleted left arm as a shield. The shadowed figure above gave ground, slashing down at Roper, who tried to dodge, and if he could not, deflected the blows with his gauntlet. Any strike that hit his arm was followed by a shock of pain from the arrow-wound, but he gritted his teeth and kept pushing. Relentlessly, he drove the defender back, and when he thought his enemy had misjudged a swing, Roper leaned forward and hooked his boot out from beneath him. The defender clattered down the stairs, and Roper stepped past him, leaving the men following behind to kill him.

And now there was nothing between him and the climb. It was dark: so dark he could barely see the steps, and he had to twist to fit his armoured shoulders up the stairs. His legs were leaden, he was gasping and at any moment he expected to run into the third defender they had seen outside the tower, but he did not come. The staircase began to glow with

orange light, and Roper knew he must be nearing the door
that led onto the battlements. That was where he found the
final defender, silhouetted in the doorway to the wall with a
shield and axe.

As Roper clattered up the stairs, the axe swung at him. He
threw up his forearm to catch the axe shaft, gasping as that
shock of pain ran up his arm once more. He held his arm up,
keeping the axe hooked up high, chest to chest with his
enemy and hauling in raw breaths. He gathered himself,
sweat spraying from his lips, and then began to bully the
defender back through the door and onto the battlements.
With another agonising jerk of his left arm, he wrenched the
axe from the defender's hand to send it spinning off the wall.

The defender had his shield pressed into Roper's chest and
tried to resist, but he was no match for the Black Lord, who
used the very dregs of his strength to half push, half carry
him backwards. The two of them, pressed intimately close,
were now on one of the walls overlooking the breach. It was
packed with archers who had been firing down at the legionaries below, but seeing an Anakim on the battlements, now
turned their weapons on Roper. He ducked low, using the
defender's body as a shield and pushing him back until he
collided with the archers standing behind. Roper's shoulder
was in the defender's chest, and he heaved him back, crush-
ing the Sutherners together until one bowman, teetering on
the edge of the wall, toppled off and plunged, arms flailing,
into the flaming chaos below.

'With him, with Lord Roper!' came Gray's voice, and he felt
bodies press against his back, helping him drive the defender
on as a ram, squeezing into the archers behind. The defender
was squirming frantically in an effort to drop to the floor, but
he was held upright by the pressure between Roper on one
side and the bowmen on the other. The pressure built until
Roper himself could barely breathe. To his right, the drop
tumbled away into nothing and his band began to grind their
opponents along the wall. They were packing the bowmen so

tightly that they could not use their weapons, and there came two screams in quick succession as one was forced off the wall, dragging another with him as he flailed to stay on the firestep.

'Heave!' Roper gasped. 'Heave!' They pressed the bowmen tighter and tighter, until their enemies had run out of space. The pressure was passed along the crowded battlement, to the bowmen at the back, who teetered at the wall's broken end, overlooking the breach.

And in twos and threes, they were forced off, into the void.

The resistance facing Roper alleviated dramatically as the bowmen stopped pushing and instead began to scramble for a good footing, each desperately aware of the drop they were being driven towards. Crushed together, they were forced off the wall and down, down, down into the breach. Some of them tried to scrabble out of the way, perching atop the crenellations, but were pushed roughly off the edge by the passing guardsmen. Roper could see the wall's broken edge drawing nearer, the drop beyond, and suddenly feared that he himself would be pushed over it by the force at his back. 'Halt!' he gasped, the drop five, four, three yards away. 'Stop! Stop!' The pressure at his back lifted, with just one defender left in front of Roper. The original man, whose axe Roper had discarded, shield still pressed into Roper's chest

The Black Lord just pushed him. The defender flailed, fingertips scratching at Roper's armour but, overbalanced by his shield, he twisted and fell, down onto the stones below.

And then, too exhausted to move any further from the void less than a foot away, Roper fell onto the firestep, throbbing left arm hooked over the battlements. His limbs vibrated minutely with fatigue, he was soaked in sweat and he coughed harshly. 'Gray.' The captain dropped next to him, one arm over Roper's armoured shoulders, his head leaning into Roper's. They panted together, the roar of battle beneath as though they sat on a cliff-top overlooking a raging iron

sea. The hay-bundles below were burning out and now
resembled smouldering coals, illuminating a bristle of
arrows and bodies. There were still hundreds of legionaries
penned against the breach, most of the fortified houses still
spitting projectiles at them.

'We must signal the advance,' Roper spluttered, gripping
onto Gray's wrist. 'The legions need to come through.' A
guardsman stooped to pick up a trio of discarded torches
from the rampart. As his comrades leaned on the battlements, staring glassily at the turmoil below, he combined the
torches, and by their joint flame, waved the legions beyond
the walls to advance.

A distant trumpet howled in response, and the drumming
changed, rippling into a marching tattoo. Roper heard a
cheer ring across the night, echoing off the walls and mor-
phing into the 'Hymn of Advance'. A glittering metal wave:
the Pendeen Legion, began to roll towards the breach.

'We've done it, lord,' said Gray hoarsely. There was wonder
in his voice. He rapped Roper's helmet, and then laughed
wildly. 'We've done it!'

Roper could not feel anything yet, but it seemed tears were
building in his eyes. His face began to warp, and exhaustion
no longer seemed the primary reason for his heaving chest.
As long as they controlled this breach, they could pump
legionaries and Unhieru into Lundenceaster. They would
still have to take the city, street by street. The defenders
would fight to the last man, but with no walls between them
and Roper's forces, it was just a matter of time.

Gray was right.

It was over.

'You realise what you've done?' Gray persisted, voice
nearly failing. 'What you've achieved? This was you, my lord.
You got us here. You did this.' The guardsmen on the wall
with them were embracing. One tore off his helmet and bellowed at the sky. Another dropped his sword with a clatter
and fell to his knees, laughing.

Relief. Cool waves of relief were flooding Roper as he sat on that battlement, overlooking the city. The air stank of smoke, but each breath of it was nectar. Roper began to laugh drunkenly with Gray, and he could no longer hold back the tears that poured down his face. 'I don't believe it,' he said. He found he was sobbing and laughing together, the pain from his wounds strangely sweet. 'It's over.' He hooked his working arm around Gray to return his embrace, and then found the tears were too strong and fell to weeping in the captain's shoulder. 'Oh Roper . . .' he cried to himself. 'Now . . . Now you can rest.'

They must have lost thousands already that night. Thousands more would die before the sun rose. But this was now inevitable. Lundenceaster was theirs.

Suthdal was theirs.

Over the buildings echoed the noise of drumming, of ringing swords and Anakim war-hymns. Roper and the beaming captain helped each other up so that they could embrace the other guardsmen, all of whom insisted on wringing Roper's hand and thumping his back. 'Well done, my brothers,' he gasped, smiling through the tears. 'Well done, all of you. What an effort.'

And though he was weary to his guts, and wanted to savour every last moment atop this wall, he found himself gesturing below, to where the dark banners of Ramnea's Own Legion waved in the streets. 'But we're not quite done yet. We cannot leave the fighting to others. Once more, my friends? Into the streets, one more time?'

Exhausted, his companions nodded.

'Come, then. This may be the last battle we ever fight.'

39

The Suthern King

By the time Roper reached King Osbert's hall, the streets were deserted, and dawn had broken over them. He was limping on an injured calf, his shot and bitten left arm held stiffly away from his side, and a patchwork band of legionaries behind him. His face was grim as he climbed the steps to the hall. He pushed through the unguarded doors, finding an upturned mess of furniture within and several sacks of beans scattered over the floor, which gleamed like rubies to Roper. The only figure inside was a man in preposterously elaborate garb, who dropped an engraved silver plate with a crash at the sight of the Anakim. He backed against a wall, sliding down into a heap of robes at its base. Roper watched him dispassionately for a heartbeat, and the man closed his eyes in despair. Roper left him and advanced to a door at the end of the hall, the boots of his companions echoing behind. He pulled the far door wide and found a dim room beyond containing five men. Four were royal retainers, one of whom lowered his halberd at Roper as he stooped beneath the lintel. He was pale, and the other retainers showed no signs of resisting. Behind them, sitting on a throne and shivering like a soaked quarry, was King Osbert.

Roper stared at the king. He resembled the fat grub at the

centre of a huge mass of wood pulp. Exposed, soft and help-less. *This*. This was who they had been fighting all this time? The gilt helmet on his head looked foolish as an upturned egg cup. A king should be a leader. A sorcerer: skilled in compelling magic. He must be able to speak words that res-onate with his subjects and persuade them that their own wishes and their lord's are in harmony. Roper could detect no power in this king that was not false and superficial.

At the expression on Roper's face, the retainers backed away. One dropped his halberd, the others following with a clatter. Roper took two slow steps towards King Osbert. He remembered the rage that had overcome him after the sick-ness that infected the Skiritai: the boiling urge to destroy. He moved Cold-Edge forward, eyes set on his enemy's face. King Osbert mewed softly, cowering into his throne, his lips work-ing soundlessly.

A voice spoke behind Roper. 'Discipline must never give way to possession. Ever.'

Roper turned. It was Gray, now standing in the entrance, looking over the scene before him. Roper gazed at him for a moment, his eyes consumed by pupils blown open in a gro-tesque exaggeration of attentiveness. He faced the king once more. 'Is this possession?' he breathed. King Osbert mewed again as the Anakim words seeped through the room.

'Of the worst sort,' confirmed Gray. 'So convincingly justi-fied that you don't even see it. You are your habits, my lord. Don't let this become one. You do not unleash your rage on an enemy king, unarmed.'

Roper thought back to the months of starvation. To the brawl through these streets, and that horrid, lethal breach where the arrows had fallen like hail. 'Think what this man is responsible for,' he said, eyes still fixed on the king.

'We were defending our future generations,' said Gray. 'He was defending his home. Kill him, by all means. But know what you are doing, and do it for the right reasons. Kill him because we must take control of this island, and he stands in the way of that. Kill him as a message to those who resist us. But don't succumb to your anger, even here. Even with him.'

Roper could not understand what Gray meant. All he saw before him was a creature so feeble and hateful that its death was insignificant. What pleasure did this soft, pale thing derive from this dark room, so insulated from the free, cold air; the sway of the trees and the flight of the stars?

'As you suggest, Captain,' he replied, lowering Cold-Edge. He nodded to the legionaries around them, who moved forward to seize King Osbert and drag him from his throne. The king began to shriek in earnest, moaning and flailing as he was gripped beneath each arm and dragged from the room. Roper cast an eye over the retainers, still standing against the wall, hands raised. 'And you,' he said in Anakim, not caring that they did not understand. 'You were sworn to this man, and offered no defence against his mortal enemies.' There was something sacred in that promise, even among enemies. 'Take them too.' The retainers were also dragged from the throne room, and Roper and Gray were left alone.

Roper advanced to inspect the throne. An ugly piece of wood, divorced from the tree that had spawned it and humiliated with frills and vulgar gold. 'Is the city ours?' he said, still looking down.

'Resistance has collapsed,' said Gray. 'But the Unhieru cannot be turned off. They're on the rampage.'

Roper only just restrained himself from saying: 'Good.' People had to know. They had to know that if the legions were required to force their way in, there would be retribution. It was the law, as surely as sea follows moon. 'But our soldiers have stopped?'

'For the most part.'

'Then we leave the Unhieru to it, as long as they don't touch the food.'

There was nothing left for Roper here. He and Gray walked back outside, Roper eyeing the noble who still sat cowering against the wall. 'Did you find Ramnea?' he asked after Gray's

sword, remembering him hurling it over the palisade to preserve Pryce.

'No, lord. I used one I picked off the floor for most of the
night.'

The sun was rising, and the two of them walked the leaden
streets in silence, passing wrecked houses and pockets of
inanimate soldiers, torn apart by the extreme energy with
which they had fought. A dead Unhieru lay sprawled in the
street, head hacked from its shoulders with evidently desperate blows. A little further on, they came upon a site Roper
recognised, where the residents had not just intervened from
windows, but joined the battle on the streets with tables and
ironware. It had been like fighting through a hen-coop. He
observed that when men fought in armour, it held everything
together. All that was left here were splinters of wood and
bone, and a soft red carpet underfoot.

They came upon a band of legionaries, Roper searching
each filthy face for friends who had survived the assault.
Tekoa was there with a dozen Skiritai, and he and Roper fell
wordlessly into an embrace.

'That looked rough, lord,' Tekoa said, as the two broke
apart. 'The breach. I saw the bodies on the way through.' He
glanced down at Roper's arm, caked in blood, and then his
shot calf. 'Are you all right?'

'I'm fine.' Roper suddenly found he wanted to talk about
the silence that had come over him in the breach, and the
strength he had drawn from it. But he could not think how to
describe it in words that Tekoa might understand. So he just
repeated himself. 'I'm fine. Was it all right for the Skiritai?'

'The fighting was mostly done when we got through. It
was just mopping up. Sturla's dead, did you hear?'

Sturla Karson: legate of Ramnea's Own. Perhaps the calm-
est man Roper had ever met, who had his own Prize of
Valour, and had turned down a spot in the Sacred Guard to
keep his legion. He had been at the front when they climbed
into the breach.

'No,' said Roper quietly. 'No I did not.'

Tekoa nodded and they stood in silence for a time, heads bowed. 'Have you seen Pryce?' Tekoa asked at last.

Roper looked at Gray, who shook his head. 'Not for some time.'

'Keep an eye open for him, if you would, lord,' said Tekoa. 'I always fear for him. He can't keep surviving, the way he fights.'

'I will.'

Gray and Roper moved on. The Sacred Guard seemed to have scattered itself across the city, and each one they encountered was a relief. They embraced, exchanged a few words and asked after those they knew to be alive. Many were reported dead, but nobody knew what had become of Pryce. Roper felt a growing dread as they moved on and the list of casualties lengthened. It seemed half the Guard had been left in the breach. Roper could sense Gray getting steadily more distracted as there was no news of his protégé, and he kept them moving, hoping to find him soon.

They did, eventually. He was not far from the breach, sitting atop an Unhieru corpse, his face covered in dried blood. He stood as they approached, holding out a sword to Gray. It was Ramnea, Gray's own blade, which Pryce had somehow recovered. Gray took the sword and embraced his protégé, Roper following suit. Pryce still had the stubs of three arrow-shafts protruding from his chest. 'Are you all right?' Gray asked.

'Stopped by the bone armour,' said Pryce. 'I'm fine.'

'More heroics from you,' Roper observed. 'If your actions on the palisade weren't another Prize of Valour, they were close. I'll need to think about it.'

'I do what I do,' said Pryce.

'I think the Prize of Valour this day would go to you, if anyone, lord,' said Gray. 'I don't know how any of us survived that breach, but we wouldn't if you hadn't been there.'

'Agreed,' said Pryce, lightning-blue eyes boring into Roper's.

'Nobody had the heart for that fight. I thought it would be the end of us. We were too weak. Too much *kjardautha*.'

'I almost got us killed as well,' said Roper.

His two companions observed him. 'In the square, you mean?' asked Gray.

But Pryce was distracted. 'Smoke,' he said, looking over Roper's shoulder.

Roper turned to see that Pryce was right: an ashen column swelling from the distant houses. 'No,' said Roper, exhausted. 'Please.'

'Do we even want this rotten city?' asked Pryce. 'Let it take its course.'

'We want the food,' said Roper. 'We need to get it out, fast. Gray: with me. Pryce: I've not seen Vigtyr. Would you see if you can find him? I think I have a memory of him falling. Or someone of his height.'

Pryce gave an impatient scowl and the suggestion of a nod. Roper and Gray hurried off, and Pryce walked back to the breach, half inspecting the bodies as he passed. There was no sign of Vigtyr and after a cursory glance at the mounds of dead in front of the breach, he decided it was hopeless trying to find him there. He could be injured, in which case he might have been taken back to camp. Pryce began to climb the breach, stiff and slow. Thousands of soldiers had passed over it now, and it was much more stable and better compacted than it had been the first time he crossed these stones.

He ambled back into camp, keeping an eye open for the big lictor among the cooking fires. But the camp was almost deserted. The first of those who had been extracted from the assault would be at the field hospital, further back. Pryce turned towards it, dragging his feet petulantly. He was diverted by the sight of Vigtyr's new tent, standing alone among the burnt-out hearths. He crossed to it, slapping the canvas. 'Vigtyr?' He fiddled with the toggles over the opening until the canvas was half-open, and ducked inside.

He was met by a scene of such order that he found himself
quite arrested. He blinked and edged further in, faintly disgusted by the level of organisation within. Even the grass
floor seemed to have been brushed so it all faced the same
direction. Only the table in the corner was in a relative state
of disorder, with a scrap of parchment on it that was not
quite aligned with the corners of the wood, and an instrument of some sort that had splattered ink over the paper.
Pryce advanced to examine it, picking it up to inspect. It was
covered in irregular, but evidently purposeful patterns,
arranged in parallel lines across the paper. A drawing of the
sea? Then he frowned.

This was writing: the Suthern art of trapping words on
paper. Pryce had seen it in the temple in Lincylene, where
there had been a strange room, like a granary for paper. It
had been stacked with vast scrolls, each etched in this same
chaotic scratching. Vigtyr could write.

He opened his mouth in disbelief, suddenly recalling the
Saxon Vigtyr had spoken in Unhierea.

There was a flapping at the canvas behind Pryce. He
turned around to see Vigtyr half-crouched in the doorway
behind, staring at him. Vigtyr's sword was buckled at his
side and he was totally uninjured. In fact, his armour was
spotless, with none of the grime or dust worn by those who
had passed through the breach.

There was a moment's pause.

'Pryce,' he said, coming inside and straightening up. 'You
startled me. What are you doing here?' He glanced at the
paper still clutched in Pryce's hand.

Pryce held it out to him. 'You tell me what you're doing
first.'

Vigtyr's eyes flicked down at the note, then he laughed.
'Oh, that?' he shrugged. 'Just practising. It seemed like magic
to me, being able to store words on paper. I've been trying to
learn, but it makes me feel sick.'

Pryce nodded slowly, letting the paper fall to the floor. 'So you're the spy.'

'What? No, no, Pryce, you misunderstand.'

'What I understand, Vigtyr,' said Pryce, 'is that if you don't back out of the tent and lie down on the grass, I will cut off your limbs like the traitorous worm you are.'

Vigtyr glanced over his shoulder, and then stepped a little further inside the tent. 'No, I don't think so, Pryce,' he said, smiling faintly. 'You've got this all wrong.' Pryce drew one of his swords, Tusk, and Vigtyr's smile changed to something more confident. 'I will not be threatened, Pryce.'

'You are being threatened,' said Pryce. 'And now, Vigtyr, I am giving you your last chance. Unbuckle your sword. Lie down outside.'

Vigtyr raised his eyebrows and laughed softly, his own hand straying gently towards his sword. 'I hoped I might get this chance one day.'

Before Vigtyr's hand had even touched the hilt, Pryce lashed out, forcing Vigtyr to step aside. With a flick of his boot, Vigtyr hooked a cooking pot from its place near his bedroll and sent it spinning at Pryce's face. He deflected it with a clang, and in the time he was distracted, Vigtyr's sword scraped free of its scabbard. There was a pause as the two reassessed, facing each other across the tent. The tip of Vigtyr's sword quivered, and then began to buzz. 'You can't beat me, Pryce,' he said, softly.

'I've heard that so many times,' said Pryce. 'And somehow, I always do.'

Vigtyr raised his eyebrows, and that movement somehow made it surprising that his sword had already started sliding towards Pryce. The motion was so direct, so clean and so perfectly balanced in arm, foot and torso, that it would have skewered any man slower than Pryce. But the guardsman's hawk-like reflexes preserved him, knocking the blade aside and responding with a hard slash at Vigtyr. The taller man blocked, and suddenly both were attacking hard, exchanging a battery of rapid violence with point and edge. The swords rang together, sparks bursting clear of each impact and a continuous shockwave oscillating the blades.

It was Vigtyr's reach, precision and coordination against Pryce's speed and aggression, and at first Pryce seemed on top. He was so fast and so fluid that he had the better of Vigtyr's parsimony, pressing forward and forcing the bigger man to retreat and give himself more time. Pryce pursued him, the two circling the tent with Vigtyr in reverse, but aware all the time of the canvas walls, of the table in the corner he would have to dodge, of the need to step high over his bedroll. Pryce, even he; was not fast enough to dent Vigtyr's defences, not while the taller man could still move and keep him at arm's length.

Meanwhile, Vigtyr was learning. Nobody could beat him at this. Nobody. In his skill with a sword at least, he had faith. He weathered the early assault coolly, assessing his enemy, probing here and there to see what he was capable of, and memorising each response. It took him longer than usual: there was little pattern to Pryce's brutal assault, but eventually Vigtyr thought he knew what was in his enemy's arsenal, and waited for his moment. When it came, it was betrayed by a flash of gritted teeth. Pryce was about to launch his hard slash, and Vigtyr knew where it would go, and where he should duck. As he had expected, the bright steel sword swept past his ear, and with an economical twist, Vigtyr managed to move his blade across his body, into the path of Pryce's wrist. Skin and edge met, and Vigtyr retracted his sword savagely, cutting deep through flesh and sinew. Pryce's had flopped backwards, fingers suddenly senseless and unresponsive, and the sword slipped from his grasp.

Whether the sprinter had actually registered the wound was hard to tell. Before the damage was even done, his left hand had flown to his belt and drawn Bone, his second sword, which he used to aim another slash at Vigtyr, who was so stunned he barely parried in time. He was forced back, then again and again by his opponent. He had been so sure that the injury to Pryce's wrist would conclude matters that he had not thought beyond it. His dodge had put him off-stride, he could not move as freely as usual, and Pryce managed to thrust him into a corner. The sprinter's right hand was useless, but his left seemed to operate just as fast, and while he engaged Vigtyr's blade, he aimed a kick at his knee. Cornered, Vigtyr could not step aside, and so was forced to take the blow, his teeth gritting as the knee jarred beneath him. The flash of white teeth seemed to be a signal for Pryce, whose next attack streaked at his mouth.

Vigtyr ducked out of the way, but as his head came down, Pryce's boot swept up into his mouth in a hard kick. The sprinter was able to place immense speed and power behind the swing of a leg, and with a pop and a splash of blood, Vigtyr's front teeth collapsed inwards. He moaned, eyes watering so that he could not see the next attack, which thrust at his breastplate. It punched through the armour, and had the blade been Unthank-silver, it might have gone through the bone plates and into Vigtyr's heart. But it grated to a halt, and Vigtyr managed to push Pryce away with his free hand so that the guardsman staggered back. Pryce bounced forward without a heartbeat's hesitation, chest to chest with Vigtyr once more, where he could supplement Bone with his brawler's weapons of feet and forehead.

But Pryce had made a mistake. Vigtyr was now a few steps out of the corner, and despite the bloody mess that had been his mouth, and the flesh wound in his chest, he had space to move once more. As Pryce lunged forward, sword driving again for the weak-spot on Vigtyr's chest, Vigtyr stepped neatly aside. Pryce's attack was too wild, too driven by rage, and his opponent was out of the way and then past him, his sword slicing down on the back of Pryce's leg. The blow carved through his hamstring, which sprang apart like a broken rope and reduced the sprinter to one knee.

There he remained, exhaling hard, Vigtyr now standing behind him.

Jerkily, degree by degree, Pryce turned himself round on one knee so he was facing his enemy. Teeth bared, he stared furiously up at Vigtyr, who prowled the tent, spitting broken teeth and returning his poisonous gaze. 'You are too thought-less, Pryce,' said Vigtyr, lisping a fine puff of blood. 'And that was too wild. You have been watching me too long. You must truly hate me.'

Pryce gave a manic laugh. 'Hate you? I don't think about you at all, Vigtyr. Killing me will not make you feel any less inadequate.'

Vigtyr stopped pacing. He met Pryce's eye, blood dribbling down his chin. 'What?'

Pryce laughed again. 'You will never be satisfied!' he said, gleefully. 'No matter what you do, you will spend the rest of your life destroying everything around you. And worse than that: you know it.'

Vigtyr took the bait so violently that Pryce was almost not ready. Almost.

Vigtyr lunged, bloody lips pulled back in an empty snarl, sword directed at his enemy's throat. And as Pryce had calcu-lated, he overcommitted in his rage. He stepped too close to Pryce, who hurled himself forward with that snake-like speed, ducking beneath Vigtyr's attack and plunging Bone into his boot. Pryce's full weight had been behind that blow, and the blade went clean through Vigtyr's foot and two feet into the ground, pinning him to the spot. With one good hand and one good leg, Pryce could not rise. He just kept his weight on his sword, driven through Vigtyr's foot, and vibrated with mad laughter. 'You're coming with me, Vigtyr.'

Vigtyr screamed, and thrust his own sword into Pryce's back. The sprinter ignored that blow, propping himself onto one elbow and reaching up with a shockingly strong left hand, using it to swarm up Vigtyr's body. 'Your swordsman-ship means nothing,' he said, voice bubbling. 'You're going to die, you bastard. You traitor. You filth.' Vigtyr thrust his blade once more into Pryce's back, but then had to leave it stuck in the guardsman as he was forced into a bow by the iron hand grasped at his breastplate. He tried to straighten, but only succeeded in pulling his enemy off the ground, closer to his face. Pryce heaved forward then, with what intention, Vigtyr could not think, until he felt the sprinter's teeth clamp onto his neck. Vigtyr screamed, hands flying to Pryce's head and trying to force it away, with no effect whatsoever.

Vigtyr could not breathe. He was spluttering and choking, growing purple and desperate as the teeth bit harder. Still Pryce was not satisfied, his fingers crawling up the side of Vigtyr's head and over his face, seeking an eye. Vigtyr could feel the moment of comprehension when the digits located one and his hand orientated itself abruptly, nails digging into the scalp for purchase, one thumb pressing into the socket.

Vigtyr dropped, attempting to dislodge his opponent, and the two men collapsed in a tattered heap. Vigtyr was trying to scream, but could manage only tiny grunts, his movements jerkier and jerkier as he flailed for a weapon. His eye bulged and throbbed beneath Pryce's thumb, his vision going first white, then red. He could feel the guardsman's teeth shifting minutely in his neck. Finally, Vigtyr's scrabbling hands landed on a handle at Pryce's belt: a dagger. He drew it, plunging it into the sprinter's neck once, and then again, and again to unleash a gout of hot blood. Vigtyr's skin was crawling as though Pryce's hands, his nails, were everywhere.

But that was an illusion, because Pryce had gone still.

His teeth had loosened in Vigtyr's neck. That insane quiver of laughter had stopped, and his thumb was no longer boring into Vigtyr's eye. At last, Vigtyr found his shaking hands could push the head away, groaning with each breath that passed his crushed throat. He wriggled out from underneath his opponent and tried to stagger back, but he fell. He tried again, and fell again, and could not understand why he was unable to move. Then he realised his foot was still pinned to the ground by Pryce's sword, and he leaned forward with trembling hands to uproot the blade and free himself. He stumbled away, backing into the canvas, drenched in blood, staring in horror at the dead sprinter lying within his tent.

Pryce the Wild had been well named. That had been like fighting a wolverine. Trying to kill him, like strangling a snake. And even now, Vigtyr could feel the vibration of his mad laughter trembling through his flesh.

40

The Witan

Bellamus sat alone by the fireside of an inn, nursing a mug of ale. He had promised himself wine, but the inn-keeper had laughed at his request. There was no wine. Trade to Suthdal had all but disintegrated with the Anakim invasion. Anyone with a ship was making fabulous money ferrying refugees into Frankia as fast as possible. There was no sense delaying the return journey to load wine, which people had no interest in anyway. The ports were stuffed with crowds desperate to trade every last possession for passage to the mainland. The roads were chaos too, and for a man like Bellamus, it had not been hard to procure money to pay for a drink and a bed upstairs.

He stared glassily at the flames, wondering if Aramilla had escaped Lundenceaster, and if she would survive the crammed roads to make it here. The town was called Wiltun: at a confluence of two clear chalk rivers, well to the west of Lundenceaster.

When a hand was placed on his shoulder, he turned only slowly, expecting another opportunistic bandit and inching his fingers towards the blade concealed in his boot. He found himself looking up into a broad face that was familiar, but so unexpected that for a moment he could not place it. Then his mouth fell open. He stood, the ale spilling from his fingers and onto the straw floor. 'Stepan?'

The knight was beaming. 'Captain.'

Bellamus laughed gleefully. 'Stepan!' They embraced, thumping each other on the back, both roaring in joy. 'By God, what is this? What are you doing here?'

They broke apart, each maintaining a grip on the other's shoulder and grinning inanely. There were tears in the knight's eyes. 'I came to find you.'

'You fool, why? What about your farm? Your wife? I am a foreign peasant!'

'You will never be a peasant, so long as you live,' replied Stepan.

There seemed so much to say, that for a long while nothing was said at all. Only when the knight had replaced Bellamus's spilt ale, bought some for himself, and the two were settled by the fire, were they able to talk.

'I never thought I'd see you again,' said Stepan, blue eyes fixed on Bellamus.

'Nor I you,' said Bellamus. 'How has this happened? How did you find me?'

'Good lord, it's been a long road,' replied the knight, shaking his head. 'I don't know where to begin.'

'The beginning,' said Bellamus. 'Where did you go after I was captured?'

So Stepan told him. How he had first stayed with the Thingalith, which had quickly become a brutal company without Bellamus's influence. 'It was Garrett,' Stepan explained. 'He took control at once. People were split between me and him as to who should lead after you'd gone, and they feared Garrett more. When it became clear that he'd be in charge, I had to leave. Thirty men threw their lot in with me, and we went to join Seaton's army.'

'Why? I thought you wanted to go home?'

'I did. Or I do. But I kept thinking you might be alive, and thought joining Seaton was my best chance of finding out what had become of you.' He delivered this information off-hand, but he and Bellamus shared a look for a long while after. Eventually, Bellamus raised his mug and toasted the knight, dropping his gaze to the floor.

Stepan went on, explaining how Vigtyr had come to Seaton's tent and delivered news for the first time that Bellamus was alive. How Stepan had lobbied to be included in the party to free him, but when Vigtyr had gone it had become clear that Seaton was minded only to murder Bellamus. In the chaos of the next morning, as they were pursued by the Anakim around the walls of Deorceaster, a disillusioned Stepan had deserted the army. 'Seaton is a villain. I had no intention of following him back to Lundenceaster. And as the raid on the Anakim camp was thwarted, I thought you might still be alive. So I waited near Deorceaster until the Anakim had marched south, then went to search for your body. No sign, and I thought you must still be a prisoner. I planned to follow you, and stopped off at a tavern to have a farewell drink with the last two Thingalith who were with me. We deserted together, but they didn't want to go any further and I can't say I blame them.'

'Where did they go instead?'

Stepan grimaced. 'Back to Garrett. Word is he's amassing a great deal of plunder, mostly from our own side, and using it to build the Thingalith into a private army to fight the Anakim. He is liberating hybrids across the north, and training them to fight too. Lord, there is no money you could pay me to go back to him.

'Anyway, in the tavern the only gossip was the invasion, and whether the Anakim could be stopped. And someone said they had had a one-eyed man in there the night before, who claimed to have been captured by the Anakim and survived.' They beamed at each other once more. 'So I knew you were alive, and they said you were heading for Lundenceaster. I followed, but my searching for you was interrupted by Garrett's band skulking around, delivering those plague-infested bodies to the Anakim. I didn't want to come face to face with him, so between that and avoiding Anakim patrols, I had to spend a lot of time hiding. I thought inns and taverns were my best bet for information, and sure enough I found one who had hosted you the night before, and knew you were heading west.' He grinned. 'It's lucky you drink so much. I followed your trail all the way here.'

Bellamus raised an eyebrow. 'I didn't realise I left such a trail.'

'You didn't?' Stepan burst out laughing. 'Oh, Captain. In most of the taverns you'd been in, I didn't even have to ask before you came up. They all spoke about the one-eyed man with the missing fingers, who drinks like a toad and has an unsettling air of capability. Subtle as you can be, you leave quite a wake.'

They purchased more ale, the panic of the invasion forgotten in their little corner. 'I can't believe I found you,' said Stepan. 'And now you can come back with me.'

Bellamus frowned. 'Back? Back where?'

'My estate,' said Stepan. 'We'll go north together, you can stay with me and we'll leave the fighting to others.'

Bellamus stared at his companion. 'That sounds wonderful, brother . . . but your estate won't survive six months.'

'It what?' Stepan was not really listening.

'Nothing north of Lundenceaster is going to survive. I'm sorry,' he added, leaning forward to place a hand on his friend's arm. 'I talked with the Black Lord a lot while I was captured. I was almost a confidant of his by the end. The Anakim have come to stay. They're not just going to exact revenge and then retreat, or rule over us and collect an annual tribute. They're here to eradicate us. Every trace of our kind will be obliterated from Suthdal. Nothing will survive what is in the Black Lord's mind. Nothing.'

Stepan's eyes were so wide as to be near bulging. 'But that can't be right. They hate to be away from their own lands. They couldn't stay.'

'The Black Lord has uncommon drive,' Bellamus assured him. 'That army is sick, but limps on to his will. They are as wretched as ever at coming south, but Roper's spell keeps them here. We have to resist, or forfeit this entire island. Everything you treasure must be brought south, where we stand a chance of protecting it.' Bellamus believed the words he told his friend, but that was not why he would not go north, to Stepan's estate. Without this conflict; without the queen, Bellamus was nobody. That did not satisfy him. He did not want the comfortable life that Stepan dreamed of. He wanted more.

All the energy had gone out of Stepan. He wilted in his chair, staring now into his ale, lips pursed. 'I'm sorry, brother,' said Bellamus. 'I really am. My hope is that I've managed to extract the queen from Lundenceaster, and she'll arrive here someday soon. When we've got her, we'll see what we can do for your wife and lands.'

'Lundenceaster's not even taken,' Stepan protested weakly. 'Those walls are immense, the Anakim may be pushed back there.'

Bellamus stared down at his own ale. 'We shall turn them back, Stepan. But it won't be there.'

The joy was gone from their reunion. They finished their ale and went out to the streets, Bellamus saying they needed to keep an eye out for the queen. Beyond the convivial tavern walls, the streets twitched, swarmed and scurried. Refugees swept for the gates, their worldly goods bundled on their shoulders, accompanied by the usual profiteers of chaos. Twice, Bellamus and Stepan witnessed bandits openly claim a wagon stuffed with food, shooing the owners to the side of the road before ambling off with their prize. Nobody reacted. Nobody helped. The stream of people parted around the scene, attention fixed on the distant invisible coast.

They found the queen the following day.

Stepan and Bellamus sat by the gates to Wiltun, each

wearing a great-sword and chain mail, provided by Stepan, to deter the brigands. The queen arrived on foot, clothes stained with dust from the road, and face sour until she caught sight of Bellamus. Then she smiled: an expression so genuine that it did not suit her. She ran to Bellamus, a plump companion on her heels, and embraced him.

'My upstart,' she broke away and regarded him. 'Great God, but it's a surprise to finally see you. What happened to your eye?'

'War,' he replied. 'Majesty, may I introduce my great friend Sir Stepan, a knight who lately served your father.'

Aramilla offered her hand, but did not introduce Cathryn. 'This collective decision that Albion is lost has been rather dramatic,' she observed instead, sweeping the crowds with narrowed eyes. 'We haven't even lost Lundenceaster yet.'

'People have forgotten what war feels like, Your Majesty,' said Stepan kindly. 'The tales of the Anakim army have been rather exaggerated. People are saying that they are massacring anyone who resists, and it is considered a matter of when, not if, Lundenceaster falls. And with your father, and the king, and so many fighting men inside, further resistance is thought futile. It is every man for himself,' he said sadly, moving out of the way of a band of horsemen galloping for the gates, crammed saddlebags bouncing at their sides.

'I arranged a horse for you,' said Bellamus.

'Now in the possession of brigands,' spat Aramilla. She gripped his arm suddenly. 'And what about you? You surely aren't abandoning this island?'

'I have no powers,' said Bellamus, shrugging. 'Beyond the man who helped you escape Lundenceaster, my spy-web is broken. I am just another commoner. But I think flight is a little premature at this stage. We need leadership and someone to rally the remaining defenders. What we need, Your Majesty, is a queen.'

Aramilla was silent a moment, looking sidelong at Bellamus. 'I am nothing without the king.'

'You could be,' said Bellamus. 'With him captured, you are our rightful leader. And if His Majesty does not survive the siege—'

'Heaven forfend,' Stepan interjected cheerfully.

'You have no children with him,' Bellamus continued. 'You are our queen.'

Aramilla stared directly ahead, frowning. 'His nephews would challenge me,' she declared at last.

'Are you certain?' asked Bellamus. 'I'm not sure there's a single noble in this land who would want to be in command when the Black Lord comes to demand Suthdal's surrender.'

She did not reply to that, and Bellamus beckoned them all to fall into step with him. They walked in silence for a time, passing into the town. 'You are leading me somewhere?' she prompted.

'To the house of the Earl Penbro: a place as rotted with cowardice as the rest of the country.'

'And you want me to stop this rot?'

'Do what you feel is right, Majesty,' said Bellamus. 'But presenting yourself to him is a wise course whatever you plan to do.'

'If I plan to flee, you mean.'

'Or if you stay,' said Bellamus.

'And you, Stepan,' asked Aramilla, suddenly imperious. 'I see you are a fighting man. Do I have your loyalty?'

'You seem to have the captain's loyalty,' said Stepan, lightly. 'And he has mine.'

The Earl Penbro's house sat opposite a river, behind a moss-covered wall some eight feet high. The gates were guarded by six retainers, all wielding polearms and shifting restlessly at the passing refugees. At the approach of Aramilla's party, they turned towards her, weapons lowering a touch. 'We are here to see the earl,' announced Bellamus, grandly. 'Step aside now. This is the Queen Aramilla, and she will not be kept waiting.'

Three of the soldiers laughed. The foremost of them

assessed Bellamus from worn leather boots to rust-speckled mail, and then switched to Aramilla, finding her no more impressive. 'Don't waste my time,' he replied flatly.

Bellamus smiled breezily and opened his mouth to respond, but Aramilla broke in first. 'Fool!' she hissed. 'I *am* your queen! Do you think alone of those who escaped Lund-enceaster, I did so with jewels and frocks in tow? How would you expect a queen who has been imprisoned by the Anakim for weeks to appear?'

The soldiers had stopped smiling.

'Admit us to the earl's presence this instant. Now. Right now, and I will not seek retribution for your insolence.' Her voice carried undeniable authority. However outlandish her claims to being queen, this was evidently not a woman used to being kept waiting. The soldiers looked mutely to one another.

'Conduct us at once, please,' added Bellamus, smiling innocently.

'Will the earl recognise you . . .' the soldier paused for a moment, 'Majesty?'

'*Of course,*' she said scathingly.

The soldiers looked to one another once more, and the one who had been speaking shrugged. 'This way.' He rapped on the gate, Bellamus winking at the other soldiers as they were admitted. Beyond the wall lay a sumptuous garden bursting with flowers, marshalled into beds by a dozen streams. They crossed arched bridges, following a gravel path to a hall, distantly visible through a screen of trees.

They were conducted inside. Servants scurried across the hall, emptying chests,dismantling tapestries and staggering beneath sacks from the kitchen. Aramilla advanced straight into the flurry, leaving her guide behind. 'Penbro?' she called, stirring the soldier to hurry forward and seize her arm. She ignored him. 'Penbro?'

An old man, a cotton shirt hanging off his stooped frame and eider-down hair framing a complexion of deep plum, emerged from a room at the back of the hall, peering at the newcomers. 'Watt?' he snapped at the soldier. 'Who's this?' Then he let out a startled cough. 'Your *Majesty*?' he asked. 'Can that be?'

'Earl Penbro,' said Aramilla, shaking herself free of Watt, who only looked relieved that the woman he had been escorting was truly the queen. She advanced on the earl, holding out a hand, which Penbro took. He brushed dry lips over her fingers, knees cracking as they bent.

'But we heard you were in the hands of the Anakim, Majesty,' he said, straightening. 'Pray God,' he added, suddenly. 'The siege has been broken?'

'I fear not,' said Aramilla. 'I escaped, thanks to the help of my servant Bellamus.' She gestured at the upstart, who bowed to the earl. Penbro's eyes widened as he heard Bellamus's name, but Aramilla left him no time to respond. 'We will need food at once, Penbro, and quarters. Then you will need to summon a witan.'

'The witan met yesterday, Majesty,' said Penbro. He explained that the council, composed of nobles and churchmen, and invested with collective executive power,had decided to retreat to Frankia. 'We are just preparing our departure,' he added, gesturing about the hall.

Bellamus stepped forward. 'You decided to flee these lands?' he clarified. 'Abandon your king and queen?'

Aramilla again interrupted before Penbro could respond. 'Some of the witan are still here?'

'Most, yes, Majesty, we will be travelling to Frankia together. But the bishops left some while ago. We will need to send word after them.'

'No time,' Aramilla decreed. 'We will eat now, while you assemble those who remain. Then we shall meet and decide a fresh course of action.'

Penbro had no choice but to obey. Bellamus did a fine impression of the loyal manservant and demanded wine, trout, cheeses, bread and smoked bacon, stating this last with undisguised relish. These things were duly produced and placed on a table, which had to be intercepted on its way out of the door. The chairs seemed to have been loaded onto wagons some time ago, and were 'quite inaccessible', so they dragged two chests to the table, Bellamus and Stepan perching on one, Cathryn and Aramilla on the other. The bacon was good but the trout, caught in one of the garden streams and covered in rare pepper, was better still.

Aramilla declared the story of their escape 'dull' and did not care to recount it beyond the indignity of having their horse stolen. So Bellamus regaled them all with how it had been to be a prisoner of the Anakim. Aramilla did not quite seem to have her usual confidence, he noted, and she would need every scrap of it if she were to dominate the witan. At once he called for Penbro, demanding clothes fit for a queen. 'And anything that resembles a crown, Lord Penbro; I trust you have something suitable?'

'My late wife had a circlet, which may do until we find something more fitting,' said the earl stiffly, answering each question Bellamus posed to Aramilla, as though it were she who addressed him.

'It may do for now,' said Bellamus, manner testy, mood gleeful. 'Gowns?'

'Some of the finer pieces are left,' he said grudgingly.

'Bring them, bring them,' said Bellamus imperiously.

'His wife was a venomous old skeleton,' said Aramilla after the earl had gone. 'Even after a week living from hedgerows I doubt I shall fit one of her dresses.'

The dresses were brought by servants bearing the Earl Penbro's apologies for his absence, evidently in the hope that Bellamus would make no further demands on his hospitality. Aramilla waited until they had finished the fish and then excused herself from the table, gesturing that Bellamus should join her. As two ladies of Penbro's house helped Aramilla change behind a screen, Bellamus paced the room.

'I can think of no more opportune time, Your Majesty,' he

said to the screen. 'Our great advantage here is that no one will want to rule. The nation is in turmoil: nobody wants to captain a ship that is so clearly sinking. Or perhaps two great advantages. Your lack of children with His Majesty makes you the clear candidate to succeed. That is fortunate indeed.'

Her magpie's laugh rattled over the screen. 'Fortunate?' she said, apparently unconcerned by the anonymous ladies who helped her dress. 'King Osbert is a more cerebral man than physical. The few times he has shown interest in me, it has not been hard to dissuade him.'

Bellamus was silent a moment. 'It was deliberate? You never wanted children?'

'Children!' she said, full of scorn. 'Can you think of any more tedious way to use your life? I think perhaps my reluctance was a relief to the king, anyway. He was not comfortable in my bed, and some rumours that I was barren preserved his masculinity. He did not want to try again. I think he saw it as some kind of sacrificial duty he must go through.'

'So he managed occasionally. What did you do then?'

'There are herbs for every occasion,' she said carelessly. Bellamus knew she would enjoy the shocked glances of the ladies helping her change. Aramilla was secure once more, and the chaos of the last few months was tempting her back. Bellamus feared how reckless turmoil seemed to make her. She knew enough to be charmed, not enough to be fearful.

When she emerged from the screen, she had succeeded in changing into a dress of green silk, so spattered with pearls and gold that if Penbro's wife had ever worn it at court, it would have been vaguely treasonous. She summoned water, washed her face and donned the gilt circlet, her face assuming the composure of a queen once more. Then she dismissed the ladies, she and Bellamus passing the time with tales. She called Stepan and Cathryn into the room with them and they waited for evening, and the assembly of the witan.

It was dark before Penbro returned to inform them that the remaining members of the witan had been gathered in the hall. He paused then, not wishing to linger, but evidently with further news to relay. 'We have also just had word from the east, Majesty,' he said carefully. 'This may be a shock—'

'Tell me at once,' she demanded.

'Lundenceaster has fallen, Your Majesty.' There was silence in the room. 'It seems the Anakim stormed the defences and have burnt the city. There are very few survivors. Those that did escape . . .' He made a dismissive gesture. 'I doubt they are thinking clearly.'

'Speak, Earl Penbro,' said Aramilla. 'What have you heard?'

'They say the king – His Majesty, God take his soul – was captured and executed by the Black Lord himself. They say the Anakim were assisted in the siege by metal demons.'

Bellamus felt something leave him at this news. 'So the Unhieru arrived after all,' he murmured.

Earl Penbro, fear evident in his every word and gesture, stammered on. 'But Your Majesty, there's more. They conjured some kind of infernal help, and the earth rose up to swallow the walls. There are stories of falcons and wolves fighting with the Anakim, of churches crumbling spontaneously, of magic incantations that overcame our forces with fear. Forgive me, Majesty, but we cannot stay here! We must leave at once! These lands are lost, utterly. We cannot stand against such powers.'

Bellamus looked to Aramilla, and found her not in fear at the earl's tidings, but oddly fascinated. She regarded him with interest for some time. 'Return to the hall, my lord. We will come and address you all shortly.' Reluctantly, Penbro bowed out of the room. 'Can the Anakim do as he said?' she asked Bellamus.

He laughed at that. 'Stories, Majesty. Hearsay, terror, speculation. They are people, like us. So too the Unhieru, though when fully armed and armoured I must admit they would be . . . daunting. As is our challenge in there, Majesty,' he added, gesturing through the door into the hall where the witan waited. 'You saw Penbro. The news will have scared the witan senseless. We shall be hard-pushed to stop them abandoning the island for Frankia.'

'Well then, we shall begin at once,' said the queen, carelessly. 'Lead on, Master Bellamus.'

'Your Majesty.' Bellamus rose with a flourish, demanding torches and half a dozen random ladies to add significance to their procession. He went before Aramilla, entering the hall to find two dozen filigreed nobles lining the walls and shining in the flickering candlelight. 'Her Majesty, Queen Aramilla,' he announced, standing aside to reveal her. There was a collective bow as she entered, and Aramilla stared around, allowing a long silence to bloom.

'Would you all allow your queen to sit with no throne?' she asked the room at large. There was an instant flurry as the nobles cast around for a substitute. In the end, the table at which Aramilla had lunched was pushed to the end of the hall as a dais, one chest placed on top as a seat, and another in front as a step. Bellamus supplied a hand so that she might ascend her chest with some dignity. There was a barely suppressed murmur at that display of favouritism for an upstart, and Aramilla cast a sudden look over the witan. Silence fell at once.

'This is my right hand,' she said, gesturing down at Bellamus and taking a dignified seat on the chest. 'He has been of immense value to us all in the war against the Anakim, whether you detected his influence or not. It is only that influence that delayed the Anakim in reaching Lundenceaster before now. It was he who liberated me from the city and brought me to safety here. He speaks for me now.' She nodded to him, and sat back to wait on his words, smiling at the shock on his face. For an instant, Bellamus was lost for words, and searched her eyes for some indication of what she wanted. But it seemed he was being given a licence to perform, so he turned to face the witan.

He was surprised, but not unprepared. He had imagined this moment. 'My lords,' he began. 'My queen has gone through

the utmost danger to be here today, and she arrives to find
you preparing for flight. You were to abandon your monarch?
Your queen? These lands? Your people?' He eyed them all,
taking a few paces into the dark space beyond the throne.

'We are weak after the failed invasions of the previous
year,' Penbro replied suddenly, glaring at Bellamus, accusation clear in his voice. 'The same invasions that stirred
Anakim retribution. Most of the fighting men in the land
were trapped inside Lundenceaster. I have recounted the
tales of what happened there to you myself, Master Bellamus. There is something terrible overtaking these lands. We
must make passage to Erebos. I am relieved my queen has
come to join us: we should all cross the sea without delay.
Better that than stay here and die in the face of this evil. We
are helpless against the Anakim.'

'We are far from helpless,' replied Bellamus, sharply. 'You
have allowed yourself to be gulled by the rumours of war,
Lord Penbro. I have seen the Black Legions first hand, and
they are starving. They have left their heart north of the
Abus. They don't want to be here. They think of their wilderness home, and we only need to give them reason to turn
back; something we have singularly failed to do. Yes, they
have taken Lundenceaster, but I know our defences were
well prepared. I assure you they will have been terribly
weakened by the effort.'

'So are we!' called a voice, to a murmur of agreement.

Bellamus nodded absently. 'Yes, that's true. We are not the
force we were. But we're all still here, aren't we?' He looked
about the hall, shadowed faces turned back to him. 'We still
live, and we're not done yet. Not until we have abandoned
this island.' His voice grew fiercer, strengthened by the darkness. It was his element. 'Our enemy is trying to frighten us
with a display of force and ruthless tactics, but they don't
have enough soldiers to subdue this country if we resist. Who
better placed to mobilise that force than those of us here?' He
spread his arms to the hall. 'And if you think Erebos will let

this island succumb to Anakim control, that they will refuse our pleas for help, then you are mistaken. You do not know the brotherhood that exists across the water, who are prepared to drop everything and stand with us against the Black Lord. We will summon allies from Erebos, and we will mobilise our people. We do as the Anakim do: enlist our population to war. We will need chance on our side if we are to hold on until then, but chance is a friend of mine,' he boasted, drawing himself upright and addressing these lords now as though they were his equals. 'You have heard my name; how could you doubt my words? Chance is a friend of mine!' He turned back to Aramilla and knelt before her. 'And I serve my queen. King Osbert died in Lundenceaster. But we have a monarch still.' He bowed his head, and Aramilla surveyed the witan beyond him.

'Thank you, Master Bellamus,' said Aramilla. 'My lords: abandon your preparations for flight. With chaos, comes opportunity. Many of our great landholders have perished. The spoils of this war shall be Albion, and all of you shall have a share beyond your dreams. Beneath me, with the rewards of this conflict, you may found a dynasty that lasts a thousand years. You may become such powerful men that your family names are never forgotten.

'We are not leaving our home to be overrun. All of you are well versed in holy scripture. This evil is not the devil's work, but a test of faith from God. It is as my spymaster says. We are not done yet.'

'But,' Penbro interjected abruptly, and then his tone became more obsequious. 'But, Your Majesty, what *really* can we do?'

'First,' decreed the queen, 'you shall all swear fealty to me in this hall. This is now the capital of Suthdal, until we have retaken all that we have lost and rebuilt Lundenceaster. Next, we will gather our men here and summon the fyrd to fortify this town. All surviving resistance will focus on us. And we shall dispatch messengers across Erebos. We will let it be known that this island is now the heart of the struggle between the Anakim and the Sutherner. That unless they want an unchallenged Anakim fortress just off their shores, and to have their own Anakim populations emboldened and ready to march, here is where they must focus their efforts. This conflict has been building for generations, and this is not the end. It is merely the beginning.

'Come now, my lords. Swear your fealty now. My spymaster – now commander of our forces, whom I name Lord Safinim – will take your oaths.'

Bellamus looked up at the sound of his own title, open-mouthed. The nobility would surely mutiny at this promotion.

But there was not a word of dissent.

With authority and reward, the queen had gained control here. It was as Bellamus had said: nobody wanted to command this failing kingdom. Whoever did was ruler undisputed. And besides, the nobility would never have taken orders from a man with no title. He felt a hiccough of triumph. 'Lord Safinim,' he murmured, unable to resist the shape of it on his tongue.

A young lord knelt first, those around him dropping hurriedly. In a wave from that point, the nobility dropped to their knees, with old Earl Penbro left standing last of all. He cast about in dismay, before snapping his fingers to two servants. They helped him onto his knees, and he too bowed his head.

With chaos, comes opportunity. The Anakim war machine rumbled on, but in Wiltun that night was crowned a queen of anarchy. Beside her, a lord of dark places.

And the great game had begun.

41

The Fire

The fires in Lundenceaster proved uncontrollable. Gogmagoc, voice gurgling more than ever after the siege bolt that had pierced his chest, but otherwise tolerating the wound, claimed credit for starting the blaze himself. The Anakim, unused to fighting fires when they only built from stone, were only just able to extract the food supplies and a quarter of their dead before abandoning the hard-won city to the flames.

Roper had time for one final act.

He led a little procession of guardsmen and prisoners into a central garden. King Osbert walked trembling and humming absently behind Roper, his royal retainers next to their counterparts in the Sacred Guard. The flames were nearly upon them, but Roper wanted to do this somewhere public.

He turned to the king. 'Kneel,' he commanded, in Saxon. Osbert did not respond, apart from to shut his eyes. Two fat tears dripped down his cheeks and he shuddered, still humming his aimless tune. Gray stepped forward and reduced the king firmly to his knees. Behind him, each of the retainers was also pushed to the floor.

Roper held Cold-Edge, the blade still filthy from their night's work, and raised it before the king. A wave of heat swept over his face, huge orange flames billowing behind Osbert, whose eyes were still shut tight. The air here was so hot that Roper could feel each breath passing into his lungs, and he knew they must leave this place soon or burn. 'King Osbert,' he said, in Saxon. 'I declare Suthern rule over these lands at an end. Your people are to leave these shores, and for your resistance to us, I sentence you to die.' The king gave a frightened mewing. 'Do you have any final words?'

The king did not.

Gray stepped back, leaving him swaying unsupported for a moment, while the king's humming grew more frantic. Roper brought Cold-Edge down on the back of his neck. His head, still strapped into its shining gilt helmet, was cut clean away and toppled to the ground. With more of a slamming noise than a slicing, the Sacred Guardsmen meted out the same fate to the royal retainers. Their bodies, their weapons, the golden chain about the king's neck: all were left to the flames, Roper turning his back on them without word or gesture.

Flames towered on two sides of the garden and Roper could feel the sweat pouring off his face as that shield of heat grew more and more intense. 'Let's go,' he said. 'Fast.'

They ran through the city streets, collecting a band of Ramnea's Own they found on the way, and passing through a screen of legionaries who protected the open gates. Lunden-ceaster had resisted, and their people must now pay the price. The few Sutherners who approached the gates were hacked down without a word, their bodies warding off any further attempts.

Roper now stood with Gray, watching from beyond the walls as a huge shimmer distorted the evening, a black cloud starred with sparks obscuring the sun's last rays. There was a howling on the air as the flames billowed and raged, and the underside of the smoke-column was stained a rusted red.

It was done.

Suthdal was as good as theirs. The vast majority of the enemy forces had been within these walls, and were now destroyed. King Osbert was dead. Earl Seaton had not been found, but was surely among those now cooking in the streets. This was a hammer blow for Suthern morale, and with no leaders, no capital and few fighters, resistance was surely at an end.

Roper could feel his heart slowing. He could feel that dread leaking out of his chest, the self-doubt lifting, and cool relief running through his veins. Ten thousand had been lost to the breach, with casualties for the whole campaign at perhaps sixteen thousand. That was worth it, for the future of their people. If he had been offered that before they came south, he would have taken it. He had known what this would be.

Gray placed a hand on his shoulder, and they embraced once again. 'It isn't over, my lord,' he said gently. 'But it's not far.' He gripped Roper's shoulder. 'With Lundenceaster taken, our supplies restored and the Unhieru with us, nothing the Sutherners have can stop this army.'

Roper just breathed, tasting the soot on the air. Every strand of him was weary. 'We will need to go west soon,' he said. 'Make certain we can overwhelm any resistance before it has time to form properly. But I doubt they are as well prepared for us down here as they were in the north. We'll be able to find food more consistently.'

'That'll cheer Pryce up,' said Gray. 'Perhaps we should send heralds west, rather than legions. Ask them for surrender?'

'Nobody asks for surrender as convincingly as a legion,' said Roper.

'The Unhieru might.'

'They might,' Roper agreed. 'They might also refuse to accept that surrender.' That was another reason Roper wanted to move the legions: to get them away from the Unhieru. The assault would not have succeeded without them. Roper himself would certainly be dead. But they could not share a camp.

Dazed soldiers ambled past Roper and Gray. There were more Anakim dead in a single battle than there had been for years, and yet pipes and murmured song were breaking out. The pressure of months; the belief that they and their unfeasible mission were doomed, had been relieved in one night's violence.

Some had come through the breach too late to fight at all. Their metal still shone, weapons clean at rest in their scabbards; the dust on their boots the only sign they had been involved in an assault. Quietly, they helped each other unstrap cuirass and helmet, dropping them unattended, just this once. Swords were loosed and cast with them, and these untested warriors laughed together softly, staying on their feet, staring dreamily at the column of smoke, soaring across the heavens.

Among them walked the petty injuries. Men clutching strips of linen to blossoming crimson slashes, their armour battered, blood-smeared and dishevelled. They reached a fire and dropped to the floor, where their peers descended on them, raising their wounds, ignoring their moans as they cleaned, sewed and bound. A rare few had fought and emerged unscathed, fouled weapons clutched at their sides, wandering aimlessly until hailed gently and sat down with hot breakfast. For the first time in months, they could fill their stomachs, and had enough rations to fill them again tomorrow.

Roper could not eat yet. He ached like he had been trampled. He stung. His calves and hips cramped with each misjudged movement. He was bewitched by the inferno and the air swimming above.

'My lord,' came a voice behind him. It sounded like Tekoa, but so broken and exhausted that Roper was filled with a sudden foreboding. He ignored the voice for as long as he possibly could, managing just two heartbeats before turning.

It was Tekoa. He stood before Roper, his face stained with tears and his helmet clutched to his chest. 'Legate?' Roper leaned to one side to see what was coming behind Tekoa. Four men, bearing a stretcher between them, a body in a dreadful state of laceration lying on top of it, and a great streak of a ponytail lying alongside.

'No,' said a desperate voice from Roper's side. 'Please, no . . .' The voice was Gray's. That was when Roper recognised the corpse. He saw it, but did not believe.

Pryce.

Gray staggered past him and into the stretcher, capsizing its burden into his arms. He bent his head over the corpse, listening at Pryce's open mouth for five heartbeats. Then leaned his head into Pryce's. 'Oh, my brother,' he said wretchedly, tears sliding down his cheeks. He uttered a moan that shook Roper to his foundations: a gentle mewing, which plucked at him like a harp-string, and set his heart rattling in his chest. 'Not you,' he whispered.

Tekoa looked silently over them, twisted face wringing tears down his cheeks. Roper dropped to kneel next to Gray as the captain emitted another noise of pure agony, one hand rising to his chest as though to hold it together. The tight reins he held over his emotions had vanished without trace. His reasonable, calm and reflective nature disintegrated, and he made again that profound noise: a gentle howl like the last wolf alive, leaning his head into the corpse. 'My brother, I'd take it for you . . . *Please.*'

Roper felt it would have been more appropriate to cry now than it had been on the battlements. But no tears came. 'What happened?' he asked, dully. 'I thought it was over . . . I thought we were done.'

Tekoa paused, gathering himself. 'He was found in the camp,' he murmured.

'The *camp*?' Roper stared down at Pryce's terrible wounds. 'Where?'

'By the eastern perimeter. No one else around. We don't know what happened. Sutherners, or traitors, or . . .' Tekoa shook his head helplessly.

Roper had no energy for wonder. He did not feel curiosity, nor the grass beneath his knees, nor the weariness in his limbs. Just the despair radiating from his side, and the tearing, visceral pain in his own chest as one of the foundations on which he had built everything crumbled to dust.

Pryce, more of a force than a man, could not be dead. Not after all they had survived together. Not after coming through that breach, those streets. Not when their great task was so nearly completed, and peace so close. A champion whom Roper had always been shocked and delighted to find at his back and his command. A soul of pure energy: inflexible, direct, unyielding.

Dead.

Epilogue

Roper sat by the hearth, head in his hands. The crumpled heap that had once been Gray lay next to him, silent at last. Tekoa, on his other side, brooded so intently that he might extinguish the fire. A few legates were with them, suffering more from the horrendous casualties to their legions than the influence of the shrouded cadaver, which lay just beyond the fire's reach. From one side of the shroud protruded the end of a long, black ponytail.

Vigtyr was there too, or what was left of him. He was limping heavily on a stuck foot, bleeding through the dressings at his neck, chest and eye, and had lost most of his front teeth. The surgeons thought he was unlikely to recover good sight in the injured eye, and he seemed a watery reflection of the man he had been. But anyone would be at passing through that breach.

Roper stared dully at a single patch of grass, the food he had prepared left untouched above the flames, slowly boiling dry. Eating was utterly impossible. Even the act of drinking felt intolerable. He just sat, unable to imagine how he had had the energy to storm the breach just hours before.

On the other side of the fire, Vigtyr stood and muttered

something about going to his tent. He limped into the dark, skirting some distance around Pryce's body. His were the only words spoken for the next hour. The fire burned low, the night grew cold, and a rotten, yellow moon rose. Gray raised his head to look at the last of the flames, and then climbed unsteadily to his feet, Roper eyeing him without the energy to ask where he was going. Gray kept his head down, and said one hoarse word: 'Sigrid.' He began to stagger away, but came to a halt after just a few steps. It took Roper some time to realise why.

There were hoof beats coming from the dark.

A horse was drawing towards them, and the gait, though fast, sounded uneven. The regular tattoo was upset by stumbles, and after a time Roper could hear the beast wheezing. Roper and Gray shared a glance, Roper wearing the hint of a frown. The wheezing grew louder and dirtier, and when the beast in question was at last illuminated by the fire, knees trembling, flanks quivering and streaked in foam, it seemed its flesh was spent. Some force went out of it and the horse collapsed onto its knees, falling to one side and pitching its rider to the ground. There it lay, utterly blown, as the rider fought his way clear and staggered upright.

Roper had never seen a horse in such a state of exhaustion, and standing above it was a face he had not seen in months. 'Leon?'

'My lord, the assault!' Leon blurted.

Roper stared at him, unable to think what he might be doing here. 'Over,' he replied.

Leon let out a breath and slumped, looking as though he was half considering doing as his horse had done, and dropping to his knees. Then he shook himself a little, looking around the fire at the blank, incurious faces, most not even returning his gaze. 'Vigtyr,' he said. 'Where is he? Vigtyr the Quick.'

'In his tent.'

Leon's chest was heaving. 'Him. My lord, it's him. He is

the spy. The traitor. I heard it from the mouth of the man who killed your brother. The assassin operating on Vigtyr's own orders. Vigtyr works for the Sutherners. He ordered Numa's death.'

Roper just frowned, not quite understanding what he was being told. Nobody else had reacted, but some power drew Roper to his feet. '*Vigtyr?*' he said, wondering at the anger in his own voice. Then he shivered a little. 'Vigtyr? You're quite sure?'

'Beyond doubt,' hissed Leon, urgently. 'That bastard ordered the death of your brothers. *He* is Ellengaest.'

The world was coming back into cold focus.

And everything was changed. Energy was returning to Roper's limbs, and he found he was panting. Gray was by his side, surprising Roper, who had not heard him approach. 'He killed Pryce,' said the captain. 'He was sent to find Vigtyr. And was murdered.'

Tekoa was on his feet too. 'He told them where our breach would be. They were prepared, because of him.'

Roper glanced at Cold-Edge, unbuckled and thrown carelessly down by his side.

'Where is the tent?' hissed Leon.

Then Gray laughed. A freezing noise, which made Roper's hair stand on end. 'I'll take you,' he said quietly. 'But he's mine, Leon.' He stooped to pick up his sword. Roper snatched Cold-Edge. Tekoa's weapon was in his hand already, and Leon's blade rang clear of its scabbard.

'We'll share him,' said Roper.

'No calls,' said Tekoa. 'Give him no warning.'

The four turned and ran together, the legates on their heels. Blades flashing, boots thumping, they prowled into the dark. The tent was not far, and sprinting seemed no effort at all. Roper was consumed by a focus he had never experienced before, eyes so wide they were starting from his head as they closed on the tent's flimsy outline.

'Vigtyr!' called Gray in a voice of horrible sweetness.

'Vigtyr! Your friends are here.' They did not slow for their approach. Gray carved an entrance in the canvas with a shriek, and ducked through. Roper, Tekoa and Leon flooded after him, into the dark. There were no candles lit inside. They could see nothing.

Nothing.

There was just the sound of their panting, of someone emitting a low, enraged growl, of a sword hacking wildly at something, of a strange and desperate keening. Roper's groping hand felt a shoulder and he pulled it suddenly close, but it was Tekoa. 'Who has him?' Roper hissed. 'Anyone? Is he here?'

Nobody replied.

It was just the four of them in the tent.

Vigtyr was gone.

They stared at what little they could see of one another. 'After him,' said Roper. 'Tear this camp apart. After him!' Gray plunged outside first and bawled at the legates, scattering them to rouse their soldiers and turn the camp upside down.

Tekoa was after him, swearing that the Skiritai would find him first and boil the flesh off him, limb by limb, for this treachery, for Pryce.

Leon followed, loping with silent intent like a dog on a trail, and Roper emerged last, scanning the night, his heart ticking once more like a clockwork spring. 'Vigtyr,' he whispered, too quiet for anyone to hear but him. 'I swear, Vigtyr, I swear we will find you. We *will* find you. Treasure the hunted moments you have left. We are coming.'

Leabharlanna Poiblí Chathair Baile Átha Cliath
Dublin City Public Libraries

Roll of Black Legions

Full Legions:
Ramnea's Own Legion
Blackstone Legion
Pendeen Legion
Greyhazel Legion
Skiritai Legion

Auxilliary Legions:
Gillamoor Legion
Saltcoat Legion
Dunoon Legion
Fair Island Legion
Ulpha Legion
Hetton Legion
Hasgeir Legion
Soay Legion
Ancrum Legion

Houses and Major Characters of the Black Kingdom

Major Houses and Their Banners:

Jormunrekur – *The Silver Wolf*
Kynortas Rokkvison *m.* Borghild Nikansdottir
  (House Tiazem)
Roper Kynortasson *m.* Keturah Tekoasdottir (House Vidarr)
Numa Kynortasson
Ormur Kynortasson

Lothbrok – *The Wildcat*
Uvoren Ymerson *m.* Hafdis Reykdalsdottir (House Algauti)
Unndor Uvorenson *m.* Hekla Gottwaldsson (House Oris)
Urthr Uvorenson *m.* Kaiho Larikkason (House Nadoddur)
Tore Sturnerson
Leon Kaldison
Baldwin Duffgurson

Vidarr – *Catastrophe and the Tree*
Tekoa Urielson *m.* Skathi Hafnisdottir (House Atropa)

Pryce Rubenson
Skallagrim Safirson

Baltasar – *The Split Battle-Helm*
Helmec Rannverson *m*. Gullbra Ternosdottir (House Denisarta)
Vigtyr Forraederson

Alba – *The Rampant Unicorn*
Gray Konrathson *m*. Sigrid Jureksdottir (House Jormunrekur)

Indisar – *The Dying Sun*
Sturla Karson

Oris – *The Rising Sun*
Jokul Krakison

Algauti – *The Angel of Madness*
Aslakur Bjargarson
Randolph Reykdalson
Gosta Serkison

Kinada – *The Frost Tree*
Vinjar Kristvinson *m*. Sigurasta Sakariasdottir

Neantur – *The Skinned Lion*
Asger Sykason
Hartvig Uxison

Rattatak – *The Ice Bear*
Frathi Akisdottir

Other Houses and Their Banners:

Eris – *The Mother Aurochs*
Atropa – *The Stone Knife*
Kangur – *The Angel of Divine Vengeance*

Alupali – *The Eagle's Talon*
Keitser – *The Almighty Spear*
Brigaltis – *The Angel of Fear*
Tiazem – *The Dark Mountain*
Horbolis – *The Headless Man*
Denisarta – *The Rain of Stars*
Hybaris – *The Mammoth*
Mothgis – *The Angel of Courage*
Nadoddur – *The Snatching Hawk*

Acknowledgements

A second book, it turns out, is harder than a first. Or it was for me; most days at work spent with the feeling that I was outrageously plagiarising myself, and suppressing a palpable sense of imposter syndrome. As a result, the assistance I received from a great many quarters was even more appreciated than last time. Huge thanks to my editors, Ella Gordon and Alex Clarke, for their splendid creative input, and great patience and understanding during the delays in executing it. I am equally grateful to Lucy Morris and Felicity Blunt for their fantastic support, and Becky Hunter for her sterling efforts and company on many publicity engagements. Patrick Insole produced another fabulous cover design which I shall be admiring for years to come, and there is a legion of others at Headline, Wildfire and Curtis Brown to whom I owe thanks, but are too numerous to name here.

Closer to home, my earliest drafts were examined (as ever) by my mother, whose judgement and input I trust very much, and which comes with plenty of sage advice too. This was also supplied in quantities by the rest of my family and friends, who have had to put up with higher levels of mania than I like to think is normal.

Finally, thanks to you, the reader, for engaging with this book and making it real. I don't take it for granted, and still feel absurdly pleased and embarrassed any time someone writes to say they enjoyed one of my books. Feel free to keep doing it, should you feel so inclined.

About the Author

Leo Carew is a Cambridge graduate of Biological Anthropology, currently studying medicine at Barts and the London Medical School. Apart from writing, his real passion is exploration, which led him to spend a year living in a tent in the High Arctic, where he trained and worked as an Arctic guide. *The Wolf* and *The Spider* are the first two books in his Under the Northern Sky trilogy.